JUN 2 6 2008

THE BELLMAKER'S HOUSE

THEODORE PITSIOS

THE BELLMAKER'S HOUSE

COSMOS PUBLISHING

Part of the proceeds will be donated to the American Hellenic Educational Progressive Association (AHEPA) to fund a Hellenic Studies Chair in the University of South Alabama.

Library of Congress Control Number 2006939495

ISBN 978-1-932455-14-4
First Published in 2007 by:
Cosmos Publishing Co., Inc.
P.O. Box 2255
River Vale, NJ 07675
Phone: 201-664-3494
Fax: 201-664-3402

Email: info@greeceinprint.com
Website: www.greeceinprint.com

Acknowledgements

My thanks and gratitude to my teacher Walter Darring, my readers Ted and Marina Striggles, David Mezner and Carl Rose. Also my thanks and gratitude to the editor Judy Frost whose comments and advice made this a better book and to Petros Kipriotelis who fanned the embers of the love for books in the early years. And most importantly, my heartfelt thanks to my family for putting up with me.

*To the memory of Elaine Bullard-Thompson
and Giannis Georgantzis*

Είδες τόνε, είδες τόνε; — Είδα τόνε — Κι ίντα φορούσε; — Άσπρη βράκα, άσπρη βράκα!
— Κι ακόμα δεν την έβαψε;
    (first lines of Karkavitsas: Πειράγματα, from the *Λόγια της Πλώρης*, collection.)

Chapter | 1

*T*he year is 1952; it is a Friday morning, in early autumn, on a mountainside in Eastern Pelion, in Greece. In the village of Taxiarhes, in a dusty schoolyard bordering the Patekas apple orchard, a group of boys is engaged in a soccer match. It has been going on for half an hour: fast, intense and noisy. There are five players on each team, in short pants, scruffy and sweaty, most of them barefooted and all of them around thirteen years old, except Nikos Pilios, the goalie. He is two years younger than the rest. At present, he's focusing all his attention on the ball advancing towards him under the control of Giannis Giannakos, the forward-center of the attacking team. His eyes are locked onto that ball, his back hunched, palms open, and he's making short, springy, in-place jumps as Giannis, eluding the defenders one by one, is getting closer.

To Nikos, all that exists at that moment is the semi-deflated, patched-up ball, propelled by a pair of bare feet. He doesn't see anything else nor does he hear any of the shouting around him; stopping Giannis from scoring is to Nikos the most important thing in the world.

The opposing guard is closing in on Giannis, but he fakes to the left, and then there is no one between him and Nikos. He glances up, another fake move — to the right this time — and with his left foot kicks the ball to the upper left corner of the goal.

Nikos springs like a tiger on a gazelle. With his clenched fists, he deflects the ball, sending it over the goal posts towards the apple-loaded tree in the Patekas orchard behind him. As he falls to the ground, Nikos hears the sweet music of his teammates' cheers and Giannis' cursing; he will be a hero again, and that's worth the scratched knee and bruised shoulder.

The ball strikes the top of the tree, raining apples on the four sheep grazing under it, and they scatter bleating. Stefanis Patekas, who hears the racket while he's clearing the field a few meters away, drops his scythe and approaches to investigate. He picks up the ball and advances towards Nikos, who has jumped the stone wall separating the orchard from the playground to look for it.

"You can load it on a rooster, all of your learning — kicking the ball all day, is all you do," he says to Nikos.

"It's a free hour, we are between classes," Nikos answers.

Stefanis Patekas is fifteen years old, much taller and heavier than Nikos. He wears long pants with mismatched patches in the seats and cloth shoes with his toes sticking out.

"All that schooling won't buy you one dry piece of shit from the store," he scoffs at Nikos.

"You would be in here too if you weren't a dumbo; it took you three years to finish the sixth grade," snaps Nikos and yanks the ball from Stefanis' hands. Walking away he pauses, raises one leg, and cupping his left hand around his mouth he trumpets the sound of a loud fart.

"You think you're smart because the teacher jumped you two classes, don't you?" Stefanis calls after Nikos. "I am going to talk to the principal, you'll pay for the apples you've been knocking down and the grass you are trampling, I've got to feed the goats and the sheep, you know," he shouts after him. Then in a lower tone: "You don't know shit, you are a bunch of sissies, all of you."

Just as Nikos tosses the ball over the wall the bell rings and most of the players walk to the side and start to put their shoes on. The rest drift towards the school entrance.

"Wait, wait," cries Giannis, "we still have a corner kick, we could tie the game."

"We said the game ends when the bell rings, and the bell just rang," says Kostas Liappis, the captain of Nikos' team.

"But it's a corner kick and the ball was in the playing field when the bell started ringing."

"That's because there was a natural obstruction, look it up in the rules, if the tree wasn't there the ball would've rolled down to the creek and we would still be chasing it," Kostas explains.

Giannis ponders the explanation. "You talk like one of those damn political people on the radio," he grumbles and he walks away.

"I never heard of this natural obstruction rule," says Nikos when Giannis is far enough away. "You should have let the sucker kick, he'd never get a goal on me."

"Why risk it if you don't have to? Besides, he believed it," says Kostas Liappis as he wipes his feet on the grass and puts on his shoes.

When the bell rings to announce the end of the school day, Nikos's classroom is emptied before the last note has died in the air. Only two students are left in the room. One is Katina Mela, the short and chubby, ugliest-girl-in-the-school Katina Mela, discussing something with the history teacher who nods his head in agreement with whatever she is pointing out in her book.

The other is Nikos, who is crawling under the desk, looking for something. When he finally finds his slingshot, he stuffs it in his bag and sprints out of the classroom. He is too preoccupied with getting the bag over his shoulder and crashes into the English teacher, who at that moment is stepping out of the office with a stack of books under each arm.

Nikos mumbles excuses as he gathers the books scattered on the floor.

"I am glad to see you are still here," says the teacher, "I need some help with this load."

"Yes sir," answers Nikos, straining to sound willing. He reaches up and takes the stack of books, feeling as if he is standing next to a giant; the teacher's long, sun-burned face, smiles down at him from behind his gray goatee and thick mustache.

He follows the teacher down the cobblestone path, hoping none of his schoolmates sees him.

In the village, the teacher is known as Kambanaris, the Bellmaker, a nickname he inherited from his ancestors; all had been bell makers and his house was called the Bellmaker's house. He had left the village when he was young, spent many years studying and working in Europe and now has returned to Taxiarhes to teach French and English in the High School.

Nikos has never been to the teacher's house before and, like all the village children, he is fascinated by it. It's an elegant, white building, with windows all around on the second and third floors and a forest of chimneys on the slate roof. It stands on top of the hill like a castle out of a fairy-tale, surrounded by a stone wall, too tall for a person to see over it. The mystery of that seclusion prompts kids of Nikos' age to circulate all kinds of wild stories about the place.

Nikos walks through the huge iron gate, two steps behind the teacher, with a stack of books under his arm, his head turning right and left, like an alert sparrow. With eyes wide open, he is scanning the area for grave markers and signs of hidden treasure. They walk on the wide cobblestone path under a grape arbor, which connects with the arbor over the large, flagstone patio. The house seems to rise gracefully among the grapevines, its top disappearing in the clouds.

"It's a castle," Nikos says, awestruck.

"We'll take the books to my study, upstairs," says Mr. Kambanaris when they pass the massive front door.

Nikos follows him up a wide staircase that has thick, intricately carved balusters and rails, to the third floor, to a corner room, with windows facing the sea on one side and the mountain on the other. Tall bookcases full of books line the walls all the way up to the decorated ceiling. In one corner is a big, polished, wooden desk set between two large windows overlooking the cove of Fakistra. As he drops his load on the desk Nikos notices that these books, like most of the books on the shelves, are not in Greek.

"They are all foreign," he marvels.

"Yes," says Mr. Kambanaris, "they are European writers, most of them. I find them easier to read and also I know the places they are talking about."

"You have been to those places yourself?"

"I spent my best years there, Niko," he answers, pulling a leather volume from a shelf.

Nikos stares at the books and tries to imagine what the places that produce such strange writing could look like. The book the teacher is holding is miniaturized in his massive hand, as he reaches to replace it on the upper shelf without a step-stool. Wisdom, strength and daring, he has it all, thinks Nikos with admiration.

Kambanaris' wife walks in the room bringing a *loukoumi* (Turkish delight) and a glass of water for the guest, and the teacher makes the introduction: "This young man is Nikos Pilios, one of my boys; a most promising young man."

Nikos pockets the tip Kambanaris hands him and races down the stairs. When he reaches the outer gate he turns around and looks at the house again. As he trots up the cobblestone path, he keeps turning for another look, then stumbles and falls on his back on top of a pile of chestnut balls. He lets out a cry and slowly stands up, grimacing as he pulls out each of the thorny balls.

"What's that I see? The great goalie, diving to catch chestnut balls?" the voice of Giannis Giannakos startles him, "what are you doing all the way down here?"

Nikos turns and sees Giannis, Stefanis Patekas and another schoolmate, Spyros Karteras, each with a cane fishing pole on his shoulder coming down the path.

"There was a huge woodpecker up that tree, didn't see the damn rock and tripped, I'm coming back from Fakistra, mother sent me to see if a boat came in — she wanted some fresh fish," answers Nikos, all in one breath. He is not about to tell them he was running an errand for the teacher.

"We are going fishing," says Giannis. "My father is coming behind with the lanterns, and we are going to fish all night. We'll stay in my grandfather's hut till Monday afternoon."

"We are going to Paraskevi. I'll be setting bird traps all weekend," says Nikos and walks off in the opposite direction, the pangs of envy hurting more than the stickers on his back.

Why couldn't he have a normal life like everybody else, he keeps asking himself.

Everybody else's farms and groves and vineyards, are at the outskirts of this village. They get up in the morning, saddle their donkey and, with their sheep and goats in tow, ride to their plot of land. They do their chores and in the evening, load some fodder on their donkey and come home before dark. Then the men go to the coffee shop to play cards and talk politics and the women prepare supper. The boys get together and play or talk about girls or what they will do when they grow up and get out of the village.

Normal things in a normal life.

Why couldn't his father be like Giannis father?

Nikos' father was born in the village of Agiates, about thirty kilometers up the coast from Taxiarhes, the son of Nikos Pilios, a sea captain who owned the largest caique on that coast.

In his younger days his father was in the trucking business. He had his own truck and was doing work for a contractor who, with a couple of clanky bulldozers, was building a road around the mountain of Pelion.

He was probably planning to return to Agiates in his shiny truck when the road reached it, to show off his *prokopi*, (success), and be the envy of his old friends and the dream of every eligible bride. But he was snared by Niko's mother's smile and her cooking. He settled in Taxiarhes, in the house that was her dowry. After a few months, the road contractor went broke and Nikos father accepted as payment a farm house and some olive groves near the sea, about fifteen kilometers away from the village of Taxiarhes, in a desolate place called Paraskevi. Deep inside he was more of a farmer than a trucker anyway.

To Nikos, the farmhouse seemed to be at the end of the world. The only people nearby were an old couple, Barba Giannis and Kyra Rini Themelis, living in a ramshackle cottage. The few other hovels were occupied only at harvest time.

Nikos' father fell in love with the two-story farmhouse, the olive groves that surrounded it and the serenity of the place. He moved his young bride there, scaled down his trucking business and spent most of his time on the farm.

Soon after, when Germany invaded Greece, the farm turned out to be the family's salvation. Since it was so far away from the village, the brave troops of the Third Reich only bothered to come once, to gather the jewelry and anything else of value they could strip off the terrified villagers.

During the occupation years, relatives from the cities of Athens, Volos and Thessaloniki, going back three generations, came and stayed with them in Paraskevi. Every square centimeter that could be scratched with the hoe was planted and when people were dropping dead from starvation in other parts of the country, the Pilios colony was almost self-sufficient. The only thing the grown-ups missed was coffee. When they could find a spoonful of it, they would dilute it with ground-up baked chestnuts, to make it go further.

When relatives come to visit now, they reminisce about where they had planted the wheat, where the tobacco and who it was that let the brown cow get away and trample the fava beans.

Now that Nikos, his brother and sister have reached school age, the whole family spends the school period in Taxiarhes at the house that was their mother's dowry. The farm is looked after by Giorgo Parsakis, an old farm hand that has been working with the family ever since Nikos can remember. Then as soon as school is off, even for the Christmas and Easter holidays, they will round up the chickens which they keep in Taxiarhes, "to have fresh eggs for the children," tie their feet, and load them in the back of his father's truck, together with the dog and the sheep, which they keep "to have fresh milk for the children" and drive to Paraskevi. They park about one hour's walk from the farm house, the closest the truck can get to it, and then with a chicken under each arm and the lead sheep on a line behind, they march to the farm house.

Nikos hates these trips.

He hates it when people see him walking down the road with chicken shit streaking down his pants.

He hates staying in that desolate place.

He hates missing time with his playmates.

He hates going back to school and hearing his playmates describe all the things they did while he was wasting his time picking olives and looking after the sheep.

His classmates talk about tourists arriving in fancy cars and strolling through the village. And of women smoking cigarettes and of girls in short, short pants and flimsy blouses that you can see clear through. He suspects they are exaggerating, but they have something to work with. Nothing exciting happens when you are hoeing potatoes or irrigating bean rows, no matter how strong the imagination.

In that desolate place, whole days can pass without Nikos seeing or talking to a person other than Dimos, his bratty brother, five years younger, and Katina, his snotty-nose sister, seven years younger than him. When he does happen to see somebody it's always some old farmer loading his donkey, or an old woman wrapped in black, tending her sheep and spinning wool.

He hates being young and dependent on his parents.

His known world is from the mountain ridge of Nehori, to the gray silhouettes of the islands of Skiathos and Skopelos. Beyond that exists the enchanted world of the battery-operated radio his father turns on for the evening news. Sometimes Nikos sneaks in the house during the day and turns it on and lets his mind wander to all those exotic places the voices are coming from.

While looking after the sheep, he watches the ships sailing in the horizon and wonders about the places they are going. He wonders: What do the people in Athens, in Africa, in

China, look like? What do they do? Are the Chinese olive trees the same as the trees in Paraskevi? Do they have sheep they have to keep from going into the neighbor's bean garden? Is there a boy sitting on a boulder looking at the horizon in this direction, wondering what lies beyond?

Using the landscape as the compass, he lets his mind travel to places he has seen on the World Map: Athens is in line with the big olive tree and the island of Skiathos behind it. Africa is a bit to the left, in line with Themeli's chimney and the island of Skopelos. Holland and England, where Kambanaris had spent so many years, are in opposite direction; in line with the white boulder and the big chestnut tree on the far hill.

Kambanaris, now there is a man who has traveled, has seen great things and must have had great adventures.

Chapter

2

"*I* like to speak to Captain George Steiner, please."

"Who may I say is calling?"

"You may say is calling Nikos Pilios."

"And who are you with, Mr. Pee-nee-lees?"

"I am with Poseidon Marine Services, in Bigport, Alabama."

"May I say what it's in reference to?"

"You may say it's in reference to the Motor Vessel George P."

"Could you spell the last name please?"

I spelled it.

"Is Te-ni-os, with an E?"

"Misses secretary, we have same conversation before one hour; my name is Nikos Pilios, with a P and an I and an L. And I am thirty-five years old, and I am five-foot-five, with brown eyes and brown hair. I weigh one hundred-fifty pounds and..."

"That will not be necessary," said the voice on the other end, dry, humorless, efficient.

"I will see if Mr. Steiner is available." Then the "elevator music" came on and I started tapping my fingers on the desk and wondering how much this call was costing Phil; starting next week I would be paying for calls like this.

After an eternity, the efficient secretary in New York came back on the line.

"Mr. Steiner is in conference. He will be tied up the rest of the evening. Do you wish him to return your call on Monday?"

"Yes, I wish him."

I gave her my number again and hung up. I scribbled "Call George Steiner" on Monday's leaf of the desk calendar. When I turned in my resignation, I worked out an agreement with Phil that let me keep the same office, share the clerical and telephone expenses and continue doing some of GESCO's work as a subcontractor. Today was my last day as a GESCO employee but, being eager to get started as my own boss, I had been squeezing in some time to work on bids for my own account.

A few days earlier, I had submitted a thirty five thousand dollar bid for piping renewal on a freighter called *George P.* It would be my first repair job. That's why I was calling Captain George Steiner; I expected to have received the order for it already.

I was already working on my second bid, a heating coil repair, on a tanker. I checked the tanker estimate one more time — four pages filled with the cost of pipes, flanges, nuts and bolts and the number of man-hours I thought it would take to do the job. It came to four hundred and sixty five thousand dollars; a big job by anybody's yardstick. I was starting out with a bang. The file labeled *ST Oil Transporter* was already bulging with smudged drawings and photographs of rusty pipes. I glanced at the letter to the *Oil Transporter* Superintendent engineer and put it on my "OUT" box with a "post-it" paper stuck to it where I had written: "Marilyn please make three copies of this proposal."

I leaned back, put my feet on the desk, lit a cigarette and let my eyes wander over the landscape outside the window, then over to the sea-scape on the wall calendar. It was the last day of May 1977. The last day of working for somebody else. "Niko, you are going to remember this day," I told myself.

I stared at the ceiling, blowing smoke rings for a while. Then while putting out the cigarette, I caught a glimpse of the note on the *Oil Transporter* letter. I tore it up and re-wrote: "*Marylin* I need three copies of this proposal."

I grinned as I pictured her pecking at the typewriter and bitching about going blind trying to read "the illiterate, foreign chicken scratch."

She had better get used to it.

I started a letter to my father on a yellow note-pad. He always complained I didn't write home enough. The fact was, I avoided writing letters as much as I could. My Greek had evolved into a unique language; a mixture of Americanized and maritime Greek vocabulary, which was good enough for communicating with the Greeks of Bigport, but writing to someone in Greece was slow going. Writing in English was even slower. I was spending most of the time trying to think of the right words for everything. Doing things over the telephone seemed much easier, but it got me in trouble quite a few times when people changed things around however it suited them, then claimed they didn't understand my accent. Phil, my boss, had insisted that everything having to do with the work be in writing.

My father never saw the need to put a telephone in the house. "That's for big-shots and show-offs and for those who are too lazy to write." So I tried to write. But after the: "All of us here are fine and we hope all of you there are fine also," I would sit staring at the page.

This time I did have something to write about.

I was laboring over the second paragraph, when Marilyn Partridge, the nosy, old-maidish secretary, came into the office.

"Hi there," she clucked as soon as her beak was inside the door, and in short, busybody steps, like a sterile hen, she moved toward my desk. She stopped a few feet from it and cast her eyes around the room. "Somebody has sure done some redecorating in here."

"It's always been like this," I said.

She walked closer to the wall, examining everything like a visitor in a museum.

"What did you do to get these?" She was looking at some Naval citations hanging over a filing cabinet. I could guess why the sudden interest in my existence.

"Saved an Admiral's poodle from drowning," I said.

She didn't laugh, just mumbled, "Now that I think of it, Norman did say something about you doing some work for the Navy before." She moved on to the wall opposite my desk.

"Ta-xi-ha-hes, how do you pronounce this word?" she asked, with feigned confusion, trying to read the inscription on the painting of the Bellmaker's house.

"Taxiarhes," I said.

"It's Greek to me, what does it mean?"

"It's the name of my village."

"What do these funny words at the bottom say?"

"My name in Greek."

"Oh, whose house is this ?"

"Mine."

"This is a painting… is there a real house that looks like that?"

"Yep, looks exactly like that."

"Is it your parents house?"

"No, mine."

"Who lives in it now?"

"Nobody."

"You have a big house like that sitting empty over there and you live in Rolling Hills over here?"

"Marilyn, there is a lot about me you don't know."

She stared at it some more, then asked: "Norman said you were starting on your own. Was he joking?"

"No, he wasn't."

"You think you can make it?"

"I know I can."

"Norman said you'll be working out of this office and will be paying Phil rent."

"That's right; I'll be paying part of your salary too." I handed her the *Oil Transporter* letter. "Here, type it on my letter-head."

She walked slowly towards my desk.

"I bet you forgot today was payday," she said, using her chirpy telephone voice. "Guess this is the last one of these for you." She put my paycheck on the corner of the desk. It was the first time I didn't have to go asking for it, put up with her stupid jokes and watch her act as though she was paying me out of her cookie jar money.

"I'll be around for a while," I said. She was not getting rid of me that easy; my turn was coming.

She looked around some more, glanced at the photograph of Margaret and the girls at the corner of my desk and walked toward the door acting as if she was going to say something but changed her mind at the last minute. At the door, she stopped for a moment, "Good luck," she finally mumbled and walked out, closing the door behind her.

She opened it a few seconds later: "It's Ma-ri-lyn, "I" first, then "Y," you always write it backwards."

"Oh, OK," I said.

That was the chummiest we had gotten since I started working for GESCO.

Norman Gardner had called me at home one day: "For the new contract, Phil Domain wants an engineer who can speak Greek and I told him you are the ticket," he said. I told Norman I would go see him the next day.

GESCO's office was on the eight floor of an office building in the middle of Bigport. I got there at nine o'clock in the morning. Marilyn was barricaded behind a large receptionist's desk, furiously attacking the typewriter while having an argument with the yellow note pad on the stand next to it.

She was a short, plump person in her forties, with a tiny head on top of a skinny, long neck, and shoulder-length gray-blonde hair. Her face was round and had a long beak for a nose. She wore a buttoned down, gray, two-piece outfit, with the sides of the upper part draping over the arms of her chair. When I first saw her, she reminded me of a hen sitting on her eggs.

A long, thin cigarette in the corner of her mouth was bouncing up and down toward the yellow note pad like a threatening finger.

I stood in front of the desk for a while, clearing my throat and saying "Excuse me," till she finally stopped. She ground the cigarette in an ashtray the size of a salad bowl, peered over her narrow reading glasses and concentrated on examining me for some time.

I told her who I was and why I was there. She asked me to spell my name and struggled to write it down. She got half of the letters wrong, then tried to pronounce it and almost

21

choked on it. I pronounced it for her, separating the syllables using the marine radio operator's code: "Pi-li-os" I said,

"Papa, India, Lima, India, Oscar, Sierra; Nikos Pilios." She stared at me as if I were a Martian.

Finally she pressed a button on the intercom: "Mr. Gardner, there is a Father Oscasiera to see you," she told the machine. Norman came out a few seconds later.

"I see you two have already met," he said, grinning.

"Not quite, maybe you can tell me his American name," said Marilyn. Norman made the introductions: "Marilyn is our receptionist and secretary."

"Executive secretary," she corrected. "I work for the president."

For an instant, the terrifying thought that she might be giving me orders almost made me turn around and run, but Norman's smile calmed me.

"Nick is the young man we hope to talk into joining us," said Norman.

"That will be nice," she said, sounding like a machine that needed greasing.

From then on, my friendship with Marilyn was all down hill.

"Never mind Marilyn," said Norman as we were walking towards Phil's office, "she has a bit of an attitude because she knows where the bodies are buried."

I didn't know what that meant but I grinned as if I did.

I knew Norman from our days at the Delta shipyard. After working as a shipfitter for a couple years, I managed to get transferred to the engineering department for the navy contracts. He was my supervisor for the next eighteen months, till Phil talked him into joining GESCO as vice president.

Norman said that Phil Domain, who was about my age, had started the company five years earlier. He christened it GESCO, which stood for Global Engineering Services Corporation.

When I met Phil, I thought he looked much older. He was also much taller, thinner and pale.

GESCO's multipage, multicolor, multi-expensive brochure said the company specialized in solving engine room problems, making the ships run more efficiently, thus saving the shipping companies lots of money and increasing their profits by heaps.

"Our experienced staff will travel anywhere to attend to your vessel's needs," read the caption under a photograph showing Phil with a briefcase, his tie blowing in the breeze, and an airplane, a steam freighter and a train in shadows in the background.

The work at GESCO was divided into two parts which Phil called divisions: The Spare Parts Inventory Control Division and the Engineering Division. I was to work in the Engineering Division.

On the propaganda sheets we were passing out, both were described as important and necessary and something that a progressive ship owner shouldn't be without.

That was four years ago; a lot of things had changed since then.

I read again what I had written to my father and, not liking it, crumpled the sheet into a ball and lobbed it into the wastebasket. I reached for the box by the desk that had been delivered earlier and pulled out a sheet of paper. I held it with my arm outstretched and looked at it for a while. I had designed the letterhead myself. The logo was a steam freighter under way, with Poseidon in a lighter shade, looming over the ship protectively, arms spread open, holding his trident and. Under it, in large, dark blue, letters: "POSEIDON MARINE SERVICES Inc.," and in smaller: "Global Ship Repairers."

The fellow at the printer's thought that the huge Poseidon, with his beard waving and the fierce look on his face, looked mean. He had suggested mermaids, on either side of the ship, one holding a pipe wrench and one holding a hammer. I disagreed.

"The company name and the letterhead should radiate confidence, imply the product's high quality, and inform the public of the company's activity," said a pamphlet I had picked up at the Small Business Development Center. I thought mine was a bull's eye.

I laid the sheet on top of the yellow note pad and started on the letter again. I wrote father about forming my own shiprepair company, about the big jobs I had waiting and about looking for some good workers to work for me. "Big things like that don't happen in Taxiarhes; renting rooms to German tourists and growing gardenias to sell in Athens is *trihes* (horse hair), I wrote.

It probably wouldn't impress him since it was happening away from the village, but I was sure he would tell everybody at the *cafenio* (coffee house).

When I finished, I folded the sheet in three, making sure the top part was showing, and put it in the envelope with two of my new business cards. They were shiny dark blue, with gold letters. On the lower left, in two lines, was printed: NIKOS PILIOS, President.

I also enclosed a twenty dollar bill, "To buy the guys at the *cafenio* a round of *ouzo*. Soon I will be sending big money," I wrote on a "post-it" note I stuck on the bill.

I closed the letter and propped it against the black telephone at the edge of the desk.

I lit a cigarette and leaned back in the chair and kept looking at the tan envelope, engraved with Poseidon Marine Service's address in dark blue letters in the upper left corner. Professional and a hell of a lot classier than the plain yellow paper that proclaimed, "*Villa* Giannis, *Jonny Giannakos, proprietor*", father's favorite nephew.

It was done; I was my own boss.

I exhaled and watched as the smoke cloud rose. For a moment, it looked like it formed a round, moon-like, glowing face that hovered below the ceiling. It had the sarcastic smile of one watching a fool march to his doom.

"So you want to be your own boss? Of all the unwise, inconsiderate, irresponsible things one could do," I thought I heard the face say.

The next time I exhaled, a long, sunburned face with a thick mustache and a gray goatee came chasing the first. It gave the moon-face a menacing look and growled: "You've got to go after success, it won't come looking for you, you free-loading lard-ass. If you are happy with the crumbs they throw you, you aren't any better than the donkey with the blinders turning the millstones."

"How can he survive? What does he know about business administration?" the moon face asked.

"My boy will make it; he's got what it takes. I know him," said the face with the goatee.

"There are lots of people who are living happy lives working for somebody else."

"That's existing, not living," answered the goatee and dissolved.

I put out the cigarette and left the office.

Driving home, the only thing I could find on the radio was news and goofy American country music. I turned the radio off and whistled my own made-up cheerful tune the rest of the way. I screeched to a stop at the end of the driveway, waved to the kids playing by the swing-set and trotted into the house.

Margaret was in the kitchen, absorbed in chopping a pile of zucchini on the counter. She was humming a church song and didn't seem to hear me reach behind her and give her a bear hug, holding my calling card in front of her. She let out a cry of fake surprise.

"You sure like to take chances, sneaking up behind somebody holding a big knife," she scolded. Then pointing to the card with it: "What's this?"

"I did it," I said grinning. "From now on, you are the wife of the President of Poseidon Marine Services, Incorporated, or PMS, Inc., for short."

She didn't laugh at the joke, nor show any excitement about what I said, and that irked me. She would act like she was having an orgasm when there was a "half off" sale at the mall, and she would jump and yell, and terrify the whole park when our eight-year-old swung the bat and accidentally got a hit, but when I came home in full sail, announcing that I had finally taken the big step — quit GESCO and started my own company, all she came up with was: "You finally went through with that cockamamie idea of yours." It pissed me off.

"I told you I was going to do it. You never take serious anything I say. Forget about cooking, let's get a baby sitter and go out to celebrate."

"Better take it easy on the celebrating; might have to tighten our belts till you strike it rich, Mr. President of P-M-S." Then seriously, as if quoting a prophecy: "Mr. Edwards says that we might have a recession; especially if Reagan gets elected."

I kicked the counter: "Shit your Mr. Edwards, what does he know? Shit him." I kicked the kitchen counter one more time and I walked away from her and lit a cigarette. At times it seemed to me that she didn't think I knew anything. The village idiot could fart and she would take it as a gospel, but I, I always had to explain how I came to know something. Where did I hear it? Where did I read it?

Tom Edwards was two years older than me, a widower who lived two houses down the street. Since his wife's death some years back he had taken up flirting as a full time occupation.

He was considered one of the pillars in Margaret's Sunday school class. The biggest accomplishment of that moon-faced buffoon was to squander a huge inheritance and a huge insurance settlement from his wife's car accident, then suck up to his wife's uncle to get him a desk job with some city license office — the kind of job where the clerks sit at their desks "on their break" while people, in a line four wide and ten deep, wait behind the window. He always seemed to have an "expert" opinion about everything. I think the only reason he was going to church was to save God the trouble of having to search for him for advice. Although he hadn't done one day's worth of real work in his life, to Margaret, he was the fountain of wisdom.

"Damn it, you haven't gone hungry yet, have you?" I said pulverizing the cigarette in the ashtray.

"But you gave up a steady job, with insurance. We have kids, you know. Katerina still needs her medicine. Where is the money gonna come from now?"

"I made a deal with Phil; I'll be doing contract work for him till my repair business picks up."

"We've got tons of bills to pay every month; not to mention that Greek bank you went and ..."

"Look, we talked about all of that a bunch of times. We discussed it, and we decided that's what was best for all of us."

"Nick, you don't discuss anything, you just tell me after it's done, and sometimes you don't even do that." She threw the knife in the sink, and scooping the zucchini with both hands, dumped it in the pot.

"Erick Burkhurst had his own business," she continued, "until he got a big shipyard job, wasn't careful how they had worded the contract, and ended up losing everything. And he had gone to college, here, in Bigport, Nick. Now he's selling life insurance."

"But damn it, if I was listening to you, I would still be a fitter at the shipyard, lugging a tool bucket up and down the ships, making half the money I'm making now, ass-kissing every redneck foreman for some overtime and getting sent home every time it rained."

"But Nick, we could barely make it as it was, then you got another noose around our

25

necks with that Greek bank loan, and now this." She slammed the pot on the stove and wiped her hands on her apron. "I knew I should've looked for another job. Instead, I let you talk me out of it."

She poured water into the pot, spilling some on the stove which made it sizzle. She picked up some left-over pieces of zucchini and shot them into the pot.

"You never discuss anything. Are all Greeks like this or did I get lucky?"

"You got lucky all right. You've got somebody who cares for his family and tries to get ahead, instead of sitting in front of the TV with a six-pack, like your Mr. Howard Demming, the great American."

"It's not just Americans. A Greek wife would want to know what her husband's up to, if she cares about her family."

"A Greek wife would be supporting her husband instead of cutting him down, damn it," I shouted.

"Maybe you should have married one, then."

Usually from here on, it's all downhill and we end up not speaking to each other for a couple of days, with me sleeping on the couch. I thought I'd cut it short this time. I blurted some Greek curses and got out, slamming the door. I kicked a couple of pine cones on the way and made the tires of the old station wagon squeal as I bolted it out of the driveway.

Damn it, I kept pounding my fist on the wheel. The woman thinks I am an idiot. She always sees the worst in everything I try to do. How's a person going to make any money so he'll amount to something, if he doesn't take any chances? I am not afraid of hard work and I am not going to allow my family to suffer; that's for sure.

And I don't expect my wife to "bring home the bacon," as the Americans say, either.

Before our third daughter was born, Margaret wanted to make some extra money, and even though I didn't agree, she got a job as a bookkeeper for an equipment rental company; the same company Linda Demming was working for. I was glad when that job was over. She was always in a hurry, never had any time to take care of the kids, clean the house, or cook a decent dinner. The money she was bringing home was not that great either. After day care, new clothes and transportation, there was hardly anything left.

It lasted about three months. One evening when I got home, I found her depressed and crying. She said the company decided to cut back and she got laid off. She was going to start looking for another job the next day, she said. I told her that I didn't want my wife working for anybody.

I took her out to dinner that night.

I kept on driving till I ran out of land and found myself staring at the tranquil Gulf of

Mexico. It always turned out that way. Whenever I felt depressed, angry, or just wanted to do some thinking, I would find myself by a shore, gazing at the open water and the horizon far away.

I parked at the edge of the bluff, pushed the seat back, lit a cigarette and stared at the boundless distance ahead. A freighter was leaving the harbor. Plumes of dark-gray smoke billowed out of the funnel, which meant the engineer on watch was increasing the fuel supply to the boilers to bring the propeller up to normal speed.

Soon the thoughts started creeping in, uninvited, bothersome and pesky, like mosquitoes on a pleasant night. Was I wasting my life? Where did all the years go? It seemed like yesterday when I jumped ship and was going to conquer the world. I wondered what became of the people I had sailed with; all those who chose to follow life as it was prescribed for them. From time to time I would run into some of them, still in the same jobs, still doing the same things, happy and proud of their small promotions and their petty achievements. I wondered what I would be now if I had stayed with the rest of the pack. But then damn it, what makes men like that any different from sheep?

The freighter was moving faster now, its superstructure glowing in the last rays of the setting sun. The smoke coming out of the funnel had become a light gray haze, barely visible; a sign that fuel pressures and temperatures were reaching their normal levels and things were settling in for the voyage.

I sat there staring at it as it was disappearing on the horizon. Pretty soon the oiler on watch would bring coffee for the engineer and the fireman and, standing under the engine room vent, they would swap stories of their adventures in the port they'd just left and tell of what they knew about the port they were heading to.

Some years earlier, that engineer could have been me.

Ah, what a wonderful life! Single, with no responsibilities, traveling from one port to the next, spending their days in the secure, care-free world of the ship, where everything has been taken care of for you. Where everybody has his rank, knows his place and there is no need for anybody having to prove anything to anybody. The biggest worry is how expensive the "girls" are in next port or if the "girls" in the last port didn't had anything catching.

Those were the fun years. Maybe it's not too bad to be the same as the sheep. Now I understand why so many seamen stay on one ship for long stretches of time without going home.

I should have done the same, or at least skipped that stupid trip to the village in Greece a few months back.

I started up the car and headed home. Margaret should have calmed down by now.

Chapter

3

*S*unday morning; I went to church. It's something I started after the Manolis Vervatos missionary visit.

Manolis is a fifty-year-old carpenter from Crete, who, like most imported Greeks, considers it his duty to butt in other people's lives. While remodeling one of the offices in the building, he heard there was a Greek on the same floor and with great persistence, managed to get Marilyn to point him in my direction.

I am sure, as she watched that crude impersonation of Zorba strut toward my office, she prayed to some God of Class and Decency to protect the place from further degradation.

I got a long lecture from Manolis that day on the benefits of "us sticking together" and a long list of reasons why I should be ashamed of myself for not being a member of the church, not supporting the Greek community in this hostile environment and not being a member of the great organization of AHEPA.

"AHEPA means American Hellenic Educational Progressive Association. It's for helping Greeks like us, here in America," he explained.

"It's a mouthful," I said.

I had heard of a fellow who had a switch under his desk that when pressed, would make the telephone ring. When he wanted to get rid of someone in his office, he would step on it, then tell the guy:" This will take a long time," or "This is confidential," and shoo him out.

I ended up buying two tickets to the AHEPA banquet, promised I would go to church next Sunday and made a note to find out more about the telephone switch.

Margaret has always been a faithful, strong and unwavering Baptist. Most of her family, other than the few who do their worshiping at the Inlet Bar and Grill, are strong, unwavering Baptists.

The few times Margaret convinced me to go to her church, I felt awkward. All the arm waving, loud praying and telling God what's on your mind out loud, for every one to hear, is definitely not for me. I prefer it the way the Greeks communicate with God: Praying by proxy. We have appointed the priest and the cantors to sing praises to the Lord and seek His blessings. And we, standing in the pews, can think of what we are going to do tomorrow, worry if we gave too many points on the Saints game, or speculate if what's-her-name, with the tight skirt over in the next pew, is having an affair with the guy across the aisle or if they just happened to look at each other funny. If the Lord did not bestow His blessings upon us, it would be because the priest or the cantors had not done their job right.

Every Sunday, Margaret is out of bed by seven-thirty, getting ready. Her Sunday school class starts at ten o'clock but she always says she is running late and needs my help: "Can you plug in the iron for me? Can you put Katerina's dress on? Can you remember to put the vegetables in with the roast?" An endless list of can-yous.

Then when they were almost ready, she would start: "Today we are having a speaker from South America, why don't you come with us?" or "We are having a spouse appreciation day," or "I am the only one whose husband doesn't come, I feel like a widow."

Since the Vervatos visit, when the Sunday morning "getting ready" panic starts, I am leaving for church. Nicole cleans her own shoes, Maria watches out for Katerina's dress and they are not any later for Sunday school than their usual lateness.

There are two Greek churches in this area, which are served by one full-time priest, two part-time cantors and a part-time choir that is in an uproar full time.

Margaret's church has a professional, school-trained, music director, and an activities director, and a fellowship director, and everything is being directed smoothly and orderly.

Usually on Sundays I join a small group of regulars at the church community hall to have coffee and catch up on world affairs, using up some of the liturgy time while doing some conscience-appeasing chore, like putting the chairs around the tables to be ready for the after-service social hour.

Leo Marks always makes the coffee. The first pot is drunk by us, the regulars, "to make sure it tastes right." Leo, whose name had started as Leonidas Makromeritis, is about seventy, thin and Americanized. He was born in Boston from Spartan parents and he is sure his family tree goes all the way back to the Big Leonidas from Sparta. During "The War" he was an army intelligence officer with three men under him; a much smaller command than his famous cousin's three hundred, but with a much larger inventory of war stories, which he keeps repeating while preparing the coffee, a task he has been doing for years, with the fussiness and dedication of a priest preparing communion.

When the first people come out of the church, just ahead of the collection plate, Leo computes the time to pour the water in the coffee maker based on some complex formula of his (so many minutes for a simple service, so many if there is a memorial, so many if the bishop is visiting and so on), and when the crowd comes out, the coffee is waiting for them, fresh and ready. His timing never misses.

We, the coffee-drinking early-comers, do the taste test on the coffee and we address all of the important world issues.

In some way it feels like being in the real coffee houses we left back home.

Manolis Vervatos comes in to get a cup of coffee "to strengthen his voice" before he goes in the church. He has newspapers mailed to him from Greece, and he feels obligated to bring everybody up-to-date on his version of the latest world events; the American foreign policy blunders, the stupidity of the Greek politicians for not seeing the obvious solution to the Turkish problem and the Cyprus conspiracy. He also never fails to brief everybody on the latest football scholarship offers to his three macho teenage sons. "I'm gonna have a hell of a time keeping the women off them boys," he chuckles as he leaves to go "help the priest."

Nick Podakakis, who must have had a very dull life, repeats the same stories every time: how primitive it was when he first came here, which, by the sound of it, was before Columbus, and how three years ago he got stuck cooking fifty chickens for an AHEPA banquet when none of the other "brothers" showed up to help.

John Papas, who is an accountant at a hospital, but acts like he owns it, makes sure everyone knows that a relative of his, from his mother's side, was lynched, and his parents got kicked out of Omaha in 1910. "They chased everybody out of town, more than two thousand of them, because somebody said the fellow did some hanky-panky with an American woman." He says his wife is planning to write a book about that "shameful event" as soon as she finds the time. "Persons in our position have so many obligations," he sighs.

Most of the men who came from Greece at an older age will go inside the church, light a candle, do a couple of up and down right-hand strokes in front of the icon, then turn around and come to the community hall. They will have some coffee and get into the middle of whatever is discussed.

Father George makes it known during the parish council meetings, that he doesn't like having to compete with the *cafenion* for attendance, but he is a domestic Greek, born in Ohio, to parents that had also been born here; he doesn't understand.

In my village, as in most Greek villages, there is a coffee house on the same square as the church. Every respectable village patriarch, dressed in his Sunday finest, will escort his wife as far as the center of the square, where she will go on into the church while he veers off to the cafenion. Some, hedging their bets, will go inside the church, light a candle and come right out to join the others in discussions of domestic politics and international conspiracies.

It is an undisputed fact that a Greek male, equipped with a good *comboloy*, (worry beads), and occupying three chairs in a coffee house, is capable of solving the most complex domestic and international problems. The priest and church deacons, not wanting to put world harmony in peril, leave them alone. When the offering plate is passed around, they make it a point to include the *cafenion* customers.

This Sunday, I was waiting for Pete Carras to show up. He was in the ship supply business and I was eager to tell him that now I was a *synathelphos* (a colleague), and ask him for some job leads. Before going into the church, Pete usually came in the community center to have an early cup of coffee with the regulars, dispense wisdom and praise the good sense of those who agreed with him.

This time Pete was escorted by his wife and they went straight into the church. He didn't come out till the end of the service with Mrs. Carras coyly hanging onto his arm, more for the purpose of shortening his leash, than for affection. I walked up to him just as Irene Papas, the accountant's wife from Omaha, was pouring it on Pete's wife about receiving "the most beautiful invitation" from them, and "how nice it was of Mr. Peter to rent the country club for the wedding reception," and how she was sure Helen must be very excited and she most definitely deserved it: "She is such a wonderful daughter," and on and on.

"You see what I am passing through?" Pete said when I got close. "You have daughters, you will be passing through the same."

"'Going through,' Peter," quickly corrected his wife, glancing nervously around her.

Pete walked away from the women's group towards the coffee table.

"Well Pete, it's done," I said. I flipped a calling card from my shirt pocket and handed it to him. "Throw something my way, don't give it all to Dixie."

Pete read the card squinting his eyes.

"Like I said on the phone," I added, "I used your Telex number. I'll be chipping in for the expenses."

He nodded in agreement, then felt the paper with his fingers. "Fancy," he diagnosed, "a rich looking card, for sure. Maybe you have job for me in your global incorporation?"

"Sure, you can head the entertainment department," I chuckled.

"Stavros do that job real good, he know all the poutan..." He cut the word short, cast his eyes toward the ceiling to show his sudden realization that he was on church property, then continued: "He knows all the *entertainment* girls in the port; he has to take the captains and the stewards there."

31

"Pete, I can use all the help I can get," I said.

"Before, when you come and talk to me, I speak to you and I say..." Pete searched for the English word, then remembering he was speaking to an import like himself, he continued in Greek: "*Vre si, what shit patriotes*, (countrymen) are we? Of course I will help you. Some day you will be a big shot and I come to you for a loan. Never know when the wife might kick me out of the house; this is America, you know? Damn women talk back in this country." He took a cup of coffee and poured two envelopes of sugar in it.

Pete was almost six feet tall, in his late fifties, with a full head of wavy gray hair and a pair of bright eyes that wanted to know everything. On Sundays, he always wore varying shades of blue suits, with bright ties, monogrammed cufflinks and a miniature red rose on his lapel. The "rich Pete," as most Greeks in Bigport called him, (to distinguish him from the other Petes in our community) was handsome enough and smooth talking enough to have convinced the daughter of a second generation Greek in the food supply business to marry him when his ship had stayed in the shipyard for repairs many years back. He got a job in a ship supply business owned by a Jewish guy, put all of the tricks he had learned as chief steward to use, and in two years had bought part interest in the outfit. A few years later, when the guy died, the Carras Ship Supply was born. At his wife's coaxing, he upgraded his name from Petros Karamaounas to Mister Peter Carras for her and her garden club and Pete Carras for the common people — short enough, so the Americans wouldn't choke on it but Greekish enough to be recognized by the ship owners. Only a few, fresh from Greece, dared to call him Petro, and then only when out of his wife's hearing.

At his wife's insistence, he tried to distance himself from the villagers of his island and — at least when his wife was around — restrain his familiarity with the fresh imports. When I got to know Pete Carras better, I could tell that he was a more timid and uncomfortable person when he was with his wife. The prevailing air of confidence, the joking, the teasing and the boasting, when he was around people who came from Greece, wasn't there when he was with his wife's crowd.

Pete, as is expected from pillars of the community, had been parish council president, was a visible contributor to the church and a conspicuous participant in lots of Greek organizations. His oldest son, much to Pete's disappointment and his wife's delight, became a lawyer. Last month he was appointed county district attorney. I am sure Mrs. Carras, thankful she lived in the land of forgiveness and opportunity, was nursing the hope that "her Steven" would overcome the handicap of his paternal ancestry and go on to the highest of political offices.

Her twenty-year-old daughter was the masterpiece of her creation. As an obedient daughter, dutifully striving to fulfill her mother's aspirations, she belonged to cultural societies and Mardi Gras societies and all kinds of societies deemed proper for persons of refinement. Her upcoming wedding to a government "administrator" from one of the old Bigport families was promising to be the social event of the year. The chosen few from our church who were honored with invitations, were boasting and rubbing-it-in to the rest of us.

Pete took a sip of the coffee, then put another envelope of sugar in it.

I asked him if I could come by his office to get the names of some of his customers. "I'd like to write to them that I am in business," I said.

"Sure, but it'll cost you," he said grinning. I promised I would buy lunch.

"I will be waiting," he said, then intercepted Christos Pittas who was walking by. "Oh, hello Mr. Christo, fancy new tie, and new shirt, business must be real good." With his fingers, he felt Christo's ordinary looking red striped tie over an ordinary looking, blue and white striped shirt.

Christos Pittas smiled, uncovering yellow teeth. He was in his late fifties, short, and almost completely bald, except for a grayish, fuzzy band around his head. He sported an oversized mustache.

"Petro, you know what they say back home: 'The cough and the wealth, are impossible to hide'. I see you've got a brand new truck: you are the one who has all the money."

"And over here they say: 'Mind you business', there isn't any wealth." It was a wimpy denial.

Most Greeks believe that admitting to having wealth or being successful, is considered boasting, and boasting is frowned on by God and also attracts the "evil eye." Pete was getting around that problem by pleading poverty in a manner that highlighted his affluence.

Christos Pittas and the "rich Pete" came from the same village on the island of Andros. Christos came to Bigport to work at his uncle's restaurant about twenty years back. He never married and never learned how to drive a car, saying he couldn't afford either of them. He always lived in a small room above the kitchen. He mastered enough English to terrorize the waitresses and keep the kitchen help of the Andros Restaurant on their toes. Even after his uncle died and he'd inherited everything, he didn't change his way of living.

When he sold his uncle's house he sent the money to his family in the village. To the villagers of Pano Hora, Christos Pittas was a great benefactor. He always sent money for repairing the church and the school and for the schooling of poor children and for paving the village square with new flagstones. "When Christos goes to the island, they ring the bell and people run to the quay to meet him," Leo told me one Sunday.

Pete Carras sent money once, to help with the painting of The Church of the Holy Cross. There were rumors that Pete had difficulty getting his wife's approval. She claimed that her ancestors came from Athens and she wouldn't have anything to do with the uncultured "fish heads."

The cultured Mrs. Carras never traveled to Greece and her only connection with the country (besides her husband, whom she tried to shield from the garden club ladies, and about whom she would say "he is European" when asked where he was from) were some Grecian-style plaster columns and naked statues that the interior decorator from the pricey Whittington's furniture store convinced her were just the thing for a lady of her noble heritage and sophisticated personality.

On the way home, I drove by the docks to see if any ships had come in. In every floating thing I saw a potential customer. There weren't any newcomers, but I saw the chief engineer of a Greek ship, whom I had met a few days earlier, and we got into a long conversation. He told me he had worked for a ship-repairing outfit before and that if he was to run my shop I would get "richer than the Bank of England, guaranteed." All I had to do was arrange with immigration for his work permit. I told him I would look into it the next day. He said he would call his company's main office in the morning and tell them that the bilge piping manifold was leaking badly and had to be replaced right away. If I were to come on board around noon he was sure I would have the order for a new one.

I bought a newspaper from a scarecrow-looking character in army fatigues at a traffic light and headed home. On Sunday afternoons, I like to sit in the patio under the shade of the wisteria arbor with a cool drink and read the paper.

Margaret walked up to me holding a bunch of streamers as soon as I stepped out of the car. During the last two days, we only spoke in the presence of the kids and our conversation had been limited to what was absolutely necessary for survival. Our sleeping arrangement consisted of getting as far away as two people can get on a queen-size bed and avoiding contact as if the other was high voltage wire.

"Church ran long," I said.

"I bet you forgot to pick up the balloons, too," she said. "Good thing I bought some, just in case."

We hung streamers across the patio, stuck posters of cute little giraffes, teddy bears and fluffy lambs all over the place and hung a big sign over the long table under the carport, announcing in glittering letters: "Happy Birthday Katerina." Daughter number three — my last attempt for a son — was turning three years old today. I inflated a multitude of balloons and tied them in multi-colored clusters in the places Margaret told me to.

She handed me a thing with a Mexican name that looked like a donkey and asked me to hang it from the top of the carport.

"Can you reach it?" she joked, never passing up an opportunity to remind me that she was two inches taller than me.

I put the Mexican donkey on the floor and reached for her waist.

"Let's go in the bedroom and I'll show you how far I can reach," I said.

"Bet you mean it too, right in the middle of trying to get everything ready; that's your way of doing things."

I moved my hand upwards under her blouse and rubbed her skin.

She waited a bit then took a step back. "Finish tying the stuff before the people start coming or you're sleeping on the couch tonight," she said. But the way she said it, I knew the storm was over.

I tied one big cluster of balloons on the mailbox, to make it easier for the guests to find the house. The Rolling Hills subdivision was a flat cow pasture that some developer had cut up into postage stamp lots and planted with identical miniature houses; all low, squatty jobs, with three tiny bedrooms and with what they called "a bath-and-a-half." All had asphalt shingle roofs whose color alternated with the two colors of the bricks: Gray shingles for yellow brick houses, black shingles for red brick. Since the houses were built at the same time, all of the surviving vegetation was the same size and in the same state of misery. The delicate white-trunked river birch planted in front of each house were slowly dying of embarrassment.

It had happened quite a few times that some neighbor who had a few drinks too many, tried to unlock the front door of the wrong house. In mine, I built flower beds on either side of the entrance door, in which Margaret planted roses. I sent a photograph of the house to my parents, with the roses in bloom, and the station wagon parked in the driveway.

Margaret had appointed our two older daughters deputy hostesses for the party.

Maria, the eight-year-old, got the job of entertaining the young guests till it was time for the birthday queen to blow out the candles and dive into the cake. She gathered all the chirping, bubbling, noisy children into the den and played school house, even giving prizes to the student who did best. In her thick round glasses, her brown hair braided in two shoulder-length pigtails and her purple button-up dress with white cuffs and white collar, she could be the poster child for the school teacher's union.

At the appointed time, the junior school teacher marched her class to where the Mexican donkey was hung, directed them to take whacks at it and watched over them as they scrambled for the candy that fell from it.

The six-year-old Nicole was mother's helper. She helped cover the long table with the frilly pink table cloth and place in the center of it the coconut-chocolate Mini Mouse cake Margaret had made. She made sure that Katerina didn't get her pretty yellow dress dirty, checked the cookies for flavor and on a corner of the cake, where finger marks were not too conspicuous, made sure the icing of the cake wasn't spoiled.

She looked adorable in her bright yellow and white frilly dress. She had big blue eyes, curly blonde hair, a slightly plump figure and a unique way of turning on the charm and snuggling up to everyone, so that no matter what she did, no one could stay angry with her for very long.

People started flocking in around four-thirty.

The first to arrive was Tom Edwards. He ambled up the driveway dressed in Levy pants, jacket and pink shirt, with the relaxed, carefree air of a government bureaucrat.

He doesn't have any children but Margaret invited him because "He is our neighbor."

Tom looked around, took in the set-up and pronounced: "Maggie, you have outdone yourself."

"Oh, thank you Tom," said Margaret and stared and smiled at him a bit longer than politeness required, I thought.

The menu for the occasion was grilled stuff. Margaret had hit a sale at Food World and stocked up on meat: steaks for the grown-ups, hot dogs and hamburgers for the youngsters and chicken for those on a diet. In the far corner of the patio, the grill, built from salvaged boiler bricks, was running at full steam. Early in the afternoon, I overheard giggly Linda Demming tell her husband: "Howard, ask Nick to show you how to build a grill like that. The metal ones don't last long and don't look that good either."

"Nick doesn't travel as much as I do. A project like that takes time," mumbled Howard.

There was a very brief moment that afternoon when a weak spark of affection toward Tom Edwards glowed in my heart. I overheard him tell Margaret while loading his plate, "This is a very good grill, functional and well constructed." Then he told Margaret her hair looked great.

He was just as generous with his expert opinion about my cooking. He loved everything, especially the roasted onions. Sometime between his fourth and hundredth extra helping, he asked me for the recipe.

"There isn't any recipe," I said. "Just put the onion by the fire, turning it every now and then, and when it's cooked, cut it up, pour a little olive oil and lemon over it, sprinkle some salt and oregano and that's it."

"That's almost primitive," said Tom. Then while re-stacking the load on his plate he said in a confiding, secretive tone: "You picked the wrong time to do it. Most definitely the wrong time."

"You can cook them any time Tom, there isn't any special time for doing it."

His round, moon-like, glowing face came closer to mine.

"I do not mean the onions, it is the other matter I am referring to."

"Then I didn't do it, whatever other matter you are referring to, I didn't do it."

"Margaret told me about resigning your position to form a service type company."

"I am going to be doing ship repairs, I am not opening a service station, Tom."

"That's what a service company is, providing a service; you do not manufacture anything." He sounded as if he had struggled to bring the explanation down to my level. "At the present, neither the political, nor the economic factors are conducive to such an endeavor. It is unquestionably an ill-timed move."

"I'll make it," I said.

"Good luck," he said, in the same tone of voice he would have said "Have a nice trip" to a butterfly flying into a hurricane. Then he walked towards a group of women, leaving me to concentrate on deciphering the meaning of his fancy words.

During the evening, Margaret kept darting in and out of the house, making sure everybody had enough food and refreshments and cake and reminding me to take it easy with the sprinkling of garlic and the oregano on the meat. "Not everybody likes things the way you do, you know?"

"I know what I am doing. You just watch the kids and stay away from Tom Edwards. Why you had to tell that windbag about my business?"

"He's just being considerate, Tom is like that," she said. There was a mischievous glow in her eyes and a faint smile as she walked away. A couple of minutes later I saw her refilling his iced-tea cup.

I was grilling for most of the time the party was going on. It kept me from having to take part in silly games, or get into conversations with people who kept asking me to repeat what I said and talked to me as if I had trouble hearing.

From the grill I could see my Maria directing the children in a ring-around-the-roses game. I admired how she convinced a shy little girl to join hands with the others and how she got a mischievous boy to behave and follow her lead. Soon she had all of them circle-dancing, falling down and standing up like the Radio City chorus line.

I knew I was looking at the future manager of Poseidon Marine Services.

Howard Demming came over, took a root beer out of the ice chest, then closed it and sat on the lid, making it creak.

"Wish I could do what you are doing," he said after taking a long gulp, "but Linda would have a fit if I said anything."

"You mean cooking?"

"I mean going into business; I've always wanted my own fishing camp." He had both hands wrapped around the can and a dreamy look in his eyes. "Yeah, that would be nice, but she'll never go for it," he sighed.

"Margaret is not exactly thrilled with what I'm doing either; she listens too much to what others say."

"Margaret will back you up. And she won't take crap from nobody neither. Linda told me what she told Miss Southern Bell when she walked off the job."

"What do you mean? Margaret said they were cutting back and laid her off."

"That's like Margaret. Linda told me that the prissy new office manager asked Margaret to start using her maiden name instead of Pilios because some of their clients might not feel comfortable with foreigners. Linda said Margaret stood up and looked that wimpy bigot right in the eyes and told her: 'You might be ashamed of yours but I am proud of my husband; you can keep your job,' and walked right out."

"I hope she doesn't regret it," I said. "Going into business is a big plunge."

"Your people always go into business and they always make it."

"Not always, Howard. You just don't hear about the ones that don't." I could think of at least four of "my people" in Bigport who declared bankruptcy last year.

"I knew a Greek in Cincinnati," Howard went on, "that had a hamburger joint in our office building.

Just a hole-in-the-wall, but by the time I got transferred five years later, he owned the whole building.

Your people are like the Jews, they stick together."

"It just seems that way, Howard."

Howard and Linda Demming lived next door and went to the same church as Margaret. Howard was fat and Linda was skinny. Their girl was the same age as Nicole, and their boy was a couple of months older than Katerina. Howard had gotten early retirement from the Air Force and was selling paper mill machinery for some outfit in Chicago. Margaret was always pointing him out to me as an example of family stability and sensible planning.

"Howard wouldn't quit a sure thing to go chase ships all over the creation," she told me yesterday.

The party started breaking up soon after sunset. One by one the guests kissed the birthday girl good-bye, hugged the hostess, saying "It was a wonderful party," patted me on the shoulder — "Great cooking" — and left.

Tom Edwards lingered longer than the others and after dispensing his starchy pleasantries, said quite casually on his way out, "One of your Oriental trees was knocked off but I put it back in the pot. It did not break. I am certain it will be all right."

It was not all right; eventually my favorite Japanese Maple Bonsai, died.

"You have a bunch more of those silly little trees; it's not like it was the only one," Margaret said, always defending him.

To me, that has been one of the great mysteries: How is it that windbags like Thomas Doubleyou Edwards always manage to snow people and get them to think they are better, smarter and wiser than the rest of us, who bust our asses to make a decent living?

Chapter 4

*O*n Monday morning I was at the office before daybreak. I made the coffee, filled my cup and went to my desk, ready to do battle with the world. From the top drawer I took out a yellow note sheet entitled "Projected Monthly Expenditures," and for the millionth time I read every single line of it, nursing the secret hope that I had over-estimated one of the items.

As I read each line, my stomach would tighten just a little more. The list read like the inescapable verdict of some high court.

Office rent: $ 250.00

Janitorial: $ 25.00

Secretary: $ 175.00

Telephone: $ 100.00 (In parenthesis I had written: Maximum estimate, will keep lower.)

At the end of each month I was supposed to pay GESCO four hundred and fifty dollars for the rent, the cleaning woman and Marilyn's pay for my work. Phil Domain had been understanding, but he wasn't going to subsidize me. Marilyn would also separate my phone calls and bill me for my part.

One good thing in this deal was that now, in a small way, I had a say-so in Marilyn's pay.

There was also an amount for "miscellaneous expenditures," which I kept changing every time I looked at the list, and one more line that read "Salary for N.P.," which did not have an amount. I didn't spend any time studying that line. Margaret had studied enough. "Looks like Phil got the best end of that deal," she had said.

Around eight o'clock I called Captain Steiner. The meticulous secretary informed me that he wasn't in yet. Yes she had given him the message. Yes, she would remind him again.

Soon after, Marilyn knocked at the door, (the first time I remember her doing it) then walked in. "I couldn't make out a couple of words on this page," she said, showing me the *Oil Transporter* proposal. "They look like dirty words." I told her what they were: they were clean words. She started to leave, then turned around and pointed to a paragraph at the bottom of the page: "This part here; are you sure that's how you want to say it? It doesn't sound right."

"It's a contract Marilyn, not a poem."

"Didn't want them to think you were illiterate."

"Just so they don't think I am stupid, I don't care what they think."

"O.K., I'll type it like this; it'll be ready in a bit."

She walked out, softly closing the door behind her.

There was some work for GESCO to be done, which I was doing on a "fixed price" contract, but it could wait. I had to get ready for the repair jobs. I would be needing supplies, material, tools and equipment. And to get those, I needed to have *established credit*, the most important component in any business, especially the ship repair business: Credit to buy supplies, to rent equipment, to do payroll; credit to survive the times of the lean cows and to keep on going in the times of fat ones. Credit is the foundation of a business.

All I had was an anemic Master Card that kept running out of breath every time I charged more than two hundred dollars.

But to open a credit account, I needed credit references, and I could only get credit references if I had a credit account.

I searched through the Yellow Pages and found one company I hadn't tried yet. I told Marilyn to take messages if anybody called and went to see them.

The credit manager of Gulf Welding Supply was a big man; built like a crude snowman, with pink, fat cheeks and an oversized nose. He looked over sixty, smoked a fat stinky cigar, breathed hard and wore a checkered black-and-white hat that sat comically on the top of his gray hair. He kept eating peanuts from a bowl at the far corner of his desk, making the chair groan every time he reached for them. He pointed to the chair across the desk and listened to my monologue without missing a beat on his puffing and chewing.

When I finished, he pulled out a credit application from a drawer and handed it to me.

"Thought all you people were in the cooking business," he said. "That fellow, Pete something, that has that little restaurant by the rail road, he is making a killing."

"It's Pittas, Christos Pittas," I said.

"Yah, something like that. Gonna need a bank reference and three credit references. If everything's O.K., we'll set you up for a five hundred dollar credit line. How long you said you been in business?"

"Next week I'll be doing my first job," I said almost in a whisper.

"Might help if you get one of your people to co-sign for you then. Shouldn't be hard, you folks are close. Get that Pete fellow that has the Andy restaurant."

"It's the Andros restaurant," I said.

Mournfully, I put the credit application in my pocket, said "Thank you very much for your time," and got up.

He stretched, reaching for more peanuts. I slid the bowl closer, but he pushed it back where it was.

"That's my exercise," he said.

Pete Carras' place was next to the Interstate, a short distance from the docks, south of the Dixie shipyard. Approaching from the river, from the highway or from anywhere, you couldn't miss the large CARRAS SHIP SUPPLY sign, in bold blue letters on a white background, on the roof of the long brick building.

Pete was standing by the loading dock, arguing with Stavro Rigotis, his assistant.

Stavros, a graduate of the Piraeus school of street hustling, was a thirty-year-old perpetual motion machine in a tanned hide, about a hundred forty pounds fully dressed. He was responsible for going on board the ships, outsmarting the competition and coaxing an order out of the captains. Then when the stuff was delivered, he got the bills of lading (*ta billia* in Greek-American) signed and stamped by the captain, and distributed the bribes and commissions. (Something for the captain, something for the chief steward, something for anybody else who had his hand out, because it was expected and because the competition is doing it.)

The only other person working there was Ramon Gonzales, a plump, easygoing, slow moving Guatemalan.

The argument was about two tins of feta that had been delivered without getting the papers signed before the ship sailed.

"Ramon forgot *ta billia*," Stavros explained, "if you call New York, Captain Stamos will O.K. it, he'll take your word."

"We'll spend more on the goddamn telephones than we make from the goddamn cheese," griped Pete, starting toward his office. I followed close behind. On the way, he stooped and picked up an institutional size can of beans that had rolled on the floor and put it back on the pallet, mumbling curses about the help that didn't give a dick about their job.

His office was a fourteen-foot square partitioned corner on the far side of the warehouse. It was elevated three steps from the floor, with big windows offering a full view of the work area. On the paneled walls, there was an icon of Saint Nicolas, some posters from a marine paint company and a calendar from a rope supply outfit showing a Greek island.

At the corner of the large leather-top desk, was a framed photograph of his oldest son shaking hands with the Alabama Governor. Pete reclined in his huge leather chair, took a cigarette out of his Winston hard-pack and tapped the filter end on the face of his gold wristwatch.

On the wall directly above his throne, in a fancy carved frame, a large photographic portrait of Mr. Pete watched over everyone below. He looked like a movie star: wavy gray hair, pointed handkerchief in his breast pocket matching the bright yellow tie, big brown eyes staring sternly into the warehouse.

I sat on a brown vinyl couch across from his desk and told him about Gulf Welding Supply wanting somebody to cosign for me.

"With who you speak over there?" Pete asked.

"I don't remember his name; it was a big man with a big cigar."

Pete lit his cigarette. "With a hat like Bear Bran the coach for Alabama?" he grinned knowingly, "I know him; no problem. I call him now."

He located his number in one of the corners of the over-scribbled desk pad and dialed the number with a pencil.

"I want speak Mr. Sam Fox." he said when someone answered.

It took one jar of feta and Pete Carras' word that I could be trusted, and I was set up for one thousand dollars credit with Gulf Welding Supply Company.

"Auburn will beat the shit on Alabama Saturday," Pete said into the phone. "O.K. we have bet for ten dollar. Pleasure to speak to you Sam. Yes, I see you in the restaurant of George tomorrow."

Pete hung up. "I buy the acetylene and the oxygen from him," he said. He puffed on his cigarette, then added: "I feel sorry for you, you open business now. Now you cannot find nobody to work. Everybody want big paycheck and no work."

"It's always been like that, Mr. Pete. My father says the same thing."

"Want something to drink?" he asked, "Coca-Cola, coffee, I got some tsipouro a captain brought to me from Andros."

"No thanks, I came to get the addresses I talked to you about yesterday."

"Oh yeah, now I remember; you promised to buy lunch too."

He unlocked the top drawer and handed me a thick, rubbed-off-brown, address book.

"Here, start from *the alpha*," he said. Then spotting something in the warehouse, he swiftly walked around the desk, opened the glass door and shouted out: "*Vre* Ramon, no put the cans to the top of the *domatoes* it get mushed."

He sat back down and sighed disgusted. "Three years doing the job and still no learn how to load the damn truck."

I leafed through the smudged, worn pages of the address book. The writing looked cryptic; the names were written in a mixture of Greek and English letters, with numbers and strange symbols next to them. I handed it back.

"You better read it to me Mr. Pete; I can't break your code."

He started reading and I wrote on a yellow pad, as fast as I could, once in a while suggesting a correction: "I think it's Lexington street Mr. Pete, not lexicon." He interpreted the coded notes on the margins: "This one pays on time, this one is slow but you no lose no money, these here, are cheap and slow sonovabitches and everybody in the company want commission."

I knew that every strange symbol and little scribble next to the names represented experience gained through years of frustration, gratification, haggling and disappointments; I was getting an education.

When we finished, Pete gave more instructions to the loading crew. Then we got in his pick-up and headed for the restaurant. We hadn't driven more than one block when he pounded on the wheel in anger: "Eh, what the hell? My goddamn brain is gone; forgot to tell Stavro to tie the pallets down, they gonna fly all over the truck."

He made a U turn back to the warehouse and walked over to where the forklift was.

"You can't get anybody good to work nowadays, that's for sure," he said, getting back in the truck. "I'm lucky my Bobby will be starting soon."

"His Bobby" was his third son, a quiet, meticulous youth, studying Business Management at Auburn University.

Fifteen minutes later, we came to the parking lot of the Wharf Restaurant, a long wooden structure on a pier that was supposed to look like an old warehouse. Inside, the walls were full of ship's wheels, lanterns, compasses, life rings: anything from a ship that George Skoufos, the owner and chief cook of the place, could get through the door.

The lunch-hour rush was over and George was at the cash register, looking inside the drawer, his thick eyebrows drawn close, scrutinizing the lunch hour harvest.

We sat at a table by the window and when George came over, Pete ordered: "Bring us your best, George, the boy here is buying. He is opening shop and gonna be a rich man."

George stopped writing. He put the pencil back behind his ear, set the order pad on the table and sat down.

"Nobody gets rich in restaurant business no more; too damn many franchises; can't compete with them." He leaned in my direction and confided: "If I was younger, I get into real estate, that's where the money is now."

His face was pink and round, in harmony with the rest of his body. "I have some American customers in real estate business and they make the money by the sack-full."

"I don't know anything about real estate, George. I am going into ship repairs."

"Oh, that's nice, that's a good business. Bravo, bravo, congratulations."

It sounded as though he exhaled heavily, or maybe it was the effort of getting up.

"I have plenty customers in shipping business. I know all the big bosses of Dixie shipyard. They eat here all the time. Bill Yeoman too, we are good friends. He eat here all the time. Come for lunch one day and I will introduce you to them."

I said I would.

We ordered stuffed peppers, the day's special, and while we were waiting George brought a plate of fried calamari and a bottle of *retsina* wine.

"Something to make a toast," he said. We toasted.

"You don't like it?" asked George, seeing that I only took a small sip of the wine.

"I never liked the smell of it, it tastes like turpentine."

"I will bring you something else then."

He came back with a half a bottle of *Ouzo*.

"I keep this for special occasions," he said, pouring into the small glass. We toasted again to my success, to my health, to George's and to Pete's health, and to a couple of other things, and by the time I paid the bill, I felt sure I was going to conquer the world.

On the way to the truck Pete got a newspaper from the yellow machine by the door and while walking, looked at the front page and started arguing with it.

"Bullshit, he no know what is talking about," he shouted. "I tell you, they no like the boy, they no like because he is not like them, that's what it is." He slammed the truck door and we shot out of the parking lot.

I glanced at the paper. The "boy" was his oldest son, Steve, the new District Attorney. Pete was having a hard time getting used to the publicity that came with the job.

"What's the paper saying Pete?"

"Bullshit, goddamn politic bullshit, that's all."

On the way back, we drove by Dixie Shipyard. Beyond the chain-link fence, I could see two small freighters tied up at the dock and people climbing all over them, like ants: chipping hammers and grinders running full blast. "This guy is stuffing his pockets with both hands. He is always busy," said Pete gesturing towards the shipyard. "He charges like hell, but he is the only one around."

"Six months from now, I'll have all of his business," I said.

"I know the right boy for your helper," continued Pete. "His name is Antonis Vrahakis I wish I could hire him but my Bobby will be coming to work soon; he is finishing with the university next month."

"I don't think he'll work for free, Pete. Right now I can't even pay myself."

Pete pulled up in front of his place.

"Next time, I buy the lunch," he said when we got out of his truck.

"I'll remember it."

We entered his office just as the Telex machine stopped clicking. Pete tore off the paper dangling in front of it, glanced at it and handed it to me.

"Here Mr. Big Shot, no forget my commission."

I grabbed it. It was from Captain George Steiner: *MV George P*. will be arriving Bigport July twenty four. Proceed with repairs per your quote. Contract mailed."

I was in business.

Chapter

5

I hadn't always planned to have my own business. That "cockamamie idea" came into my head a few months back, after my visit to Taxiarhes, the village where I grew up. I had been away for twelve years. I waited to visit till I had a job that I could brag about and make all those who stayed behind jealous. I didn't want to be like a lot of people, who watch every penny when they are on vacation.

And damn it, I was sure I was ready.

I had what the Americans call a "white collar" job. I worked in an office, wore a tie, was called "Mr. Nick" and had an expense account. I was going to show the sheep herders and the farmers in the village that I was living "the good life."

I rented the biggest car Hertz had in Greece.

First, I took Margaret and the three girls to places they had talked about at school and read in the bible: Philipi, Corinth, the Parthenon, explaining in detail everything they saw. (Margaret said I bragged as if I had something to do with it.)

After the touring, I drove our big car to Taxiarhes. On the way, Margaret asked me quite a few times to stop to take pictures of the beautiful scenery or to let the girls pick pretty wild flowers growing near the road. None of them wanted to admit that the winding mountain road was making them carsick.

At the village, I parked under the old chestnut tree. A young boy pulling a white goat stopped and looked at us briefly, then took off running up the steep cobblestone path. I placed a rock against the back tire and spent some time discussing with Margaret which suitcases we should carry first. Then with careful, city-dweller's steps, we walked up the same path the boy had taken.

When we were within a few yards from the house I saw the same boy going down the front steps, while counting some coins. My mother was right behind him. Margaret asked me what the boy was doing but there wasn't time to explain about the old custom of running ahead to announce good tidings, such as the arrival of loved ones; my mother had reached us and she was smothering me with tearful hugs.

We returned to the car later, escorted by both my parents and Dimos, my younger brother to pick up the rest of the suitcases. When we stopped for a breather at the half-way point before starting up the hill, my father, glancing at the multitude of suitcases, said: "You must have sailed with men from Hios. You know what they say about the seamen from Hios when they come home, don't you?"

I did but told him I didn't.

"When crewmen from Hios return to the island, they bring lots of shining new suitcases, so it'll be talked on the island that so and so's son returned rich, but each one of them only has a shirt and a change of underwear in it."

Dimos broke out into a loud laugh. I could tell it was to please father; he always did that.

"In mine I got socks and handkerchiefs too," I said and we both laughed. It was a lukewarm laugh, intended to make both of us more comfortable, to make us think that nothing had changed.

At the dinner table, Margaret and the girls spent most of their time re-arranging the pieces of roast lamb with orzo on their plates. It's mother's specialty and my favorite but for them it had too much garlic, and there was no mint jelly. After a while they said they were tired and went to the room mother had prepared for us. They sat up talking till I went to bed about three hours later.

"How come you left so early?" I asked. "You should've stayed and talked with mother some."

"She don't talk like our regular grandma," said Katerina.

"Talk? Talk with who? You never bothered to teach us how to speak Greek. Remember how many times I asked you to? Eh? do you?"

"Oh come on Margaret, you know enough Greek by now."

When we went for a walk the next morning, I was stunned by how much the village had changed. Every hovel and goat barn had been given a thick coat of whitewash, called a "villa" and offered for rent. Hand-painted signs nailed on chestnut trees and fence posts were advertising "rooms to let", in English and German, with arrows pointing up the winding cobblestone paths to "Villa Giannis" or "Villa Katina." The tranquil silence I found so unbearable when I was growing up and was now looking forward to, had been replaced by the cacophony of chain saws, concrete mixers and overloaded motorcycles that were making up in ear-splitting noise what they lacked in horsepower. Huge trucks with thundering, smoke-belching diesel engines were constantly struggling to make the steep climb up the freshly bulldozed roads that scarred the mountainside. The displaced red clay streaked down the hills: the bleeding, open wounds of the mountain.

At the square, the general store that used to stock everything a person in the village needed had been enlarged and divided in two. A metal Coca-Cola sign said one side was now a "Supermarket." Below the bold black English characters, somebody had written the same word by hand in Greek. Gone were the salted cod and loops of sausage hanging from the ceiling and the open sacks with rice, lentils, native beans, the crates of smoked herring and the barrels of nails that used to be along the walls. Now, there were instant coffee pouches, toastbrot loaves and breakfast-cereal boxes stacked in neat rows on metal shelves, like in a 7-11 store, only the signs were in Greek and German.

The other half of the building was a "Hardware Store," its shelves stocked full of things I never knew existed when I was growing up: small electric fans, hair dryers, electric extension cords and plastic garden-hose fittings.

Later that evening, I went to the Festorias' coffee house at the end of the square. Most of my old playmates were there and acted glad to see me. I had expected to find them aged, needing a shave (since it was only the middle of the week), with calloused hands and clothes showing the scars of field work and livestock handling.

None of them looked like that. One or two wore baseball caps, all were clean-cut and their clothes looked like they came from the same stores as mine. After the greeting and the hugging they started bombarding me with prying questions about my job and my life in America. They listened to my answers as if they were hearing a fish story, and before I'd finished, they started telling me what they were doing.

Stefanis Patekas, the same one who took three years to pass the sixth grade, clean-shaven, in denim pants and jacket, showed me a colored brochure of *Hotel Kalithea*. "Recognize the place, Niko?" He didn't wait for my answer. "It's the old house by the school. I added another floor, cleaned up the old stable and connected it with the house. I've got twelve rooms now. Keep them rented almost half of the year. Easy money. Don't bother with sheep no more." His thin, greasy mustache was stretched straight by the grin.

A few minutes later, cousin Giannis Giannakos entered the *cafenio*, with the roar and handshaking of a politician running for re-election.

He was a runt of a man, weighing no more than a hundred-forty pounds, most of it in his mustache, a bundle of brown straw stuck under his nose. His clothes were new and shiny and two sizes too big. When he saw me he stood for a moment and looked me over, then in a shaky voice he brayed: "*Vre, vre, vre Niko*, at last, you got enough courage to come back." He gave me a wimpy hug, stepped back and examined me again, pinched me on both cheeks, declared he was glad to see me, and loudly enough to be heard across the mountain, ordered a round of drinks for everybody.

One hour later we left the *cafenio* together. Walking slowly, he blabbed about his shrewd planning and the timely moves of his buyings and sellings that made him such a great success.

"I knew this place was going to be something big one day. The foreigners are buying everything. The more run-down a place is, the more they like it. All a smart man has to do is wait for the right time. Did I give you my card?"

I told him he had, but he gave me another one anyway. It was like the one my father had sent me: A bi-fold, cheap looking yellow card, showing a two story whitewashed house. Under it, it read: *Villa Giannis, Jonny Giannakos, Proprietor*.

"You did a good job fixing up Maneta's old barn," I said.

"It was part of the dowry. That, and the bean field in front of it. Now I have better parking than anybody else. That's why I can get more for my rooms."

"That's good," I said.

"Did I tell you I have two sons? They are eleven and ten, aces, both of them. In a few years they'll take over and I'll have nothing to worry about." He took out a pack of Marlboros, offering me a cigarette and then a light with a gold-colored butane lighter.

"You tried, you did what you thought best, I'm sure," he said exhaling. "And your daughters are very beautiful, anyway." He was patting me on the shoulder, as if consoling a child who came last in a race.

We had stopped at the straight, half-way point of the path to my house, by the old chestnut tree with the hollow trunk, catching our breath before starting up the steep hill. A considerate full moon frugally shed some of its light on the old stones in our path. It conserved most of it for Giannis' oversized gold watch, his three gold rings and his gold cross, big enough for a Bishop, dangling from a gold, battleship-size anchor chain around his neck.

He turned and faced me.

"I am going to confess something to you," he said. "I see you as more like a brother than a cousin. I was always jealous of you. You were the best goalie in the school. I could never get a goal on you. You seemed to know exactly when to jump. You had perfect timing. If you had stayed in the village I am sure you would be something now. You would know when to jump on the dumb foreigners." He laughed, a hearty, self-satisfied laugh.

In the moonlight, his two gold teeth glowed like fireflies in a cave.

"I've done all right," I said.

He pulled on his cigarette and turned his head up as if to look at the moon while he exhaled.

"To believe is to see, Kambanaris used to say, remember?" he said after a while. "No matter how much we swore we already knew how to spell his crazy words, he still would drag us up to the blackboard to write them."

"'Seeing is believing,' he used to say," I corrected.

"That's it. *Bravo Niko*, you remember the old goat after all these years." He sounded like a grown-up admiring a first grader's painting.

"Kambanaris was a great man," I said.

"He died eight years ago," he said.

"Is that so? He was pretty old when we were in his class. Most people do nothing at that age; he was not teaching for the money."

"A year later his wife went. That great house of his has been up for sale ever since." He was pointing with his cigarette-loaded arm toward the edge of the village, where the dark silhouette of Kambanaris' house towered over everything else.

He drew the last puff on his cigarette. "It'll never sell; it'll take somebody really rich to buy it," he mumbled while concentrating on grinding out the stub with his boot. After a while he stopped, inspected the remnants of the cigarette and said as if to himself, "But if it's fixed up, it will be the best

house this side of the mountain; in its day, that house was the king of all the noblemen's houses." We walked to where our paths separated in silence and said our good nights. As I crawled into bed, I felt tired and regretted that I'd made the trip.

It started from the very first day I arrived in the village. Any time my father got me cornered, he would recite a litany of names of all the sensible village boys who married nice village girls that could communicate with their in-laws and had big *prika* (dowry), which the sensible boys used to get into business and become the pride of their parents.

"Did you see Kostas Liappis? He got an industrial loan and built a bakery on the Patekas apple orchard behind the school. He sells bread to all the villages around, winter and summer. Real convenient for the old folks, everybody loves him. He got elected village president last month, did you know? There is a guy that has done good *prokopi* (success)."

"And Spyros, Apostolis Karteras' son, he married Lenio, Progidena's daughter, got the chestnut grove by *Profitis Elias* as *prika* and turned it into a plant nursery. His oldest son is his right hand. He goes with him as far as Athens to sell their gardenias. His youngest one, a smart little fellow, eight years old, looks just like Apostolis. I bet he's going to be a carpenter like his grandfather. He's always by his side."

He would let out a mournful sigh and add: "Your cousin Giannis Giannakos, now he came out a very smart man. What have you made? Nothing. A hole in the water."

When father slowed down, mother would pick up the slack, repeating the same things in her own words. "Everyone your age that had the good sense to *sit on their eggs* has made *kali prokopi*." (Good success). Then she would list all the girls whose husbands

50

either stayed in the village or got respectable jobs nearby in the city and visited their parents at least once a month, with their wives and children, all speaking the same language. "Do you remember Katina Mela? Marika's daughter, the one that wasn't good enough for you? She married Stefanis Patekas. She is the brains behind the *Kalithea Hotel*. If it wasn't for her, Stefanis Patekas would never have gotten the loan to build the hotel. Marika is so proud, nobody can talk to her anymore. You used to make fun of Katina, remember?"

Yes, I remembered. All the teachers loved her. She not only knew the names of kings and the dates of all the battles, but what day of the week it was and what the weather was like. She could even find mistakes in our textbooks. She was quite big back then and with the typical cruelty of children towards each other, we used to call her "Mount Katina" and say she had a nose like a cucumber and a mustache like a pirate. I was glad to hear she had managed to marry somebody and was doing all right.

"You should hear Katina's girls," mother would say, "they are about the same age as your oldest ones. They come and stay with their grandmother over here," she gestured towards the house next door, "and it is such joy to hear them talk. They're perfect young ladies; you'll see."

I saw the next day. Katina visited her mother next door, and since her mother was visiting my mother, she came over with her two daughters in tow "to say *kalosorisate*" (welcome). The girls hit it off right away. Soon, my Maria had them playing "follow the leader", and Katina's "perfect young ladies" were teaching mine Greek obscenities and showing off the foreign words they learned from the guests at their hotel.

I couldn't stop looking at Katina. I was amazed how all those large, amorphous lumps had redistributed themselves to just the right places. The Katina I was staring at, had the kind of body that should be kept away from flammables. She gave me a hug and I thought I would melt. Who would have thought. Lucky, dumb Stefanis. Who could have guessed it.

I had left the dull, slow-moving village life twelve years before to join the merchant marine, eager for adventure in faraway places. A few years later, finding the shipboard life too dull and too confining, I stuffed everything I owned in my pockets and one rainy night in Long Beach, where the tanker "Olymbos" was unloading crude oil, I jumped ship.

It was October of 1966.

I became very good at dodging immigration inspectors and haggling with bosses who thought they could get you to do anything for nothing because you didn't have a green card. Most of the guys in the same predicament ended up marrying some alcoholic old hag with one foot in the grave, or coughed up about a thousand dollars to some Puerto Rican to pretend they were married and hoped she would agree to a divorce when the green card came. Most of them outsmarted themselves; the Puerto Rican hookers took them for everything they had and got them kicked out of the country.

I was doing fine and marriage had never crossed my mind. I had weaved my way through the country to South Florida, and I was finding plenty of companionship among the women in Miami. Then one day, about three years after I jumped ship, the superintendent of the Flagler Dry-dock Company, sent me to pick up a set of ships' drawings from the Caribbean Shipping Company. The receptionist, a cheerful blonde with brown eyes, smiled at me and kept on smiling. She said her name was Maggie. "Short for Margaret," she clarified.

She said her ancestors were European too, they had come from Ireland.

She said she just graduated from high school.

She said I spoke good English and had the sweetest accent she had ever heard. (Silently, I thanked Kambanaris for that.)

She understood everything I said; never asked me to repeat anything.

I wrote my father three months later that I was getting married to a nice girl from a nice family with a large *prika*, who spoke the language as if she had grown up in Taxiarhes. It was almost true. She said she would learn Greek and she did get some bed sheets and bathroom towels at her bridal shower.

We got married on Saturday, November nineteenth 1969, at the Second Avenue Baptist Church, in Miami. Margaret looked like a princess out of a fairy tale. I have the wedding date on the back of a card that I keep in an inside pocket of my wallet. Margaret would be very upset if I forgot our anniversary. She did manage to learn some Greek, enough to make me be careful what I said in front of her, but she didn't feel confident enough to get into a conversation, especially with my parents.

On my third day in the village, when mother started telling me how Pavlos Stenos, Kyra Amalia's nephew, had become a contractor and was getting rich converting old hovels to villas, I felt I had enough. I jumped up, told her I had promised Margaret and the girls to show them the village and started to leave.

"The truth is always painful," said mother, then she made me take a windbreaker with me because, "It's always drafty by the ravine."

We took the narrow cobblestone path that wound its way through the village, down to the cove of Fakistra.

The department of tourism had gouged a car road to the cove and the path was seldom used anymore. Nature was slowly reclaiming it. The goats and sheep, the best path cleaners, had been displaced by rooms to let. The long, thorny blackberry vines snagged our clothes and the nettle weeds stung the girls' legs. After a while, we stopped to rest on a large, flat boulder overlooking the mountainside. I took Katerina off my shoulders and concentrated in taking out a piece of thorny vine stuck on Nicole's shirt.

"Why couldn't we go on the big road like everybody else?" whined Maria.

"Your father doesn't do things like everybody else," said Margaret while leafing through the Greek-English dictionary she always carried with her. Then she asked me: "What's so great about making boxes?"

"I don't know. Why?"

"You parents seem to make a big deal about it. Kostas made *to-ko-ti*, and Giannis made good *to-ko-ti*. What kind of boxes are they making?"

I almost smiled. "It's *pro-ko-pi*," I spelled, "not *to-koti*"

"It sounded like it, what does it mean?"

"It means, to do well, to succeed: to get rich in other words."

"Oooh," Margaret reflected. "I guess to them, you haven't made a very good *to-koti*, eh?" She put her hand on my shoulder and squeezed the back of my neck.

It was what my mother had said as we were leaving that got Margaret asking about boxes. She had said: "You went to the other end of the world, stayed there as if you threw a stone behind you, and where is your *prokopi*? All you came back with was some trinkets and fancy clothes. You got your grandfather's name, but didn't get his smarts, that's for sure; that Nikos Pilios had the biggest caique in his village when he was half your age. He made great *prokopi*, he left his mark; his house was the biggest in his village, as big as Kambanaris, till the Germans burned it." And that was not the first time she said it.

I broke away from Margaret and walked down the path, kicking chestnut balls as I went. I picked up some stones and started throwing them, hard, as if I wanted to hurt the nettles and the chestnut trees ahead.

Who in the hell made the rules that determine when a man is a failure or a success? The way I see it, I have done all right. I have done more than all right; I have been in places and have seen and done things that these peasants, who never went beyond the mountain ridge, can't even comprehend.

After a while we moved on. As we continued toward the outskirts of the village, I showed the girls the places where I used to graze the sheep, the trees I climbed to cut fodder and the spring from which I had to bring water, when I was their age. Nicole wondered why I couldn't get the water out of the faucet and Katerina asked if the refrigerator was broken.

Everywhere, new buildings were sprouting among the chestnut trees. Most of them were still a long way from being finished, concrete monstrosities with rusting steel spikes pointing towards the clear blue sky, smudging the velvety green of the mountain slope: the frames of future *Pensions* and *Rooms to Let*, under construction.

Near the end of the road, we came upon the Kambanaris house. It took me some time to recognize the place. The huge grape arbors had collapsed into a big tangled mound, interwoven with blackberry vines and nettle weeds. The glass of all the windows was broken and the surviving shutters dangled on one hinge. The massive front door was gaping half open. The whole house had the pained look of someone dying a slow, agonizing death. The ivy, like a loyal guardian, covered all the walls in a protective embrace, shielding the disgraced king of all noblemen's houses from cruel public eyes.

I stood there staring at it, till Margaret asked: "Did you know somebody who lived there?"

"Kambanaris," I said.

"You look as if you'd seen a ghost," she said.

"He was the best teacher I ever had."

"Oh, yeah, I remember you telling me about him."

I lit a cigarette, sat on the remnants of the stone wall by the iron gate and stared at the house.

Kambanaris had worked many years in Europe, then lost everything during the last war and returned to the village and the old house. All he brought back from his years abroad, was a lot of books and a Dutch wife who spoke Greek with an accent which the people in the village entertained each other by mimicking. My father would point him out to me as an example of the futility of anyone going abroad. "Look at that goofy professor, he wasted his best years in strange places, and where is his *prokopi*?"

He taught French and English at the village high school. Back then there were no hotels, tourists, or even electricity in the village. Our side of the mountain was unknown to the world. France and England could have been in another galaxy. It took all of his resourcefulness to get us, a bunch of rebellious village boys, to study those strange sounding languages.

It was at this house that I saw Kambanaris for the last time. He was sitting at his corner desk in the upper corner room.

I was hypnotized by the view.

The ordinary sounds of the village blended and floated up, reaching the room as music from some distant, enchanted place. I felt as if I was above the world, that I was superior to all the creatures scurrying below; their problems seemed so insignificant.

I was leaving to join a ship in Suez and had stopped to say good-bye. When his wife brought us coffee he re-introduced me to her: "Remember this young man? One of my boys. he's going overseas." I thought I detected a tone of pride in his voice.

We chatted for a while, then I said good-bye and he wished me luck. I told him I was going to be an adventurer, like him. He said he was sure I would do well, he had confidence in me.

I flicked away the cigarette, carefully stepped over the rusty rails of the iron gate and the thorny blackberry vines growing between them and followed a narrow footpath between the tall nettles to the house. I made it to the weed covered patio and tried to peek inside the massive front door.

"What are you looking for?" A woman's voice from behind startled me.

I turned around and faced Kyra Amalia, the stubby, elderly widow who lived near by. I told her who I was, and after the customary pleasantries — she said she was so happy that Marigoula's son had turned out so handsome and with such a nice family, and some other all-purpose flatteries — I asked her about the house.

She started with the usual old villager's prologue: "Ah, the children of today. None of them want to stay in the village anymore; nobody respects anything old nowadays." Then she went on to say that since the death of Kambanaris and his wife, their only daughter who lived somewhere in Europe never came to visit. She wanted to sell the house, but it wasn't easy with everything being so high and the house being so run down.

I asked if I could go in and she said to be careful: some boards had rotted away. Margaret didn't think it was safe for the kids and stayed in the yard picking cyclamens with them.

I squeezed around a bundle of chestnut tree branches stacked inside the front door (the remnants of goat fodder), stepped on some fresh manure and cursed the goats.

Kyra Amalia heard me and quickly made excuses: "I let them go inside sometimes when it rains, they couldn't hurt anything."

Stepping gingerly between bird droppings, on boards that looked the safest, and hacking my way through sticky cobwebs and scaring roosting pigeons, I made it to the third floor study. I brushed aside the leaf-loaded spider's web on one of the windows and looked out.

It was as if no time had passed.

The sun was sinking behind the village of Xourihti. It painted the tops of the chestnut trees golden yellow and brushed large orange patches on the pale blue sea. A sailboat at a distance was cutting a path through one of them. The islands of Skiathos and Skoppelos were glowing in the horizon. Under the huge chestnut trees, the village was settling for the evening. Somebody was returning home from the field, the donkey's bell keeping the rhythm of the pace. A group of children were playing war on top of the ruins of the Venetian castle. The bell of Agios Taxiarhis started to toll, announcing it was time for vespers; its heavy sound rolled down the mountainside and spread out over the sea.

Margaret's calling snapped me out of my daydreaming. I went back down the shaky stairs and joined them, the girls eager to show me the pretty flowers they had collected.

As we were walking away I kept turning back every few yards to look at the house.

That night I tossed in bed for a long time, till I gave up on sleep and went out on the balcony. The crickets were singing their hearts out. A full moon hung high over the island of Skiathos, shining a golden path over the calm sea to the cove of Fakistra. I leaned back on the chair, put my feet on the railing, and gazed at the Kambanaris house, plainly visible from the balcony, glowing at the end of the golden moon-path, like some great monument.

The villagers used to tell stories about the first Kambanaris, who was famous all over the world for his bells, the sound of which no other bellmaker could duplicate. The house that he built, a long, long time ago, had kept his name immortal. It was the tallest structure on the east side of the mountain and could be seen from miles out at sea. The caique captains used to navigate by it. Our parents were told by their parents of the feasts at the Kambanaris house that lasted for days, with important people coming by boat from far away places. Acetylene lanterns, mounted on the house walls and under the arbor, lit the place up brighter than daylight.

Now there was a man who had left his mark on the land; his *prokopi* (success), has been shining for years.

After some time, the crickets called it a night, the breeze felt cooler, the moon moved closer to Skiathos; its path got narrower, concentrating all its glow at the Kambanaris house.

Yes, Giannis Giannakos was right: it would take somebody *really rich* to buy the *king of all noblemen's houses* and bring it back to where it was in its glory days. But then it would be the best house this side of the mountain.

I stood up with decided firmness, flicked my fifth cigarette into the bean garden below, and went back to bed.

I slept well the rest of that night.

Early the next day I drove to the city. I told everyone I had some errands to run. I spent most of the day between the lawyer's and the banker's offices and returned to the village late in the afternoon.

"That's the stupidest of all the stupid ideas you have had up to now," my father bellowed when I told him, during supper, what I had done. Until then, the idea of marrying a foreigner and staying in America had claim to that title. "Now I am sure I have been cursed to have a son who will never, ever, amount to anything."

Later, a very distraught Margaret would ask me over and over. "Why did you do it? Why did you buy that... that... white elephant?" But I couldn't come up with a convincing answer for her, or even for myself. I had a reason for it. I felt it, I just couldn't put it into words.

I boarded up the windows, patched the roof and with the help of my brother Dimos, dragged the huge front gate inside the building for safe keeping. (It had hand-forged ornaments and riveted joints, there aren't any craftsmen that could build them like that anymore).

I told Kyra Amalia she could graze her sheep in the property if she kept an eye on the house till I started the restoration. She kept wishing me *kaloriziko* (may it bring you good fortune), over and over, trying to disguise her disappointment that some day she would lose the free use of the place.

I had been trying to see Kostas Liappis since my arrival, but we kept missing each other till I caught up with him at his bakery one day before I left.

The years had taken away some of his black curly hair at the top and added some weight on him, but he was as energetic as when we were young and seemed sincerely glad to see me.

We sat at a small table in the corner behind the counter and between telephone interruptions and waiting on customers, we tried to catch up with our past. I congratulated him on his election as village president, told him about my life in America and he told me about his in the village and what he planned to do as the village president. "Need to set some controls, some order, on this wild construction that's going on, need to preserve some of the character of the area," he said. "And what we need most is to develop something that will create permanent jobs for the people." We clinked our *tsipouro*-filled glasses and toasted *Kaloriziko*, to the Kambanaris house. "I am glad you got it instead of somebody from Athens or Germany," he said. Then he got up to give two loaves of bread to a customer.

"I had asked the council to buy it, but they didn't think it was worth it," he said when he came back. "I thought it would be a good place for a hospital. The building is too far gone but it's six acres of land in a good location: good access to the road and the sea. Maybe we get lucky and some rich American from our village will donate it to us." He was looking at me smiling.

"That will be my mark, like a monument; from now on people will know I've been here," I said. A spark appeared in his eyes and I wondered if he misunderstood me.

"It would give permanent work to a lot of people from the village. The hospital in Zagora closed after the earthquake. A good hospital in a beautiful location like that, would become famous."

"It will be famous anyway," I said. "The way I am going to fix it up, it will become known all over the country; and the Taxiarhes along with it. It will be like the Pharos of Alexandria, like the Colossus of Rodos."

He poured more *tsipouro*. *"Kaloriziko"*, he said and we clinked our glasses again.

We returned to Bigport the next day; my two week vacation was over and in a way, I was glad. In a place where you can ask somebody how many children they have, and they'll answer two and a girl, since daughters only count as bad luck, I could imagine what the people in Taxiarhes were saying as I weaved through the village with a string of women in tow.

Soon I was back to the grind, busting my ass and making cartloads of money for Phil and the rest of the GESCO stockholders.

On a trip to New Orleans, I showed a photograph of the Bellmaker's house to a bearded sidewalk artist and got him to paint it the way my mind saw it finished.

"What are you going to call it?" asked the painter. "Every big house has a name."

For something that important, I needed to think about it for a while. For now, I told him to paint TAXIARHES on the top and at the bottom, GORDIOS DESMOS (Gordian Knot). I don't know why, it just popped into my mind.

I framed it and hung it on the wall across from my desk.

Two weeks after I came back from Greece, GESCO sent me to Lisbon, on a job for ESSO Petroleum that had two tankers in the shipyard.

That was the trip that convinced me to change the way I was going about my life.

The port captain for ESSO was a big, robust, hard working, hard-partying individual named Eric Stewart. Every night, after our dinner at one of the restaurants at the "Praga De Restoradores," he would make the rounds of the strip joints around Lisbon. "That's food for the spirit; it keeps you young," he would say. A couple of times he talked me into going with him, each time blowing a weeks' per-diem. After the second time, I told him that I was not getting the huge per-diem he was and from then on I was taking up book reading. He had to go to the New York office a few days after that and the second day he was gone I got a yard-long Telex from Phil, chewing my ass out royally.

It surprised the hell out of me and I wondered what it was all about. The mystery was solved when Captain Stewart returned to Lisbon a week later and told me that he had tried to call Phil Domain at his office. Phil was on his way to New York, so Captain Stewart had a long talk with his secretary.

I am sure, since the lover-boy-captain was not paying for the call, and since he has never seen Marilyn, it was a very long and driveling, long-distance flirting session. (The bitch can sound sickening sweet over the telephone.)

"Told her, 'You people should raised the poor guy's per-diem, poor Nick is doing a great job but he's starving in some ways. Like the book says: a man can't live on bread alone you know,'" he chortled.

"I don't think she got the joke, Cap," I said and showed him the Telex.

He paused a few seconds to read it, then mumbled: "Yep, I was right, she didn't seem too bright."

It turned out that Marilyn had had Phil paged at the Atlanta airport and told him that I had been complaining to the client about not getting paid my allowance. Phil, who was laboring hard to make everybody think GESCO was bigger than IBM and more solid than a Swiss bank, got pissed off and sent me the long Telex from the Ionosphere club in Atlanta.

That incident made it very plain to me that no matter how much I busted my ass making everybody else rich, my future, the Bellmaker's house restoration, my triumphant return to the village and the fulfillment of all of my dreams and high aspirations would always depend on what other people, people like Phil and Marilyn, thought of me. It was hard to swallow, but I had to admit, the dumb, ignorant, vain, Giannis Giannakos was accountable to nobody.

I turned in my resignation one day after I got back from Lisbon.

I guessed that some day, when I was rich, sitting at the balcony of the renovated Bellmaker's house, sipping ouzo and watching the sunset over the Aegean, I would be thanking Marilyn and Phil for it.

Chapter

6

I waited like a new bride for the July twenty-fourth, which would bring the motor vessel "George P." with the busted sewage pipes, which would launch Poseidon Marine Services into the ship repair business and get me started into my great *prokopi*, my success, that would make me the envy of the villagers and my father prouder than an English Lord.

While waiting, I worked on a ships' inventory project for GESCO. I had some questions about the contents of a storeroom and I went looking for Scotty to clear them. I was told he had not been in that week. I said I'd see him when he came in. It felt odd, still being in the same place, doing the same thing, yet not being part of the crew. Phil's complaints about a job running over budget or Scotty's excuses for missing another day seemed so remote now.

George Jones, who went by the name of Scotty in honor of his Scottish origin, joined GESCO as head of the Inventory Control division two years after I was hired. He was about fifty-five years old, semi-retired, semi-intellectual and fully alcoholic. He stood about five-and-a-half feet tall, with a full head of graying hair that was once red and a thick reddish mustache, which he twisted and curled up almost to the middle of his cheeks. Scotty and Phil had a common watering hole they frequented and during an attack of benevolence caused by half a dozen bourbon and waters, Phil offered him a job.

Scotty had been for many years with Lloyds of London, till he became disgusted with the bureaucrats and quit, he said. He averaged about two weeks of work a month; the rest of the time supposedly he was working on putting together a big shipping deal, but everyone knew that he was either drunk, or getting there, or recovering from it. Despite that, Phil kept him because he believed having an ex-Lloyds of London man on the crew was raising GESCO's prestige. If a visiting client asked for Mr. George Jones, he was usually "on a job out of town."

Inventory control was tedious work. It involved digging into spare parts boxes piled high, in hot, dusty, noisy store rooms, trying to identify every strange looking piece in there, cataloguing it and entering it into a computer program.

Very boring stuff. Fortunately I only had to do it when work on my department was slow. The only time I remembered anything exciting happening was when we did inventory on an Italian tanker en route from Charleston to Aruba. I found a bundle of letters in the parts box of the Boiler Feed pump and since none of us could read them, I thought the next logical thing to do was to take them to the captain.

About a half-hour later, a thunderous commotion got everybody running to the starboard side, in time to see the chubby chief engineer in his flowery boxers, running for his life, with the old captain at his heels, looking wild, waving a pistol and yelling something about a "petite Luchia." Tumbling close behind, like an oversized toddler just learning to walk, was the chief's mountainous wife waving a twenty-four inch pipe wrench.

"The captain swears he will kill the chief for... you know... with his wife," translated a crewman next to me, winking and gesturing with his bent finger to show what the chief had done to the captain's wife. For the rest of the voyage, the chief stayed locked up in the spare cabin and the captain stayed drunk in his. A few times, the chief's wife would stand in front of the spare cabin door, call her husband dirty Italian names and throw whatever she could lift against it, which the mess-boy would pick up later. The steward, who like any good steward, knew everything about everybody, told me that the chief engineer had had a long love affair with the captain's young wife. When the chief's wife showed up unexpectedly last week, in his rush to get rid of Luchia's letters he probably stashed them in the box with the feed pump parts which was near his cabin.

The guys at the inventory division were talking about it for months.

My business card said I was the head of GESCO's Engineering Division. Most of the time I was representing shipping companies who did not have their own port engineers or they needed additional help while the ship was in the shipyard. I could inspect repairs and supplies and approve invoices on behalf of the people who wrote the check. I was wined and dined by those doing or trying to do business with the ship and I don't remember any shipyard superintendent or ship supplier ever having difficulty understanding my accent.

During GESCO's early years, regardless of the title on the business card, everybody would pitch in to get the job done. The president, vice president and all the in-between wheels, worked together with a spirit of comradeship and confidence that our little company would grow. And GESCO did grow. By the time I started my own company,

GESCO had seventeen employees, but by then the spirit of comradeship had begun to fade. Phil seemed distant and unapproachable, Marilyn got promoted to office manager, which pissed everyone else off, and most of the people were more concerned with pleasing the bosses than making money for the company.

I was glad I became independent.

A couple of times I went to lunch with Phil and we talked about "payables" and "receivables" and "overhead" and unreliable help. I was like him; I was *an entrepreneur.*

When the repair jobs started coming in I was planning to move to a building where I could have a shop, besides an office. A shop is an essential part for any ship repair outfit.

I bought an old service van at a Southern Bell surplus equipment auction, which I was going to use for transporting material and people during the repairs.

The middle of the month seemed to have come overnight and with it the realization that I wouldn't be getting a paycheck this time. I rushed to finish one of the GESCO's jobs and wrote on the invoice: *"For conducting spare parts inventory onboard the Motor Vessel Philadelphia, while in the port of Bigport, on July third through July tenth. Forty-one hours @ $ 10/hr."* I was following the same style Phil used when writing his invoices. Marilyn typed it on plain blank invoice form. I was planning to have my own fancy invoice forms, with my company name and logo on the top and: white-customer, yellow-accounting, green-shipping, printed at the bottom, like the big boys, but that would be later.

I handed the invoice to Phil as soon as it was typed, instead of trusting Marilyn to "put it through her system."

"I thought we agreed you were going to be billing us at the end of each month and get paid in thirty days," said Phil.

I told him that I expected to be busy later and billed him early, for his convenience.

He promised he would try to get me a partial payment the following week. "That should hold you till your ship comes in," he chuckled.

It seemed that the twenty-fourth of July was taking forever to arrive. I kept checking the list of tools that I would need, made sure the large credit manager at Gulf Supply, in his grief over Alabama's loss, didn't forget to approve my credit application, and stayed in touch with a couple of guys I was going to hire as soon as the ship got into port. It was my first job; I wanted everything to go right. After the *George P.* was done, the four hundred sixty five thousand piping job I had quoted for the *Oil Transporter*, would be ready to start and soon after, I would start renovating the house in Taxiarhes just the way I wanted it, tall like a castle and shining like a beacon. On a marble plaque by the main entrance, I will have carved: RESIDENCE OF NIKOS PILIOS. Any idiot would see who had made great *prokopi.*

The motor vessel *George P.* ran into a storm and kept getting delayed. When she finally got in port, on July twenty-ninth, she docked inside the Dixie shipyard.

I went on board as soon as the yellow flag came down. People from the shipyard were swarming like vultures on a dead donkey. Every one of them was either talking into, or listening to a crackling walkie-talkie and armed with measuring tapes and flash lights, were busily inspecting, writing and figuring.

The captain said that the storm he ran into off Key West did a lot of damage and he had orders to go to the shipyard. "Looks like we are going to be here for awhile," he said. "There are more surveyors running around than I have crew. George Steiner is gonna get a new ship out of this."

"How about my piping?"

"Oh, that's *trihes*" (horse hair), he said, "You can do it anytime. Go see the Chief Engineer."

I went to the Chief Engineer's cabin, waited till he finished reading his mail, and we went down to the engine room.

"That's half of it," he said pointing to a group of rusty pipes snaking their way downward next to the ships' skin, "the rest is in the Ballast tank and it'll have to wait till we take on cargo."

Nothing to it, I thought.

I was at the shipyard gate before sunrise the next morning waiting for John Mavros to come. He was the rest of my crew. He drove up a half-hour late, in a beat-up, rusty Toyota with more duct tape on it than metal and a new sticker on the dangling front bumper: *"If you are rich, I am single."*

John had sailed for a while as a wiper, then jumped ship, married some alcoholic hag for the green card and became part of that special group of ex-seamen found in every port, doing part-time work for ship-related businesses in the day, and hanging around strip joints at night, mooching drinks from guys whose ship is in port. They claim to have the inside scoop on everything going on in the waterfront, are always just hours away from the "big break" always "temporarily" short of cash, always in need of dental work, and abhor steady work because they are "nobody's fools."

Stelios Panagiotakis, who calls himself Telis, and owns the Casablanca Bar and Grill, had recommended John Mavros to me, hoping to get him out of the bar where he was mooching drinks and pestering the strippers.

As far as craftsmen go, John was an insult to craftsmanhood, but with the shipyards, fab shops and the papermill shut-downs around Bigport sucking in anybody that could breathe, it was hard to find people willing to work for what I could afford to pay. I was planning to do the engine room piping with John, and when the captain got the ballast tanks empty, I would round up more people and start the big part of the job.

We went down to the engine room and with wrenches, hammers and chisels, we attacked the rusty bolts and had the first section of pipe loosened up in less than an hour.

Smooth sailing. The pieces were easy to get to, and all I had to do was transport them to the shop, build new ones and install them. Easy money. Why didn't I start my own business earlier? I could have been rich by now.

We snaked that long, twisted, rusty, foul-smelling piece of pipe, full of rubber patches and clamps, up the ladders, across the main deck and down the gangway. We almost got as far as the spot where I had parked the van, when running out from the superintendent's yard-office came a monster of a man; a mountain with legs and a yellow hard hat, yelling at us in some incomprehensible language.

We slowly lowered the pipe to the ground and stood rubbing our shoulders, waiting for him to get closer.

"Where the fuck you think you're going with that pipe, boy?"

I told him where I was going.

"You can't come in here and work how the fuck you please, this is private property."

"I got this fuckin' job before the ship got here," I shot back.

"Nobody can come here and work in the yard without our say-so; you ought to know that."

"I got the contract one month ago," I said. "Anyway, it's a small job, just a few pieces of pipe, you guys are going to make a killing on this ship."

"Makes no different, you got to OK't with the office. C'mon, get your ass over to see Anderson; leave the fuckin' pipe here." And he nudged me on the right shoulder toward the main office. He smelled of sweat, tobacco and beer.

We zigzagged across the yard, between piles of scrap steel, welding machines and scaffolding, with the monster two steps behind. Shipyard workers turned their heads as if to take a look at a condemned man heading to the gallows.

Anderson's office door was open. The smelly mountain nudged me in. Anderson was at his desk studying some papers. In the center of the desk was a bronze rectangular block, with two-inch black letters engraved in it: Thomas S. Anderson. Probably the handiwork of some resourceful machinist vying for brownie points.

"Yes Bubba, what is it now?" he said in a bored voice without raising his head.

"This fellow here," Bubba nodded his head towards me, "him, and another one, were toting a pipe out of the yard. Says he's got a contract to do a job on the Greek ship. Told him I sure as hell didn't know nothin 'bout it."

"OK. Bubba, I'll take care of it." Smooth, friendly; I felt relaxed.

"Be on the ship," said Bubba and left.

Mr. Anderson put down the papers and turned to look at me. He seemed to be in his late sixties, with thinning gray hair, and a round, reddish face. His eyes were cold and penetrating. He was smiling, a foxy, conniving kind of smile that immediately made me uncomfortable. Normal people in the ship repair business don't smile; they walk around with a frown, growling, always poised for attack, like wolves guarding a kill. The only ones smiling are the inexperienced and naive; and also the hardened, scheming ones, who wear a sly grin as part of their uniform.

"Now then, who are you, young man?"

"My name is Nikos Pilios," I said and showed some teeth as I handed him my card.

"Poseidon Marine Services Inc.," he read aloud. "So you are the one starting up. Don't mind Bubba, he gets carried away sometimes." Then in a soft, confiding tone, as if giving advice to his grandson: "You picked the wrong time to get started son. Business is not what it used to be. Not that many ships come here any more, and from those who do, if you get any work, you never know when you're gonna get paid. Your people got the right idea; restaurant business; everybody's got to eat. Cash dealings, no invoices, no worrying if the check will clear and nobody knows how much goes in the cash drawer."

"Never worked in a restaurant, ship work is all I know," I said.

"You picked a tough business to get into, son," not so softly this time.

He pulled out some papers from a drawer.

"In this country, we have to put up with a lot of paper work, son. Our insurance makes us have these forms filled out by everybody who is going to do any work in the yard." He handed me the papers. I looked at them trying to figure out what they were, and reached for my pen.

"You might want to take them home and read them. Need to have the company stamp on them anyway. It's a pain, but we have to do it," he said. He stood up and I realized he was a tall person. "Nice meeting you and good luck in your business, son." He had walked around the desk, put his hand on my shoulder and started me toward the door.

"Fill out the forms, bring them back and we will work something out. I will tell Bubba to get somebody to put that pipe back up on the ship so it won't get lost."

He was speaking slowly, separating the words and lightly patting my shoulder. "Nice to meet you, son," he said again and then I was led out.

I found John Mavros leaning against a light post, whistling a Greek tune and flipping his key chain like worry beads. "Pick up the tools," I told him. "We are stopping for today," and seeing it was necessary, I added: "I'll pay you for four hours."

The bundle of forms from the pesky insurance company that grandpa Anderson wanted filled out was titled: HOLD HARMLESS AGREEMENT. There were six pages of fine print and the only filling out to be done was at the bottom, where there was a place for my signature and the company's name and seal.

The gist of all that legal gobble-gook was that no matter what happened to me while in the Dixie yard, it would always be my fault; I would not sue Dixie shipyard, their affiliates or their officers. I would apologize for getting killed on their premises and pay them for mopping up what was left of me.

Margaret pressed the company seal on the page, typed my name and "President" in the title block, and I signed it. I took it back that afternoon but Bubba said to come the next morning; Anderson was gone for the day and he couldn't let me in the yard without his say-so.

In the morning Mr. Anderson was in a meeting and I sat outside his office till almost noon when I finally caught him going in.

"Please come back later, when we can talk, we are very busy now." Soft, sweet, grandfatherly; no room for doubt.

Late in the afternoon, I forced myself in his office.

"I need to get started on that pipe," I said. Anderson gave me a serious, solemn look that immediately made me nervous.

"My superiors have instructed me, from now on, not to allow anyone in the yard with a conflict of interest." He paused a bit: "What it means is, we're not letting people in who do the same kind of work we do."

"I understood it the first time," I snapped.

"I know how you feel, but I don't have any control; you see I am not my own boss like you, I work for somebody else. Very sorry." Always smiling, always calm.

Captain George Steiner was not much help either.

"I can't interfere with shipyard policy," he said, then added, "The yard says they can include the engine room piping in the insurance claim, so I'll let them do it; you understand. You can do the ballast tank piping when the ship gets out of the yard and starts loading. Yes, I know, it's the hardest part of the job, but there will be many opportunities to do big jobs for us. We come to the area quite often. We are buying another vessel that needs a lot of work; you will make it up soon."

The next day I went back on board the ship. I couldn't stay away, I was burning to see what they were doing to my piping job. There was a new guard at the gate, and he probably thought I was part of the crew.

The Dixie people were all over the ship like fire ants on a dead caterpillar. Each one of their so-called "craftsmen" represented twenty dollars an hour charge to the insurance for weather damage repairs. On my engine room piping that I was going to do with only John Mavros, they had about a dozen guys: fitters with helpers, riggers with helpers, welders with helpers; even the helpers had helpers.

It made me sick.

Bubba came in the engine room while I was having coffee with the chief engineer, watching the yard workers goofing off.

"I thought we told you to stay the fuck out of here," he growled.

"I am just visiting," I said.

"I don't give a rat's ass what the fuck you are doing, I want your wet-back ass out of here."

"Ok., I'll leave when I finish my coffee."

Some shipyard workers stopped what little they were doing to watch the show.

"I said I want you out of here now. Come on, *vamoose*."

"In a minute, when I finish my coffee." Calmly, I took a sip out of the Styrofoam cup.

"God damn it, I said *now*," and he grabbed the back of my shirt and dragged me toward the door, the coffee spilling on my hands.

"We go see Anderson right now," he said, and with him behind me, half-pushing, half-chasing, we got off the ship and marched to Anderson's office.

"We don't want you in the yard, not for a visit, not for work, not for nothing, is that clear?" were the concluding remarks of the loyal vice president. His voice was hard, no grandfatherly stuff this time.

Bubba followed me to the gate. "Don't let his ass or any of his crew get in the yard again," he told the guard.

"Yes sir," said a uniformed dimwit and stared at me as I walked by, as if trying to print my looks in his memory.

"I didn't think you could pull it off," said Bill Yeoman a couple of days later. "Ever since the old man paid through the nose to buy out two upstarts that had worked for Dixie before trying it on their own, he'll crush anybody trying to get started in this business."

The ship stayed in the yard for an eternity. The closest I got to her was across the street. In the evenings, I would meet some of the crew at the strip joints and get an update on the shipyard screw-ups and the shafting Captain George Steiner and the insurance company were getting. She finally came out of the shipyard two weeks later and started taking on cargo right away. I was waiting with my crew at the dock and as soon as the gangway hit the dock we climbed on board. I attacked the piping with all the energy overdue bills can produce. The loading time had shrunk from the three weeks to two. I had to pay overtime and bust my ass to get the damn job finished before she sailed. The pipes were in hard-to-get-to places inside the muddy, slippery, foul-smelling ballast tanks. Every flange bolt was rusted solid and had to be chiseled off taking three times longer than loosening it up with the wrench.

The total job came to sixteen thousand dollars and the net profit out of all that was seven hundred dollars; and that was because I was there almost twenty-four hours a day.

On one of those days, a fellow who said was the port engineer for a shipping company whose ships were calling in Bigport often, came to look at the ship for a charter his company was negotiating with Captain George Steiner. He saw the work we were doing and seemed to like it. He said the next time he needed any work he would keep me in mind.

I gave him a bunch of my cards and told him that my crew could travel anywhere and do the best work of any body at the lowest prices. In the few seconds he seemed willing to spend listening to me, I told him about my work as a port engineer when I was with GESCO and my shipyard work, before that. "I know every phase of the ship's operation," I emphasized.

He gave me his card, after I asked him for it: Gene Mudrawski, Senior Port Engineer, Berres Shipping Inc., 2210 Choupitoulas St. New Orleans La.

Maybe something good could come out of the miserable job of the George P.

Chapter 7

I was catapulted out of bed by the sound of the neighbor's car backfiring in the driveway. The blinking red numbers of the electric clock on the nightstand confirmed it: I had overslept; one of the few times in my working years, and certainly the first time in the ten months I had been in business. (Being my own boss hadn't produced the abundant, care-free hours I had thought.)

Rushing toward the bathroom, I stepped on a doll that squealed and I cursed.

"What's the matter?" Margaret sprung up in the bed.

"I am late, that's what's the matter."

"I asked you if you set the alarm last night and you said you had."

"I thought I had; all these damn buttons."

Why in the hell did the damn oversleeping have to happen today? I threw some clothes on, while mumbling curses and ran to the van. I turned the ignition key, but all I heard was the sickly whining sound of a dying battery struggling to turn a cold engine over. On the second attempt it sounded even sicklier and after that, nothing; just the hopeless, resigned, clicking of the ignition. Pounding the wheel, cursing and kicking the floor boards didn't help any.

I went back in the house, emptied Margaret's purse on the kitchen counter and sifted through the tons of strange stuff in there, looking for the keys to the station wagon. The racket brought Margaret running downstairs and she complained about my scattering her stuff.

I pulled the car next to the van, jumped the battery, and got the damn thing cranked.

I am sure the poor van, as it struggled down the interstate, was cursing the day it became property of Poseidon Marine. To be sold to an overworking deadbeat, get dented and scratched up, forced to carry heavy, greasy tools, and then to suffer the ultimate humiliation: to be painted an ugly gray color, with left-over, lumpy inorganic zinc paint, making it look like it had run wet through a cloud of ashes: what a curse.

The guys at the old warehouse I now called the Poseidon shop affectionately called it "The Graveyard Ghost."

Its poor six-cylinder heart must have sputtered with envy whenever we parked at the docks and saw its sister, who had been sold at the same auction, to the Dubois sisters. They had painted it a shiny pink color, with red and yellow stripes, covered everything inside with fuzzy pink carpet and installed fancy little lights and a big, soft, fluffy bed with smooth silky sheets. They removed the ugly load-rack from the top and put in new, gentle, shock absorbers that made it bounce cheerfully up and down whenever some sailor was playing a game with Candy or Stormy inside.

In this unlucky thing, instead of the laughter and soft music, there was cursing and the rattling of tools in the beat-up tool box. Instead of the sweet smell of perfume, there was the stench of tobacco juice and cigarette butts. When the gas cap got stolen two days after I bought it, I stuck a green pine cone in its place.

Limping along the highway, with every moving part on its last leg, I made a silent promise: When I get my next job, I am definitely getting a new truck.

This morning, all I wanted was to get to the shop as soon as I could get there. I told Moe to come in two hours earlier to finish the pump foundation for Berres Shipping. The truck to pick it up was probably already there and I needed at least four more hours of welding on it. I would rather have pulled teeth than ask for another extension. Mr. Gene Mudrawski, the "Senior" port engineer for Berres Shipping had all the charm of a drill sergeant and didn't listen to excuses.

I screeched to a stop in front of the shop and when I jumped out, I saw Moe sitting on his tool bucket by the entrance, smoking; the door wide open.

"Did I forget to lock the damn door, Moe?"

"No boss, you didn't, the welcome wagon made us a visit. The lock's been busted and the door left just like you see it."

I turned loose a streak of curses and rushed inside.

"What did they take?"

"Took the welding cables, don't know 'bout nothing else."

"Do you know if they took the new grinder?"

"I ain't seen it, boss."

"Let's look, you know what it looks like, it's about the size of a Wild Turkey bottle," I said.

"Wouldn't know 'bout that, I'm a Wild Rose man myself."

We walked to where the welding machine was. Both cables had been cut off right where they came out of the casing.

"Somebody tried to get some party money for the weekend," said Moe.

"They must have come this morning, I was working on the damn pump base till midnight, supposed to deliver it today. Sonovabitch!"

"Bet 'twas over a hundred pounds of copper in them lines, boss."

"Yah, and they'll get about twenty dollars for them. It'll cost me over two hundred to get another set. Let's see if they took the grinder."

We looked all around the pump base, the bench, even in the little cubicle I used as an office; no sign of it.

"The only damn new tool I had and I didn't get to keep it more than two days. How the fuck are we gonna smooth the edges and grind all the fuckin' stubs of the fuckin' foundation? It cost two hundred and fifty dollars. I had to kiss ass to Gulf Supply to let me have it on credit. Think I can get a loan on the van?"

"Yeah, they might pay you to keep it off the streets, boss."

"Shit, why all this rotten luck? Did I piss in the well?"

"Did you what, boss?"

"Nothing, it's a Greek saying. Keep looking, see what else them fuckers took."

I went to take another look in the office while trying to remember where it was I used last. Damn it, why me? And why today, when I need to deliver the fuckin' job? I lit a cigarette and calculated my chances of borrowing one from somebody: They were slim.

"Hey boss, that was smart, I wouldn't think to look in here neither," I heard Moe say.

He had picked up my over-alls with his chipping hammer, holding them as far as his arm could stretch, and was looking at the grinder under them.

"Margaret was gonna wash them, it's a good thing I forgot to take them," I breathed.

The final burglary tally, beside the cables, was the battery of the welding machine, the coffee pot, and Moe's radio. The rest of the tools I kept in a box in the van.

When the cop came, he scribbled a few things in his note book, gave the place a bored looking-over once, wiped the sweat off his forehead and complained about the hot weather this late in the year.

"We will notify you if anyone is apprehended," he said, walking to his car, then added "It happens all the time around here."

The neighborhood had seen better days. Across the street was a used truck dealership that was moving because they'd gotten tired of being broken into. Next to it was a big warehouse that I never saw opened. At the corner of the block was an old, two-story stucco building with a faded "For Sale or Lease" sign by Magnolia Realty inside the lower corner of a broken window. Over the door, with some effort, one could still make out "Riverfront Cafe," one of the last remnants of the good old days, when this area was called Magnolia Park and was buzzing with activity.

There used to be shops, a movie theater and a park with a long pier. Alekos Vardaris got his start to riches by selling hot dogs to the people promenading on it in the afternoons.

The streets were paved with red bricks, still visible where the asphalt peeled off. All of that was before the Interstate chopped up the neighborhood and sent everybody to the outskirts of Bigport. The movie house had been converted into a chicken processing plant, with packs of dogs roaming around it all the time. The promenading pier had been dismantled.

I had moved from GESCO's plush office to this rustic, miner's-shack-looking place exactly one month earlier. The building was an old warehouse, on a dead-end street. It had concrete floor and wooden walls that were patched with many boards of different sizes and colors, and with lots of shelves and hooks left from the multitude of previous tenants.

The whole shop was about forty feet wide by sixty feet deep, with a sliding door that would open up half of the shop. I thought that would come in handy when I worked on large pieces. To the right of the door was a ten foot cubicle, which I made into my office. I installed two big windows on the inside walls so I could have a full view of the shop floor from my desk.

In the far corner, there was a toilet with a smelly burlap curtain for a door, which I replaced with a green tarp.

Behind my desk there was a hole where an air conditioner used to be, closed with a piece of galvanized tin. I replaced the tin with a glass window. Until I could afford an air-conditioning unit, at least I wouldn't feel like I was in a cave.

The place was much bigger than I needed, but I was confident I would be using every bit of it when my work picked up. It was close to the docks, three blocks from Andrew Carras' office, whose telex number I had in my cards, and the rent seemed low enough, so I signed a two-year lease with Magnolia Realty Company.

Next door, in an antebellum-style house with three pink flamingos in the front yard, lived a middle-aged, heavy-set man on some kind of disability income. He would spent most of the day shining his Chevy Impala with his radio on full blast, listening to some fiery preaching till late in the night. He came over to meet me the first day I moved in and greeted me as if we were long lost friends.

"Mighty glad to have some neighbors, mighty glad. I'll be your watch-dog, I will. No thieving man is gonna get pass me, no siree, praise the Lord, praise the Lord."

The cop was getting in his car when I saw the Lord praiser drive up. I asked him if he had seen anything.

"Been on an all night revival. Sorry to hear about the burglary, real sorry, I am. God will punish the thieving man, He surely will, praise the Lord."

So much for watch-dogging.

I paced a few times, kicked a few things, cursed some more, then told Moe I was going to see if I could find some welding cables.

"Grind all the sharp edges of the pump base and if anybody calls, tell them to call back in one hour," I said.

"Sure thing boss. Reckon it's gonna be a while before we get another coffee pot, hey boss?"

"I'll bring you some coffee," I said.

Moe was my only employee at the time. I hired him during the job of the George P. I was desperate for welders and was hiring anyone who walked in from the street. Moe had sashayed in one day, said he had just gotten in town and was looking for any kind of work.

When we finished the job, I laid everybody off except him. He was a good welder and had sailed as an oiler for a while so he knew his way around ships. He seemed dependable, was pleasant company and was happy with what I was paying him.

He said he was forty-five but looked at least ten years older. He was tall, skinny, with skin the color of rust and arms that looked longer than normal, covered with dragons, hearts and anchors. He walked with a slight swaying motion, from right to left, like a sailboat rocking at anchorage. He said it was because of a bullet stuck in his right hip. A long knife scar ran from the bottom of his left ear almost to his chin.

His full name was Moses Abraham Taylor. His mother must have had high hopes for him, he said. He drove a shiny silver Cadillac the size of a locomotive.

I asked him what he was doing before this job.

"I was serving," he said.

I told him my neighbor had been in the service. "He was in Germany, then transferred to Cincinnati, then the Pensacola air base before he retired. Where did you serve?"

"Leavenworth, then Atmore," he said.

Howard Demming laughed for ten minutes later that evening, when I asked him where those bases were. Then he told me those were the names of jails. It pissed me off.

The phone rang as I was about to leave. It was Gene Mudrawski, the port engineer of Berres Shipping. He said that the driver coming to pick up the pump base had never been to my shop before, and wanted me to give him directions.

I poured my heart out, telling him about the burglary and about all of the equipment that was stolen, of the steel supplier delivering late and of the...

"If the fuckin' base isn't ready by tomorrow, you eat it. I'll get Arcadian Metal to make it," he cut me short.

I said: "It will be ready sir, you know we do good work sir, I apologize for the inconvenience, sir, thank you for understanding, sir," then: "Fuck you, Mister fuckin' Polack, sir," but I had already hung up.

I drove off to see Bill Yeoman.

Bill Yeoman, beside having the good taste to be a regular customer of the Warf Restaurant, owned Yeoman's Shipbuilding and Repair, a small shipyard about a mile upriver from the Dixie shipyard. George Skoufos seemed to have a high regard for him and kept telling me I should try to meet him. "He is a good man, he could give you help."

I am always suspicious about help coming from people in the same business, but I said I would go and see him when I got a chance. Then one day when I went to the Wharf Restaurant for lunch, Bill Yeoman was there and George dragged me over to his table and introduced us.

He seemed to be a likable fellow, about fifteen years older than I was, with a few gray hair on the sides and a strong, bony face. We talked about his business and mine with the vagueness of competitors, and about other, non-business things while munching on "Chicken à la George" and "Athenian green beans."

He told me that he grew up in Montgomery, next door to a Greek family with two children. "Mike and I were the same age and we were inseparable. Never got the hang of pronouncing his last name right thought. In the end I gave up and called him Bla-blakis. Hell of a nice fellow. His sister was two years younger. Hell of a good-looking woman."

When it was time to go, he offered: "If you ever need any help, come see me."

On quite a few occasions later, I found out that he meant it.

The secretary said I could go right in. "Mr. Bill is in his office."

I found Mr. Bill hanging a watercolor featuring a flight of mallards rising from a foggy swamp.

"You should send some of your paintings to a gallery; it's beautiful stuff," I said.

"Then it would be work; I paint for relaxation."

He put the hammer in his desk drawer.

"I got a card from Mike Blablakis yesterday," he said and showed me a post card from the Panama Canal.

"After we got out of the navy he went to work for the Corps Of Engineers. Did I tell you I almost married his sister? Hell of a good looking-woman. Her folks married her to some Greek from Greenville in South Carolina."

I told him what happened and asked if I could borrow a set of welding cables for about a week.

"No problem," he said. "Got the coffee pot too?" he chuckled. He called the secretary and she brought me a cup and a refill on his and we continued talking about Mike

Blablakis and his sister, and about paintings, and Bonsai trees, and undertakings loftier than ship repairing. About a half-hour later we went to get the cables.

In the center of the yard was the half-finished hull of a tugboat covering almost all the work area. It loomed over the office trailer and the couple of dozen workers, like a termite queen in her nest.

"How is the new construction going?" I asked.

"Not fast enough."

"It's a big one," I said.

"So are its headaches."

The welding machines were next to the dry-dock. About a dozen of them, with their welding cables piled in front of them in a tangled mess, like spaghetti in a pot.

"Get what you need;" he said, "I'm gonna have to kick somebody's ass; keep telling them to roll up the lines when they are through."

We pulled a line from the pile and coiled it in the van.

"They come by here all the time," said Bill, "they bring welding cables, oxygen lines, all kinds of tools. They say they are from out of town, just finished a job here and don't want to haul the stuff back. About two weeks ago, three guys came by with a trunk-full. I told them: 'wait here, I'll go inside to get the money,' and called the cops. Hell, most of the lines still had Dixie's name bands around them. I am not too crazy about the Dixie sonovabitches, but I hate a thief even worse."

He sat on a welding machine and wiped his hands with a rag.

"Saturday, a week ago," he continued, "I had some men come in to work on the new tug. It's not really any use trying to bring people in at the start of deer season, but my ass is in a bind big-time. When I came in, there was stuff scattered all over the place. They had cut the hinges off and dropped the gate, drove their truck over it and loaded up everything.

The crates with the engine parts for the tug were stacked over there." He gestured toward the construction site. "They busted them and took everything out.

I hot-footed it over to Frank Colley's junk yard; the only one open on Saturdays. There is a line of winos of every shape and form in beat up cars, trucks and shopping carts, going clear around the block. All loaded with anything metallic, from hubcaps and lawn chairs to sawing machines.

I walk up to the guy standing by the scales and ask him where they are putting the day's buy.

'I tell them to dump it over there, what is it to you?' he asks. I tell him what it is to me and he mellows.

'I tell them to dump it in front of the crane — I am Ed; if you recognize anything, come see me,' he says. I walk to where he pointed and sure enough, between a pile of

75

aluminum tire rims and a pile of stainless urinals, are my engine parts: the machined babbitt bearings costing me six hundred bucks apiece, the motor mounts, the hydraulic cylinders, my whole Merchant's Bank loan, piled up in a heap, busted, bent and scratched all to hell. What they couldn't lift, they cut up with the torch.

'You know who unloaded this stuff over here?' I ask this Ed character.

'I knew it,' he says, 'that sonvabitch didn't fool me for a minute.' It turns out the guy didn't like what they paid him for it, claimed his stuff was number one grade and dragged Ed to the pile to show him. Ed got suspicious and asked him for his I.D., so he gives him his real address and phone number; real smart, eh? They picked him up a couple of hours later. Ed and I had to go in and give a deposition. The damn idiot, as much sweat as he had poured into it, could have made more at a hamburger joint. He got seventy bucks from the junk man and will end up doing a couple of years in jail, and I am out over ten thousand dollars. Dumb sonovabitch."

We finished loading the cables, Bill gave me cup of coffee for the road and told me not to be in a hurry to return the cables. I will always have a feeling of gratitude towards the Blablakis family, whoever they are.

After Yeoman's place, I drove to Vasilis' Gulf Oil station across the Bay to get a new battery for the welding machine. Everybody else wanted either cash or credit and all of my cards had been recalled.

Vasilis Larkeas came from Larissa, a town about four hours drive from Taxiarhes, at the opposite end of the same province. Because of this closeness of our home towns, he always called me *patrioti* (fellow country-man), and acted as if we were related. It had been six months since he'd come back from a four-week vacation in Greece and he still hadn't run out of stories. While he was there, the local newspaper wrote a story about him, describing him as "a great philanthropist, a visionary businessman and the owner of a thriving liquid fuel distribution company." Somehow copies of the paper found their way to the community center here and made the rounds after church service.

I found him under the car lift, cursing and trying to screw the oil plug back in a Cadillac.

He showed me a shelf-full of batteries the size I needed. "This one is already charged," he said, picking one up.

When I told him I'd pay Friday, he put it down and bombarded me with hardship stories. He had to pay the gas invoice, the tire bill was due, he was behind on his taxes, the... He paused briefly, wiped his plump hands on an overloaded rag, waited for the effect of his speech and seeing I was not counting out money, he released another barrage: The *mavros* (black helper), had to be paid, the car lift had to be fixed, the... So much for the *patrioti* bit.

In the end, he let me have it after I swore that I definitely, for sure, without fail, would be there Friday morning with the money.

I gassed the van up and added it to the tab.

"I got gas caps," he said when he lifted the pine cone to put the gas nozzle, "they are only five bucks," but he didn't insist.

Moe was snoring full throttle, his feet on my desk, his arms dangling limp on either side of my chair. The small desk fan was fixed where it was blowing straight at his face.

He was startled when I kicked the chair and jumped up, tense, like someone caught sleeping on his watch.

"I was just resting my eyes boss, came in to catch the phone."

"You've got to cut down on your partying Moe; you don't get enough sleep on the weekends."

"I sure tried boss, but them that put the days in the week messed up; they put Mondays too close together and Fridays too far apart."

"It's a world full of mistakes, Moe. Now, let's get these cables hooked up and finish the welding; and be careful, don't let the damn machine get overheated."

"Sure thing, boss. I'll be stopping it every so, to cool off. You know, you shoulda let the junk man make razor blades out of it; it's probably older than you and me both."

"It's running fine, just have to be careful with it." I connected the battery while Moe dragged the cables off the van.

"It shoulda been put out of its misery, boss; it's done for. Painting it purple didn't help it none."

"It's dark blue; and anyway, that's what we had left over. Did anybody call?"

"That 'third' dude; said he hasn't got the rent check yet."

"Great."

"And the cat from the steel outfit called, he said: 'tell that wet-back from now on it's gonna be cash up front or we won't unload.'" Moe finished fastening the welding cables. "You know boss, that boy got too much mouth. You say the word and I'll take care of him."

I clamped the battery and started the welding machine. Moe adjusted the amperage, got ready to strike an ark, and the damn thing quit. I checked the gas tank: not a drop in it.

"Damn, what the hell else is gonna happen?" I flung the crescent wrench away and it hit the acetylene bottle, almost breaking the regulator.

"I'll get some out of the van, boss, I know how to use them Georgia credit cards."

He came back with a piece of plastic hose.

"Don't let it get to you boss, it'll all work out." He wormed the hose down the gas tank.

The phone rang and I dashed over to the office. It was a wrong number. I slumped in the chair, feeling the breeze of the little desk fan on my face, staring at the calendar on the wall across from the desk. It had been almost one year since I had started the business and there seemed to be no end to the struggle. It had been a hell of a lot tougher than I thought. It was not only the Bigport Steel Supply that I owed money to; I was late on paying everybody. GESCO was also having cash flow problems and they were slow in paying me.

The benevolent Captain George Steiner had given me more work the second time his motor vessel *George P.* came to Bigport, "To make up for the loss of the engine room piping to the shipyard," the kind-hearted captain had said. It consisted of replacing a lot of rusty steel plate in the ship's ballast tanks. It was hot, dirty, slow-moving work, for which the Dixie Shipyard had probably quoted him a fortune. The job had run way over budget and I would have been a hell of a lot better off if I had never heard of Captain George Steiner and his motor vessel.

On top of it, he refused to pay a big part of the invoice, claiming it was lousy workmanship from a crew that didn't know what they were doing. (The scheming bastard, was all praises about my workers and their workmanship till I sent him the bill.)

I went to see a lawyer, who told me that I needed to put two thousand dollars in escrow before he could look into the case. I dropped it, but hoped I'd run into the sonovabitch some day in a dark alley.

The mailman brought a bundle of mail held together with a rubber band. I stood up and grabbed it from his hand. I went through it, looking for any checks or work orders. I had been expecting payment from Coastal Shipping for a small job I did two months ago. Also Marilyn from GESCO said she had mailed me a check. And the port engineer of Berres Shipping had promised me he would be mailing a purchase order for ten cargo hold ladders, which would keep Moe and me busy for a week. (That was before he got pissed off about the pump foundation.)

In today's bundle there wasn't anything I could take to the bank. There was a letter from Greece in my father's handwriting. The address was copied exactly as it was in my calling card; even the word "president" in big, shaky characters under my name — was he trying to be sarcastic?

I sat down, put Father's letter aside, and started tearing open the envelopes. It was mostly junk mail, bills and overdue notices. Usually I read all the junk mail. Often there would be invitations to seminars where I was guaranteed to improve my administrative skills, get the various departments of my corporation to work more efficiently together, manage my cash flow more profitably and invest my surplus funds where they would bring the maximum returns.

I didn't think I could get much more work out of Moe, if I paid the three hundred bucks to go to a "How to Delegate and Motivate" seminar, but for a very brief moment it felt good to be addressed Chief Executive Officer, to be offered memberships in "Who's What" publications and gold credit cards, because as they put it: "I had arrived, I was on my way up."

Most of the overdue notices were of the type: "Pay up or else!" but a few were trying to tackle the dirty job of collecting with some humor. They'd send cute reminder cards, showing a Sherlock Holmes character holding a magnifying glass with a message at the bottom: "We have been searching for your payment, but we can't find it. Can you help us?"

Usually after the second cute reminder, they would call up and start threatening.

There was a fancy letter, in a large envelope with gold and silver trim, congratulating me for being selected to join the "Exclusive Registry of Corporate Executives." My name was engraved in large gold letters. "Just as it will appear on the registry page reserved for you," said the note under it. "The form below," it continued, "should be signed and returned promptly to take advantage of the extraordinary discount."

There was a spot where I should sign; "verifying correctness of the name," it said. It was right below the three boxes where I should mark how many books I wanted to order. I could have one for two hundred and fifty dollars, four for nine hundred, or six and up at two hundred apiece.

Why couldn't I think of a racket like that?

I put all the bills in the cardboard box labeled "Bills," threw the rest of it in the trash and with a heavy heart I went to the van and got the check book. I dumped the load of the "bill box" on the desk and started picking through the mountain of multicolored invoices:

Gulf Welding Supply: 1 Black & Decker 7 inch angle grinder, $ 166.45" That could go back in the box, it was only twenty-eight days old.

"Sherwin Industrial Coatings: 5 gallons industrial primer: $ 41.25." That one was over two months old. I wrote the check but I didn't sign it. I would enclose a note apologizing for the oversight when they sent it back. That would stretch it a couple of weeks.

"Bigport Power Co.: $ 455.63." That had to be paid, these guys didn't fool around.

"Gulf States Fasteners: $ 186.55 I knew Frank, he was a supplier of nuts and bolts. He had started in business about the same time I did and like me, he was trying to keep his payables and receivables on speaking terms. His invoice was over sixty days old. In the bottom of the overdue notice he had scribbled: "Pay me, so I can pay them, so they can pay him, so he can pay you." It went back in the box. I could plead with Frank, he understood.

Two or three over-ripe bills for tools and steel totaled a thousand dollars. I wrote checks for all of them, but made sure I put them in the wrong envelopes. I would apologize for the "clerical error," when they sent them back.

There were a couple bills from Gulf Welding Supply for a box of welding rods and two bottles of oxygen, totaling $86.88. I paid those. The fat manager was friends with Andrew Carras and if I didn't pay, all the Greeks in Bigport would know it in no time. There were a bunch of others for which I wrote the checks but made the amount written longhand completely different from the amount in numbers. The "new secretary" would be blamed for that.

I licked the envelopes closed, took the check book to the van, and feeling as if I had been swinging a twenty-pound sledge hammer all day, went to see how Moe was doing with the welding.

"Forgot to tell you boss," he yelled over the noise of the machine, "a woman came by looking for you."

"What did she want?"

He stopped the machine. "Needs to cool off... She didn't say; said she wanted to talk to you."

He lit a cigarette.

"She was...fine,... real... fine." The last three words were drawn out to emphasize that the woman was more than just ordinarily "fine."

"She smelled good too. Said she will come back."

"I don't owe any money to any women like that," I said.

"She was fine, real fine," he repeated nostalgically as he walked toward the toilet, then started humming a blues tune.

Nothing worried him lucky rascal; he seemed so content with his life. He didn't have the third dude, the steel selling cat and the Berres Shipping cat, breathing down his neck. And he didn't have a Margaret at home, hammering on him about the mistakes of quitting a steady job and of throwing hard earned money on a pile of rubble, in another country, where "God knows when we will get to go back again."

It was almost noon.

I decided to go see Pete Carras; maybe I could talk him into another small loan. I told Moe I was going to be back in an hour and started to leave.

Two steps short of the van, Edward Hamilton the Third drove up in his red pick up, his radio blaring a wailing country song.

"Just happened to be driving by," he said, "I thought I'll stop to see how you were doing."

My shop was on a dead-end street.

Edward Hamilton the Third was the son of Edward Hamilton the Second, who had inherited the Magnolia Realty Management Co. from Edward Hamilton the First. The original Hamilton had founded the real estate company that managed this and about a dozen other structures like it, now old and semi-dilapidated, around the city's slums.

The third Hamilton was about thirty-five years old, but the stretched skin on his plump, white cheeks made him look much younger. He kept turning his whole head slowly toward whatever he was going to look at, like a surveillance camera on a pedestal. He was of medium height, with big, brown eyes and a very big, round body.

He wore a gray suit, white shirt and a red tie with the word "BAMA" on it, each decorated with various sizes of food stains. His shirt collar (the part that was not covered with neck skin) was yellowed with perspiration stains. He waddled into the shop and looked around.

"It looks like you're getting settled," he said, after his head had scanned the shop.

I told him about the burglary.

"That's too bad, did you call the police?" He was tearing open a Three Musketeers bar. I told him I had.

He noticed the two windows I had added. "I'll have to check what the lease says about alterations," he said.

"It says that when I leave, if the owner doesn't like the changes, I have to make it as it was before. I have the pieces saved, if the building doesn't fall down by then, I'll put them back."

He was looking at my face and I noticed his lips moving silently, following my words.

"It won't collapse. These old buildings are strong. They don't make them like this any more." He tried to sound knowledgeable and confident like his father but he didn't have the old man's convincingness.

His father, the Second Hamilton, was a thin, tall man, around seventy, and what the locals called "Old South." He had negotiated the original lease, but he let junior handle the less important details, hoping, I guess, that someday he would take over the company that the First Hamilton had founded and expand it into a conglomerate, stretching beyond the railroad tracks.

So far the only thing the third Hamilton was surpassing the old man was weight; about one hundred fifty pounds of evenly distributed, loosely attached, blubber. He wiped the perspiration from his forehead. "Almost middle of November and it's still hot," he complained. He took the last bite of the candy bar and threw the wrapper on the floor.

"I checked with the girl before I left; she said she hadn't gotten the check yet. Guess with all the moving and working, it slipped your mind," he said, when he stopped chewing.

"No, I haven't forgot, I was waiting for the bank to print the new checks. I was on my way there when you drove up."

"I can stop by later and pick it up then, if it's O.K."

"I'll save you the trip, I'll bring it by your office, I'll be that way, any way," I volunteered, and before he had a chance to say anything else, I started toward the van. "I'll go there now, see if they got them ready."

81

I drove off and took a deep breath. Damn it, this is getting tight.

At Carras, Ramon said Mr. Pete had just left for lunch.

At the Wharf Restaurant, George said he hadn't seen him for a couple of days. "I think he started eating at Andros restaurant. He's trying to get on the good side of Christos because he plans to go to the village in the summer."

I said I wouldn't go chasing him, but before I sat down to order I called Phil Domain. Marilyn said Phil was out of town. "Stop by and see us sometime, don't be a stranger," she added with all the warmth of a machine. I said I would, and told her to ask Phil to call me.

"I'll tell him for sure, the minute I hear from him," she said.

The waitress came over as soon as I sat down. Her gray uniform was tight around her plump figure.

"Can I get you something to drink, honey?" she asked in a sweet, seductive, very southern voice. I had known her long enough to know that that was her working voice. The kind of voice that prompts men to forget about diet and order dessert.

She was about thirty years old, with dyed blonde hair - the original black could be seen emerging from the roots.

"Miriam, I need you to do me a favor," I said, "I want you to call this number and ask for this guy; he's been dodging me." I handed her my napkin.

"Got you, honey."

We walked over to the phone by the cash register and she dialed the number while humming a country song.

"Honey, let me tell Phil something," she said when somebody answered; her voice, smooth, lusty, full of seductiveness.

"Yes honey, just tell him it's Suzy, he knows." She waited a few seconds and then she handed me the receiver.

"Hi," Phil's voice came from the other end. When I answered, there was a brief puzzled silence, then he recovered and we swapped hardship stories for a while. In the end Phil promised he would pay part of one of the outstanding invoices. It was just enough to keep the third Edward off my back. I told him I would stop by after lunch to pick up the check.

"Thanks for the help," I told Miriam when she came to take my order. "You did good."

"Don't mention it honey. I've got lots of practice getting child support out of that deadbeat ex of mine."

The "fine" woman sashayed in, around three o'clock that afternoon.

I asked her who she was and she acted surprised: She was Cindy, didn't I remember her? the dancer at the Safe Harbor Bar and Grill. She was wearing her work uniform: a tight leather job, hardly enough material to make a welding apron, with boobs and thighs overflowing. Her bleached blonde hair reached down past her bare shoulders.

She sat on the tool box near where we were working and the considerate Moe stopped the welding machine and offered her a cigarette. When she asked me if I knew when the *George P.* would be coming back to Bigport, I remembered her: She was the girlfriend of Demetris Varvanis, the second engineer of the George P. They were inseparable the whole time the ship was here.

"We're getting married when his ship gets back," she announced, playfully blowing smoke in Moe's direction. "Jimmy is going to open a night club and I am going to manage it."

I told her I would let her know as soon as I found out something.

"Come by tomorrow, we'll know something for sure," volunteered Moe.

"*Arhidia Calavrezika*, Stop by the club, I'll buy you a drink," she said as her trembling, parts headed for the door.

"Did Demetris teach you Greek?" I asked.

"No, I learned that from somebody else. It means: 'See you later,' no? I know how to say: 'Pretty girl' too: '*poutanaki*,' right?"

"Maybe," I said, "I don't remember, I've been gone a long time."

"Looks like little Cindy is serious about this Demetri guy, she's learning the language," said Moe when she left.

"Nah, that's some stupid saying, haven't heard it in years," I said, reaching for my cigarettes and finding the pack empty started towards the office for another. I had real problems to worry about instead of Cindy's ass; still I wondered who taught her to say *Calavrezika Testicles*, (a stupid saying among Greek men, when they want to emphasize something small and insignificant — I guess the men from Calavria whom the ancient Greeks defeated eons ago, have small balls.) The poor thing thought she was saying 'See you later' when she was really saying "tiny balls" — and calling herself a "little whore" for "pretty girl."

I saw Father's letter propped against the phone and after lighting a cigarette I sat down and tore it open. In the standard by-fold correspondence paper, only half a page was written from father: "We wish God keeps all of you healthy as all of us here — praise God — have our health. We finished the chestnut harvest. This year was a good harvest but the prices are low so we put it in the cold storage of Stefanis Patekas. Did you know that he got an industrial loan and built a cold storage plant and making money by the sack-full? Who would expect it from the idiot Stefani. Don't understand why God is punishing me."

Mother's letter occupied the other three and a half pages; all in one sentence with no commas and no periods. She had only four years of schooling — the maximum a girl in the village could get at her time — and she was proud of it.

She too wished us health, wished *Maria* and *Nikoleta* were doing well at school and hoped my wife, *Margarita*, dressed them warmly and didn't let them play out in the cold weather.

She mentioned the Patekas cold storage and how lucky dumb-Stefanis was to marry Katina Mela. Maybe he wasn't so dumb after all (like some smart-alecky son, who married a foreigner with the name of a flower). And Kostas, the son of Vagelio Liappis, donated a huge chandelier to the church of Agia Marina, all gold and crystal. When they lit it up last Sunday for the baptism of his son, it made the whole church glow as if the sun was shining right through. "Father Pantelis said it was as if God was smiling at us. Everybody is grateful to Kostas."

I lit another cigarette. Leave it to Kostas Liappis to know how to get votes. He was the captain of our football team and most of the time we won the matches because he could confuse the other team about the rules and the legality of their goals.

"Boss, need you to come and hold this piece of plate for me." Moe snapped me back to reality.

We worked on putting the pump base together the rest of the day. I cut the pieces and held them in place for Moe to weld them, while running through my mind what companies I hadn't approached for work or who I hadn't asked for a loan. A couple of times my mind's wandering got in the way of what I was doing and Moe burned my fingers.

"Got anything lined up after this pump gizmo, boss?" he asked when he stopped again to "rest" the welding machine.

"Don't worry, I got lots of irons in the fire, Moe."

"I could put in for my pennies, ought to be good for a couple of months," he said.

"Something will come up, Moe," I answered, but I didn't know from where. The big job on the tanker *"Oil Transporter,"* despite my fancy proposal and my repeated phone calls that cost me a fortune, went to a fellow named Stathakis that ran an outfit out of Brooklyn.

Everybody that I spoke to about work said they were glad to know I was in business and the next time they needed something they would definitely give me a call. But the calls never came.

That's not how they show it on television. Having your own business is supposed to be a fun-filled adventure; the biggest worry is supposed to be sheltering all those profits from taxes. Instead, I was driving the Graveyard Ghost with the pine cone for a gas cap and Moe a shiny Cadillac with a Playboy tag on the front. I was one month behind on my house mortgage, I owed every supplier that had given me credit, and neither I nor GESCO had any work scheduled any time soon. In two weeks, the third Hamilton would be camped at my door again and I was running out of ideas.

We finished with the pump base late in the afternoon. Instead of going straight home, I drove to a spot by the waterfront and parked on a small bluff overlooking the Gulf.

There was a light breeze blowing from the east. The water was calm, glassy, its orange and grayish colors reflecting the sky and the setting sun.

A shrimp boat was heading east along the horizon, with a flock of seagulls trailing behind her. One of them broke off and headed north.

I puffed on a cigarette and watched it.

After a while, the shrimp boat was almost out of sight; just a small golden speck on the horizon. I reckoned Greece would be straight ahead and to the left of it. And in a small village, somewhere over there, a young boy was probably sitting on a boulder watching his sheep grazing below, and looking at the blue sea and the ships on the distant horizon, dreaming of someday traveling to far-away lands, having adventures and doing great things.

How I would love to trade places with him.

When you are young, it's enough for you if your team wins the match, or you get a good part in the school play, or write an essay that the teacher will read in class.

As long as the sheep don't stray in the neighbor's beans and the goat doesn't eat the grafts of the fig tree, there is nothing to cloud the joy of life.

I tried to put it out of my mind, but the thought kept returning: "Maybe I should go back to the shipyard." They probably wouldn't give me my old job back, but I could be a fitter again. It would be a big bite of "humble pie" as Margaret's priest calls it, but we wouldn't lose the house, the kids could stay in the private school and the Greek bank wouldn't foreclose on the Bellmaker's house loan. If that happened, I could never go back again.

I'd almost gotten used to being my own boss and not taking orders from anybody.

As I sat there looking at the sea, behind the cigarette smoke, through my mind ran some of the stupid mistakes I had made and the opportunities I had squandered in my earlier years. I thought of old Captain Pandelis, the captain on my first ship, and I remembered his folksy wisdom with newfound appreciation. One time I had overheard him tell the chief engineer:

"Want to get revenge on a cocky hand? Promote him, keep him for three months, then get rid of him."

I cranked up the Graveyard Ghost and drove home.

As I was nearing the house, I saw Erick Burkhurst's Cadillac backing out of my driveway. He waved at me and smiled, that annoying smile that's glued to the faces of insurance peddlers and people happy with themselves. I waved back. I grinned and was glad I missed him.

Margaret had introduced Erick to me at one of her "pastor appreciation" church dinners. He gave me his business card, told me that he had had a steel fabrication business in Chicago (but the good Lord delivered him from it), and that he was a regular at a Greek restaurant up there. The next day Erick Burkhurst was at my house with a briefcase full of papers that Margaret and I signed, while he was blabbering corny jokes and mispronounced Greek dishes. Since then, Margaret has been giving him a check every month for our health, home and car insurance. She always manages to have the money to cover those checks, no matter how tight things are.

During dinner, I hinted about going back to the shipyard. "Maybe for awhile, till we get some of the bills paid up," agreed Margaret. She didn't seemed as relieved as I thought she would.

"Anyway, having your own business is not a hell of a lot better than working for others; you just take orders and ass-kiss different people," I reasoned.

Margaret put down her fork and looked at me across the table. "Nick," she started, ignoring Nicole's complaint about getting more broccoli than Maria, "to be your own boss is what you always wanted, isn't it? Sure it looks easier from the outside, but once you are in it you need to stick with it and give it a chance." She turned toward the kids, snapped "Quiet you two," then continued. "Maybe you go back to the shipyard till we get caught up with the bills and I'll be praying for God to show us the way."

For a very brief moment, I felt like reaching across the table and kissing her right in the gravy-stained lips.

"I'll go talk to them next week," I said.

On the television, it seemed as though every channel was talking about a hurricane that was somewhere in the Gulf, and everybody was making a big deal of it, trying to guess where and when it would make land fall. "It must be nice," I thought, "not to have anything to worry about to be able to entertain yourself by tracking a little wind storm."

I went to bed. It had been a long day.

Chapter 8

*H*urricane Sheila attacked Bigport twenty-four hours later, with all of the fury hell can turn loose when she feels playful. It roared ashore blowing more than 120 miles an hour and pouring enough rain to float the town out into the Gulf.

The kids spent the night in the corridor, between the bathroom and the stair-walls. The man on TV said that was the strongest part of the house and Margaret wouldn't have it any other way. We watched the television people in yellow rain coats broadcasting from different parts of the shoreline, being pelted by rain until the power went out. Then we listened to the radio and the wind the rest of the night.

This was the first time I had weathered a hurricane since I quit sailing. Margaret kept suggesting we go somewhere out of the way, like lots of other people, but those lots of other people were unseasoned, soft-living land lubbers. When I was sailing, I had been caught in many storms. We tied everything down, pointed the ship into the weather, reduced speed and let it pound the waves. The wind howled through rigging, the waves came over the bow swallowing the whole deck and the cook had to revise his menu and serve us sandwiches and cold cuts. But all these were minor inconveniences, part of a trade that was famous for its hardships and the high demands on those who worked in it.

Tom Edwards and Howard Demming had left several days ago, probably looking for an excuse to miss work for a couple of days. Howard Demming said he was taking his family to Six Flags in Atlanta, and Tom Edwards was going to visit his sister, elevating a couple of points their standing in Margaret's judgment and plunging my popularity with the kids into the abyss.

The wind got serious soon after dark. It screamed through the trees, snapping their branches and shaking the house. Every so often something would hit the roof or the walls of the house and terrify the children. The rain came through the keyhole of the door as if somebody was holding a hose on the other side. I watched in terrified anticipation as the aluminum frames of the two windows I hadn't boarded up, (I run out of lumber), first bent inward and then outward when the wind shifted. I was expecting them to pop out any second and for us to be sucked into the darkness.

Some time in the middle of the night, when it blew the hardest, we were spooked by a thunderous metallic sound, like the steps of an iron monster. It clanked first in the back yard, then on top of the carport, then on top of the house, then landed in the front yard, and after a lot more clanging, seemed to stop across the street. The girls hugged us tight.

"It's the tin man, looking for Dorothy," I told the kids in a lame attempt at a joke. I looked at their terrified faces and I vowed: "From now on, when the hurricane warnings are out, I'll be leading the convoy out of town, heading for the hills."

At the first daylight, those who had stayed behind came out, numb and dazed, and surveyed the devastation.

Every bit of ground was covered with debris. At the house next door, a large pine tree was driven through the living room roof and was standing straight up, as if it had been growing there all along.

Pine needles driven into tree trunks made them look like strange, hairy worms. The metal storage shed from next door was crumbled and wedged into a bay window of the house across the street.

"There is the monster that was going to crush the house," I told Nicole, who was holding my hand.

I went over to Howard Demming's house and walked around it. It was boarded up tight and didn't seem to have any damage. Further down, at Tom Edward's house, the plywood from the living room window must have been blown away, (all the other windows were boarded up,) and a pine tree branch had gone through, piercing the leather recliner in front of the television. I went back to the house, got my saw and one piece of plywood and cut up the tree and boarded up the window. Somebody could haul off everything if the house was left open like that, next to the road. Later I told Margaret about it. "You mean the tree went through the chair?" Margaret had exclaimed.

"Yeah, too bad he wasn't sitting in it."

It took almost two hours to travel the fifteen miles to the shop. Downed trees, broken power poles, flooded streets and stopping to look at other people's misfortune made driving slow.   At one point, I detoured trough a pasture because part of the road was blocked; a DC-3 was laying in the middle of Airport Boulevard upside down, like a giant dead bug. Chain saws were buzzing all over town.

A radio advisory gave the locations where generators, chain saws and ice were sold.

It advised people to boil all drinking water and to avoid fallen power lines. Then the sheriff came on and said that the police would be on the look out for looters and people who were overcharging for goods and services. I knew better. If there is a buck to be made, people will find a way to get it.

When I got to the shop, I found a pink plastic flamingo wedged in the window of my office its neck broken and hanging down limp, as if it had been shot. The walls, floor and ceiling of the little cubicle were covered with soaked paper and pine needles. I closed the hole and left everything else the way it was. The bills, overdue notices and the calendar girls could dry where they were.

With the electricity out at my house we were faced with the problem of keeping the medicine for Katerina's ear infection cold — An antibiotic called *Amoxicilin* that came in a little bottle with a big price. Without it, her ears ached and although she didn't complain, it was heartbreaking to watch her being miserable.

The Dixie Ice company was one of the two places in the area that sold ice, and I spent a half an hour weaving my way there only to be told that the trucks bringing it from out of state were late because of all the debris on the roads. I joined a huge crowd in a line four people wide, that ran around the block. People sat on boxes and crates, while others came prepared for the long wait; they brought along folding chairs, ice chests, knitting projects, books and crossword puzzles.

An old couple behind me, sitting on yellow beach chairs knew the old couple in front of me sitting on green beach chairs and they got into a long conversation, swapping horror stories about the night before. My standing between them didn't seeming to bother them at all. The couple behind said, and the couple in front agreed, that they "hadn't seen a storm the likes of this one, in all their born days."

"Kotronas lost all four of his boats; two of them sunk right next to the dock and two washed up on the bank; all smashed up. It'll cost a heap to get them running," said the old man behind.

"Heard from your son in-law?" asked the old man in the front.

"Talked to Cooter this morning, said his boat got all tore up. He'll be patching and welding for weeks. Good thing he knows how to do welding himself, Cooter does."

I spent my time scribbling on a brown bag, trying to come up with a budget that would get me out of the hole I was in. After adding up what I had coming, then subtracting it from what I had going, it looked like I would have to work around the clock in the shipyard for a couple of hundred years before I got my head above water.

Around Bigport, there were many quaint, small fishing towns, whose docks, marinas and boatyards used to be crowded with shrimp boats, oyster boats, snapper boats and whatever other kind of boats it takes to catch the creatures living in the Gulf, in the rivers and the lakes.

Every normal male around here is supposed to have some kind of a boat to give him an excuse to be away from the house while waiting for the hunting season to open. Before the storm, all sorts of floating contraptions were crowding the marinas, fishing camps and driveways. Anything from the foot-soaker size with a trolling motor about the size of an egg beater, to catch catfish and bream around the lakes, to the big, deep-sea jobs, for catching marlin, sharks and mermaids in tiny bikinis.

Now, they were all scattered on roof tops, on top of trees, in the middle of cow pastures and on the highways. Yachts lay on top of the docks in a pile, or sunk alongside the pier with many expensive holes on them.

Many of these boats would never float again. Some, would be renamed *SS Hurricane Sheila* and decorate the parking lots of souvenir shops and sea food restaurants.

It was afternoon when I got my block of ice. Driving home, I was thinking about the two old chattery couples. By the time I left, between the four of them, they had given a full report on every boat, barge, tug and anything else that used to float in the bay. Nosy old farts.

I took a different route home hopping it would be faster. Two blocks from the ice place the road was blocked and I joined a group of five other people helping an old couple drag some of the branches of an oak tree off the road. The old couple looked just like the couple behind me in the line for ice: in their late seventies, short, plump, grandparently. The fallen tree had torn part of the front porch of their house on which two rocking chairs could be seen under a pile of oak leaves.

At one point, as four of us were pulling on a branch to dislodge it from the porch, the old woman, doing her feeble best tugging with the rest of us, said with heart-breaking sadness: "Me and paw used to sit on that porch and watch the people go by. Now look at it, it's all splinters; it is."

"Don't you worry none, Ma'am" said the guy holding the branch next to me. "The insurance company is gona pay you to build a brand new one, it's gonna be just like it was before."

That's when it hit me. "That's it," I shouted, "Damn it, that is it."

Everybody gave me a startled look and took a step back as if I had something catching. I turned around and walked to the car, feeling their stares piercing my back.

Sometimes a problem seems so big, so impossible, and all along the solution is right in front of you, staring you in the face. I guess that's what the Americans call not being able to see the forest for the trees. Why the hell didn't I think of that before? I drove straight to Erick Burkhurst's office.

It was about time he did something for me.

I found Erick and a middle-aged secretary scooping up the broken glass from the floor — the remnants of large door and two windows.

"*Giassou Amigo,*" he greeted.

"I know a good insurance man you could talk to," I said.

"He's probably looking for another line of work right now," he chuckled.

"Listen," I said, "I figured how to get the premiums I owe you paid up and maybe even do some more business together."

"Let me see, you gonna open a *souvlaki* stand."

I told him what I had in mind.

"Bravo Mr. *Mousaka*, that's smart, you are a smart *baklava*, but you need to talk to the fellow they're sending down later in the week; I'm gonna have my hands full with cars and houses." He walked over to a chair, glass crunching under his feet, and opened a brown briefcase.

"I have the guy's name here somewhere; call him to make an appointment." He found the name and wrote it on the back of his business card.

"These are my new cards," he said, handing it to me.

I looked at it. It read: "ERICK W. BURKHURST Independent Insurance Broker, Home, Auto, Boat. We have you covered."

There was a shadow drawing of a big man looking like Abraham Lincoln, with his arms stretched protectively over a group of people consisting of a black woman that looked like Aunt Jemima, a Chinese man, with robe and pig tail, an *euzone*, probably copied from a Greek Fest flyer, a Mexican with a huge sombrero and a woman with a hat made out of tropical fruit.

"O.K. *Senior Pastitsio*? Talk to the Mariner's Fund guy, I'm sure he will give you all the work you can handle."

I told him I'll be there.

By the time I got home, the block of ice could fit in a whisky glass.

I camped in front of Erick Burkhurst's office till the Mariner's Fund guy showed up. When he finally did, he said he was too busy to talk and suggested we meet for lunch the next day.

I thought having someone from Lloyds of London with me the next day would boost my standing, so I went looking for Scotty Jones, who had been laid off from GESCO.

"He will make you a good man," Phil said when I asked for his address. "Only keep him from reminiscing about the good old days and the bulker *Mirella*; and let me know when he has a paycheck coming."

Sometimes, when Scotty had a few drinks in him, he would get melancholy and start rambling about crooked ship owners, who bribe crooked insurance bosses, who override the reports of honest insurance agents about unseaworthy vessels, then blame the agents when there's an accident. He knew what he was talking about, he would insist, he got blamed for the sinking of the *Mirella*, and given a desk job in a crummy little office next to the broom closet. He, who had been a field man since graduating from the Maritime Academy at the top of his class, who had been in every major Lloyds' office, from Calcutta to Rio. That's why he had told them to stuff it.

Those who knew Scotty could sense when the lamenting was coming on and would remember that they were urgently needed somewhere else.

I went to pick Scotty up thirty minutes before the lunch meeting with the Mariner's Fund man. The Southern-bellish woman who answered the door said Scotty was in the shower and I was welcome to wait in the parlor. She was middle-aged, tall and thin with traces of an aborted makeup attempt.

Some loud opera singing was coming from a record player in the parlor. I moved a woman's jacket from a chair and sat down.

"The girl didn't come in yesterday," she apologized.

Theirs was one of those old houses that has a historic plaque in the front and at some time in the past was owned by somebody rich. Everything in the house had seen better days.

There were lots of large framed photographs showing a tall, distinguished-looking man, shaking hands and accepting plaques from people who looked important. One I recognized as a past state governor. In a couple of photographs, I thought I recognized the woman standing next to the distinguished-looking man, as the one now pouring drinks across the room.

On the wall next to my chair, a framed front page of the *Bigport Herald* was showing the same man, accepting a plaque from another aristocratic-looking man. The headline above it read: "Judge William Oscar Hamilton named Bigport citizen of the year."

"Will you have a drink?" the woman asked.

I said: "No, thanks."

"I'll just refresh mine, then." She poured bourbon in a water glass from one of the bottles on a small table loaded with drink-making stuff in a far corner of the room, next to a sofa occupied by two cats and a full laundry basket. She took a pair of silver tongs and tried to extract an ice cube from a little silver bucket and when that proved difficult, scooped one up with her hand and put it in the glass. She scooped one more and put it in another glass, added some bourbon, then dried her hands on her dress.

"I fixed you a drink, Scotty," she yelled out over the singing. "He keeps that blasted thing so loud," she apologized as she fussed with the record player knobs.

George came in, walked over and turned down the volume. "It's Maria Callas, in Carmen." His voice had a tone that was part scolding and part patronizing.

He wore a pair of freshly-pressed brown pants and a starched white shirt.

"Wonderful voice, very talented woman, he should have married her," he continued while working on the tie.

"Who should have married her, Scotty?" asked the woman.

"Onassis. He should have, but was too shallow, the bum." He finished with the tie.

"Don't know anything about them; the judge only listened to gospel music; the ice is gonna melt; mine already did." She scooped another ice cube from the bucket and refilled her glass. George took a long gulp from his, put on his jacket, then searched his pockets and came up with two dollars, which he stared at for a few seconds as if trying to remember what had happened to their companions, before putting them back.

"I'll need a twenty from you, Pet, till Monday; forgot to stop by the bank yesterday."

Gingerly the pet went to the sofa and dug in a large black bag.

"Bring back something to eat," she said, handing him two ten dollar bills.

We started towards the door and he leaned over as if to kiss her.

"I'll be back in a couple of hours," he said as his lips almost touched her left cheek.

"I might be lying down, don't feel very good," she said.

She was pouring herself another drink as we were leaving the room.

The representative from the Mariner's Fund Insurance Company was young, with delicate features and thick glasses. He was from New York city and he acted as if he had been dispatched to unexplored territory. It was obvious he was new in the business; he picked up the lunch bill, including Scotty's two vodka martinis.

I cringed every time Scotty lifted his glass, fearing he might get melancholy and start his usual rambling about *Mirella*, but this time he behaved like a professional. He rattled off insurance terms and sea stories that impressed the hell out of the greenhorn agent. By the time lunch was over I had a yard-long list of boats he wanted us to work on and a promise of just as many next week. All we had to do was to go where the boat had landed, make an estimate of the repair costs and send a complete report to his office, including photographs, copies of the policy and the replacement costs. Then if the boat was repairable, we'd coordinate the repairs with the owners.

With each survey report, I would be sending an invoice to the insurance company. Nothing to it. Scotty was going to be doing all of the inspecting and report writing and I would concentrate on the repairs. And there were plenty of them: Lots of damaged hulls to be welded and lots of engines that had been submerged in salt water and had to be replaced.

Maybe I wouldn't get rich on this contract, but it would bring in some badly needed cash and keep me from going back to the shipyard. And the Bellmaker's house in the village was safe for a while. The storm, together with the grief and devastation, had also brought an economic boom to the area. The way I saw it, the hurricane was the white knight that had saved a little damsel in distress called Poseidon Marine Services.

Having Scotty handle the surveying and the report-writing part made the job go fast and smooth. When I was in the merchant marine, surveyors from Lloyds of London were to the ship's officers what the Pope is to the parish deacon. Now, I had a Lloyds of London man working for me. I had come up in the world. I never missed a chance to mention in a conversation that I had an ex-Lloyds man on my staff.

People and equipment poured into Bigport from every corner of the country, and in most places, electricity and all the other utilities came back after a few days. I saw a picture in the newspaper of a postal collection box at the other end of town that had been knocked over and its load scattered in the ditch. I used that piece of news for as long as I could get away with it. Every time somebody called asking for payment, I would answer, "The check must have got lost in the storm. If you don't get it the next couple of days, give me a call and I'll cut you another one." I even stretched three extra weeks out of the landlord.

For about six months, I milked the hurricane for as much as I could get out of it. Margaret complained that I was working long hours but I kept telling her that you have to get it while you can. I hired three new guys, bought a used Toyota pick-up, in good enough shape that it wouldn't embarrass Margaret when I parked it in the driveway, and I kept the Grave Yard Ghost for shop use. I even got Gulf Welding Supply to sell me on credit an "almost new" welding machine for the shop and kept the old one for field work.

I was supervising all the repairs, Scotty did what he was supposed to, and things were moving along as normally as possible in my kind of business.

Sometimes we would come across a boat or yacht whose repair costs would be more than it was worth. Then it was declared "total loss": the owner would get a check from the insurance company for whatever the value of it was determined to be and we would either haul what was left of it to the scrap yard, or work out a separate deal with the owner for the repairs and he would pay us out of his pocket. Quite a few owners made money on deals like that.

Once in a while, usually when he got paid, Scotty would disappear, then show up a few days later with some excuse that neither of us took seriously. Scotty was honest; he just couldn't resist the booze.

One day, when I hadn't seen Scotty for a whole week, I got a phone call from someone who sounded very pissed-off. Sorting through the cussing and the shouting, I made out that Scotty had surveyed his boat and told him it would be declared a total loss. He had been waiting for the check to come in.

"It's been two weeks since he's done looked at the boat and I ain't got nothing yet," he roared through the wire. "Called the insurance today and they said they ain't got no report, no nothing from him, neither. What kind of flimflam operation you got going there?"

I told him we were a reputable company and we stood behind our work. "Mr. Jones is on a job out of town, but I'll come over myself and make a new report," I told him.

"Better get something straightened out here: that fellow got my money and I ain't gonna put up with no thieving outfit," he growled.

I coaxed some directions to his place and told him I would be there in an hour.

As I was walking towards the truck, the new man, Lloyd, caught up to me: "Remember, got to leave early today, got to go see the kid's teacher."

"Yeah, I remember," I said.

"Floyd is gonna leave too, he is riding with me." Then seeing I didn't grasp the importance of the event, he added, "The onliest left here, will be Moe."

"I know, don't worry, Moe can look after the place," I said and drove off.

Loyd and Floyd, the country cousins, walked in one morning, a week after the hurricane, looking for a job. Standing side by side, one tall and tanned, the other short and very white, in their bib cover-alls and bright, multi-patched welder's hats, each holding a five gallon plastic bucket with their tools in it, they were like two characters out of some old Hollywood comedy.

They said they came from the north part of the state and had served together in the navy.

I happened to need some welders right then and I hired them both. They were sharing a rented house out in the country and a beat-up Camaro, loaded with junk and smelling of marijuana, in which they came to work every morning.

At the time, that's all I thought they shared.

Floyd was twenty-five years old, single, tall and athletic. He did his job, seemed to mind his own business and spoke little in quiet tones. He was a pretty good mechanic, and he could also do welding and fitting. The odd thing about Floyd was his small brown eyes. They were always darting from side to side and there was a glow in them that betrayed more brain activity than the docile, countryish image he projected.

Loyd was short, skinny, always tense, always sticking his nose in everybody else's business and always bragging about how great he was, as a mechanic, as a hunter, as a lover and as everything else. He seemed to think that I wouldn't survive without him.

He was married, had a cute six-year-old daughter and a wife with a body that would make a saint give up sainthood. Sometimes she needed to keep the car and dropped them off at work, she always wore a skimpy halter and very short, very tight shorts that brought all work to a screeching stop. She flirted with everybody.

I didn't believe Loyd's bit about leaving early to see the kid's teacher. More likely they were working on one of their shady side deals.

I drove off to see the unhappy customer who lived in the woods a few miles from the shop. It was a mild, sunny day, with the few leaves that had survived the hurricane turning beautiful fall colors; a nice day for a ride in the country - if one was in the mood for it.

I zigzagged through pecan groves on clay roads, looking at the scars left by Hurricane Sheila.

Lots of houses still lay crumbled in piles; their owners, having salvaged what they could, either gave up and moved away, or were still haggling with the insurance companies. Some declared their determination to rebuild in simple and effective ways. On top of one mountain of rubble the owner had spray-painted on a chunk of flooring: "Down but not out." A block further down, someone had painted on what used to be a white interior door: "Decorations by Sheila" and his neighbor, not to be outdone, had scribbled on a piece of plywood: "Just like a woman." Disaster brings out strange humor in people.

Row after row, pecan trees were laying on their side, their roots sticking up in the air like the webbed feet of a giant bird. The pine trees were snapped off near the ground and lay in a jumble. The country was buzzing with the sounds of chain saws and logging equipment. Crews had come in from all over the country, and were busy chopping trees and clearing roads.

At one point I had to stop and wait for a mule team that was moving a tree out of the way. Two black mules with blinders, walking behind a guy with a wide straw hat, were dragging a long pine tree out of a tangle of branches and shrubbery between two houses. The guy directing the traffic said the team was from Missouri. "They can pull logs out of places machines can't get to, and they don't tear up a place neither," he said. The mules, with their heads lowered, sweat running down their necks, were moving in slow, humble, steady steps, unaware of their special talents.

I noticed my gas gauge was showing empty. When the road block cleared I drove in to Vasilis Larkeas' service station. It was the only structure in the middle of acres of farmland. Traces of the hurricanes' passage were still fresh around here; the Gulf Oil sign post was bent in half and the sign seemed planted upside down among the azaleas. The windows were still taped in a diamond pattern with brown tape, and part of the roof was still covered with blue tarp, held down with cinder blocks.

Vasilis walked up to the truck, wiping his hands on a filthy rag.

"Wanna fill up, *patrioti*?"

"Not at this price," I said, pointing at a large, handwritten cardboard sign, which in misspelled scribbling, said the price of "reglar gas" was a "dolar twenny" a gallon.

"Just put two dollars in it."

"That's the hurricane price," he explained. "If I don't have power and use a generator, the state OK's to sell high, but to you, I sell regular price."

"I though you got power last week," I said.

"No, not yet. You don't hear the generator?"

I listened to the noise of a small gasoline engine in the back.

"It sounds like a motorcycle."

"No, it's Japanese generator, that's why."

"Just put five dollars in it."

I wove my way through the shop, stepping around old tires and oil puddles and when I finally got to the bathroom, the damn thing was locked.

"Be right out," someone grunted from inside.

I took a leak at a spot behind the station and on the way back I noticed an old lawn mower, close to the door but well out of sight, without a muffler, running full throttle.

"Your Japanese generator is almost out of gas," I told Vasilis as I signed the gas ticket.

"You got to make it while you can my friend; you won't be telling anybody about it, *eh patrioti*?"

Navigating by the directions of the unhappy boat owner, plowing through miles of dirt road, I found his hideaway: an old camper trailer, hardly visible from all the bushes growing around it, propped up on cinder blocks a couple of feet off the ground, next to a creek. Large oak trees, with Spanish moss dangling from their branches, surrounded the camper.

A tangle of concrete rubble and weeds served as stairs to the front door and next to it, half-buried in kudzu vines, was a rusty pick-up truck, with cinder blocks for tires and a load of firewood in the back. The driveway was just a goat path, with a truck parked at the end, identical to the crippled one, but with tires and without a load of fire wood.

I had taken only a few steps towards the trailer when two huge black dogs of some man-eating breed popped up from under the middle of the trailer and with long leaps, barking viciously, headed straight for my throat.

They had that "show no mercy" look which prompted me to turn around, almost tripping over an old tire, take some galloping strides and dive in the truck, just as the biggest of the two was catching up. It pressed its mouth, wide open, against the door window, showing long, lethal teeth while frothy slobber streaked down the glass.

I leaned on the horn until a stocky fellow, with a long unkempt beard, somewhere between thirty and sixty, wearing farmer's style blue cover-alls, came out from the trailer. He walked up, peered inside the truck, thought for a while, then shouted something to the dogs that made them retreat behind the trailer.

"What you want?"

I cracked the window an inch and slid my card through it. He held it at arms' length, squinting his eyes, then looked me over.

"You Cuban?" he asked when I got out.

"No, I am Greek."

He scrutinized me some more. "Sure no look no Indian; I knew some Creek folk when I lived in Atmore."

His left cheek was puffed out and every so often he turned his head to the right and spat out part of what he was chewing, making a squishing sound.

"You got the money?"

"Could I see your papers?" I asked.

"Got them inside," he growled, "I'll fetch them."

I followed him, making sure I stayed on his left side.

"Wait here," he said when we reached the door.

He went inside and I stood by the steps, keeping an eye on the dogs and trying to guess where he had the still. He came out a few minutes later, holding a large, wrinkled, brown envelope with grease stains.

"It's all there." He handed me the envelope. "Elmer had all the papers."

I laid the papers on the hood of the truck and looked at them. He stood by my side, looking me over.

"Sure you ain't no Cuban?"

"Yep, I am sure."

"Do this kinda work all the time?"

"All the time."

He kept staring at me.

"That other fellow, he talked queer too."

"He's not Cuban either," I said.

I looked at his papers, wrote down what I needed and put everything back in the envelope. Then I asked to see the boat.

We walked behind the trailer, weaving between empty propane bottles, old appliances and broken lawn furniture. At the edge of the creek, tied to a cypress tree, was a twenty-two foot bass boat.

"How long have you had the boat?" I asked.

"Week before the hurricane. Elmer couldn't pay me back my money and said I could keep the boat. Said everything was paid up to the end of the year. He's the one that sent that other Cuban here."

I looked the boat over.

"You haven't got any damage," I said, "not even a scratch."

"It could have been; all of them trees falling all over, one of them could have hit right smack on it."

"The insurance is not going to pay anything if there is no damage, especially total loss, that's for sure."

"Shit, I could've got a limb and poke a hole in it; that would've make it total loss, and nobody would know no different."

"But you didn't, did you?"

"That would sink the boat; what kind dumb-ass talk is that?"

"Some folks would call that fraud, you know?"

"Now, you look here," he shouted. "I paid good money to that other fellow to take care of this. He got two hundred dollars of my money. I ain't gonna be flim-flammed by no thieving Cuban. You go back and take care of this or it'll be hell to pay. I ain't kissing my money goodbye, hear me boy? I sure as hell ain't."

The dogs had come out from under the trailer and were clearing their throats.

"I'll go back and check with the insurance," I said. "What's your phone number? I'll call you in the morning."

"I ain't got no phone, I'll call you; I got your number."

I started toward the truck. The two dogs followed a few feet behind.

"Better come up with the money tomorrow," he yelled, as I was getting in the car.

Driving back I tried to figure out the mess Scotty had gotten me into. One possible explanation was that this Elmer character, who was a bartender at one of Scotty's hangouts, bought some moonshine from the cave man and instead of money, gave him the boat, which was probably going to be repossessed anyway. Then this guy figured he would bribe Scotty to declare it total loss, pocket the money and keep the boat. I was sure Scotty never intended to defraud the insurance, it was against his nature. He probably was hard up for money, saw a sucker and figured he could make an easy two hundred dollars. Now he was either still drunk or drove that clanker of his into a ditch, which might be better than the moonshiner catching up with him.

I called the insurance company the next morning and I was relieved to hear that the premium had not been paid and the policy had lapsed a month before the hurricane. I passed this on to the fellow with the man-eating dogs when he called the next day and told him I would get his two hundred dollars back to him. He let loose an avalanche of curses for Elmer, me, the insurance company and "every thieving Cuban," which I am sure continued long after I had hung up.

Chapter

9

*T*he key kept slipping through my cold fingers as I struggled to open the office lock before the phone stopped ringing. Just as I reached for it, it stopped. I cursed the contraption and went to make coffee. It couldn't be a customer this early in the morning anyway. The East Coast shipping offices wouldn't open for another hour and the offices in Greece were in their midday siesta. It was probably one of my guys, calling to say that his car wouldn't start or he was coming down with something, which meant that he was either hung-over or looking for another job.

A few minutes later, it rang again.

"Good afternoon your excellency. About time you got to work, Mr. Big Shot." Pete Carras must have had a visitor in his office, his sarcasm was in English this time.

"Pete, it's only six-thirty."

"They tell me you work three shifts now, have big jobs."

"Don't even have enough work for half a shift. I got one man's worth of work and four people doing it."

"I have a Telex here for you, for big job."

"I'll be over in a minute," I said.

I trotted the three blocks in one breath.

Pete was arguing with somebody on the telephone. The vegetable man had just unloaded and was sitting on the couch across from Pete's desk holding his papers. I walked over to the coffee pot and poured myself a cup of coffee.

"No, I no want manila," Pete shouted into the phone, "captain ordered three inch nylon rope. I speak to you father two weeks before, not know about requisition forms. You ask you father and call back, O.K.?" he hung up.

"Requisitions and *arhidia Calavrezika*," he muttered, reaching for his cigarettes.

"That is the son of Petro Zervas, in Baltimore," Pete said to both of us. "Good boy but he can not ... like they say in Andros, *feed hay to two donkeys*, he not get the smartness of his father. His father opened Atlantic Cordage same time I open this business." He pointed to the calendar on his wall showing a Greek island. "We was on same ship; I was chief steward and he third mate; very good man." Pete finished tamping the back of his cigarette on his thumb-nail and lit it. "Now Petro got the bad sickness and must retire, but I no think his boy will make it." He took another puff, "Ah, kids today, they get spoiled with easy life. Very few of them make... good people." He didn't seem satisfied with the word. "How you say in English *prokopi*?" he asked me.

"Success," I said.

"Yah, that's it, very few make that now. I was lucky with my Bobby, he come out very smart boy." He ground the cigarette in the ashtray.

Boby had started working for his father full-time, six months earlier, right after he graduated from the university with a degree in business administration.

"Oh, here," he said, remembering why I was there. "It was on machine this morning. I already send them you name; no forget my commission. Soon you be rich man and I come to you for loan, OK?"

I glanced at the Telex on my way to get a refill on my coffee. It was from a London shipping agent Pete had been doing business with. In the word-stingy style of the telegram, it was announcing that the *MV Ocean Lady* would be arriving in Bigport the last week of December, to take on cargo. There was a brief list of stores and provisions they wanted Pete to supply and then the last sentence: "Arrange competent shop assist chief engineer with propeller repairs."

I refilled my cup and got back with the others. "How come you are alone Pete?" I asked when I sat down.

"Stavro is gone to a ship and Ramon is late; lazy bum." He paused a bit as if he was expecting another question, then volunteered the answer. "Bobby gone to London; he called this morning, he gone and see Panos Skiafakis of Progress Shipping and he collect full payment from the sonovabitch." Pete's face glowed. "The sonovabitch give me the running around over one year. Bobby goes there and tells him, if he no pay we tie his ship next time it comes to America. He pay... *amesos*,...(immediately) right there."

"That college education is paying off, Mr. Pete," said the vegetable man.

"Bobby is smart boy. That was smart idea he have, to go to England. He go to see two other companies yesterday and they promise will give me business. Today he go to see more people and when he coming back, he will sit two days in New York to go to see companies. He has a book full of appointments. I will have to built bigger warehouse, this here already small." Pete waved his arm to emphasize the small perimeter of the place. His eyes were shining and I am sure in his mind he already saw the large warehouse and a fleet of trucks in front of it, all painted in avocado green and fire house red, with large blue and white letters declaring: CARRAS SHIP SUPPLY INC.

"Well Pete, everybody visits customers. You should have been doing it too all these years," I said.

"I know, I know, everybody goes to New York. My competitions go up there, minimum two time a year, but I no like the damn *aeroplanes* and I no like to go to fancy offices talking to big-shots. Bobby do that real good."

Bobby was only twenty-four years old, but he had the levelheadedness of a much older man. He was short and thin, with steel framed glasses on a delicately featured face. He was meticulous and soft-spoken, but when he spoke, there was a reason and purpose to it; he didn't go for idle chatter.

The old fox, Panos Skiafakis, knew that Bobby's soft, frugally dispersed words were a bigger threat than the bountiful but harmless verbiage generously dispensed by Pete Carras. He realized he couldn't give Boby the "running around."

"I not see you, Mr. Big-shot, doing much visiting," said Pete.

"I am going to go to New York as soon as I can afford it, then later, maybe I go to Poseidonia. Want to come?"

"What is this Poseidonia?"

"It's a trade show. It happens every two years in Piraeus. Everybody that has anything to do with ships is there; shipyards, repair companies, shipchandlers, from all over the world. I'll go and try to get some customers."

"Maybe I will come with you. I have not been to Greece from sixty-nine. That time, I go with train to New York and from there with the passenger ship *Olympia*. How many hours to fly?"

"It's not long. You have a couple of drinks and go to sleep and when you wake up, you are there. Let's plan to go together, O.K.?"

Pete's phone rang and he tried to answer it but pressed the wrong button and disconnected the call. Pete cursed and slammed the receiver.

It rang a few seconds later and this time Pete kept saying: "Halo, halo," but there was no answer.

"Press the button that's blinking," I offered. He did and it worked.

"All these godamn lights and buttons, too godamn complicated," he said when he hung up. "I liked my old telephone better."

"It's progress, Mr. Pete, progress," quipped the vegetable man.

"That's what my Bobby say, but I say to him, 'Progress is for young people, when you take over you put all progress you want in here, I no like you change my things.'"

102

Pete's tone was mild and his displeasure had all the sincerity of a father loosing a wrestling match to his toddler son.

"Your Bobby has a good head on his shoulders, you are a lucky man, Pete," said the vegetable man.

"He is a good boy, only he want to make everything modern fast, I am an old man."

Pete Carras' face was beaming. Even a blind person could sense the pride for his Bobby.

On my way back to the office I wondered if my father would be as proud as Pete, had I stayed on the farm. That's what he wanted me to do and was disappointed when I left.

On December twenty-eight I was standing at Pier Six-South, one hour before the *Ocean Lady* docked. Pete had shown me the Telex he sent the shipping agent: "Arranged Poseidon Marine meet vessel on arrival."

There was a light drizzle and a cold, northerly breeze blowing and everyone waiting for the ship had crowded under the stevedore's shed, a twenty-foot metal container with the long side cut open and turned up, to make a canopy.

Everybody was talking about the weather. Some were saying it was the coldest they remembered and others that it was not near as cold as it gets where they came from, where they worked out in the open all day, with the thermometer so far below zero they were reading it in China.

No one believed anything anybody said on the waterfront, but they listened, waiting for a break to tell their piece. Once in a while they would throw in some remark like "Yah, I heard you folks spear-fish on the ice in Cuba, come winter time," or something like that, to let the other guy know they were not fooled.

"It's too damn cold for me, damn near as cold as back in forty when the Bay froze over, and I was a damn lot younger then." That was old Simon, the oldest of the linehandlers. The linehandlers were the ones who caught the heaving line when the ship got near. Then three or four of them together pulled in the rope and put the eye over the mooring bit. They took it off again, when the ship was leaving, so the crew running the capstans would winch it on board. For that simple chore, the ship agents were billing the shipping company the equivalent of brain surgery.

A fresh gust of wind brought the strong stinky smell of the paper mills.

"Shit, they must be making toilet paper today," said a short, fat linehandler with missing teeth, then spat by his side.

"Damn, there are gonna be more damn people on the dock than the damn ship has crew," old Simon mumbled, looking for a spot to spit his tobacco juice. Some times it seemed that way, especially when a ship was coming from a foreign port. There were the immigration, the customs, the health officials and the ships' agent, all of which would go on board as soon as the gangway was lowered. The rest of us would wait for them to leave and the yellow flag hoisted down, before we were allowed to stampede up the gangway, each trying to outrun his competition.

That day on the dock, beside Stavro Rigotis, were two other shipchandlers waiting to get on board, all of them armed with price lists, brochures, note pads and next years' wall calendars showing naked curvy girls in seductive poses, trying to hide what was between their legs behind some miniature ships' part.

Stavro, who had this one in the bag, stood by the side of the shed, smoking and staring out toward the river, calm and expressionless like a high stakes poker player. Occasionally he would glance at his two competitors, probably rejoicing at the thought they were wasting their time.

The other shipchandler was Felipe, from Olsen Ship Supply; a short, fast-talking Spaniard, and according to Stavro, a slimy, lying, no-good sonovabitch.

The third one was a new addition to the cutthroat field of ship supply: Suzie Wong. Rumor had it that everything about Suzie was fake; she was not even Chinese, just a stripper and a hooker in the waterfront till she shacked up with a Norwegian steward, and they started the ship supply business. She always called on ships wearing the same outfit; a tight, low-cut Oriental dress with a slit on the side that went up — way, way up. On rainy days, she wore a clear plastic raincoat over it. She always managed to get some kind of an order from most ships. Then her assistant would make the delivery wearing an even skimpier outfit. "The rottener the vegetables, the more raw meat showing," Stavro had said.

Then there was Sam Richards, the representative from Dixie shipyard. Gray-haired, clean cut, dignified, grandfatherly, with what looked to the uninitiated like a kind, gentle smile. You wouldn't hesitate to put your head on his shoulder and pour your heart out. He was always there next to me, meeting every ship that came in, at all hours, ass-kissing the captain and the chief engineer for any repairs they might need. Most of the time he would beat me, because his boss could afford to pay bigger bribes. Hell, everybody was pulling for the sonovabitch; the agents, the stevedores, even the tug-boat crews. If they were handling a ship they thought had engine problems, they would call Sam on the Walkie-Talkie he had glued to his side.

The cigarette salesman was also there with his free sample packs with six cigarettes in them, his Marlboro wind breakers and T-shirts which he would exchange for the carton tops the crew had collected. He would make sure the ships' store had a large supply of his brands and linger around, talking down the competition till it was time to join them for lunch. He claimed it was part of his marketing strategy, but we all knew he was just a cheapskate.

There were two Pakistanis with boxes full of radios, cassette players, video cameras and other electronic gadgetry. They would go on board, spread their merchandise in the crew's lounge and sell it to those who got detained by the immigration, or were too dumb to go ashore and buy the same stuff at half the price.

Manolis Tringas, who had sailed for a few years as a deckhand till he decided there were more thrills ashore, was there with his Argentinean partner. They operated a kind of all-purpose store for seamen. They would pick them up in their bright red and yellow van with "Seven Seas Emporium" painted on the side, and take them to their shop stocked with everything a sailor's salt-cured, homesick heart would desire. There were rumors that they made most of their money by selling porno movies and other shady deals, but rumor circulation is normal on the waterfront.

The DuBois sisters, one black and one white, in jeans so tight they must have grown up in them, were sitting in their pink van, parked next to the shed, smoking and listening to strip joint music. They were waiting to pass out flyers with photographs of smiling mermaids with names like Misty, Stormy and Candy, each one of them inviting "the good looking men of this ship for a fun time at the Happy Mariner, your home away from home." The DuBois sisters were not really sisters, it was just a marketing gimmick they came up with, saying they had the same mother but different fathers.

Next to them was a guy from International Ministries. He, too, was going to pass out flyers, but his warned of the wrath of God for the sinners and of His blessings and rewards for those who resisted temptation.

The fellow from the seamen's club was there with his van. He was going to pick up those who wanted to go shopping, to church or to a soccer game.

Some days there were also service technicians, port engineers, cargo representatives, replacement crew, girlfriends, stamp collectors, hookers, queers, free-loaders and con-artists.

We all stood there, trying to get shelter from the cold and the rain, each one of us examining the ship, its hull, its paint and her crew shuttling back and forth tying up and getting the hatches open or leaning on the bulwarks looking at us. Each one of us searching for clues and each one of us giving his own interpretation of what we saw.

"You ain't gonna sell many cigarettes to this one, I ain't seen nobody smoking yet."

"It looks like an all Oriental crew, they'll buy a lot of electronics."

"Look at the stains on the cook's apron, ain't gona be selling them T-bone steaks, that's for sure; cabbages and noodles, that's all."

"The ship looks pretty rusty, bet they don't pay any overtime; another deadbeat crew."

Finally the customs and immigration people left, the quarantine flag was lowered and we sprinted on board. I let Sam Richards get one step ahead of me. He handed his card to the chief engineer but he didn't even get to say they were a big shipyard, doing work around the clock, when the chief interrupted him.

"The office has already made arrangements with ... Poseidon Marine Services, Incorporated," he read the name from a note on the agent's stationary. I loved the sound of it.

"That's us, chief," I said handing him my card and three of my new wall calendars.

"Thank you," he said. "Could please wait until I get finish with fuel report?"

Sam saw my triumphant smile and I am sure he vowed to get even.

I sat at the couch and leafed through an Italian women's magazine.

The chief, a short, pudgy, balding Italian around sixty, got busy calculating the fuel consumption for the voyage. When he finished, he telephoned the numbers to the captain, then took another look at my card and turned toward me.

"*Allora Nicola, parlare Italiano*? No? Well, about the propeller repairs, the representative from the company that makes this type of 'controlled pitch' blades, is supposed to be here." He pronounced "controlled pitch" with a dislike, as if naming a disease. "The propeller is under warranty, we cannot do anything without him. Do you like some coffee?"

I said I would.

A few minutes later, a Filipino steward in a starched white jacket brought three coffees.

"*Sa la mat, poh,*" I thanked him.

The plump, middle-aged chief's wife joined us and the chief showed her my calendar. "Classico Swiss Cheese Fondue," he read, pointing to the recipe for January. He added something in Italian and they laughed.

"Clever Switzerland people, they steal the *cusina* from us," he said to me and the three of us laughed.

I was glad I had picked the "World In Color" calendar, with pretty landscapes and unusual recipes from different countries. Since it wasn't surplus money I was spending, I wanted something that would hang in the office instead of the bathroom walls.

The chief engineer's office was a large room with aspen-color paneled walls and carpeted floor. There were clear plastic corridor strips laid over the dark green carpet, leading from the door to the chief's desk and to the bathroom.

The curtains on the portholes, the soft-cushioned, cloth-covered chairs, the still-life portraits on the walls and the little decorative things around the room made it feel snug, cozy, and homey. After the coffee and some small talk about Italy and Greece, I said I would come back when the rep for the fancy propeller was here.

I met the propeller representative at 8:30 the next morning.

"William Petersen," he said, and reluctantly accepted my hand.

"How do you do Mr. Peterson." I gave him a hearty shake.

"It's Petersen, with an E," he corrected and handed me his card. It read: "Mr. William

F. Petersen, Technical Consultant, authorized representative for Skewed Profile Propulsion Systems, US Gulf and Central America." It was the larger, European size card, with shiny silver background and gold letters.

I gave him mine.

He was a tanned man in his early fifties, with gray, perfectly combed hair. He wore a striped brown suit with a bright colored shirt and a tie. The hand that reached for my card had three gold rings on it.

He wrinkled his bushy eyebrows, squinted his eyes and gave me an appraising look. In a voice mixed with equal parts of boredom, regret for wasted time and low expectations, asked me if I was familiar with this type of propeller and how many of them I had worked on before.

He didn't seem convinced when I told him that I wouldn't have any problem getting the job done. He kept smoothing a gray clump of hair on his chin with his right hand.

He asked if I had a rate sheet and I gave him a page Margaret had typed with the hourly rate of foreman, craftsmen and helpers, for straight time and overtime.

"I specifically requested an experienced repair shop; I am not running a training school," he griped, reaching for the page.

He looked at the rates. "But if that's whom they sent, I guess you'll have to do. You are the foreman I presume?"

I assumed my rates, the lowest in the area, had something to do with his mellowing. His English did not sound American, more like that of a snobbish Northern European educated in England.

We discussed how many people I was going to use and how many hours we would be working.

"Let us try to keep the overtime down as much as possible," he instructed.

I said "Yes sir."

The "consultant" and I went to the lighted drawing board where the chief engineer had spread the hull drawing and, pointing with a long stick, he explained: "By loading the Number One and Number Two cargo holds first, and by moving some ballast forward, the propeller hub should be out of the water ready to be worked on in twenty-four hours.

"Chief," the consultant commanded. "Make certain you have a complete set of seals; once we open the hub we cannot use the old ones. They are special seals and it will take six weeks to get another set."

"I know, I know, I have worked with this crazy type of propellers before," answered the chief. "The boxes are like the shipyard bring on board; nobody open. We all go look now." His tone of voice prompted his wife to look up from her magazine, probably concerned about the chief's blood pressure.

We followed the chief to the store room and he opened the spare parts box. The special seals and the special screws and the special tools needed to put the special propeller together were all there. Mr. Petersen examined them and pronounced them suitable.

"I don't see the torque wrench," he said when he finished the inspection.

"It is in that box," answered the chief pointing to a box on the upper shelf, the thin shipyard sealing strip still undisturbed around the hasp.

"Is it calibrated?" Mr. William F. Petersen inquired.

"We never used, it is as delivered."

I reached up to pull it off the shelf.

"It is safer there. We get it when we need to tighten the bolts," said Mr. William F. Petersen.

We started working the next day. The work area was between the ship's hull and the rudder, just a couple of inches above the water surface. A shipyard would have spent a couple of days building a platform to work from and if the pompous representative complained, they would have told him to take a hike. But when your whole operation consists of Moe, Rufus, the two country cousins, the Graveyard Ghost and a purple welding machine, it's hard to be intimidating.

So we worked standing on the round, slippery hump of the stern tube, with barely enough room for one man to get a foothold and swing a twenty-pound sledge-hammer.

We used the ships' paint float to shuttle from the pier to the propeller. A steady icy breeze was blowing from the north the whole time we worked.

"Boss, somebody left the refrigerator door open," said Moe, when we made the first landing on the stern tube.

"Refrigerator, hell, it's the deep freeze they yanked wide open," countered Loyd.

"You guys get to work and you'll warm up in no time," I said.

"Bet you there're gonna be ice chunks floating down river any minute now." Loyd always tried to have the last word.

The plan was to loosen up each of the eight twelve-inch nuts that held the massive propeller-blade to the hub. Once loosened, the blade, about the size of a Volkswagen would have to be carefully removed We'd then renew the manhole-size seal, put the blade back and tighten the nuts. Then the engineer would rotate the propeller with the turning gear till another blade was vertical and we would do the same thing all over again. Talking about it, in the chief's warm, carpeted office, it seemed simple. In the summer, it would be a fun job, but on the last days of December, with a cold front passing through, it was a job one wishes to his enemies.

Every tug-boat going by made waves that splashed around us, soaking our feet with freezing river water.

The shape of the ship's hull and the size of the rudder made the spot we were standing seem like the bottom of a funnel, with the top facing north, gathering the icy wind and freezing mist, which penetrated the sweaters, coats and everything else we had piled on. It made the exposed skin burn, as if being dry-shaved with a dull razor. Our bodies ached, our gloves were wet, our fingers were stiff and the tools were slippery. After a hammer slipped off Moe's hand and went flying over my head into the river with a big splash, we tied a line on all the tools.

It took anywhere from thirty to fifty firm, wholesome blows with the sledge hammer hitting the blunt end of a three foot wrench, to loosen up each blade nut. Only Rufus could loosen them up in less. He was twenty-two years old, fresh off the farm, six feet tall and about two hundred pounds of hard muscle. In his meaty hands, the twenty-pound sledge looked like a tuning fork.

We would struggle, two men at a time on that balcony of hell, as Moe called it, for about half an hour and then row back and dive into the Graveyard Ghost, parked on the dock with the engine running. We sat in front of the heater fan trying to squeeze all of the warmth from it, while drying our gloves and shoes with the acetylene torch and talking about times spent in the tropics. Just when some of the numbness was beginning to go away the two on the propeller would start shouting to be relieved.

It took all the pleading, promising, reasoning and threatening I could muster to keep the guys from walking away.

We finally loosened up all of the nuts of the first blade and, holding them as if they were priceless gems in our frozen hands, we put them in a drum. Using a rigging arrangement that would be the envy of the pyramid builders, we lifted the blade up and removed the damaged seal. Under the watchful eye of "Mr. William F. Petersen, Technical consultant", dressed as if he was on the ski slopes of Switzerland, with care, and as gently as our numb fingers could do it, we installed the new and improved seal. We lowered the blade in place, tightened the nuts as much as we could with the long wrench, then took a break to get ready for the final step.

It was six o'clock; it had taken us ten hours to get this far, which I thought was pretty good. I was charging a good hourly rate and an even better overtime rate and I could just hear my bank account exhaling when I deposit the check. I just wished it was not so damn cold. When I am sipping my evening ouzo, under the patio grape arbor at the Bellmaker's house, staring out at the blue Aegean toward America, I will remember this job.

"We are almost done, tomorrow we'll get the other four blades for sure," I told the guys sitting in the van. I didn't believe it, I was just trying to keep their spirits up.

"What are we waiting for now, boss?" asked Moe.

"Waiting for the chief to bring the torque wrench; we have to tighten these nuts by the book," I said.

THEODORE PITSIOS

"I got a torque wrench for my Camaro, it's Sure Grip, they are the bestest," said Loyd. Then since nobody spoke, he went on. "Bet this torque wrench is a big mother."

"How much longer after that?" asked Rufus.

"We got about an hour and we will be done for the day," I said.

"Bet it will take more, takes me 'bout that long to do my Camaro," Loyd butted in.

"Can't it wait till tomorrow? We are beat," said Floyd.

I walked toward the gangway to get away from the complaints. The chief had been gone a long time, but I was too tired to climb all the way up on deck to see what was keeping him.

First I saw Mr. William F. Petersen coming down the gangway in long, stiff, pissed-off steps. Behind him was the chief, red-faced, talking with both hands and struggling to keep up with him.

"The seal on the box was not been broke. You see yourself," the chief kept repeating.

"You have to use a dynamometer to finish the job. They have misplaced the torque wrench and it will be days before I can get another one," Mr. Petersen announced when he got near me.

"You see I break shipyard seal; the box was empty, shipyard bring empty box on board," the chief protested.

"You will need a dynamometer that has a scale up to twenty thousand pounds and a ten-ton chain hoist," Mr. Petersen continued, ignoring the chief.

A dynamometer is a super-heavy-duty round-face scale, about the size of a hub-cap. It's used to measure the strength of cargo rigging and to weigh big, heavy items. It's an expensive gadget and only outfits who absolutely need one, have it. I said I didn't have such a thing, but would try to find one the next day, which seemed to piss off Mr. Petersen very much.

I told the crew we were knocking off for the day.

"Thank you Jesus," cried Floyd.

On the way to the shop nobody spoke; we were all too tired, too wet, too cold for conversation. As soon as the van stopped they ran to their cars and took off.

I called Bill Yeoman at home, told him what happened and as I expected, he said I could borrow the ten ton chain hoist, but he couldn't help with the dynamometer.

"Most of the shops that could have one are closed for the holiday," he said. "The only one I know for sure that has one of those is Dixie Shipyard. I don't envy you."

"I'd rather pull my front teeth," I said. "Are you sure nobody else has one? I'll drive to New Orleans if I have to."

"Nobody that I know; you still want the hoist?"

"I'll be there in the morning; now I am tired, I'm going home and the Petersen

110

character can fuck himself; it's his problem anyway. The ship is supposed to furnish all special tools."

Early next morning I went to Yeoman's place to pick up the chain hoist. He was waiting for me by the door, looking like an army commando, dressed in a camouflage outfit with a pair of binoculars hanging from his neck and holding a coffee cup. I apologized for getting him to the shop so early.

"I needed to get an early start anyway," he said, "the club is going to the Fort Morgan preserve; hope to take some good pictures."

I would have never thought when I was looking after the sheep in the village and entertained myself by watching the industrious sparrows and the squabbling blue jays hop among the branches, that in a far away strange place called America, people would be forming clubs to do just that.

We went to the storeroom and together, half dragging, half lifting, we loaded the ten-ton chain hoist in the van.

Walking through the yard, I noticed there was not much progress on the tugboat.

"How's the new construction coming?" I asked.

"We don't talk about that," he answered and I didn't ask any more.

We wished each other a Happy New Year and I left.

Driving along the practically deserted road, I was trying to think where in the hell I could find a dynamometer. Bill said the stevedores had one they were using to load-test the cranes, but they were not working today and he didn't have anyone's home phone. Maybe I could try somebody in New Orleans; anything to keep me from having to ask Dixie Shipyard.

The bone-chilling sound of a siren jerked me out of my thoughts. In the rear view mirror, I saw the motorcycle cop, with his blue light flashing, signaling me to pull over.

He parked behind me and with slow strides came by my window. He was tall and heavy-set, in a brown leather outfit at least two sizes too small.

"What's the matter officer?"

"See your license and registration," he said.

"Is there something wrong officer?"

"You know what's wrong."

He took my license with his leather-gloved hand, walked back to his motorcycle and talked on his crackling radio while looking at my car tag. I lit a cigarette and tapped on the wheel, silently cussing.

He came back, handed me my license and asked me to sign the ticket.

"What's this for, officer?"

"Failure to come to a complete stop at the sign."

111

"I did stop," I protested.

"You arguing with the law, fellow? I saw you go sailing passed it. Big red sign, says STOP, in English; maybe they ought to have it in Mexican."

I've never won an argument with these guys. I signed and headed for the shop, cussing as I went.

At the corner of Water Street and Broad, I saw the Chief Mate returning to the ship. He had helped with the rigging and the paint float, the day before. I offered him a ride. I always give a ride to seamen whenever I see them walking. I guess it's something left from my sailing days.

As soon as I stopped by the gangway, Mr. Petersen's silver Mercedes pulled up next to me. He was wearing a tight brown leather jacket and matching gloves. He came over and asked where the rest of my crew was.

I told him I was still looking for the dynamometer.

"Blast it," he pounded his gloved palm on the side of my door, "I had specifically asked for a competent repair shop. Instead I got *Senior Fixit* and his mariachi band."

I jumped out of the van slamming the door behind me. I was going to kick that pompous buffoon's ass clear to the other side of the river and to hell with his job.

The corner of my jacket got caught in the door and as I tried to walk away I was yanked back. I opened the door, freed the jacket and re-slammed it. In that tiny increment of time, through my mind flashed the Kambanaris house, the Greek bank holding the note, my parents mourning their son's inability to make any *prokopi*, all of the characters at the Festorias *cafenio* laughing behind my back and Margaret telling me Tom Edwards was right.

I lit a cigarette.

"Mr. Petersen," I said, as if I was talking to a judge, "what you have requested is an expensive, special tool which not many people keep around. I am not saying that anybody was dishonest, the shipyard guys probably made a mistake and your guys probably forgot to double-check and make sure the torque wrench was in the box, but if we had advance notice we could have one available. Now, on a Friday, New Year's Eve, it is a little difficult. I was on my way to the office to make some more phone calls."

He said he would come too; he wanted to see "my operating facilities."

He followed me to the office and made it clear as soon as he got there, that "my facilities" were below his standards.

I started calling all the people I thought might have one of those contraptions. Most places didn't answer and those who had an answering service either didn't call back or didn't have what I was looking for. Some suggested, more often than I cared to hear, that I contact Dixie Shipyard.

I paced in the little room a few times, poured myself a cup of coffee (the consultant didn't want any) and asked again if he was sure the blade seals had to be replaced. He repeated, I think for the zillionth time, that the agent was going to hear from him, which meant Carras was going to hear from the agent, which meant all the Greeks in Bigport were going to hear from Pete Carras. What they would probably hear would be that Nikos Pilios, who had ambitions to start his own business, bit off more than he could chew. He didn't have enough sense to have the right tools for the job and caused Mr. Pete to lose face and probably a client too, because he stuck his neck out and recommended him, and what do you expect from seamen who jump ship and marry foreigners to get the green card?

I picked up the phone and dialed the number for Dixie Shipbuilding and Repair, Incorporated.

Bubba Smith answered on the second ring. He laughed when I told him what I wanted, then he said that it was their policy not to deal with anything smaller than a bicycle shop.

"You can't get in the ship repair business with a hammer and a pair of pliers. We..."

"I'll pay you rent for it," I cut him short.

There was a brief silence. "We get three hundred dollars a day rent for it," he said finally.

I put my hand over the mouthpiece and turning to the representative who was looking at the calendar, tapping his ring-loaded fingers on my desk said: "He wants four hundred dollars a day for that thing." He almost swallowed his cigarette. "Ask him if it has been calibrated," he said when he recovered.

"Yah, it's calibrated, it's got papers and had all it's shots." Bubba was gloating.

"I'll send someone over to get it," I said.

"Well, can't let it out of the yard by itself, got to have a rigger with it."

If anybody else from that shipyard had answered the phone, I stood a slim chance to work out a normal deal.

"O.K." I said, "I'll get the rigger too, how much for him?"

"You know, today and tomorrow is the holiday rate, thirty-two an hour."

I knew what the sonavabitch was doing.

"O.K., O.K." I said.

"You'll have to get a foreman with him also; that's how we always send it out." He was on a roll.

I took a deep breath and relayed it to Petersen: "He wants thirty-six an hour for a rigger and a foreman.

"Send the blasted thing, we need it," he growled.

"I need it at Pier Six, south side," I said.

"I know where you are, they'll be there in an hour. Pleasure doing business with you."

I hung up the phone and stared at it for a moment, wondering why I wasn't feeling glad I had found the damn dynamometer.

Two primitive looking characters with hairy faces, missing front teeth and emitting a light fishy odor, showed up alongside the ship around noon, each holding on to a leather strap on either side of the dynamometer's wooden case.

Mr. William Petersen measured the length of the wrench handle, calculated how many pounds of force it would take to give him the foot-pounds of torque he needed, and drew a bold red line on the face of the dynamometer marking the spot where the dial should be when everything was right.

We dragged the chain hoist over to the propeller, coming very close to capsizing the paint float, and slipping and sliding all over the place we connected one side of the dynamometer to the end of the wrench and the other to the chain hoist. Then we started the tortuous effort of pulling on the chain to bring the black needle of the dynamometer to the red mark.

It felt a lot colder than the day before. A steady freezing breeze from the north was driving a fine drizzle directly to where we stood, turning our faces blue. We struggled to pull on the hoist chain and it kept slipping through our wet, cold gloves. With each pull, the needle would make a nudge toward the red mark; a movement detected more by wishful thinking rather than by actual distance covered. The red mark was at about four o'clock on the face of the gauge. Might as well have been in another continent. It took forever to get the needle from one line to the next. I don't think anybody has ever traversed so small a distance with so much agony.

When the black needle eventually reached its mark, we called Mr. Petersen who looked at it uttered, "It will do," and returned to his Mercedes.

All this time, the two shipyard characters were sitting in the front seat of their beat-up truck with the engine running. Once in a while they would lower the window, shoot a mouthful of tobacco juice in the river and roll it back up.

We finished two blades that day.

New Year's day was a repeat of the day before, only the wind felt even colder, the tools heavier, the icy river-water, icier. If it happened that we needed something from the shop, everybody would volunteer to go get it, enjoying the warmth in the van for the thirty minutes it took to get there and back

We finished the last bolt of the last blade at eight o'clock that evening. There wasn't enough strength among all of us to drive a thumbtack into melted butter. I would definitely remember this job.

Next morning I got Margaret to type the invoice. It came to a pretty respectable sum. There were lots of man-hours at the time-and-a-half rate, plus the cost of the Dixie characters and their gismo. Enough to keep the wolf away from the door for a while and maybe pay for a couple of new windows on the Bellmaker's house, the kind with big panes that don't block the view.

Petersen had suggested that I meet him at the cafeteria of the Sheraton Hotel to sign the invoice. Then I could take it to the agent who was going to cut me a check. Things were looking up. It was about time too.

Petersen stopped spreading marmalade on a piece of toast, read the invoice real slow, sipped some coffee, then read it again. I was sitting uncomfortably; I changed positions on my chair a couple of times. He read the invoice again, then scribbled something on his napkin and pushed it to my side.

"That's a more realistic number," he said.

His "realistic" number was about twenty percent lower than mine.

"If you are joking, it's not very funny," I said.

"Your men worked very slow, the workmanship was extremely poor and because you didn't have the right tools, the job took much longer."

The wolf was reappearing at the door and the windows with the clear views, were in jeopardy. I told him that the weather was bad, we didn't have enough advance notice, it wouldn't have taken as long if he had let me build a work platform, and anything else I could think of at the time. Every time I protested he would remember something else he didn't like and would deduct some more from the invoice; soon I would have to pay him for doing the job.

By the time he signed, he had deducted almost thirty percent, which, after I paid the Dixie bandits and my guys, left about four dollars an hour for my time.

A hell of a way to start the new year.

A few days later, I saw Bill Yeoman at the Wharf Restaurant. He looked depressed. He offered to buy me a drink. He said that shipbuilding is a shitty business and anyone getting in it should have his head examined. The tugboat he was building had run way behind schedule. The customer had given the job to Dixie Shipbuilding to finish and was suing him for all kinds of revenue losses on top of it.

I thought it would cheer him up if I told him my hard-luck story with the *M.V. Ocean Lady*. He grinned. "Welcome to the world of ship repairing," he said. "You just got acquainted with what is called: "Discount by intimidation," all the sonovabitches do it. Don't feel bad, we all go through that in the beginning; you've got to plan for it."

Chapter 10

*E*very respectable outfit has a company brochure. The big companies have multi-page, multi-colored jobs with glossy photographs showing happy workers with spotless work clothes and smiling big wheels in suits and white hard-hats explaining why they are the best.

Dixie shipyard has an eight page brochure that looks like a small town newspaper. They found some half-way normal looking guys, dressed them in clean clothes, and took their pictures while they pretended to be welding and sandblasting. They also have pictures of their dry-dock and their two cranes, taken from an angle that makes them look huge. They even have a place with a "partial list of our valued customers" and half a page of quotations, supposedly from shipping company big wheels, saying all kinds of nice things about those vultures.

My workload was nothing to brag about and my bank account couldn't afford any splurging, but I had been in business over three years now, long enough to be called "established" by those who had reasons to flatter me. I figured it was time I advertised my company's name in colorful print. All the marketing experts were telling me: "You got to spend money to make money." I'd already spent for calendars. I swallowed hard and decided to spend a little more.

I picked out the photographs I would include in my brochure: One had Moe welding on a pump base in the shop. Another showing Loyd and Rufus working on the propeller of the Ocean Lady. I thought that demonstrated versatility. An outside shot showed the shop with the sign over the door and me standing under it. I thought that showed personalized attention. I talked to the office supply guy about the brochure, who told me to talk to the guy who printed my business cards, who told me to talk to a commercial artist, who couldn't understand me and took a while to figure out what I was talking about. When his price quote came in, I was shocked. All I wanted was something that would show prospective customers I was not a bicycle shop. When I told him I couldn't afford it, he too recited, "You got to spend money to make money." I was brought up to believe it was the other way around.

We did away with the photographs, (even with the one showing me under the sign), and the multicolors and the multipages and finally, just before we did away with the whole idea, we settled on a two-color bifold on glossy white paper. A few weeks later, he brought the preliminary work for my approval and he explained, "You want to project an image of depth and stability; to imply competence and individual attention, as well as experience and quick response." He proposed to do all that by showing in shadows the outline of three ships: an old freighter, a tanker and a modern bulker, — the kind that has the bridge and engine room aft and looks like a slipper from a distance. In the foreground, he had an anchor, a propeller and a windlass, in three shades of blue.

I gave him my approval and a fifty percent advance.

When the brochures came, I spent a couple of days writing an introductory letter. I said that we do excellent work at reasonable prices, that we have a multi-craft crew able to travel anywhere at short notice and that we have many important satisfied customers, "the names of which we will gladly provide upon request." It took a lot of writing and arguing with Margaret about the meaning of the words and what I was trying to say, but when it was finished, it was a nice one-page letter. I made copies and mailed them to "the Superintendent Engineer, Repair Division," of every shipping company I could get an address for. It cost over two hundred dollars in postage.

Then I waited for the inquiries and the orders to start coming in. Having spent a ton of money to keep my part of the bargain, I waited for the second half of the American prophecy to come true.

And I waited, and waited, and waited. Finally, one day I got a phone call. The guy on the phone spoke Greek in slow measured sentences, like an old fisherman in an island cafe. He said his name was Captain John Emons with Hios shipping from New York. One of his ships was going to be in Bigport for a couple of weeks taking on cargo, and wanted to know if I could do some repairs while she was here. Nothing big, just renewing a few shell plates and a few feet of fire-line piping, on deck.

My surefire marketing drive was finally paying off.

"Like I said in our brochure, Captain Emons, we do all types of marine repairs, in port as well as with our riding crews."

"Haven't seen any brochures," he said, "never read the junk mail; wouldn't have time for anything else. I got your number from Petros Carras. I only deal with big outfits, but I've heard good things about you so I'll give you a chance. If you are interested, I'll send you the job package."

I told him we were real busy, but I would take a look.

I went to Pete Carras' soon after I hung up. Stavros was reading the Greek Maritime News and Pete was having coffee and talking about football with Sam Fox from Gulf Welding Supply.

Pete's face was glowing red, the color of fresh sun burn.

"What happened to Pete? He looks like a Yankee tourist," I said to Stavros.

"He went fishing with John Papas."

"I thought Pete hated fishing."

"Yeah, but people here think it's an honor to be asked to go fishing with John Papas; he usually invites doctors and people from his hospital and only Greeks that are born here; strictly upper-class stuff."

I got a cup of coffee, went into Pete's office and when he finished bugging Sam Fox about Alabama's loss to Auburn last week, I asked him if he knew Captain Emons.

"I know him many years, he is from Hios, where all stingy people come from, his real name is Giannis Manopoulos, but change to John Emons when got American papers; to save ink. Watch your... your... *pazaria*," he said after some hesitation.

"Negotiations," I translated for the benefit of Sam Fox who looked puzzled. "I am always careful with my negotiations, I cover every contingency, *pithanotita*," I quickly translated because it looked like he didn't understand the word.

"Contingency and *arhidia Calavrezika* - bullshit." This in the direction of Sam Fox, as if translating the Greek saying, then in my direction again: "Be careful vre, many shipyard bosses, *exipnakias*, like you, lost their ass working on his ships."

"He means smart aleck," I explained to Sam Fox, "but I am not one of them."

"You be careful, that's what I speak to you, don't be an *exipnakias*," repeated Pete.

I said I would be careful and I wasn't an exipnakias, and left.

It upsets me when people call me an *exipnakia*. I get a feeling that something very bad will happen to me, that I will suffer some kind of punishment if I am found out to be an *exipnakias*, has been with me almost for ever. I think I can trace its origin back to the time immediately after Kyra Rini's accident when I was a child.

Kyra Rini was the wife of Barba Giannis Themelis. They were the elderly couple that lived near our farmhouse in Paraskevi.

I was probably eleven years old that summer. One afternoon, I was sitting on my lookout spot watching the sheep graze in the Lithos field. For entertainment I was making the sound of *mbourou*, the shell that sailing ships use as a horn. I had finally mastered the trick of cupping my hands around my mouth the right way, and I was blowing with all the strength of my lungs sounding like a real *caique* passing by.

The next day was baking day, when Mother would bake the bread for the week. She made me help her fire the oven and when the bread was done, she said we were going to visit Kyra Rini, who had had an accident the day before.

Mother killed a hen that had quit laying eggs and put some of the chicken stew in a pot, which she wrapped it in one of her aprons, tied on top so the lid wouldn't come off. Holding the pot with one hand and Katina, my sister, with the other, she started up the narrow path to Themelis' house. I followed a few steps behind, munching on an apple and carrying the bread under my arm, still hot, wrapped in a red checkered napkin. Dimos followed behind, shooting with his sling shot at everything that moved.

Kyra Rini was sitting up in bed, knitting. A blood stained white cloth with yellow stripes was wrapped around her head and under her chin, making her look scary. Her left hand, from the elbow to the wrist, was wrapped in the same kind of cloth. I remembered seeing Barba Giannis wearing a shirt like that.

Mother put the pot on the table and sat at a chair next to the bed. I put the bread next to the pot and waited for my earned cookie.

"I can't get out of bed my precious," said Kyra Rini, "Barba Giannis will be coming in any minute now, he will get you some sweets."

"They don't need any," Mother cut in. "They just ate some apples I baked for them."

"These are chocolates from Volos," said Kyra Rini, "besides Nickolakis is such a good boy."

Occasionally, I would fetch water for her or do other small chores which always earned me some cookies: "One for me, one for my little brother and one for my little sister." The little monsters; every time I came back from her house they would be looking at my hands.

"Barba Giannis will be in any minute," she repeated. Everybody called him Barba Giannis, (Uncle Giannis), whether he was their uncle or not. He was a tall, stout man, about sixty at the time, with a gray, walrus kind of mustache and a large wine barrel mid-section. When he was not busy making wine, he would either be sitting at the edge of the cove entrance, waiting for a school of fish to go by to dynamite, or helping his forty-year-old son, Apostolis, hew chestnut tree logs, which they sold to the city. Barba Giannis' part of that job was to sit under a shade tree sharpening the axes and giving advice to his son on the quality of each log.

"How did this terrible calamity happen to you?" asked Mother.

"It must have been an evil hour, that's all I can say," said Kyra Rini. "We have been waiting for a week for the *caique* to come to take a load of logs to Volos, but the sea was too rough. Yesterday looked like was going to be a nice day so I thought they might show up. When I woke up in the afternoon, I heard the mbourou and I said: 'They are here.' They always blow the *mbourou* when they are coming, so we go and help them tie up. I went out to the balcony but I didn't see anything so I thought I was hearing things. Then as I turned around to go back in, I heard it again, clear as a church bell. So I climbed up on the railing to see around the olive tree. I was standing on my toes, leaning out, when the rail broke and before I could grab hold of anything, I am coming straight down, right on top of the two skins he had just unloaded. They burst and all the wine gushed down the yard. It got in the flowers, in the water trough, even in the pan I had put some molded bread for the chickens. It soaked the bread and then the chickens were staggering all over the place." She tried to smile at the last part.

"Did you get hurt bad?" asked Mother.

"My head got a big gash back here, my knee is swollen and hurts and my hand is scratched some, but I say *Doxasi Kyrie*, it was not worse," and while saying that, she put down her knitting, crossed herself and showed Mother her injuries.

Mother repeated: *"Doxasi Kyrie,"* and crossed herself also.

"I kept telling that blessed man of mine: 'Need to fix that rail, before somebody gets hurt', but he would never do it. Now he is crying because he lost all that wine; it serves him right, I say."

"It certainly does," concurred Mother.

I went and stood by the corner, pretending to look at an old musket hanging on the wall. It was the darkest spot in the room and the farthest from Kyra Rini's eyes.

Kyra Rini leaned over closer to Mother: "To tell you the truth, I don't mind this, it'll give me a chance to rest a bit."

"You deserve it," agreed Mother.

Barba Giannis came in, walking as if he just gotten back from burying his best friend. He broke a piece of the bread I brought, poured himself a glass of red wine from a jug, sat at a bench against the wall and chewed it slowly.

"This is good bread," he said to no one in particular, then addressing Mother: "It was the best I'd made in years. I unloaded the skins and went to tie the donkey before I emptied them in the barrel down the cellar; it was going to be for the whole year."

"It would be a miracle if it lasted you three months," interrupted Kyra Rini. "Now get some of those chocolates Apostolis brought from Volos and treat the company."

He strained up and shuffled to the cupboard.

"What made me set them right there?" he mourned. "It was probably some kid, some *exipnakias* playing games and she thought she heard the *caique*."

"It was a real *mbourou*," said Kyra Rini, "I could tell."

He brought the box to his wife and sat back down. She opened the box and my eyes saw heaven; a multitude of round chocolates the size of plums, each wrapped in a different color of shiny foil, glittering in the light like jewels in a treasure chest. She held the box out to Mother, who after some coaxing, took one and said she would save it for later. We snatched ours, after a quick scan to spot the biggest one, and opened them slowly, saving the shiny foil to play with later.

"I am sure it was some kid, some *exipnakias*, playing games, and if I ever find out which one it was, I'll work the belt on him so hard, he'll never forget it," said Barba Giannis, and pounded his fist on the bench which made the wine glass rattle and scared little Katina.

I said I was going to check on my bird traps and took off running. The chocolate tasted bitter and I spat it out as soon as I turned the bend. I never told anybody about it, but every time I went by their house I would always run, afraid that some angel would swoop down, grab me and deliver me to Barba Giannis.

* * * * *

I spent a lot of time studying the Emons job-package. It would be the largest job I had tackled up to now. It would take about twenty-five people to do it, which meant I had to find twenty more. But if I could pull it off, I would be getting up there, in the same league as Petros Stathakis and the other big boys of Topside Repairs.

There used to be stories circulating on the waterfront, about the big jobs and the big money that were handled by Stathakis and the other "top side" repair outfits out of Brooklyn. They transported busloads of workers out of New York: Cubans, Puerto Ricans, Greeks, Scandinavians ("a nut from every tree" as the old timers used to say), to wherever the job was. They put them up in some flea-bag motel, and then turned them loose on some rusty ghost ship, to have her transformed into the pride of the seven seas, saving tons of money for the owners and making a bundle for themselves.

One story had it that Stathakis brought a large cabin cruiser to his little island in Greece and was showing it off during the summer. When he tried to store it at a shed he had built by his house, he discovered that somebody's building made a narrow spot on the road from the port, too narrow for his yacht to pass through. The village council had been trying to buy that property for years. They wanted to tear it down and widen the road so trucks could reach the little harbor, that way generating some business in the poor village, but the owner of that building was asking a fortune to sell it. Stathakis didn't even haggle with him. He gave him the millions *of drachmas* he was asking, had it torn down and even paid for widening the road, which made him the village hero. They even named the street after him.

I bet his parents pranced around the village, proud as peacocks of the *prokopi* their son had made.

I called Captain Emons' office a couple of days later, when I thought I had calculated everything about the job. His secretary said he was on the phone but would be off shortly if I cared to hold. I told her he could call me back at his convenience. He called about an hour later and jumped into the haggling without a warm-up. He said my price was way too much before I even got to the small numbers.

I told him we were a small company and we paid higher prices for material and supplies.

He told me he felt uncomfortable dealing with a small, unknown outfit like mine; maybe he should have Stathakis do it after all.

I told him I was confident I could do a first-class job and finish it on time.

He told me this was not an insurance job, he was paying for it out of his pocket.

I told him we had to pay more for welders and fitters down here because we were surrounded by big shipyards.

He told me freight rates were low, and ships were losing money.

I told him I could go just a few hundred dollars lower; no more.

He told me he would think about it and call me back.

When I got back from lunch, Moe handed me a message: "This captain fellow called and said for you to call him." It was Captain Emons.

"Didn't I tell you guys when someone calls long distance, to tell them you can't find anything to write with and ask him to call back in an hour?"

I called him, hoping his secretary wouldn't put me on hold. She connected me right away.

"I need to finalize this thing today. What's the best you can do, so I won't go to Stathakis?"

I told him and it was not good enough.

Finally we settled on a price and both of us swore we were going to go broke.

"I'll tell the secretary to send you the contract," he said.

The ship would be in port in two weeks.

By the time the *Aegean Glory* docked, I had fifteen guys waiting at the dock. I told the Hios Shipping port engineer that I had another fifteen on another job and that I could bring them on later if needed.

This job was big enough to require a "ship's superintendent": somebody who would wear a white hat with Poseidon Marine Services decal on it and walk around the deck with his walkie-talkie and measuring tape strapped to his side, making sure everybody was working. Just like Dixie shipyard.

I hired a retired chief engineer named Wayne Fitzerald. He was going to be my right-hand man. According to him, he had sailed for many years, had worked in shipyards for many years, was responsible for all the advancements on ships and nobody in the maritime industry would move a finger without first consulting with him. In the idle days before the ship arrived, he talked for hours about how he was going to organize the "repair division" of Poseidon Marine Services and how we were going to conquer the ship repairing world.

The first day of a repair job on a ship is always hectic. There is material to be brought on board, scaffolding to be built, work to be assigned, equipment to be put in place, bribes to be negotiated and freebies to be settled: The cook wants a crack in the stainless sink welded, the bosun wants to know where he can buy a good radio, "one that can catch Greek stations," somebody wants a money order made, someone wants to know if he can call his island from my office, and a couple of others need a ride to the nearest whorehouse. It kept Wayne and me running.

The second day was a bit quieter. Wayne spent most of it in the ships' lounge drinking coffee and telling sea stories with the representative from Lloyds of London.

Every time I asked him how our crew was doing with the bilge pump repairs down in the engine room, or the anchor windlass brakes, or with the binnacle base welding at the bridge wing, he would say he was just getting ready to go check on them.

Back in the shop at the end of the day, Wayne asked to speak to me in private. When someone wants to speak to me "in private," it can only mean that he is quitting, wants a raise, or a loan. We went in the little office and closed the door.

"Chief," he said, "my back is acting up on me again. It's never been right since we got torpedoed off Gibraltar. Did I tell you how that U-boat got us? I was in the water for twelve hours, in the middle of the winter. This climbing up and down on the ship trying to keep all them guys working, it's too much. To tell you the truth, I was looking for a job, not work. If you don't mind I am going to call it quits."

So much for conquering the ship repairing world. I said I would mail his check and that I hoped his back got better.

I told Antonios Vrahakis that he was the new "ship superintendent" and from then on he walked on deck like a ten star general.

I had hired Antonios about a month earlier. Andrew Carras was very pleased with the decision. "He is a good boy, it's a shame to be working for foreigners," he had said.

He was almost ten years younger than me, about the same height, born in a small town outside Athens, and had a Turkish kind of complexion. He insisted on being called Antonios, not Tony, or Anthony or any other compromise. He made sure nobody was goofing off and the job was progressing, although we were constantly short-handed.

As it always happens when you have a lot of work, you have a hard time finding people to do it. The shipyards were very busy, a couple of paper mills were having "shutdowns" and construction in the area was going strong. Every day, big ads in the paper were promising welders and fitters a hell of a lot more than I could afford to pay. I was constantly interviewing people. They would shuffle in, and while I or Antonios told them about the job, they would stare at us as if lip-reading, then turn around and go to work for Dixie, who treated everybody like crap.

"Ain't working for no Cuban," I heard one of them tell the other as they were getting in their truck. I had read in the paper that they had found fifteen Mexicans suffocated in a trailer by the side of the road in Texas and a bunch more had been shot at by the border patrol. It just didn't make sense: Here I was, begging people to come to work, paying damn good money and a few miles down the road, people were dying trying to cross the border so they could get a back-breaking job on a farm for less than the minimum wage.

Seven days into the job, when Moe came back from the ship on an errand he informed me, "Boss, the purple welding machine done burned up."

"It's blue," I corrected.

"Done burned up, anyways."

Antonios, coming in behind him, got more detailed:

"Lloyd tried to cut off the windlass supports by arc-gouging them. As soon as he turned up the amperage, the machine started smoking; didn't see it in time to shut it off."

"The stupid sonovabitch! I told him to be careful with that machine."

"Boss, you ain't gonna start that Greek cussing again are you?" asked Moe.

In cases like that, curses come up by themselves, instinctively, like crying "Ouch" when you burn your finger, or blinking in the bright light. But they don't get the purple-blue welding machine running.

"We need equipment that'll work," Antonios said for the millionth time, "torches, hydraulic jacks and for sure a couple of new welding machines. Everything we got is on its last leg."

"I'll ask the tooth fairy," I said and went into the office.

I slumped into the chair and reached across the desk for the telephone to call the Dixie Equipment Rental Company.

Next to the painting of the Bellmaker's house, hung the Gulf Tool Supply calendar. Miss May, blonde, with boobs to spare, leaning on a pipe threader on a windswept tropical beach, was smiling sinfully at me. "With the right tools, the job is a breeze," said the caption below it. Further down, Sunday, May twenty-eight was highlighted in red and on the margin, in bold red letters I had written: "Departure of *Aegean Glory*." That's when the job had to be finished. Captain Emons had slipped a two thousand dollar penalty clause in the contract for every day his ship was kept beyond the deadline. If I missed the deadline, I could almost hear Andrew Carras: "Vre si, didn't I tell you smart Alecky people get burned?"

I had twenty days to do with fifteen guys a job that normally would take twenty-five people over a month to finish.

Seven days before the completion date it started to rain, slow, steady drizzle: enough to make the deck slippery and the welding miserable. One of the jobs was to renew about sixty feet of half-inch-thick plate, four feet high, around the steel coaming of the starboard side of the number two cargo hold; a fairly easy job if it didn't rain.

I called Captain Emons and asked for an extension of the deadline but he said there was no way he could get the charterers to agree. "Have to be at the grain elevator ready to load Monday morning of the twenty-ninth. Didn't I suggest you tackle the coaming job first?"

He had, but I couldn't buy the material then because my account at Bayway Steel Supply had passed its limit and they were asking for a payment before they sold me anything else. They had delivered the steel just when the rain started.

I asked the ship's captain for permission to swing the cargo booms over the work area and drape the hatch tarps over them to keep the rain out, but he said he was afraid the tarps might get torn or burned from the welding sparks. In real language, it meant what I had offered to pay him wasn't enough. Probably John Mavros, while driving the captain to the agent's office, had told him that I was making money by the cart-load.

John Mavros, after working for me for a few days on the sewage pipes of the motor vessel George P. some years back, concluded he was underpaid for his talents and went back to what he was doing before; mooching, pimping and occasionally driving for a ship's agent, taking crew members to the doctor, or picking them up from the airport. During those drives, he displayed his knowledge of life in America and dispensed advice about being successful in this country.

It was distressing to think that the country's reputation in the eyes of a new-comer, hinged on a chance meeting with John Mavros, but I guess it has always been that way. I remember getting reports on the country's economy from rickshaw drivers in Surabaya and boat launch operators in Manila and scrutinizing the tugboat crews and the line handlers' clothes in the ports I was visiting. That's something that has been overlooked by the foreign relations department of every country. They don't seem to realize that the stevedores, taxi drivers, hookers and everybody else who works on the waterfront, are the windows through which a visitor looks into the country. And these people, because they are ordinary working people like us, are more believable than the fancy-talking bureaucrats

We strung wires over the cargo hold and over it we spread heavy duty, bright blue plastic I bought from Sears, making a dry canopy to work under.

We got the job completed one day ahead of the deadline and I am sure, all the shipyard spies who hung around the dock watching us work were heart-broken.

On the last day, at lunchtime, I had pizza delivered for everybody.

Chapter

11

*P*ete Carras hovered over me: "Hey, Mr. Big Shot, you are working yourself? What are you going to do with all your money?" Let somebody else make a living."

I was lying on my back under the air compressor, trying to put the engine together so we could use it the next day on the ship. Moe, lying next to me, was holding up the oil pan, grunting from the weight and trying to keep the oil from dripping into his eyes, while I lined up the holes to put the screws in.

I didn't say anything, didn't feel like searching for the right answer to his sarcasm.

"Listen, Mr. Rich man, I have a Telex here from Captain Emons for another, bigger big job. Come, we go for lunch, need to speak to you about something."

I crawled from under the compressor and wiped my hands.

"Is your talking going to cost money?"

"It is for good reason *vre*, don't be a *cheesecake*, like the Americans say; you can't take it with you, you know?"

I got cleaned up and got in his truck.

I read the Emons Telex on the way to the restaurant.

"Big job, eh?" asked Pete.

"It could be a nice one," I said.

We went to Andros restaurant.

"You must join AHEPA," he said when we sat down, "it will be good for you."

"I thought you wanted to talk about something important. They called me to join the chamber of commerce the other day. It was going to cost two hundred dollars a year."

"This is only thirty-five a year. If you not have, I will pay. AHEPA is an organization of Greeks living in America. We meet every month and talk, have food and help people.

It started in Atlanta in 1922 to help those coming from home with the language and with the citizenship."

"Manolis Vervatos already gave me that speech. It sounded like something you guys put together to have an excuse to get out of the house."

"You come next week when we have raffle and see, you will like, I am sure. I got ten tickets here for you." He handed me an envelope. "Only ten dollars apiece, you can give me a check."

I bought one, after he paid for the lunch, and told him I would be out of town next week.

It had been six months since we finished the job on the *Aegean Glory*, but I hadn't forgotten Captain Emons' negotiating maneuvers. The agony of trying to meet the completion deadline and avoid the penalty was etched permanently in my mind. This time, when we went through the negotiating ritual, I was prepared.

The *MV Aegean Spirit* was coming to Dixie shipyard for dry-docking and bottom repairs, and he wanted a price for replacing the crankshaft on the starboard main engine. As far as engine repairs go, this is pretty ballsy job, and if I could pull it off, it would be "a big feather in my cap," as the locals were saying. But at the Dixie shipyard, all the supervisors, foremen and security guards knew me and every one of my crew. We couldn't get past the gates even if we dressed as Gregorian monks. They had strict orders not to let the Greeks from "that bicycle shop" inside the yard for "no reason whatsoever." Maybe they didn't have posters of us at the guard shacks, but our description was passed on from guard to guard at the end of each shift.

It got to where they wouldn't let anyone in the yard who spoke with an accent. A few weeks earlier, they wouldn't let Carras' Ship Supply make a delivery to a ship on the dry-dock because Stavro and Ramon fit the description. Pete had to rush back from a wedding, see the vice president and get everything straightened out. They lost a whole day of work sitting by the yard gate.

I told that to Captain Emons, and he said getting in the yard was a minor problem that he could take care of, if we agreed on everything else. The "everything else", was the price and the penalty if the repair went beyond twenty days.

As is customary and expected, from Captain Emons side the freight rates had gone down, the shipping companies were losing money, and the insurance only paid a small part of the job.

From my side, wages had gone up, supplies gotten more expensive and this particular kind of work required specialized, more expensive craftsmen.

Had the Salvation Army been eavesdropping on our negotiations, they would have dispatched food packages to both of us immediately.

We agreed to do the job on "time and material" at an hourly rate of sixteen-fifty an hour and no penalty clause.

By now I had learned to analyze carefully every single word he said. Captain Emons made important and expensive tasks seem trivial and simple. Many shipyard estimators had lost their bonuses and had their careers shortened because of negotiators like him.

The only other guy I knew who was as slick was Eugene Goodhart, the port engineer for Bay Shipping, an American company. He lived in a farm east of Bigport and whenever he came to see me about doing work on one of his ships, he would bring whatever he was growing at the time. He dressed and spoke like an old-fashioned farmer and when he was discussing business, his big black eyes would stare at the other person wide open, full of innocence and bewilderment. Those who didn't know him wondered how he managed to survive in this cut-throat world where even your ass must have eyes.

He walked in my office about three months back, carrying a roll of drawings in one hand and a plastic bag full of fresh zucchini, scallions and tomatoes from his garden, in the other. At that time I was building pontoons for the U.S. Corps of Engineers. The "Final Inspection and Acceptance Specifications" for that job were a separate section, thicker than a small town phone book, with long, legal words that sounded like some kind of military proclamation. I added twenty percent to my original price, just in case they found something I had missed.

We spread Eugene Goodhart's drawings on top of the ones for the Corps of Engineers. Eugene's drawings were for an Inert Gas Deck Seal, a much more complicated job than the pontoons and he spent a lot of time going over it with me and Antonios.

In the end, as he was walking out, he said in a casual, nothing-to-worry, kind of tone: "When that contraption gets built, I'll send one of them engineering boys from the office come take a look at it, to keep the boss off my ass."

"He said in one sentence, what these guys took half a book to say and he made it sound so simple," I told Antonios afterwards.

"Watch him," Antonios warned, "he can sell you 'kelp as silk ribbons,' as they say back home."

I wasn't there when they closed the deal, but from what I'd learned about Captain Emons, I had a pretty good idea how the conversation between him and the Dixie shipyard representative went, in getting them to agree to let me do the job.

Captain Emons, in his thick, Hian accent and grandfatherly tone, probably told the shipyard estimator that he would be sending some men to change a few pieces on the main engine; nothing big, just routine stuff, and if they needed any help, which he didn't think they would, the shipyard might give it to them. He was going to ask one of the junior pencil-pushers to send down a Telex with everything they'd talked about and if he would just sign it and send it back to keep the paper shufflers happy and his picky boss from chewing his ass out.

"Don't worry too much about the fancy words; those college boys always try to make their job seem important," he probably told the Dixie estimator.

About one week after our bleeding negotiations I got a letter authorizing me to proceed with the main engine work on the *MV Aegean Spirit*. Enclosed was a copy of the Telexed shipyard agreement giving us permission to go in and do the work.

Reading it, I couldn't keep from smiling at the way Captain Emons' "junior pencil-pushers" had worded it. On the bottom right hand corner was the accepting signature: Edward "Bubba" Smith, Superintendent, Repair Division.

I sent Antonios and Loyd to New Orleans to board the ship and start the preliminary work.

"This ain't another of them ships that feed you fish with their heads on, is it?" whined Lloyd. He pestered me to give him preference on out of town jobs, because he liked the per-diem and the travel time pay. But then he always found something to gripe about.

By the time the ship docked at the shipyard, they had disconnected all the piping from the starboard engine, and they were ready to start pulling the pistons out.

The docking of the *MV Aegean Spirit* caused a lot of commotion at the shipyard. The ship superintendent assigned to the ship, after seeing my two guys on board, called the yard superintendent, who called the shipyard vice president, who called me and told me to get my ass down there right now before they get them two Mexicans of mine locked up for trespassing.

As soon as I stepped out of the truck, Bubba Smith strutted up to me like a marshal on a Western movie, his "walkie-talkie" strapped to his right hip and a huge measuring tape to his left, and, stooping to get his face even with mine, shouted:

"Listen you, told you a thousand times not to set foot in this yard! This is private property and you are not allowed in it. You understand me?" The last sentence was pronounced slowly, as if addressed to someone reading lips, every syllable emphasized by a jab to my left shoulder, like a physical exclamation mark. Mr. Anderson, the vice president, was looking on. A circle began forming around us. I didn't answer him, just stared at him, trying to look bewildered.

"I want you," he continued, "to get your shit and get your ass out of here right now, or there will be hell to pay; comprende?" Bubba's face was getting red, his breath smelled like sauerkraut. I moved my head back trying to get out of range of the spit and tobacco juice spray.

"If you are still here half hour from now, I am calling the law and have all of you arrested for trespassing. You understand me?"

There was a small red wart on the left side of his nose. "You should have that lump checked," I said, "it could be serious."

He stopped and stared at me, probably startled by my inability to grasp the importance of the situation.

"What seems to be the problem?" I asked after a couple of seconds of silence, trying to sound puzzled. "Didn't you read your contract?" Another brief pause. "I just happen to have a copy of it in my pocket, I'll read it to you, since you don't have your glasses on."

With slow, ceremonious movements, I pulled the copy of the Telex from my shirt pocket, unfolded it, held it with both hands and clearly and slowly, as if reading a royal proclamation, started: "Repairs on main engine and its auxiliary components, will be carried out by the owners, or their appointees. Shipyard to cooperate and provide crane service and assistance, ex-pe-di-ti-ou-sly, on 'as needed' basis."

I waited a couple of seconds, then said: "You see Mr. Smith, I am their appointee. It looks like somebody from your outfit has signed this agreement."

"Let me see that, can't understand pidgin English." He grabbed the Telex and looked at the signature. "I'm gonna get this shit straight right now," he growled and with long strides, headed for the "O.K. Corral."

"While you are at it, I will need a crane at one o'clock to unload the liners from the truck," I called after him. "Ex-pe-di-ti-ous-ly," I couldn't resist it.

Beside the crankshaft, we ended up repairing everything that was in the engine room: pumps, pipes, electric motors, anything we could pass as an auxiliary component of the main engine. I had twenty people, going in and out of the yard, pissing the guards off. Every time we were going to take a piece out of the ship, we would wait for some big wheel to be around, then we would walk by Bubba's yard office real slow and watch him cringe.

At the Safe Harbor Bar And Grill, every night most of my guys and most of the ships' crew entertained themselves by telling stories about how pissed-off the shipyard wheels were. Cindy had been promoted to manager of that place and used her connections to give us the inside scoop on the waterfront. She told me that Bubba got fired and had it not been for his wife, who was the sister of Anderson's wife, he would have stayed fired.

The sonavabitch, it was his turn in the barrel.

Chapter | 12

W hen Hios Shipping asked me to look at a conversion job on one of their ships discharging in Hoboken at the end of that April, I had been in business for almost four years.

I had calendars, brochures, pens and baseball caps with my company name and logo on them. And I had some good equipment and bank loans up to my ears; all of the ingredients of an "established" small company. The seasoned business people I knew were telling me that it was time I made a sales trip to New York. I should be making the rounds of the shipping companies at least every six months, they advised; wining and dining the engineering and purchasing wheels, and handing out brochures, business cards and trinkets with my company name on them.

Phil Domain was making sales calls in New York at least once every two months. I had gone with him a couple of times on some consulting jobs, when I was working for GESCO.

"You have to keep your name fresh in their minds," was his motto.

It sounded like a good idea. I am sure the barmaid with the rose tattoo on her left boob, at the Irish pub at the corner of Forty-eight and Lexington, kept Phil's name fresh in her mind.

I didn't think of myself as any kind of a salesman. As an engineer, I could more easily talk people out of something than into it, and a trip like that would take a big bite out of my budget, even if I stayed away from Irish pubs.

Every time we had a leisurely moment together, Pete Carras would trumpet the benefits of marketing trips, prompted Boby's triumphant return from London and New York a year earlier.

"One more year; then Bobby will be ready to run the business and I go visiting," he would start, and then the nostalgia of home would move in. "Bobby says we can take the trip expenses out from taxes. I will spend the summers in Andros and go visiting companies in Piraeus."

He would pause for a moment and then continue. "My sister stays now in the house my mother left to me. In the front yard there is a lemon tree. My father used to sit under it after dinner and smoke his pipe. From there, the whole village is in front of you; you can see the harbor and the boats, coming and going."

It was the same story every time.

"When I go, I'll stay in the big room, at the corner of the house. At night, I always sleep with the window open; there is always breeze coming from the sea and the sound of the trates fishing outside the harbor, is like a lullaby. When I was there in sixty-two, I used to sleep like a baby."

He would look away and be quiet for a while and I could tell, in his mind, he was sipping coffee under the lemon tree, watching the fishing boats bobbing in the harbor. Then he would snap out of it. "Bobby wants to put computer in office. He says will save money. The damn thing costs a cartload of money, will have nothing left to go visiting."

Captain Emons wanted to add more bulkheads to the holds of the *Aegean Dawn* for some high-paying cargo they were going to transport, and the best time to take measurements for the job was when the holds were empty.

"I have to be in Greece for a few days," he had said, "but talk to Captain George Kamenos, he is collecting all the bids."

I lined up some appointments, planning on staying in New York a couple of extra days to make sales calls and took an evening flight out of Bigport.

I spent the whole day on board the Hios ship looking over the bulkhead job. The ship's chief mate offered to be my assistant in taking measurements. His name was Thanassis Krassas, but everyone called him *Papou* (grandfather). He said he was only six months away from retirement and couldn't wait. He was a stout old-timer with broad shoulders, a thick white mustache, a full head of white hair and bushy white eyebrows, under which two brown eyes stared suspiciously at the world. He descended into the cargo holds with the agility and surefootedness of someone who had been doing it for a long time. He seemed to appreciate the prospect of making some extra money before retirement and kept repeating how glad he was "one of our own" was bidding on the job.

I asked him if any body else had been looking at it.

"Just three guys from the New Jersey Shipyard; and they didn't seem very interested."

When I was leaving, he walked with me down the gangway. "You bring the pieces alongside and I'll get them down the holds in no time; just give a little something for the bosun and the guys. The Jersey shipyard fellows said they would bring a big crane; that's expensive, no?"

In my room at the Roger Smith Hotel, (same place I stayed when I came with Phil), munching on a pastrami-on-rye from the corner delicatessen, I worked on the estimate. It's always a gamble trying to figure out how much it will cost to do a job. There are rules of thumb for how many feet a welder can weld in a day and how many pounds of steel a fitter can fit, but there is no formula for figuring out when the welder will be hung-over, or when the fitter can't read the drawing right, or when moody sailors will try to squeeze you for extra money to get your material down the hold. Most estimators put a number at the bottom of the cost column for "miscellaneous unforeseen expenses." But there is always the possibility that somebody working for a shipyard or a big company, fresh out of college, spending someone else's money, not having a clue what the job looks like, goes in with some crazy low number and you are out of a job.

After two full ashtrays, and half-way through the late, late show, I concluded that I could do the job for sixty-five thousand dollars. It included everybody's tips and bribes and left enough for Nicole's braces and maybe the paneling for my study at the Bellmaker's house.

Walking out of the Rector Street subway station the next morning, I tried to find my way to the Hios Shipping office. The first time I was in Manhattan was in the sixties, soon after I went to sea. I was being transferred from a tanker laid up in Curacao to a freighter that was loading in Staten Island. It was January, the snow was knee high and I quickly discovered that a suntan was no substitute for an overcoat. In the years that followed I'd come to New York many times, but my first visit left me the strongest memory: me and another engine cadet in flowery, short-sleeved shirts, arms stiff, hands planted deep in the pockets, teeth clenched, staring at a guy who had been hit by a car, lying between mountains of dirty snow. People were standing around in a circle; no one reaching to help him. The company representative who was escorting us said people were afraid of being sued.

This time, sheltered in my gray business suit that Margaret had decreed was appropriate for a young executive, I was walking slowly, enjoying the springtime breeze and walked slowly, looking at the buildings on both sides of the street. Number fifty-nine, its' address on a polished bronze plaque, had a glass and black marble facade with a huge revolving glass door, which kept spinning as people went in and out. As I watched, I suddenly recognized the place.

I entered behind two suited guys speaking German, into a large, cool, white-marbled lobby. There were six elevator doors on the wall across from the entrance. On either side of them were boards stuck small white plastic letters telling in alphabetical order who was on which floor. Hios Shipping was on the eleventh floor.

A plump receptionist stopped typing long enough to inquire if she could be of help.

Captain George Kamenos, she told me, had not made it in yet. I said I would come back later and went back down to the lobby.

At the far side of the lobby was a concession stand, no bigger than a closet, overflowing with snacks, newspapers and magazines. I bought a cup of coffee and sat on a bench near some potted plants that formed a smaller, more secluded area of the lobby.

A few feet from the concession stand was an elevator with fancy bronze doors and a bronze plaque next to it that read: "Global Bulk Carriers Inc." When I was sailing, everybody was trying to get signed on their ships. The food was good, the pay was above average and the overtime plentiful.

In the center of the lobby, surrounded by four marble benches, a marble statue of Atlas carried a bronze Earth on his shoulders. Six Oriental guys, half of them standing and the others sitting cross-legged on the benches, were having an animated discussion. From the few English words I caught, I guessed they were trying to sign on one of Globals' ships.

Not much seemed to have changed. I stood on that same spot, years earlier, before I made up my mind to jump ship I was with three other Greeks, rehearsing what to say to Captain Joseph Clayton, the personnel manager for Global: a big, burly man, about sixty.

Captain Clayton spoke like a longshoreman, in a rough, gravely voice and I remember how my legs got weak when he started asking questions the first time I went to see him. My classroom-trained ears couldn't catch his waterfront English. He stopped speaking to look at me and under the gray canopy of his eyebrows I saw a pair of wolf-eyes shooting right through me. He had thick, wavy gray hair, an untamed white beard and a full, smoke-stained mustache. A long pipe at the side of his mouth bounced up and down as he talked, with thin smoke rising from it like an incense burner.

I mumbled "excuse me" and "I beg your pardon" a few times, then he sent me away, growling something that sounded like: "You've got to be able speak English to work on our ships, fellow."

Ten days later, I returned with two other guys who were applying for deck officers. In the lobby we met Petros Tsantis, a third mate, already part of the motley Global crew, who was being transferred to another ship. He had promised to coach us for the interview with Captain Clayton. "He wants to know what kind of license you have, what kind of ships you worked on and specially, how long you stayed on them; they don't like people who leave after a few months," Petros had said.

Buoyed by this inside information we got busy rehearsing our opening lines. The idea was to throw at him everything he had to know up front so he wouldn't have a reason to ask questions. Petros gave us the right words and corrected our pronunciation. We were like school children trying out for a play.

When we thought we were ready for the performance we took the elevator to the sixth floor. The receptionist, a sweet young thing in a tight dress, with breasts the size of grapefruit, recognized me. She escorted me to Captain Clayton's office and wished me luck. I said "thank you" and winked at her as if we had been old comrades. I closed the door behind me, took a deep breath, stepped forward and started:

"Good morning Captain Clayton, my name is Nikos Pilios, I have license of Third Assistant Engineer for steam and motor vessels of unlimited horsepower, here is my passport and copy of my license, my last ship was the *Ionian Sea*, a steam tanker with fourteen-thousand horsepower steam turbine main propulsion engine, I served on *Ionian Sea* one year and one month, I work hard and I like to get employment with your company because..."

I was about to run out of air and out of things to say, when a tall, slender fellow walked in holding a file. He tapped on the paneled wall and before Captain Clayton answered, he walked up to his desk without closing the door behind him.

"Excuse me, Joe," he told the hairy captain who was looking at my papers. "We are taking the *Global Transporter* out of lay-up. The old man got a hot deal in Orinoco and she has to be under way pretty bloody soon. See what men you can come up with, quick like, will you? Here is what I need right away."

His words were crisp and clear like Kambanaris'. I understood everything he said.

The captain glanced at the list and put it aside.

"Here," he said, "you can have this one," and nodded in my direction as he handed him my papers. "He just walked in; I'll see what else I got on file." Then he pressed the intercom button: "Lynda," he told the machine, "if any officers come in today, deck or engine, send them straight up to Operations, to see Mr. Crackit."

"Yes sir," sang Ms. Grapefruit. Then a couple of seconds later: "Sir, there are two deck officers out here now, should I send them in?"

"Have them follow Mr. Crackit." Then to Mr. Crackit: "Lynda can pick up their paperwork if you hire them, Mr. Crackit."

Mr. Crackit asked me to follow him and did the same with my two rehearsal partners on the way out. Lucky bums, they didn't even have to do their monologue in front of Captain Clayton.

After some routine shop talk, Mr. Crackit told the three of us to see somebody two floors below, for the travel arrangements to Maracaibo the next day, and report onboard the *Global Transporter*.

On my way out, feeling invincible, I gave Lynda my most seductive smile and oozing with charm, I leaned over her desk and asked, "I and you, maybe go to night-club tonight? You like? Eh?"

She giggled and picked up the phone that was ringing without answering me.

It was years ago, but it seemed like yesterday.

I threw away the empty coffee cup, gave the rehearsing Asians a sympathetic glance, and took the elevator to Hios Shipping. I had killed forty-five minutes. The plump receptionist said Captain George was in now but he was on the phone. She suggested I take a seat and asked if I wanted any coffee. I said yes, so she would have to stand up. She was about twenty-five and curvy. On her way to the coffee pot she asked if I wanted cream and sugar and I told her in Greek that if she touched it, it would make it sweet enough. "I don't speak any Greek," she apologized, "I'm a temp, the regular girl will be back Monday."

I sat on a leather couch, picked up a copy of the Maritime Reporter from the coffee table and pretended to read while observing the temp struggle to get supplies from the lowest desk drawer and answer the telephone at the same time.

I could hear someone in the office next to the reception area doing battle with the Greek telephone system.

"Halo?... you are breaking up again... Halo, Captain Emons,... yes they looked yesterday. Krassas said three guys from the shipyard spent three hours on the *Dawn* looking the job over... Yes, they called yesterday... It's one hundred twenty-five thousand and some change... twenty-five, yes, well... it's a big jo. ... big job, they said they included a lot of overtime because we are in a hurry."

I got interested. He was talking about the job I was quoting. I took my eyes off the temp's cleavage, stared at the magazine and concentrated on listening.

"Halo...still there?... lost you again. No Todd shipyard is booked solid for three months... No I haven't seen him. Krassas said he was on board yesterday, spent the whole day on board... Ya... it's still early over here. Yes, I'll try to keep it under a hundred but I don't know... Are you going to be in Piraeus tomorrow?... OK, I'll call tonight if I hear something. Yea...ì maybe a better phone too."

I stood up.

The receptionist raised her head from her typewriter, moved aside one ear phone and with a strained look she pointed to the phone whispering, "I am sorry, I have two more, holding for him."

I told her I had to go down to feed the parking meter and I would be right back.

I went to the lobby, found a quiet spot and spread my notes on the bench. What the hell did I leave out? How could my estimate be that far off from the other guy's?

I went over every single item again. I added some to the cost of the material and the labor, I adjusted the percentage for the "miscellaneous" and the "tips" to the crew, and came up with a new figure of seventy-five thousand dollars; still a long way from the other quote. I re-checked and concluded the other outfit must have somebody that hasn't done any actual work himself.

After a while, I saw the temp going to the concession stand and I thought it was a good time to see Captain Kamenos. That way she couldn't tell him I've been waiting outside his office when she showed me in. I dashed into the first elevator that opened.

I knocked and a bald, plump man with red suspenders and a red bow tie came out of the office next to the reception area.

"I am looking for Captain Kamenos," I said.

"That's me," he said, then made some apology about the girl stepping out for a minute and ushered me into his office. It was a small, cozy space, with the walls covered by bookcases and reproductions of classic Greek architectural details. On top of one bookcase there was a small plaster statue of Pericles.

"One of our ships was involved in a collision in Greece and most of our people had to go there. I am in personnel, but I was asked to handle this conversion project." He had the funny Greek accent of one who had learned the language outside of Greece.

I told him I had looked at the job and we could do it for ninety-seven thousand dollars. He looked at his notes and said that Captain Emons had told him it could be done for around eighty.

I went through the ritual of looking at my notes and doing some scribbling and gave him a new and improved number.

He took some contract forms from a drawer and typed while talking about his last year's visit to Delphi and Santorini. He asked me to sign on three copies and I walked out of there with a purchase order for the conversion of the Motor Vessel *Aegean Dawn*, for $ 87,920.

I called the office from a pay phone in the lobby, and told Antonios to order the material.

Next to the phone booth, on the marble benches in front of the Global Bulk Carriers elevator, three Greeks were discussing their last ship. One of them was trying to light a cigarette from a lighter that wouldn't cooperate. He saw me smoking and asked for a match when I hung up. I gave him a light, he said "thank you," in English and I just nodded. At an earlier time, maybe even an hour ago, I would have told him I was Greek too, asked him where he was from, what he was sailing as, and showed off by recounting some of my experiences at Global.

Now, I didn't feel the urge to do it. Somehow their world seemed too small.

I called Margaret and asked her to check with the bank about a ninety-day loan.

"Another one?"

I told her about the Hios job. "You can start picking the wallpaper for the house in Greece."

"We got to fix this one first — we haven't painted it since we moved in." Always the sensible one, always yanking me back to reality.

"We are rolling now," I said.

My next appointment for the day was at two o'clock with the Vafakis shipping company, two blocks down from Hios shipping. I went to a luncheonette around the corner, ordered a ham-and-cheese sandwich and a Coke, and sat by a window with a view of a small grassy triangle at the intersection of three canyons, with a few dusty trees desperately reaching for sunlight.

On the next table, three Norwegians and a Greek were talking about chartering a ship. On the table behind me, a woman and two guys with note pads were talking about some building contract.

I was a businessman among businessmen. I put my note pad next to me and started drawing an outline of the Bellmaker's house.

The senior port engineer of Vafakis shipping was professionally polite and preoccupied with something else. Scotty had told me, back when we were doing work for the insurance company after hurricane Sheila, that he and the Vafakis senior port engineer were really close because he had saved his ass many a time from blunders he was about to make. I hastened to mention that Scotty Jones was now on my staff, but that didn't seem to have any effect on him. He kept looking at maps, bright colored hotel brochures and travel guides, piled high on his desk. He asked questions as if reading them from somewhere and kept grunting agreeably while scanning a stack of pictures. Then the answer to his mechanically asked: "Where are you from?" brought him back to the office.

"You are really from Taxiarhes? I just got back from there. When was the last time you were there? How far from the square is your house?"

He was throwing the questions at me in bunches, sometimes not waiting for the answer. "What do you know about Marika Lakonidis? Do you recognize the house in these pictures? Isn't this a strange coincidence? That's a beautiful area — very popular. We spent four weeks in Taxiarhes. Mr. John Vafakis, from the London office, bought a house near the square; he is going to be a regular there. I had my lawyer draw up an offer on the Lakonidis house. I'll be spending a lot of time in Taxiarhes, I'm sure."

I told him I had a big house there with a beautiful view and he was welcome to use it any time he was in the area. That seemed to score me some big points; I would think of the excuses when the time came.

By the time I left, I had been assured over and over that the next time one of their ships needed work, I would be the first they would call.

That night, I went to the Acropolis Restaurant to share my jubilation with an old friend. The restaurant was on the ground floor of an old building at the corner of Forty-seventh and Broadway. Next to the entrance door was mounted a framed copy of the menu. Everything started with the word famous: Famous Stavro's Greek salad, famous *souvlaki*, famous *pastitsio*, famous *galactobourico*; only the soft drinks at the bottom were not famous. Inside, the walls were covered with autographed pictures of movie and theater stars going back a couple of generations. The restaurant had been there since the forties, started by Stavro Moustakas, a steward who jumped ship and married a rich young Irish girl from New Jersey.

Fotis and I used to sail together. He was a third mate, ambitious and convinced he was the reincarnation of Apollo. He decided the long sea voyages were interfering with his love life and married the Acropolis Restaurant that came with Katina and a house in Astoria. Fotis thought that Katina's looks were not worthy of an Apollo, but that was seen as the compromise one has to make when getting a bargain. Like buying a table at half price because one leg is a bit shorter. A skillfully placed block will eliminate the flaw and everybody will be happy. Fotis' block was a curvy Puerto Rican that he provided for.

It was late and the place was almost empty. Only two couples in the corner booths, whispering and holding hands. The dining room was dimly lit, with most of the light coming from a display case by the cash register, loaded with "famous" pastries and pies, which were making the whole place smell of lemon and nutmeg.

Fotis was on watch behind the cash register, stiff and alert, like a helmsman on a supertanker, keeping a sharp eye over his dowry. The black hair he used to let cascade in curls over his forehead, like Tony Curtis, was now almost straight and combed back, trying to cover an emerging bald spot.

We greeted each other and I sat down in a booth. He locked the cash register, said something to a waitress and came over.

"You look great, the South agrees with you," he said sitting across from me.

I told him he looked great also and then we talked about business, Greece and about other people. The waitress had brought a carafe of red wine and a plate with feta, Kalamata olives and *dolmades*, his famous appetizers.

"Did you ever learn how to skate?" I asked when our reminiscing drifted to the New York days.

"No, never had the nerve after that incident, but the kids did. Sometimes we take them over to the same place. How about you? I guess you don't get much ice down in Dixie."

"What you saw that day has been my life's skating experience, on ice or on anything else."

"We were a crazy bunch back then."

While we talked, we were nibbling on the appetizers and emptying our glasses.

"We were lucky, it could have been a hell of a lot worse," I said.

"It was your idea," he said refilling the glasses, "you were the engineer." The wine was sweet and going down easy.

"It was a good plan, only there were too many captains in the group."

He made hand signals to the waitress and she brought over a new carafe and another plate of dolmades and feta.

"Katina still laughs when she remembers it. Last week Eleni asked her how we met and they both ended up rolling on the floor laughing. Eleni wrote it for her school work and got arista for it and the teacher asked her to read it in class. Katina put it in my pocket last night and I read it today."

He went to the cash register, unlocked the drawer and took out a folded piece of paper. "Here, read it, I got to go tell the guy in the kitchen to start cleaning up."
I unfolded the paper. On top was the title:

WHY MY NAME IS ELENI,

by Eleni Kondos

My dad was born in Greece and he was a captain on a big ship. In December one year before I was born, he was in New York waiting for a ship. One day he, two other captain friends and one fellow that was an engineer and one other guy that was something else, all waiting for the same ship, were in the Central Park watching the people ice skate. My mom says they were ogling at the girls. Then they decided to try ice skating themselves, because watching the other people do it seemed real easy but when they got on the ice they couldn't stand up because none of them knew how to skate. (My dad says in Greece they don't have dumb things like ice skating.) So they were falling down all the time and they were knocking other people down too. Then one of them got the idea to hold hands in a line, like doing a Greek dance, but that didn't work either. When one person fell, he took the others with him. In the old days they were playing music in the ring and everybody skated in circles in one direction, like they do now. My dad and his friends were bumping into everything and knocking every body down all over the place. Then they got the idea to make a circle and lock hands behind their backs to be more stable, and that's when the disaster happened. They started spinning faster and faster and they couldn't stop and they were knocking people down and everybody was yelling at them and three men that worked there went on the ice and grabbed them trying to stop them but they couldn't, so all were spinning together real fast and then, like a big mountain they came crashing on the benches. My dad was on the bottom of the pile and they had to take him to the hospital where my mom worked because he had a broke leg. Grandma Dorothy said only a Greek would try a stupid stunt like that. My mom married my dad when his leg was O.K. and then I was born. And that's why my name is Eleni. The Greeks suppose to give their kids the same name their parents have, so I got my dad's mom's name and my sister got my American Grandma's name. I wish they didn't have that stupid rule and name me Dorothy instead of my sister who is a brat anyway."

There were a few corrections, a big red "A" and some compliments by the teacher.
"How old is Eleni now" I asked Fotis when he got back.
"She is in the seventh grade. Not bad for a twelve-year-old, eh? It got her ten dollars from my mother-in-law too."

"Funny how time flies."

We finished the carafe.

My first appointment the next day was with the Bay Shipping Company, in New Jersey.

Was at the building a half hour early, playing it safe, not knowing exactly where the office was. I lingered in the lobby for twenty minutes, watching the elevator traffic and draining a large cup of coffee to soothe the effects of Foti's "famous house wine."

The receptionist looked at my card and dialed a number.

"Mr. Romero, your nine o'clock appointment is here."

A brief silence; then she read him my card. She broke new ground in mispronouncing my name. She was about forty, small breasted with black hair and tanned skin.

I walked over to where three couches were surrounding a glass top table, sat down, picked up a magazine and held it open.

Nobody seemed to know much about Bay Shipping, other except that they were paying top dollar for everything and on time. They showed up in Bigport about a year ago with an old tanker which they tied up in an out-of-the-way spot upriver, and started overhauling it. A couple of Greek "top side" repair outfits out of Brooklyn had an army of people running all over her.

After the repairs on the first tanker were finished, they brought another and did the same thing to that one.

There were rumors that the owners were some Greeks and Jews out of New York and that they owned ten tankers under the American flag, but everybody was tight-lipped about who I had to see to get a job. Finally Cindy, from Safe Harbor Bar And Grill, using her contacts, got a name for me, which got me an appointment.

Cindy had been quite helpful through the years. She had become half-owner of the bar and she had a good ear about waterfront gossip. I found out accidentally, that she also owned some rental property and that she was supporting a handicapped child in a private school, which earned her in my respect.

When I was working for GESCO, someone advised me to try to be early for appointments – advice I found to be useful. Watching the people coming and going, looking at the office decor and catching bits of conversation, is like feeling the pulse of the company. It's possible to sense if a company is an old, established one, or something that sprouted up in good times and might disappear as soon as the freight rates drop a couple of points.

I glanced around the Bay Shipping office. It could have been the office of any business. All the furniture was chrome and beige imitation leather. On the walls, the only decoration was two large posters of sailing ships in chrome frames. The lone white orchid in the center of the glass coffee table only added to the chill of the place.

I browsed through an old *New Yorker* magazine, occasionally glancing at my watch and at the receptionist absorbed in her work. I saw a credit card advertisement in the magazine, showing a group of people at a Mediterranean-style patio overlooking a beautiful cove. It was covered with large rectangular flagstones and had a low stone wall where people sat holding drinks. When the receptionist wasn't looking, I cut the page and put it in my briefcase. It would be added to the box marked "Taxiarhes house" I kept in the bottom drawer of my desk.

Finally, forty-five minutes after the appointment, the receptionist escorted me to the conference room: a plain rectangular space with a long table in the middle.

"Mr. Romero will be right out," she said and left.

It was like visiting a doctor's office.

He came ten minutes later and sat across from me without saying anything about being late. He was of medium-build, around fifty, dressed like a mannequin in a store window. Everything on him was new, fresh and crisp; his gray pin-striped suit, his light blue shirt, his yellow and blue tie with small red anchors on it and the yellow handkerchief in his breast pocket.

He had wavy, brownish-blond hair and a delicate triangular mustache of the same color, with a white spot right in the middle that made it look as though his nose was running.

We exchanged cards. I thanked him for taking the time to see me and gave him my brochure (the one costing a dollar seventy-five for a two color bifold, on glossy white paper, a thousand copies minimum), and the loose page, titled: "a partial list of some of our valued clients." He glanced at it, said "hum" in a bored voice, and put it next to his yellow pad.

He was holding a fancy pen and kept scribbling with it on the yellow pad; nothing legible, just scribble, as if checking to see if the pen had ink. From time to time, he would look at the back of his hand with his fingers stretched out, then the opposite side with his fingers folded. He got from his pocket a small silver nail clipper with lots of attachments and corrected whatever imperfection he had spotted.

When I am at someone's office, I look for clues of that person's preferences that I can claim as my own. On many occasions I have confided that I too have a collection of bonsai trees, or that I like deer hunting, or Jesus is the answer, or whatever it was that gave me the hint I might bond with the other guy. It had worked well when I was with GESCO.

With this sterile person it was impossible to start anything. The room was bare, he didn't wear any pins or medals, Margaret was buying all of my clothes and I didn't know anything about fingernail grooming.

I kept talking, he kept making agreeing grunts and scribbling on his pad, and when he ran out of fingers to inspect, he started looking at his watch. Finally, I thanked him again for seeing me, he mumbled that he "will be in touch," and I left. I was sure if someone had asked him thirty seconds later who it was he had talked to, he wouldn't remember. I walked out of there feeling incompetent and discouraged.

On my next two appointments the men I saw were good at their job; they knew how to look attentive, show interest and act impressed. They kept saying they were glad I visited them and yes, definitely, I would be hearing from them. The tone of their conversation seemed confiding, intimate, as if we were old friends. They made it sound as if it was a miracle they had survived up to now without my services.

I tried to tone down my optimism by reminding myself that these guys were professionals and they talked like that to all vendors, but something Phil Domain had said kept coming to my mind: "It's like looking at a pair of large boobs — you know it's silicon but you hope you are wrong."

My last appointment was with the Berres Shipping company, one of my first customers. After a loud-mouthed port engineer named Gene Mudrawski got fired, I did many small jobs for them, but all of my dealings had been with their New Orleans branch office; the big wheels were at the headquarters in New York.

The headquarters were in a modern building at the corner of Forty-eighth and Lexington, away from the traditional shipping-office neighborhood at the tip of Manhattan. I guess the younger Berres figured out that he could be in waterborne business without having to look at the water. Some said that he did it because he kept getting sea-sick when his father made him go to sea in the summers of his college years.

I met with the head of the purchasing division and the head of the freighter division and the head of the tanker division and a lot of other heads of divisions, all professionally cordial and polite, who saw talking to vendors as part of the chores in a day's work.

While I was in the office of the vice president of engineering he took a call from one of their port engineers at a shipyard, leaving the phone on the speaker. The guy on the other end, sounding as if he was talking from the bottom of a well, said that the insurance man had just finished inspecting the hatch covers of the ship and found them all corroded beyond repair.

"We've got to get new ones and quick. Lloyds' will only give us a conditional for sixty days," were the last words of the voice in the well.

The vice president flicked the speaker switch off, sighing at the drudgery of never-ending problem solving, and, turning to me, asked as if he already knew the answer: "You can't build hatch covers, can you?"

"Oh yes, we have built lots of them," I rushed the answer, "let me take a look at the drawings."

Half-heartedly, he asked somebody to get me a set of the drawings and said I could use the empty desk in the corner. I looked at the drawings, added and subtracted and then added something for a safety margin, then a little more to be discounted later, and after three pages of calculations, I showed him the bottom line: "I can have the whole ship-set built in three weeks," I said.

"You said you have built hatch covers before?"

"We built lots of them for Kesler shipping, a German company." (I had only repaired one of them, but the ship had sunk and the company was out of business).

"I know them, their office was one floor below," he said. "You know the hatch covers have to be inspected by Lloyds'?"

"No problem," I said.

"One of our port engineers said you've had trouble meeting deadlines — we've been doing business with a company in New Orleans."

That damn Mudrawski.

"That was over three years ago, it was..." I threw whatever excuses came to mind, but he harped on it, till he got an almost five thousand dollar discount.

After assuring each other that I was going to go broke and he was going to get fired, he told the purchasing guy to write me an order.

I used the phone on the empty desk to call Antonios, give him the news and tell him to order the material.

I felt like I could fly home.

Three weeks later, we loaded the brand new hatch covers, painted a glossy hunter's green with orange border lines on four flat-bed trucks, for delivery to New Orleans.

"That's the mahogany front door and the curved staircase of the house in Taxiarhes," I thought as I watched them go down the road till the last truck disappeared on the west-bound lane of the interstate.

My corner room at the Bellmaker's house will have bookcases going all the way up to the ceiling, full of thick books, and people will be asking me if I've read all of them.

I was basking in the gratifying feeling and the unbridled optimism that comes when one outsmarts the competition and finishes a job profitably and ahead of schedule.

Chapter

13

*M*argaret decreed, in a manner leaving no room for negotiations, that this year's Christmas holidays would be spent in Pompano Beach.

"I told mama we will be there Tuesday evening, the twenty-third," she said the morning after Thanksgiving.

It had been a quiet Thanksgiving dinner, without any friends or visiting relatives, most of the conversation at the table consisting of telling the kids to behave.

Margaret got up early that morning, barricaded herself in the kitchen and sliced and diced and mixed with concentration and fervor, as if we were having the groom's parents over. Then, when everything was ready and the table set, came the realization that this year — again was going to be just the two of us and the girls. No one else would see that the turkey had turned out just like the one in the picture of *Southern Living*, or how pretty the new china was. No one would know that she made the biscuits and the cranberry sauce from scratch and how she improved on grandma's stuffing recipe.

She knew that the girls and I wouldn't really appreciate how she made the cornucopia, the beautiful centerpiece, based on a picture in the *Good Housekeeping* magazine and how she got the colors to match the place mats perfectly. What's the use of laboring to make a turkey design with marshmallows on top of the sweet potato souffh, when all the kids will do is play with it?

By the time we were ready to eat, Margaret had lost her appetite. In the afternoon, she called her sister Sandra, in Pompano Beach. Sandra said that she had fifteen people over, that she had baked a huge turkey, which they ate outside where Joe had made the back yard look like Pilgrim's hall, with long tables and benches. (Joe Carroll, is a quiet, almost meek carpenter, whom God sentenced to be Sandra's husband.) Sandra also said that Joe's sister Gloria brought a huge ham and Archie with his wife and kids came over dressed like Pilgrims, and they had this and they had that; about forty-five minutes worth of phone bill.

Later, after I had gone to bed, Margaret called her mother. And so, this year we are heading south for Christmas.

The work in the shop had slackened and it would be fine if we closed for a couple weeks. Might as well. Usually on workdays sandwiched between holidays, half of the guys don't show up and of those who do, most of them are hung over and do more damage than work. Also, Captain Emons had asked me to take a look at a ship in Miami and that would make the trip tax-deductible.

On the last working day, Margaret brought to the shop some cold cuts, soft drinks and Christmasy paper plates. We made a table out of saw horses and plywood and covered it with a Christmasy table cloth. Tuan Nguyen, the Vietnamese welder who was working double shifts putting his wife through college, brought a bucket of boiled shrimp. Other guy's wives brought fried chicken, meat balls, fancy vegetables and lots of deserts. (Antonios' wife brought a carrot cake that was the best I ever tasted).

We stopped working around noon, cleaned up and we had our first "company Christmas party." Just like the big boys. I made a very short speech, thanking everybody for their good work and their contribution in keeping the doors open, wished them "happy and safe holidays," thanked them for their thoughtful gift (a model of a three-masted sailing ship that probably cost them five dollars each), gave everybody their paychecks, and in a separate envelope marked "Season's Greetings," their bonus checks.

Using strange maneuvers so it wouldn't seem obvious, each one peeked in their bonus envelope and then one by one, remembered they had to be somewhere, and in five minutes they were all gone.

In that day's mail there was a card and a letter from mother wishing all of us Merry Christmas and bringing me up-to-date on the village happenings. They expect a heavy winter this year, one of Katina Mela's twin daughters won an award for calligraphy, Giannis Giannakos said the other day he was going to make more rooms to rent and Marika Lakonidis was all set to sell her house to somebody from America who had something to do with ships and go live with her daughter in Volos. She was all ready to go to Volos, but the man that was going to buy it got robbed and killed by gangsters just as he was walking home from work in New York. I should be careful, "Xenihtia, (foreign land), is full of criminals, not like our peaceful Taxiarhes."

I loaded the car the night before, hoping for an early departure. When I go on a trip alone, I like to leave early. I find it comforting to have the sunrise meet me on the road and to know that I have the whole day ahead of me to get where I am going. That's when

I am traveling alone. With the wife and kids, early departure is any time before sunset.

I shuttled back and forth, carrying packages to the car for hours: big ones, little ones, rectangular, square and odd-shaped ones, all wrapped in shiny green paper, with red ribbons and gold bows. I was proud of the way I had stuffed the back of the Ford station wagon and the rented box on the top. The back seat was laid down and by cleverly arranging some luggage, I made it into a cozy bed. That way, all they had to do was crawl out of bed and into the car. Didn't even have to open both eyes.

I was nursing the secret hope of every father traveling with children: They would fall asleep as soon as the car starts rolling and wake up when he pulls into the driveway at the other end.

Next morning, when I tried to get everybody in the car, Katerina couldn't find Laura-Lee, her homely Cabbage Patch doll, Nicole wanted to bring her favorite pillow, the one with The Fonz on it, Maria didn't like the cozy bed and Margaret thought I looked like a bum in my comfortable traveling clothes.

When the doll was found and the pillow changed and the bed rearranged and my ironed shirt matched my pants, we got in the car and discovered we didn't have enough room for the cake Margaret had made the night before. She ended up carrying it on her lap.

It was almost noon when we pulled out of the driveway.

So much for planning.

I drove along, playing poker and silly games in my mind with the mile markers and the car tags, trying to keep from screaming at the kids, ignoring Margaret's remarks that it was my fault they were misbehaving.

"All you do is yell at them; that's not teaching them any discipline."

"This is the last time we are doing this," I would swear, pounding on the wheel.

"Oh, daddy, you say that every time we go anywhere," Maria, the witty one, would remark.

"But this is absolutely, positively, the last time, for sure!" I would shout, and repeat it, every twenty miles.

I remember reading about a couple from Florida on their way to California who abandoned their two kids at a rest stop in Alabama. They were eventually arrested in Texas and sent to jail. Their lawyer should have tried to get on the jury some fathers who traveled more than twenty miles with two or more kids.

All the years I'd been driving this stretch of road, nothing has changed. Every mile seems to be the same as the one just passed. The same flat, empty pastures, the same skinny pine trees, the same dead armadillos.

Grandma was waiting for us. We hugged, we said we had a nice trip and that we were not hungry. The kids told about their soft-ball triumph, the school trip to the television station, the big smelly truck loaded with cows we passed on the road and the Disney World visit daddy promised on the way back, and finally we went to bed. I dreamed about the car running off the road and Margaret yelling at me for getting her covered in lemon meringue.

The day after Christmas, while Margaret and Sandra were at the mall returning presents, I drove to Miami to take a look at the freighter Captain Emons was thinking of buying. He had asked me for a cost estimate of some changes he was contemplating. Sandra's husband, Joe Carroll, came along for company.

We got there about noon. Miami had changed a lot since Maggie and I lived there. It made Bigport look like a small village. Where Flagler Drydock Company had been, there was now a passenger ship terminal. Tall condominiums and office buildings lined Flagler Boulevard, where cheap restaurants and seamen's bars used to be.

The ship I wanted to see was tied up at the east end of Dodge Island, on the water side of two other rusty hulks. We climbed a steep, rickety catwalk and walked aft, across the deck that looked like the skin of a creature with psoriasis, toward the accommodations housing. Big rust-blisters were crunching under our feet as we walked gingerly, trying to avoid the weak-looking spots.

"The agent said there was a watchman on board," I muttered, looking for someone to stop us.

"Got to be some Cuban around, I hear a radio blaring," said Joe, nodding in the direction of the cabins.

The radio was inside the forward door of the deckhouse, on top of a Shell oil drum. Next to it was a flashlight and a clipboard with a piece of paper titled "Visitor's Log" and a stubby pencil tied to a short, knotty string. I signed the log.

"This is Public Radio Florida," the radio announcer came on. "Stay tuned for the second half of Aida from the Metropolitan Opera, brought to you by Texaco."

"Anybody home?" I called out. There was no answer.

The cabin door next to the entrance was on the hook. I heard someone coughing and I called out again.

"Just one bloody minute," came an answer in an accent that was definitely not Cuban. Then there was more coughing.

Joe was looking at the oil spill prevention poster on the wall. He asked if the instructions were in Greek. They were, and I started to translate.

"Nickola, what a surprise," I heard a phlegmy voice behind me. I turned around and in the cabin doorway, I saw a shaggy figure resembling George Jones. He coughed again, turned the radio off and stepped toward me with his hand extended.

"It's really nice to see you, Nickola," he repeated.

"Scotty, this is a surprise. How are you doing?" I shook his hand with both of mine and said I had been asking about him and couldn't understand why he disappeared.

"I was going to call you, Nickola, but I have been so busy," he coughed again, took a sip from a pint bottle he got out of his pants pocket and continued, "I've got the deal to run these two ships here, only I've had this blasted cold and haven't been able to do a bloody thing."

"You should have called, Scotty, why did you disappear so suddenly?" He seemed embarrassed and uncomfortable with the question and sought refuge in coughing.

He looked a hundred years older.

I told him why I was there and asked if the fo'c's'le was open.

"I run a tight ship, Nickola, nothing is left open or laying about." He coughed again, then got a string of keys from the back of the cabin door and we followed him forward.

I started sketching the changes Captain Emons was planning and Joe offered to help by holding the "dumb end" of the measuring tape. Scotty sat on a coiled rope, sipping his cough medicine and explaining how the group he was putting together was going to convert the two rusting hulks next to this one into livestock carriers and transport sheep from Australia to Saudi Arabia.

"They have to be delivered live you know, Nickola, something about their religion."

While working we talked about old acquaintances in the business. I told Scotty about the senior port engineer of Vafakis Shipping who was planning to buy a house in my village but got mugged and killed.

"That's too bad, Nickola, he was a good man. That's why I'm careful where I go, I plan to live a long time."

When we finished with the measurements about an hour later, we were all hot and sweaty. Scotty walked with us to the top of the gangway. I put a ten-dollar bill in his hand as we were starting down the shaky steps: "to buy a beer on me," I said. He called from the deck when we got on the dock and were walking away and told me again that I would be starting work on his ships as soon as he got over "this bloody cold."

There were three cruise ships docked on Dodge island disgorging passengers and causing a huge traffic congestion. It took us almost thirty minutes to inch our way out of the docks.

"I could go for a cold one," said Joe, adjusting the air conditioning vent.

"Let's see if Conky Joe's is still in business," I said, and turned right on Flagler boulevard and right again in to a small alley, half a block long, terminating at the water. Conky Joe's Bar and Grill was still there, next to a yacht supply store.

"He used to make the best conch fritters anywhere," I said, as we sat at the bar.

"Some place," said Joe, looking around. "How did you find it?"

"The owner is an old friend, I used to come here when I was working with Flagler Drydock."

"Is that him?"

"Yah, that's Charlie."

Charlie Callahan was sitting behind the counter with his feet resting on the sink, reading a book. He hadn't changed a bit; the same tall, tanned, outdoorsy type, who had about as many years on his back as Scotty, only not as abused.

"He used to be vice president with an old shipping company in London," I explained, "till one day he decided he had enough, bought a house boat and bummed around the Caribbean for a while before settling in Miami."

"That's the life," sighed Joe.

The place was decorated to look as if it was built out of stuff collected on the beach. There was plenty of driftwood, old lumber, fishing nets, Portuguese floats and old ships' lanterns, installed in a way that made you think it just happened to land there. The bar was a stack of lobster traps, topped with old hatch covers, coated with clear resin. Part of the harbor with some yachts bobbing in the water could be seen through a large window behind the bar. There was a faint sour smell in the place, a mixture of old wine, spilled beer, smoke and food. A large overhead fan made a faint rustling noise.

We were the only customers. Charlie and I reminisced for a while, and before we got another round I ordered a plate of his conch fritters. "To show the natives here how they're supposed to taste. (I was referring to the latest craze in bumper sticker humor appearing on cars with Florida license plates, "native," "semi-native," and my favorite: "so what?", with an outline of the state of Florida on the left side. Joe's car had "native", on the driver's side.)

"My wife put that sticker on," muttered Joe.

A few minutes later Charlie brought a heaping plate of steaming fritters, and another round of beer.

"Scotty tells me you've got a big operation in Houston; a big shipyard or something," said Charlie, and took a sip of his beer.

"It's in Bigport," I said, "and it's not that big of an operation; the bank owns most of it."

"Every Greek I know can out-poormouth the poorest Irishman. Scotty says you are doing big insurance jobs."

"How long has Scotty been around here anyway?" I asked.

"This time, about a year-and-a-half. We were mates in the Academy, you know?" He wiped a wet spot on the counter and walked back to his chair.

"What happened to him?" I asked.

"Poor bugger, the *Island Merchant* got to him."

"The 'Merchant'?"

"A tanker that went down in the North Sea."

"Oh, yeah, that was, what? ten years ago? What did he have to do with it?" I asked.

"He was the one who signed the papers for the ship to leave the shipyard. How do you like the fritters?" he asked Joe.

"Spicy, make me thirsty," answered Joe.

"That's the idea mate."

"Tell me about Scotty," I asked.

He refilled the glasses and took a sip of his.

"Scotty was a good inspector, had a sharp eye and was not taking shortcuts. When the *Island Merchant* was at the shipyard in Lisbon for quadrennial, Scotty was one of Lloyds' surveyors for the ship. He was supposed to have checked the sea chests, but was drunk that day and the guy that did it didn't see one of the penetrations that was over-corroded. A month later, crossing the North Atlantic *in ballast*, a week before Christmas, the sea chest broke and she sunk. They found one lifeboat with twelve men in it, all frozen solid. The captain had his wife and six-year-old son with him. Never found them. Scotty was the kid's godfather." He took another sip of his beer.

"They gave him clerical jobs after that, but his drinking got too bad and they had to let him go."

"What about the bulker *Mirella* he used to talk about?" I asked.

"It's the same ship."

A middle-age man walked in and sat at the far end of the bar. Charlie wiped the counter in front of him and took his order.

"Care for more fritters?" he asked when he came back.

"No, we'll be leaving soon," I said.

The new customer came over and asked for change.

"Since then, when it hits him, Scotty walks off from whatever job he has and I find him sleeping in the back." He raised his voice as he walked toward the cash register. "He is always putting some big deal together in his mind, which gets bigger and bigger with the years."

The middle-age guy was putting coins in the jukebox.

"The harbor master is a pal of mine," Charlie went on. "I got him to put Scotty as watchman on those ships. It's the best job for him. Hope they don't scrap those rust buckets anytime soon."

The jukebox started crying about somebody leaving somebody.

We said our good-byes and headed north.

We took highway A1A on the way home; Joe said he wanted to stop at the Dania Marina and Boatyard to show me something. He took me to the far end of a pier where a squatty, over-aged houseboat was lazily rocking with the waves.

"What do you think of her?"

"She looks like an unmade hooker, on Monday morning," I said.

"Ah, the looks is small stuff, I can rip this old superstructure and put up a new one in no time. I get the wood for nothing, the hull is good though," Joe's face was shining.

He said "Hi Carl, how's the family?" to a fellow who looked like he might have something to do with the yard and we went on board. Joe showed me which bulkheads he was going to knock out and where the new cabins were going to be. He would pock the timber with his knife every so often to show me how hard it was and repeat: "Don't make them like that any more, they sure don't."

"Carl says she can be had for a song. The owner died and his wife doesn't care for the boat."

"What the hell are you going to do with it, Joe?"

"I can retire in three years. By then I'll have her all fixed up and me and Sandra can spend our time going from one island to the other in the Bahamas: Cat Island, Exuma, Eleuthera, all over the place. Have you seen how clear the water is over there? How pretty those little coves are? You can see the lobsters and the conch walking on the bottom. The coconut trees come right down to the water. Everything is so simple, so peaceful."

About an hour later, after some coaxing, I got Joe back in the car and we headed north. "Ah, that will be the life," he said leaning back, stretching his arms over his head. He spotted a post card I had clipped on the visor and picked it up. "Where's that?" he asked.

"It's in my village, an old classmate sent it to me for my name day, it was on the sixth of this month."

It had really choked me to get a card from Kostas Liappis, just a day before my name day. And to be that particular card on top of it; the thoughtfulness of a true friend.

He examined it. "Prety," he said. "Look how clear the water is, like in the Islands."

"That's the cove of Fakistra, my house is on a hill beyond those rocks in the corner."

"Nice," said Joe softly, "nice and peaceful."

For the rest of the way we were silent. Joe, in his mind, was probably moored in one of the coves of Exuma, diving for lobsters, or sipping rum with coconut water and watching the sunset from his mahogany deck and I was sipping ouzo at the patio of the Bellmaker's house.

Chapter | 14

*L*loyd was a good mechanic, an average worker and a huge pain in the neck. His boasting, scheming and ass-kissing were getting on my nerves. And when he teamed up with Floyd and pulled some of their pranks, he was costing me money on top of it. Their "Georgina" matchmaking stunt ended up costing me Rufus and George, two damn good workers and putting me one week behind on a conveyor job.

Lloyd had discovered that George, a punctual, hard worker and a hell of a good lathe operator, was a drag queen after work. He convinced George that Rufus, the shop helper, a twenty-two year-old farm boy who was renting a room in Loyd's house, had the hots for him, but couldn't make the first move because he was shy.

The "country cousins" had concocted a scheme to overcome this problem. One Saturday evening, Floyd, Lloyd and Rufus drove to where George lived and sent Rufus up to his apartment to pick up some deer meat George was supposed to have for them. The innocent, gullible and a touch "simple", Rufus, walked into a set dinner table, complete with candles and soft music, and a perfumed George with two gallons of make-up, dressed in a fancy evening gown. When Rufus finally figured out what was happening, he bolted out of the apartment and ran the seven miles back to his room. Neither George nor Rufus ever came back to work after that.

Sending Lloyd on out-of-town jobs was the easiest way to get him out of my hair and make him happy too, since he liked the extra money. It seemed a simple solution at the time.

One Monday morning, just as the rest of the crew was piling into the van to go to the docks, Floyd drove up in a taxi. He had a big lump on his forehead which he said he got by running into a door. He said Loyd was sick and wouldn't be coming.

"His wife needs the Camaro to go somewhere," he explained, and hopped in the van.

A couple of hours later, I got a call from Lloyd, sounding wild and telling me he was coming over to beat the crap out of me and that he was going to sue me and throw me in jail and kill me, and ... and ...

"You got hold of a bad batch, Lloyd, go sleep it off and get your ass to work in the morning," I cut short his raving.

When Floyd got back from the docks, I asked him what the hell was that all about, but he didn't say much.

The next morning, Moe, who always came to work about thirty minutes ahead of the others, told me that Lloyd had finally found out that Floyd was fooling around with his wife and kicked them out of the house. Then he got really messed up and was threatening to kill them and everybody else.

"You know, Lloyd lost one of his balls in an accident and I reckon that cut down on his stud service; Floyd just happened to be there," Moe said.

Lloyd kept calling me about three times a day for the rest of the week, then stopped. His wife filed for divorce, Floyd moved out, and I thought that was the end of it.

Lloyd came by the shop a couple of weeks later when Floyd was out of town. He was sober, sleeker than a Cuban pimp, with a stripper from the Happy Mariner hanging all over him. He said he was getting into a different line of work; he just came by to return something to one of the guys. He sounded mysterious.

The stripper transported the trembling contents of her undersized outfit over to where Moe was working and chatted for a while.

"She says they are going to open a bar together," Moe told me after they left.

"She must be desperate to have her own business, poor woman. She deserves better than that asshole," I said.

"She said Lloyd wanted to come to give Antonios his measuring tape back, but I think he just wanted to show that his "ball" is still working."

"I hope that's the last I see of him," I said. "He has been a pain in the ass."

"Don't think so, boss."

"You know something I don't?"

"Just got a feel, people that kind like to stir things up."

The notice arrived in two overstuffed envelopes, via an overstuffed deputy marshal two weeks later.

"Looking for Py. ly., ah. this guy here," and he pointed to my name on the envelopes.

"You found him," I said.

"Well, looks like this is your lucky day, sign here."

I signed.

154

"What kind of name is that?" he asked walking to his car.

"It's Irish," I said.

"It sure is a weird one. Can't keep track of them no more, too damn many foreigners," he mumbled and struggled to squeeze himself behind the wheel.

I tore open the envelopes:

"Lloyd N. Jones, plaintiff, vs. Poseidon Marine Services Incorporated, and Nikos Pilios, defendants."

The curses poured out, flooding the office.

The company, and I personally, were being sued by Loyd Nathaniel Jones for four million dollars.

The gist of all the legal jargon was that I was responsible for his marriage problems because I was sending him out of town so much, in violation of the original employment agreement, which caused marital stress and forced his wife to be unfaithful. To overcome his grief, some shyster lawyer had determined that Lloyd needed two million dollars from me and another two million from Poseidon Marine Services.

I threw the papers across the room and used my entire inventory of cuss words on Lloyd Jones, the shyster lawyers and the horny bitches. I kicked everything I came across and when I finally ran out of things to kick, I called my insurance man and told him about it. It took him awhile to answer me.

"I think it might be covered under liability," he said when he finally stopped laughing, "but hell, we can sell it to the Enquirer and make a fortune," then had another laughing fit.

For a long time, it was the hottest item in the shop. During the next six months my guys kept going back and forth to the lawyers' for depositions, on my time, of course. I had to pay them while they were sitting in a carpeted, air-conditioned office, sipping Cokes and talking about Loyd's wife's ass. The insurance lawyers got John Alepakis, a history professor at the university, to act as an interpreter for me and Antonios, and they seemed to get a laugh out of every answer.

They asked Antonios what he thought of Loyd's wife.

"I think, if he put her in a bottle, she would do it with the cork," he answered. Alepakis translated and all of the men burst out laughing and all of the secretaries blushed.

Eventually, "my lawyers" offered "his lawyers" a settlement, which "his lawyers" grabbed, kept most of it for themselves, and threw the left-over crumbs to the semi-castrated country cousin, who dumped the stripper and moved to New Orleans.

When the ever-cheerful insurance agent brought the policy renewal bill a couple of months later, I almost choked seeing how much it had gone up.

"I got nothing to do with the money," he said, his smile taking up half of his face, as if he was wearing oversized dentures. "The big boys in Cincinnati decide all that. I still think though you should've call up the Enquirer."

"You have raised the fuckin' premiums over two hundred dollars a month; that's a lot to pay for Loyd's ball."

"It's not just that — you are growing Nick, you are getting up there," he explained. "The premiums are based on the sales and your sales have gone up way up."

"I just don't' understand it: My customers complain that I am too expensive, my suppliers say I Jew them down too much, and my workers gripe they are under-paid. My wife on the other hand, says I am working too much and bring home too little. Then the accountant says I owe taxes because I made too much money last year, which I didn't, but something about the "acruables" and the "depreciables" and the "work-in-progress" being out of kilter, made the bottom line, the way the revenuers see it, too big. Then damn it, how come I am always broke? I am dreading for Fridays to get here; making payroll and paying bills is the scariest thing I've done."

"It's normal Nick, it's called 'growing pains'."

"It's a hell of a fix," I said. "I can't get the big jobs because I don't have the money it takes to do them, and I don't have the money because I can't get the big jobs."

"You are in a Catch-22," said the grin.

"And how do I get out of this catch?"

"Just hang in there. Be like the bulldog, once it grabs hold of something, it won't let go."

So I hung in there, with my nails and my teeth and with all the strength I could find in me, I hung in there.

Chapter

15

*P*ete Carras and I were having coffee in his office, chanting the usual song: Doing business with ships is not what it used to be; it takes forever to get paid nowadays; Bigport used to be full of ships; this country has gone to pot; nobody trusts anybody any more; creditors are getting more persistent when the Telex machine started clicking. Both of us jumped up and went to take a look.

"It's for you," said Pete after the first line got printed. "Maybe I need to change my name to Pilios enterprises."

It was from the senior port engineer of Caribbean Shipping, a barge operating outfit out of Miami. A few years back, when Scotty was still on my staff, at one of the Propeller club meetings someone had pointed out that senior port engineer to me and told me his company ran the big barge that came to Bigport every month. For the rest of that evening I kept trying to get close to him but Bubba from Dixie shipyard stuck to him like a limpet. A bunch more estimators and superintendents from Dixie were orbiting around him constantly.

"Looks like every free-loader from Dixie is here tonight," said Scotty, scanning the crowd.

I always took Scotty with me to the Propeller Club meetings. I introduced him around as a retired inspector from Lloyds of London, presently on my staff. He appreciated the attention.

"It's a Propeller Club meeting, Scotty; it's open to anyone making a living in the waterfront. Besides, they might have come to hear the lecture," I said.

"My friend, as long as it's free, the Dixie vultures will go even if somebody is giving away a case of clap," said Scotty.

I followed the port engineer of Caribbean Shipping to the bathroom and faked taking a leak a couple of times, but I couldn't get to a urinal next to his; the Dixie guys always surrounded him.

Finally, late in the evening, Scotty started an argument with Bubba about the quality of a repair job Dixie had done a few weeks earlier, which distracted Bubba from his guard duties. I managed to slip into the can and talk to the Caribbean port engineer on the next urinal.

I handed him my card and in the short time we were neighbors, I told him that we did the same work as Dixie, only better and a hell of a lot cheaper.

He said he would give the information to the responsible party, zipped up and left.

I hadn't spoken to the Caribbean port engineer since. One of his underlings asked me a few times to go on board the barge and give him a price for some work, but all those turned out to be dry runs. The guy never really intended to give me the job, he did it so he could tell his boss he got more than one price.

The Bigport route wasn't successful. A few months back they had tied the barge up and I gave up on trying to get any work from them. Now the senior port engineer himself was asking me to contact him about quoting on repairs on that barge.

I trotted to my office and called him right away. He said that he had fired the port engineer and had taken over the barge operation himself. They were going to do a major conversion and use it on a different route. Would I be interested in giving them a price?

"You can pick up a set of the hull drawings from the agent," he said.

I said I would have him a price by this evening, before he had even finished talking. Then after I hung up, I remembered that the barge was docked inside the Dixie shipyard and they wouldn't let me look at it, even with binoculars. If I managed to get past the guard at the main gate, I would be stopped by another over-zealous, over-armed redneck at the bottom of the barge gangway who would ask for a pass from the security office, my identification and probably the O.K. from Bubba or his boss.

No way to fake it.

After some thought, I drove over to Bill Yeoman's place. I hadn't seen Bill since he sold Yeoman's Shipbuilding and Repair to a group of investors out of town. They changed the name to Bayou Towing and Repair and kept Bill as manager, on a very short leash.

He was at his desk, behind stacks of computer print-outs, with only the top of his head showing. A ribbon of thin gray smoke was spiraling toward the ceiling. There were no new paintings on the walls.

"I thought you cut cigarettes two years ago," I said.

"How did that saying you told me go? 'You may want to become a saint but the devil won't let you,' wasn't it? Sit down; what's on your mind?"

I told him what was on my mind.

"That's why I need the skiff for a couple of hours this evening, I'll pay you rent for it."

"Don't worry about rent; glad to contribute to a good cause; and socking it to Dixie is the best cause I can think of right now."

"It's a hell of a way to get a job, but my work is real slow right now," I said.

"At least it's *your* company. You don't have a bunch of accountants sitting in New Orleans telling you how to run your business."

At about three o'clock that afternoon, during the shift change, Moe and I quietly eased up on the barge from the riverside. The thing was huge. The drawings said she was four hundred feet long and one hundred feet wide, with the deck about forty feet above the water and a deck house twenty-five feet tall on top of that. Looking up from the little skiff, I got a sense of how an ant must feel looking at the top of a skyscraper from the sidewalk. I climbed on board using the emergency boarding steps and Moe took the skiff out of sight. All of my past visits on board were not wasted; I remembered my way around and immediately got busy measuring and taking notes. I was drooling; there was so much easy work on the thing.

I finished in less than an hour. I got on deck and looked for Moe. He was dozing off in the skiff a few yards away. I found some screws on deck and threw them at him to get his attention. He woke up on the fourth screw and brought the skiff alongside.

"Bubba will have a conniption when he finds out we got on board," he said on the way back.

"Couldn't happen to a better guy. Hope they fire his ass, and this time, he stays fired."

I did my figuring as soon as I got in the office. Motivated by the multitude of overripe loans and the golden opportunity to aggravate Dixie, I sharpened my pencil to the limit. I called the port engineer as soon as I finished.

"We can get everything done on your list, for $ 68,947," I told him. Somebody had advised me when I started in the business, that if you quote in round figures, it looks like you guessed at the job. But if you put a lot of little numbers trailing the big ones, it looks as if you have taken every detail into consideration and you have gone as low as it's possible.

"Are you sure about your numbers?" he asked. That always means that the price is way below everybody else's. The fellows at the Dixie shipyard, secure in the belief that no one else had looked at the job, had probably given him some number three times as high.

We went over the work list, line by line.

"When can you start?" he asked, when he was sure I had all my ducks in a row.

"Right now," I answered.

"The barge needs to be in Jacksonville as soon as possible; the charters are waiting. I'll Telex the contract to the agent. He can sign it for us and you can get started."

I drove over to the agent's office as if mine was the only car on the road. In the lobby, I pressed the button for the elevator, but it was taking too long and I took the stairs to the fourth floor, two steps at a time.

"You must have flown over here," said the agent, putting down the phone; "I was just talking to Miami."

It was the first time I had been in his office. I looked around in awe. It was a big room, and everything in it was big: the black leather sofa, the matching leather chairs, the oil paintings of sailing ships in gold carved frames and the globe on a brass stand. The agent was reclining on a leather chair, behind a fancy, leather-top desk the size of a ping-pong table, in front of a window with a panoramic view of the river. Beautiful. But I could never have something like this, even if I could afford it. I would have to keep changing clothes and getting cleaned up every time I came in from the shop. Then when the guys came to see me, they would track dirt in the carpet and Margaret would have a fit.

I gave him my bid and while he was making copies, the Telex machine started clicking. I ran over and looked. It was my contract. I stood there watching the little ball hammer out the characters that formed my company's name and I could feel the pride, warm and tingling, rushing through my veins. That was my little company there, dealing with big corporations and coming out a winner. The clicking of the Telex printer was at that moment, the sweetest music I had ever heard.

"You got one over the guys at Dixie didn't you?" said the agent.

"Yep, I guess I did." I was suppressing the urge to shout. We both signed the Telex and he made copies.

"Good luck with it," he said, handing me my copy. "Are you sure it's not too big a job for you?"

"I can handle it," I said.

"I wish I could be a fly in Bubba Smith's office when I call him to turn the barge over to you," he said with a grin.

I waited till he made arrangements with the tugs to pick up the barge from the Dixie yard and bring it to a public pier, a quarter of a mile from my shop, then I floated out of the office.

I made up two shifts; I had the first and Antonios the second. For once, I didn't have any problem getting workers. Bay Shipping, the hot-shot outfit out of New Jersey, had gone belly-up, stranding the work crews, mostly Greeks and Puerto Ricans, broke and hungry, in Bigport. There were rumors that the FBI, the IRS, the CIA and the rest of the alphabet were looking for the owners.

I never got any work out of the sales-call I made to the too-perfect Mr. Romero in their sterile offices a year earlier, but now when their name came up, I was quick to say: "I knew there was something fishy about those guys, that's why I wouldn't do any work for them, even though they asked me a bunch of times."

Early on the first day of the Caribbean job, walking by Floyd, who was changing an expansion joint on the steam piping, I noticed his helper, a young Greek fellow I hired from the stranded crew, sitting on the tool box watching him grind the flange. When he saw me, he jumped up and started explaining:

"He told me to sit down, I tell the truth. I want to work, you are not going to fire me, are you? I need the job, I need it very much." He spoke in Greek and could get a prize for speed talk.

"Can't talk with him, he can't understand English," yelled Floyd over the grinder noise.

"I understand, I understand, but he don't speak regular people English," he defended.

"Try to speak plain, use simple words," I told Floyd.

"I speak, same as always." He stopped grinding. "Here," he said, handing the grinder to the helper, "Hang on to it while I check the fit."

The helper took the grinder and, looking perplexed, searched around, probably for a hook.

"You could have said: 'Hold it,'" I told Floyd.

"Can't stop and think how to talk when I am fixing to do something."

We shuffled some people around and after the second day, the work moved much faster.

From a bankruptcy auction, I bought two "flux core" welding machines for welding in the shop. The weldments came out smooth and shiny and I would make sure anyone visiting the shop got to see them.

I was thinking: a few more jobs like that, back to back, and I will be up there with the big boys in New York. I'll be starting on the house renovation in Taxiarhes next year. The flagstone-covered patio will have an arbor over it with two kinds of vines: red muscadines and white seedless. Under it will be a large table from solid slate from the Propan quarry, where I'll have my morning coffee, my after-siesta snack and my evening ouzo, while gazing at the blue Aegean.

The job took three weeks with thirty-five people. On the second week, the harbormaster said we needed to move the barge to another dock because there was a freighter coming to unload on this one. Two tugs came and pushing and pulling gently, moved us about a mile down-river. As we were passing by the Dixie Shipyard I saw Bubba standing on top of the dry-dock wing-wall looking at us. I couldn't resist it: "Eh Bubba," I shouted from the top of my lungs, "still looking for the barge? Come see me later, I might have some work for you."

The senior port engineer of Caribbean Shipping came up from Miami for the final inspection. He was an old salt about sixty five, who grew up on the waterfront. I took him to dinner at George Skoufos restaurant. Trying to make conversation, I mentioned Conky Joe's Bar and Grill in Miami and his famous conch fritters. Told him that I was there six months ago.

"I was there two weeks ago," he said. "Somebody put a bug in the old man's ear about converting one of those old hulls into a livestock carrier." He ate some of the calamari. "This is good stuff." He emptied his wine glass. "A hell of a thing about those ships, they are tied three abreast and had one watchman looking after them. When I went on board I looked all over for him. Then I walked in the aft house of the last one; it stunk to high heaven. They said later the guy had been dead for three days." He dipped a large piece of calamari into George's special cocktail sauce. "I had seen the guy at Conky Joe's, a funny talking Scotsman, that kept saying he was an ex-Lloyds' man."

He refilled and re-emptied his glass. "A hell of a way to go for anybody, though."

"Yah, a hell of a way to go," I echoed, and I knew it sounded hollow.

Chapter 16

*F*our and a half years into the life of Poseidon Marine Services, Inc., I had another cockamamie idea to add to my huge collection: I moved the business into a bigger place, a couple of blocks down the street. Edward Hamilton the Third, in one of his "coincidental" visits that always happened a couple of days after rent was due, told me about the building going on the market.

I went and looked at it, then begged and pestered everyone at the Merchants Bank, till they loaned me the money to buy it.

The new shop was a tall metal building, almost double the size of the old one, with strong steel columns that could support lifting hoists if it ever got to where I could afford them. It even had a foreman's office and break room.

The main office was a Creole Cottage style building, about fifty feet away from the shop, connected by a covered walkway. It had a reception area, private bathrooms, central heat and air, and four separate rooms, the biggest of which became my office.

I had a new sign painted and mounted on a tall post in the front. Soon after, I came to the conclusion that it was time I hired a receptionist to go with the reception area. Sending calls to an answering service or putting the phone on call-forwarding to my house didn't work out very well. The people I dealt with were not too happy when they called my office and one of the kids would pick up the phone at home and they'd have to spell out the whole message. Many times I got home and our ten-year-old Nicole, who loved to imitate the telephone operator of the TV show "Laugh In," would give me the message:

"Some man called about a ship coming in tonight."

"Did you write down his name?"

"No, because he didn't sound like a nice man; he said a cuss word."

I needed someone who would sound professional, take messages, say that I was in a meeting when I was in the bathroom and say I was out of town to those I owed money to. A secretary with a cosmopolitan accent who would ask: "May I say what this is in reference to?" and: "Let me see if Mr. Pilios is available," just like regular companies.

Margaret didn't think much of the idea. "You are going to pay somebody to sit there, maybe answering the phone once in a while, when you can't afford to draw a decent paycheck yourself."

Always throwing cold water on my hottest aspirations.

"You have some miniskirted bimbo from the docks in mind?"

I told her I didn't, and tried to explain that besides answering the telephone, the secretary would be doing the invoicing, the accounts payable and payroll, and all kinds of other important stuff.

"You only write a couple of invoices a month and a handful of checks. You are going to let some stranger stick their nose into your business?"

And so, Margaret became the office manager at the salary of $ 350 a month. Four hours into her first day, I realized I'd made a big mistake.

Right after I moved into the new shop, my workload took a nose dive. Now on top of all my other headaches, I had to listen to Margaret's griping about keeping my office messy, about my lousy planning and about me wanting to play big-shot, and how Mr. Tom Edwards had predicted that the economy was going to slow down and how Howard Demming would never made a rash move like that.

I didn't care what those two drones would do, I was sure I had made the right move. The old place had gotten crowded. In the little office, the filing cabinet and the vendor catalogs I had accumulated left no room for an extra chair. And in the shop, the old Monarch lathe took up half of the floor. It had taken all of the resourcefulness we could muster to do the hatch cover job for Berres Shipping.

"Necessity is the mother of invention," said a paint salesman looking at the strange rigging we used to move the hatch cover out of the shop, without a forklift.

'Being broke, is more like it,' I thought.

If I was going to grow, I needed a bigger place and in my mind, the move was a necessary one. But the ship repair business has always been either feast or famine; and that summer, right after I made the June mortgage payment to the Merchants Bank, the famine period started. I laid everybody off except Moe and Floyd, because I was expecting an order from Berres Shipping for a piping job any day. They spent most of their time standing in front of the floor fan trying to stay cool, each holding a broom, and when they saw me coming, they would start pushing it, going around whatever was lying on the floor. Later, when I made them pick up the tools, there would be dirt impressions of sludge hammers and pipe wrenches on the concrete.

My heart bled when I was adding up their hours on Fridays. I kept inventing reasons to call Berres and casually ask if they'd made a decision on the piping job. They kept saying they were still evaluating it.

A week before the fourth of July, on a very slow day, Howard Demming strolled into the shop. He said he just happened to be in the neighborhood and stopped by to say "Hi." We chatted for a while about our kids' ball games, our wives' shopping habits and his new job promotion, and since this was his first time to my place, I showed him around and tried to explain what we were doing.

I told him that the foreman and fifteen more men were working on a ship at the docks.

He acted impressed, but I think he was doing it out of politeness. At the end of the tour, while walking outside, Howard drifted toward his car and, acting as if he just remembered it, asked me if I could take a look at his barbecue grill, which just happen to be in the trunk, and tell him if it could be fixed.

I looked at it and told him it could be fixed. While waiting for Moe to weld it, he leafed through the photo album lying on the table in the reception area. In it, besides the photographs showing my crew in action, I had photographs of everything we had built; vent cowls, pump foundations, manifolds. Howard glanced at each one of them.

After a while, Moe came in and said he was finished.

Howard looked at the repair and exclaimed: *"Wunderbar, wunderbar."*

Then while we were lugging the grill back to his car, he asked: "Why didn't you tell me you do steel fabrication? You could be doing some work for us."

I didn't know what he meant. I suspected he was trying to get out of paying for the welding. I was not planning to charge him anyway. If I did, I would never hear the end of it from Margaret.

"We build parts that go on ships," I said. "Your company has ships too?"

They didn't and he went on to explain, tenderly, like a kindergarten teacher, that what I was doing, making things out of steel pieces, was called steel fabrication in this country.

"Like the stuff you have in the photo album," he said. "We have a manufacturing plant for the paper machines outside New York, but they are subbing work to shops like yours all the time. Hell, they have to, they are paying union wages up there; can't compete. The Finns are eating our lunch as it is."

I told him that I was interested in anything "that was legal and I was getting paid for it." Howard said that the production manager would be coming through town in a couple of weeks, and if I wanted, he could bring him by the shop.

"Ya, sure," I said, "just let me know a few days ahead of time to make sure I am in town, we have been pretty busy lately."

Like most conversations with Howard, I forgot about it soon after he left. A few days later, Margaret told me that Howard was going to New Orleans to inspect some machinery a company called "Arcadian Metal Works" was building for his company. He was going to take Lynda with him and they were going to spend the weekend at a hotel and go shopping and go to the theater and why couldn't we ever do something nice like that? Secretly I wished some Cajun would knock Howard over the head; then I remembered: Arcadian Metal Works was the outfit Mudrawsky, the damn Polack port engineer of Berres Shipping gave all the work to after he got pissed off at me for being late on the delivery of a pump foundation, four years back.

Howard called two weeks later, apologizing for the short notice, but he'd "been busier than a hooker on a battleship." He said the production manager was going to be in town the next day and he wanted to know if it would be O.K. to bring him by.

Among close friends, the immediate, reaction would be: "Oh, shit," but in this case, I coughed, blew my nose, cleared my throat and then I said: "It's gonna have to be in the afternoon; in the morning I have the representative from the Loyds' of London inspecting the shop for a big job we are getting ready to start."

He said they could come by at two o'clock.

"He is a real nice fellow, I'm sure you will like him," said Howard.

"Does he know anything about ships?"

"No, I am afraid you won't be able to swap sea stories with him. He was a procurement officer in the army; but he knows his stuff, he has been with the company ever since high school."

"Well, I will be waiting for you."

Before I had even hung up, I was wishing for a hurricane or an earthquake, or any disaster that would give me a face-saving excuse to cancel his visit. The business was going through the longest dry spell I could remember. If the phone ever rang, it was either a salesman or somebody asking for a donation, or a fast-talking New York stock peddler who kept repeating my first name as if we had grown up together, trying to get me to buy some "hot" stock.

I had laid off everybody, even Moe; there was nothing going on in the shop.

Executives of large corporations didn't get there by sticking their necks out. They don't change vendors unless they are absolutely sure that the outcome will make them look good.

I could be telling the Chicago Big Wheel that I had the best craftsmen and that we do excellent work till I was blue in the face, but if all he saw was an empty shop, he would brush off my talking as another sales pitch. He would be polite, take my card and the company brochure, tell me that he would give me a call next time a need for my services came up, and half-hour later, he would have forgotten what the place looked like and would either be pissed off for my wasting his time, or thinking that sly Howard was trying to pull something.

People believe what they see.

Some old sea dogs had known that years before I figured it out. An old chief engineer on one of the tankers I sailed on, spent the days in his cabin or in the officer's lounge, in his starched khaki uniform, playing cards and running the steward ragged keeping him supplied with coffee and snacks. A couple of times during the day, he would open the engine room door from the cabin deck and peek down through the catwalk grating at those standing watch down below. That's the closest he came to working during the voyage.

But when the ship got into a port where someone from the office could be coming on board, he would spread machinery drawings all over his office and put on a pair of coveralls that hadn't been washed since he signed on. Looking as if he had been up all night, he would explain to the visiting wheel that he was working on locating a heat loss in the fuel oil heater, or a pressure loss on the superheater, which when corrected, would reduce the fuel consumption by at least two percent. The pencil pushers from the home office thought he was the most dedicated man in the company.

I needed to show the visiting manager that we were an efficient, small fabrication shop doing work of the highest quality and fussing over our customers like an overprotective village grandmother.

I called Moe but the woman who answered said he was locked up for child support. I didn't do any better with the rest of the people on my phone list; Antonios was in Greece and the others were either working, fishing, or drunk. It was the middle of the hurricane season, but there was not even a strong wind anywhere. The chances for an earthquake were slim too.

I called Manpower Temporary Services and asked if they had any welders and fitters available. A well mannered, sweet sounding southern lady said that they had plenty, how many did I need? I made arrangements for two welders, two fitters, one grinder and one helper. I asked her to make sure they were in my shop by ten o'clock the next day.

"How long is the job going to last?" she asked.

"It's going to be a long-term project; I will be needing plenty more in a few days, but I'll try these guys to see what kind of craftsmen you people have."

She said she was going to send me some good men.

I switched the phone to call forwarding and drove to the junkyard, four blocks away. I found Jack Kraman, the owner, half buried in a large pile of old plumbing material next to the scales, sorting brass bathroom fixtures.

"Some guy brought this load an hour ago; these fittings are antique, there is a treasure in here," he was salivating.

I told him what I wanted and he pointed me to the right scrap pile on the far side of the yard across the street.

"Watch out for the snakes," he said.

A tugboat superstructure with the name of the tug still legible through the peeling paint, was by the entrance to the yard. A dog had made a home under it and she was quick to let me know that she wasn't ready to show off her new puppies. I gave her a wide berth.

I walked between mountains of steel pipes, rusty ship's plates and car frames, all waiting to be cut up to furnace size pieces for the foundry. Further in, there was a pile of ship's anchors and next to it, a pile of anchor chain.

I found a batch of new steel plate that Jack had bought from a steel processing outfit in sizes that I could handle. It was next to a heap of store fixtures, metal shelves and tables, all jumbled and rusting; the price stickers of whatever they held were still taped to some of them.

The sun was baking everything. The heat, bouncing off the metal, hit my face as if I had just opened an oven door. The sweat drops sizzled when they hit the steel plates. In about an hour I had loaded as much as the little truck could carry.

Next day, when the Manpower guys showed up, I told them what to do and made sure they were doing it the way I wanted it.

Howard and the production manager of Chicago Modern Machinery arrived at two o'clock sharp. They found a busy group of people absorbed in their work: welding, burning, fitting and grinding. On the work tables lay open the drawings of ships' parts from old jobs.

As we walked through the shop, I explained to the production manager what we were doing: "this guy here is building a sea chest for a freighter, this guy here is building an anchor windlass foundation and these pieces here are going to be made into a cargo hold ventilator cover, to be installed by our field crew."

The production manager examined everything with the eye of someone who knows what he is looking at. He read the label on the welding wire spool. "We use the same kind in our plant," he said. Then further down: "We use Argon for shielding gas also, it splatters less and doesn't leave pin holes." He scrutinized a piece that was supposed to be a foundation: "Good fit-up, good surface prep."

"On ships every component is critical," I said, "because of the harsh working conditions we have to make certain that everything is done right. We are very strict on quality control."

"You have a clean, neat shop," he said when we walked outside.

I laid off the guys from Manpower as soon as Howard and his boss turned the corner. I told them I would call them later, which they didn't believe and I felt sorry for them. Next day, I returned everything to the scrap yard and told Jack that the customer canceled the order. He gave me full credit.

A week later, Howard brought a drawing of a simple steel platform that I could build with my eyes closed. I priced it like a starving lion and a few days later I had the order.

That order led to a bigger one and after that, an even bigger. I bailed Moe out of jail, Antonios came back from Greece, I talked Floyd away from where he was working and slowly I rebuilt my old crew.

Soon after, I bought a forklift, a yellow Hyster that could pick up four thousand pounds, from somebody going out of business. The Merchants Bank of Bigport loaned me five thousand dollars to pay for it and after a few days, we all wondered how we had managed without it.

Doing work for Howard's outfit opened up new horizons. It was work I could plan and schedule ahead of time and do in the shop, out of the weather during normal working hours.

In ship repairs, I either had lots of work and I was begging every wino and skid row bum to come to work, or I had lots of winos and skid row bums standing around while I was begging the shipping companies to give me something to keep them busy. Ships, it seemed, always broke down on weekends, or during holidays, or while we were packing for a trip to Disney World.

The papermill guys would ask for the best and final price, and if they liked it, I got the job. There was no talk of the price of paper being down, or whether it was an insurance job or if they were paying out of their pocket.

And they paid on time. I didn't have to be calling Piraeus, or New York and be told the check was in the mail, or my invoice got lost, or they didn't like the job and they were taking twenty percent off.

On my next company brochure, this one in multi-color, with five photographs, under work performed I added the line: "Steel fabricators for marine and shore-based industries."

Maria started spending time in the shop on the days she didn't have school. She would put on my coveralls and would drill and tap and get all dirty and sweaty, making me proud and her mother furious. In a few years, she would be able to run the place, the house in Taxiarhes would be finished and I could spend my long vacations there, showing the guys at the Festorias cafenio my prokopi.

The shop stayed crowded. Now, in addition to ships' parts, we were building catwalks, hand rails, platforms, ramps, kickers, slitters and all kinds of strange looking things with even stranger names.

I never griped again if somebody used too much paper.

We made a multitude of attachments for the forklift and we were doing things that the guys at Hyster had never thought of.

The subcontracting administrator of Chicago Modern Machinery was sending the job drawings in boxes, via United Parcel Service. Each box meant at least a couple of weeks work. After some time, I discovered that every time I saw the UPS truck approaching, my pulse quickened in anticipation. It was the same as seeing the postman when I was a teenager in the village and had a pen-pal in the States.

I had rented a small part of my shop to Constellation Shipping, a Norwegian shipping company, to store and service their container loading equipment. They had a ten ton overhead crane which I offered to install for their technicians in my place, at my expense, if they let me use it. They did and when the ever-fickle shipping market changed a year later and Constellation Shipping moved their operation to the West Coast, I bought the crane for six hundred dollars.

I was getting to be like the big boys.

Chapter 17

*P*ete Carras got me to join the AHEPA organization using a simple, effective method: pestering.

When I went to see him for another short-term loan, he told me I was going to their next meeting. "You already know everybody. It's not as if you are going to be with strangers," he said. "Our boy Antonios, is vice president this year."

AHEPA stood for: American, Hellenic, Progressive Association and anything with "progress" in it was sure to attract "our boy" Antonios. This time I couldn't wiggle out of it; it was going to be the interest payment for my loan.

AHEPA met once a month, on Sunday evening, at a house across the street from the church. It was an old, antebellum-style home in constant need of repairs, with big rooms, big porches and a big mortgage that the organization was struggling to pay off.

The meeting started very formally. The council sat on green metal folding chairs behind a long table facing the rest of us who sat on brown metal folding chairs. Manolis Vervatos, being the president, sat in the center. To his left was John Papas, the treasurer and to his right was Antonios, the vice-president, looking as if he was sitting on a throne. To Antonios' right was Tony Philips, the secretary.

Pete stood up and introduced me as his guest and everybody welcomed me as if they hadn't seen me before.

The invocation, in mispronounced English, was recited, then the minutes of the previous meeting were read. The president gave his report and then the treasurer gave his: "Cash on hand, $79.43; bills due, $ 327.53. I would like to remind some of the brothers who are late with their dues, to please pay up. We need the money."

The treasurer was an easy-going, soft-spoken fellow by the name of John Papas. He was a domestic Greek but not related to the Papas from Omaha who was a hospital accountant. To most American Greeks, "Papas" is what's left after Americanizing whatever last name they came with. His father had migrated to Chicago from the island of Crete at a young age. Some of the Cretan resourcefulness and mule-like perseverance had been transferred to the son, although a bit diluted. During the war, he had taken part in the raids over Germany as a tail gunner, which turned out to be useful training for the AHEPA treasurer's job. Ground fire started before he had even finished with his report.

"What happened to all the money you said we had at the last meeting?" somebody shot from the left side of the room. The old tail gunner turned around and let him have it.

"Last month's balance, Brother Pittas, was $ 248.99, out of which we paid the following bills..." and he started listing all the payments till someone from the other side of the room interrupted: "Who authorized twenty-one seventy-five for charcoal? We not vote for that."

John swung to the right and unloaded: "That was for the church barbecue brother Tony, the one where some brothers who promised to help didn't show up till it was time to eat."

"George Skoufos don't need help. He knows everything, and can do everything, and he is better than everybody," answered Tony, pouting.

It's an old trick that we, Greeks have refined and use it whenever there is a need of a face-saving excuse for getting out of doing any work. When they ask for volunteers we sign up eagerly. We decline to be in charge of the project, modestly saying that there are others better qualified for that. With strong, indisputable, and at the time, sincere words, we assure whoever gets stuck with the top job that he can count on us for all the help he might need. We participate in all planning meetings and generously offer our opinion (whether asked or not). Then when it comes time to do the work, we either manage to get our feelings badly hurt, or our dignity heavily insulted, or we are so appalled at the inferior work the project chairman is allowing that we refuse to have our good name associated with anything so far beneath our standards. "I am not going to have anything to do with serving beans straight out of a can," or something like that.

We usually stay angry for about a week after the project is over and then we will accept the apology, (offered or not), and forgive the perpetrators. "Brother" Tony Philips was an old master at that.

Tony's parents had lived in Brooklyn for a year before they moved to Bigport. All they brought from the little Aegean island was their six-year-old Tony and the yard-long last name: Hadzifilipidis. Tony, now in his late forties, a short, fast-talking, fast-moving, balding stub of a man with a shifty look, shrunk the last name, expanded the Brooklyn accent and the Yankee moves and kept them as part of the inheritance.

The treasurer went on with his report.

Eventually big Jim Farmanis, authentic Greek mountain-man, stood up, unglued the thick cigar from his lower lip, spat a couple of times, and in his thick island accent, announced: *"I make emotion to pay bills as money come available."* Somebody seconded it and the old gunner came in for a landing.

When the meeting got to the new business part, Tony Philips spoke up. "I make a motion to have a raffle for a pick-up truck, to raise money," he announced.

It got very quiet. Christos Pittas nudged Pete Carras sitting next to him: "You second it, you like to hear your name when they read the minutes." Pete didn't answer.

Finally, John Papas, the hospital accountant, raised his hand and seconded it.

"If he didn't, his sister would give him hell," Pete whispered to me. John's sister was Tony's wife.

Tony got up and explained how he was going to do it.

"We sell five hundred tickets at a hundred dollars a ticket, that's fifty thousand dollars. I can finagle a good deal from Bigport Motors, maybe pay no more than fifteen thousand bucks for it, we pay a little for expenses, then we have a big banquet; real first class stuff, with prime rib and open bar and we have the ticket drawing. We gonna make a killing."

"Where are you gonna sell five hundred tickets?" someone asked.

"We sell to the Americans, real easy, I know plenty guys that will buy ten at a time," said Tony, "'specially when I tell them it's tax-deductible."

"Where are you going to have the banquet?"

"Who is going to be the chairman?"

"How long will it take to sell the tickets?"

The questions were coming from all over the floor.

"Who is gonna sell the tickets?" Nick Podakakis asked, "I am not selling any tickets any more. Last time I sell tickets for mink coat at Greek night, my neighbor win and when she go to pick up, the store don't give it to her because they say is not paid."

"That was a mix-up," explained Tony, "it was a new manager. He didn't know the arrangements I had made with the other guy."

"I no get mixed-up in monkey business. Last time I not look my neighbor in the face for months. My wife almost give me divorce."

I was sitting in a corner with Big Jim Farmanis, Christos Pittas, Pete Carras and John Alepakis. It seemed like those born in Greece always ended up clustering together without really trying. Alepakis was born in Utah, but he liked to be around us more than the domestic Greeks.

Christos leaned over and in a low voice said to the rest of us: "He sounds like a New York hustler, he finagles other people's money and then he brags how much he spends on the junk he throws riding the floats with all the bigshots on Mardi Gras."

"He's president of the Roman Cavaliers, you know," said Alepakis with a hint of admiration.

"*Arhidia Kalavrezika*. It's that damn finagling and high society living that got his ass in trouble with the tax people," said Pete Carras, mostly for my benefit.

"Haven't heard anybody say that since I left home," said Christos Pittas. "You know they auctioned his shop off, sold the fixtures to the scrap man and threw his ass in jail. If it wasn't for his brother-in-law, he would still be there. And he's bitching he didn't get any sympathy from the Greeks and started going to the Main Street Baptist church. Don't have any respect for those Greeks that give up their own religion. I call them prodotes."

Alepakis looked perplexed.

"I call them *traders*," repeated Christos for his benefit.

"You mean *traitors*," the enlightened Alepakis corrected.

"All this fancy talking and showing off, is to pass himself as an American-American. He is ashamed to be one of us; that's what I think," said Big Jim Farmanis.

When Tony's motion came to a vote, the nays had it.

The next item was to find a chairman for the celebration of twenty-fifth of March, the Greek independence day. John Alepakis was nominated. He accepted and started saying what kind of program he had in mind.

"I would appreciate any help or any suggestions any of you might have," he said.

"Keep the fancy speeches short," was Big Jim Farmanis' contribution.

Big Jim Farmanis was about fifty, tall, rugged, macho, garlic smelling, imported directly from a Greek mountain ten years earlier. He was working as a mason for his brother in-law, and because he came by the shop once in a while to have some steel lintels made, he acted as though we were partners and the closest of friends. Jim chewed thick cigars, had the rural Greek habit of making spitting sounds to keep the evil eye away from those he liked, and still pinched one's cheek as a show of affection. Whenever he saw me, after the handshake, he would pinch my cheek and say: "You look good my friend, you look real good, *bravo, ftou, ftou, ftou*." The more I told him it bugged me, the more he did it.

Antonios Vrahakis, "our boy" the vice president, reconfirmed that he would chair the Easter Day picnic. "I am going to need more help, this year we are going to cook two lambs. The *Pasha for the Mericani* is the same Sunday. Gonna have more families. That's how it should be every year." Then turning to me: "Right Nicko?" Antonios' wife was Baptist and he considered our wives' common religion a point of comradeship with me.

"You go tell the Pope to change it, brother Antonios," said Manolis.

"Maybe when one of your sons becomes a Patriarch, he can change it," Antonios shot back.

"My sons are going to marry young, they like girls too much. They are like their father; they like that pussy."

Anthony asked me if I wanted to be in his crew preparing the Easter Day picnic; I could help with the roasting of the lamb in the spit. I had heard that his roast lamb was one of the best, and I could pick up a few pointers, but I wasn't going to play second fiddle to my shop foreman. I said we were going to Florida for Easter this year.

Eventually, somebody made a motion to adjourn, somebody else seconded it and that marked the beginning of the social hour. There were cold-cut sandwiches and potato chips and drinks and everybody swapped fish stories, bragged about accomplishments, and under the guise of friendly interest, tried to pry some information that would provide fodder for gossip.

The secretary took me aside, filled out some papers and said at the next meeting I would be inducted into the chapter of AHEPA.

In our church the responsibility to assist the priest in singing the praises to the Lord and asking for forgiveness of our few, insignificant sins, was shouldered by two cantors: Christos Pittas with his soft, frugal voice and Manolis Vervatos, whose *"Kyrie Eleison"* could pierce the farthest clouds and reach even the hardest of hearing saints.

Then when the liturgy part started, the choir began their singing. Vervatos considered this his signal that he was done for the day and went back to the community hall to help humanity.

Ms Anastasia Kastelarou, fiftyish, sweet, good looking, intelligent and hard working, who called herself Sia Casters, "with a C" and about whom there were lots of rumors as to why she never married, played the piano.

Mrs. Eleni Vervatos, the amateur opera chorus singer and music instructor at a local high school, was doing the directing. It must have been that fine thread of music that tied this petite, nervous, delicate creature to Manolis Vervatos. Eleni refereed the squabbles between the tenors and the bases, and managed to blend everyone's voices harmoniously, sounding like a bee hive during migration. Only Big Jim Farmanis, who kept missing the hints to find some other way to serve God, sounded like a wasp trapped in a green house.

This Sunday, the Bishop was visiting and the cantors and the choir were showing off, chanting everything twice, once in Greek then in English, stretching the *Kyrie Eleison* and the *Alleluia* till they were out of breath, making the service last for ever.

Volunteering for small chores offered a good chance to step out for a smoke and a face-saving way out of the long sermons.

I got out and helped John Alepakis and Mrs. Cleo Athan, the Hellenic school teacher, with the preparation of the Lenten lunch and the decoration of the hall for the March twenty-fifth celebration, which this year was celebrated two days earlier, on the twenty-third, because it was Sunday.

We hung blue and white paper ribbons from the ceiling, put little Greek paper flags on the tables, and stuck posters of Greece on the walls. We couldn't find portraits of heroes of the period, so we had to settle for the posters of Greek beaches the bureau of tourism had sent us for last year's festival. (Mrs. Athan pinned small flags over the topless bathers.)

The American and Greek flags were placed on either side of the stage.

When the service was finally over, and the bishop seated at the place of honor, the ceremony began.

The Vervatos couple sang the national anthems. Eleni sang the American, clear and melodiously, and Manolis sang the Greek, loudly and badly out of tune. Then the boys and girls of the Hellenic school, ages four through twelve, dressed in traditional costumes of the period, marched around the hall to the tune of a marching song on an overused tape.

One by one, they came to the microphone and under the coaxing of their teacher and parents, overcame shyness and stage fright and recited poems full of pledges to shed their blood to the last drop and fight to their last breath to free the country from the barbarians. Their Greek was accented, which made the sad poems sound funny and those that Alepakis tried to translate into English didn't rhyme and sounded strange.

Kyria Katina recited a poem in Greek about a maiden whose husband had gone abroad, *stin xenihtia*, and then returned to find her married. Everyone applauded loudly; those who understood it were moved by the words and those who did not, by the rendition.

The patriotic fervor was flooding the place. There was no doubt: Any barbarian foolish enough to cross the borders today would be crushed into oblivion.

After the performance, we served a Lenten lunch of fried fish, pickled beets with *skordalia* (garlic sauce, shunned by most teenagers) olives and baked potatoes.

Surprisingly, Margaret and the girls joined me for lunch when their church was over. We had talked about it a few days back but after the big fight we had in the morning I didn't expect to see her.

I didn't think it was my fault and I still think she owes me an apology. It started when she showed me the program from Katerina's ballet recital. My Katerina's picture was just a quarter page, squashed below the half-page photograph of Tony Philips' daughter. I told her she should have gotten a full page add. What will the people say, my daughter's picture being half the size of the Philips' kid?

"If you cared so much for your daughter why didn't you come to the recital? Everybody else's father was there."

"Damn it I told you I couldn't come because we were trying to finish the boiler work on the Berres ship; they wanted her to sail the next day and they are my best customers."

"It's always some deadline, always some rush job, you are never around them; poor Katerina was heartbroken."

"Damn it, I bust my ass to provide for all of you, to keep you nice and comfortable and instead of thanks I am made to look like a villain."

"Listen Niko," Margaret's voice got firm and even. "You are busting your ass all right, but it's because you want to, because you want to prove some cockamamie point to yourself or to somebody but for sure it's not for me and the kids. As a matter of fact sometimes we are made to feel that we are in the way."

"You are an ungrateful bunch, all of you," I shouted and left slamming the door behind me.

When the March twenty-fifth program was over, Father George made a brief speech thanking all those who worked for the preparation of the day's events. He even named me.

Funny how some acts of mischief are turned completely around. A few weeks later, in a parish council general assembly meeting, when it came to electing board members, somebody stood up and said how I was always around to give a hand in the hall and in the church, and how that showed I cared for the community and a bunch of other nice things. By the time he had finished I was too embarrassed to say that I declined the nomination and the next thing I knew, I was the new member of the parish council.

Chapter

18

"The old man doesn't have much left. If you want to see him alive, better hurry over here."

It was five o'clock in the morning. Kostas Karpelas hadn't wasted any time with congenialities.

Kostas was my sister's husband, was about my age, had gotten rich in the olive business and lived in a fancy new house about forty kilometers from my parents. Another one with great *prokopi*.

After I hung up, I lit a cigarette and called my brother, Dimos. His wife said that he was at the farmhouse with my parents. She was getting ready to go there also, Father was indeed not expected to make it.

It seemed the worst time to take off from work. I had a job in the shop for Chicago Modern Machinery that had a tight delivery schedule and I was in the middle of preparing a bid for a big Inert Gas installation job, to be done with a riding crew. There were material prices to be gathered, equipment to be located, work crew to be scheduled. If only I could put this trip off for a few more days.

"You say that every time I ask you to take some time off to do something," Margaret reminded me. "You think nothing will get done if you are not there all the time."

Interesting how some people think that all there is to running a business is to tell others what needs to get done and they'll jump right to it.

"Delegate the tasks, an executive should not micro-manage," a professor of an evening business class I took had said. I would like to see him tell my guys what to do and expect it to be done when he got back from his country club. It might seem to work fine when it's somebody else's money, but when there is only a couple of hundred bucks between you and poverty, micro-managing is what keeps your head above water. I don't think I would last very long if I wasn't there every minute.

I told Margaret about catching one of the helpers sleeping behind the lathe and about walking into the shop just in time to stop one of the fitters from butchering a piece of plate that cost six months groceries, and that if I hadn't been there, they would have welded the conveyor frames for Chicago Machinery with the wrong kind of welding wire. "And that was only yesterday. If I am going to be away for a while, might as well close the doors, because the bank is going to do it for us, for sure. They are going to be using more welding rods for lighting their cigarettes than welding."

"You have your priorities mixed up, you will regret it later," was Margaret's answer.

For most of the morning, I agonized about taking the time off. I could leave Antonios in charge; he had been with me for five of the seven years I had been in business. He could run the shop and deal with the customers - in some cases better than I did; he didn't seem to be as much of a soft touch as I was. I liked the time when a ships' captain, thought that because I was out of town, he could renege on the price we had agreed upon for repairing an electric motor. Antonios kept the motor dangling on the crane thirty feet up in the air for four hours, till the captain counted out the full payment.

Lately though, I had an uneasy feeling about him. He ran the second shift for a while and the production had dropped way off. Some mornings I would find metal shavings on the lathe, when I didn't have any lathe work going on. Moe said that he thought Antonios was taking jobs on the side but I didn't take it too seriously.

At noon, Pete Carras and Stavros Rigotis came by to drop off a Telex and Pete asked me if I wanted to join them for lunch at the Wharf Restaurant.

"Today is the day of the raising of the Holy Cross, It's the name day of all the Stavros, big panigiri (festival) in the village," said Pete when we sat down. Then while staring at the menu, he mumbled: "but my big-shot district attorney son, don't celebrate; his mother made him change his name to Steven." He set the menu down resolutely and patted it with his palm: "We can have anything our heart is craving; Stavros here, kernaye."

"What was that?" asked Stavros alarmed.

"I said you are treating, stingy Hioty; today is your name day and the custom is to treat the guests. You have same name like my father, but he was not tsigounis like you, he spent all his money."

"I'll buy you a drink," Stavros said, conceding.

"You mention your father, I got a call this morning, mine isn't doing so good; I wish I could arrange it so I could go for a few days," I said.

"Don't wish about it, just get on the aero-plane and go. You'll regret it later if you don't," said Pete.

179

He took a sip of the water and lit a cigarette. "My father died on his name day, twenty years ago," he went on, "I was in Rotterdam then, my uncle had to pay the priest to bury him."

The waitress was standing by our table.

"I'll come back," she said after awhile.

"He got the bad sickness and it ate him slowly," continued Pete. "My mother said he was asking for me. I had been on the ship for over a year. I was chief steward on the Glaros, of Manakis Lines. I was going to go home from Lisabon but the company offered a five hundred dollar bonus if I stayed another three months till the ship got to Piraeus. I got the telegram saying he died right after we left Rotterdam. He was a good man."

"Will it all be on one check?" The waitress had returned.

"Yeah, I'll have the soup," said Pete.

"Me too," echoed the rest of us. For a while nobody spoke.

"Five hundred dollars was a lot of money those days, but... don't think about it, do it, get on the aero-plane and go," said Pete.

When I got back to the office, I told Margaret to get a ticket for the earliest flight to Greece.

She got one for the next morning and for the rest of the day I kept bombarding Antonios with instructions and advice on how to run the shop and which man to put on what job.

"Don't you worry," he said. "Haven't I done it before?"

He had, but it was never more than a couple of days.

It was an early flight from Bigport to Atlanta. I sipped coffee and leaned back, running through my mind everything that had happened since I had last visited the village. I was working for someone else then, which didn't impress Father. I started my own company soon after I returned from that trip, hoping to make a lot of money, renovate the Bellmaker's house, make him feel proud of me and show him that all the years abroad had not been wasted.

It has been a constant struggle: dodging bill collectors, meeting payroll and keeping up the payments to the Bellmaker's house. There were many times I felt like dropping everything and going to live in a cave somewhere, forgetting about Taxiarhes, the business and the world.

It was turning around now. It wouldn't be long until I'd get caught up with the bills, start the renovation and show him my prokopi. Just a little longer.

The bump of the landing jarred me back to reality.

I called from the Atlanta airport to tell Antonios what material I had ordered for the Chicago Machinery job, and again from New York, while waiting to board, to tell him not to work anybody overtime. Then I called my sister to tell her I was on my way. With the time difference I figured they would be finished with dinner.

180

"Zoy se logo sou" (Long life to you) said her mother-in-law, recognizing my accented Greek. "He left us a couple of hours ago, everybody is at the farmhouse, I'm looking after the young ones."

I stood there, silent, unable to think of anything, just staring out of the narrow window at the airplanes disappearing in the sky. It was raining.

"Thank you," I said finally, "I will see you tomorrow."

In Atlanta, it was twelve noon, Saturday, September seventeen.

I boarded the plane moving along with the mass of nameless strangers, mechanically going through the motions of showing my boarding pass and finding my seat. I sat by a window and gazed out, oblivious to those around me.

The stewardess touched my shoulder and asked me if I wanted anything to drink. I ordered a scotch and water and when it came, I drank half of it in one swallow and returned to looking out at the sea of puffy white clouds below and the blue emptiness above.

It had been almost eight years since I saw my father.

I tried to imagine how it would be returning home with Father gone. I had never thought that there might come a time when he wouldn't be there. I had been to many funerals and had consoled many friends saying: "None of us will live for ever," or "His time had come," but that was for other people. My father was always going to be there, just like the old fortress of a farmhouse, and the olive trees that surrounded it.

I don't even remember Father getting any older. He always had a gray, prickly, triangular mustache, thin gray hair and walked leaning slightly forward, with his hands behind his back. When he hugged me, his face felt scratchy and smelled like cigarettes.

If he had only lived a little while longer. The Bellmaker's house would have been finished and he would have seen that I was right, that I too had made *prokopi*, better than all the others.

Once in awhile I would get a letter from him bringing me up-to-date with the news of the area in his order of importance. Always some father's son in the village had opened a store or bought a big truck or did some other great thing that showed how well he had succeeded and he became the envy of the villagers and the pride of his parents.

To my news about moving into a bigger house where each child had her own room, about getting a big new car and my business successes, my parents would always remind me of the order of things according to them: "What good are all of those things over there?"

We were not very close, my father and I, but then we were not that far apart either. We disagreed a lot, but I guess in our own way, we did care for each other. I thought that all this talk about his health getting worse was just something they were making up to get me to visit.

181

I tried to remember the good times we had together, but I could only recall the times when I got the switch because the goat ate a fig tree graft, or because the sheep got to the neighbor's bean garden, or because I didn't clean the trash from the irrigation ditch and wasted a whole cistern of water in the middle of the summer. He was a caring and loving father, but I guess when young, one takes the good times for granted, feeling entitled to them, and the only things that remain in the mind for long are the discomforts of discipline.

I wondered what my kids will remember of me.

I had another drink and then I dozed off. I skipped the dinner and from the breakfast tray, I only took the orange juice and the coffee.

The plane landed in Athens just before noon. I changed some money, rented a Ford Escort from Hertz and headed north. Since it was Sunday there was not any traffic on the roads and I drove the little car as fast as it would go.

Passing through the market area of Volos, I bought a black tie from a push cart vendor. A half-hour later, I stopped at my sister's house. Her mother-in-law was the only one there, baby-sitting my sister's two daughters. I changed into a suit and with her reminding me to hurry but to be careful, I continued on. I zigzagged up the steep road, scaring old farmers on their donkeys as I went and sending goats and chickens running for their lives.

As I rounded the last bend and saw the village across the mountain, I could hear the church bell of Agioi Taxiarhes announcing in its mournful toll the death of a parishioner. Each toll, deep and coarse, like the moan of a dying giant, spread over the mountainside, slowly fading. Then, before that sound was completely gone, a new one would leap out of the bell tower and follow.

The house was overflowing with people. They were standing on the balcony, the stairs and the slate-covered patio. They whispered among themselves as they moved aside to let me through. Some shook my hand and murmured condolences.

My brother's wife met me at the door. She gave me a hug, said *"zoy se logo sou"* (long life to you), and put a black arm-band on my left sleeve. My father's casket was on the table in the middle of the living room. My mother and sister were sitting by him, with their backs to the wall. We hugged.

"He kept asking for you," Mother said. "He tried to hold on till you came."

I kept swallowing and I wished I was somewhere alone. I looked around and through the mist in my eyes I saw everyone staring at me. I couldn't think of anything to say. I gave Mother another hug and stood next to her, my hands folded in front.

Father Pandelis started his prayers as soon as the commotion of my arrival subsided. He had been my classmate at the high school but this was the first time I had seen him since he became a priest. His hair were tied in a bun behind his head, outside his tall black hat. His priestly clothes seemed too big and his beard was scraggly. He looked nothing like the sleek, mischievous teenager I had remembered. His first words of chanting startled me; he was way off-key.

He walked out the door chanting the prayers and behind him the cantor and the boy with the censer. The pallbearers picked up their load and followed.

When I was growing up, the procession would follow the three kilometer cobble stone path through the village, pass the Filaretou overlook and the Kartalion elementary school, then struggle uphill for about a kilometer to the church. Now we went in the opposite direction; to the new black-top beach road, about a quarter of a mile away. They put Father in the back of Kostas' truck and everybody squeezed into the available cars. Father Pandelis gave a ride to the cantor and three other people in his battered Fiat.

At the church, the memorial service was brief. We lit candles, the priest and the cantor asked God over and over to forgive all of Father's sins, and then the pallbearers carried him to the cemetery across the street. A couple of guys walked ahead and stopped the traffic of tourist cars and trucks loaded with chestnuts and building supplies, till everyone had crossed. Tourism and commerce don't stop, even for one's death.

The priest chanted: *"aionia i mnimi"* (may his memory be eternal), a couple of times, then said to Mother: "He is not suffering any more, he is with God, Kyra Marigoula," and to me and Dimos: "He was a good man."

Then one by one, the people walked up to Mother and the rest of the family, told us *zoi se logo sou*, (long life to you), and left. George, the deaf-mute, about fifty years old, who used to help on the farm, seemed to be the most heart broken.

My brother and I helped Mother and slowly walked back to the car. My sister's husband stayed behind and took care of the financial obligations: something for the grave digger, something for the priest, the cantor, the boy with the censer, the boy who rang the bell and anyone else that had anything to do with the funeral.

At home Mother asked if we were hungry; she could make some trahana. None of us was. She felt tired, she whispered "good night" and with slow, short steps, she went to bed. The rest of us: my sister Katina and her husband Kostas, my brother Dimos and his wife, sat up late into the night reminiscing about Father.

We were sitting in the *himoniatico*, the winter room, with the big fireplace in the middle of the north wall and a bed on either side of it, the same beds from the time I was growing up. Father's bed was the one on the west side and I shared with Dimo the one on the east side. My mother and sister slept in another room.

The only time I remember my parents sleeping together was when my sister got sick and traded with Father because she had to have her own bed. During the night I heard noises and my suspicious imagination thought they might be working on bringing us another sister. In the morning Mother said that Father kept going to the bathroom for most of the night. "That goat meat we had for supper didn't agree with him," she said.

We never got another sister, so maybe it was the goat meat.

We kept talking and smoking and flicking the ashes in the fireplace. It had turned quite chilly outside and Dimos had a roaring fire going. He always kept a large supply of olive tree firewood in the storeroom and a small one under the bed, for replenishment. He preferred olive wood because it burns with a clean bright flame, unlike chestnut, which pops and smokes and doesn't give out much heat. He would expertly stack the short pieces on top of the grate and around it stand some of the long ones upright and some horizontal, sticking out of the hearth and moving them closer as their ends burned.

"This is where you two tried to boil me, remember?" said my sister when Dimos was putting some fresh wood in the fire. The others hadn't heard the story and asked what it was about.

For the sake of accuracy, I undertook to tell it. I told them that when our Katina was four years old, around this time of the year, on a rainy day, Mother had a strong fire going, to heat up a kettle of water to cook lentils. Dimos and I were playing war, each having one of these beds for a castle and bombarding each other with pillows. Katina was playing in front of the fireplace, totally unconcerned by the heavy artillery flying overhead. At one point, one of us cried "Attack!"

"It was you," interrupted Dimos.

"No, it was you, I'm remembering it," I said. Anyway, we jumped down from the bed, stepping on the wood that was sticking out from the hearth. That tipped over the kettle with the boiling water, dousing Katina from head to toe.

Mother heard her screams and came running up. She took Katina's clothes off, and with them came most of her skin. Her face was turning purple from crying so hard. Mother sent us to bring the tomato paste from the store room and she covered Katina's body with it. Back then we used to make enough tomato paste in the fall to last us for a year. We kept it in jars with a layer of wax on top. She used almost the whole year's supply. Eventually all of her skin came off, but there were no scars left.

"Funny how time flies, can't believe our little Katina is a grown-up, married, with kids," I concluded.

"I've been married five years now."

"You are still on your honeymoon then. I've been married sixteen," I said.

"Yes, I remember the day you got married," she reflected. "It was Saturday, we were picking olives behind the chapel of Agei Anargiri, in Paraskevi. Father looked up at the sun and said: "It's getting evening, Nikos will be getting married about now. Why don't you go over to the church and light the candles?" Till then, he always hoped you might come back; his biggest fear was that nobody would stay to look after the farm; that everybody would leave the village."

Next morning, Mother said that it's the custom to do a good house-cleaning after someone has died in the house. It was the first time I had heard of such a custom.

"You were in such a hurry to leave the village, it's no wonder you haven't learned anything about your roots," she said. I guess the wise ancestors did it for health reasons, or as a distraction from grief, or maybe as a way of getting smart alecky sons to help their mothers with the house chores.

So once again, we locked up the house in Taxiarhes, piled into my car and drove to the farm house in Paraskevi. A few things were different this time; we didn't have the chickens and the sheep with us; Mother had somebody looking after them at the farm.

On the way out of the village, we drove by grandfather's monument: a marble obelisk by the side of the road, with a wreath carved near the top and a list of twelve names below it. A small star of David was next to one name. The monument used to be in a prominent spot by the square, but some members of the village council feared it might offend the hordes of German tourists and they moved it to a less conspicuous place.

As we went past it, Mother crossed herself and murmured: *Eh patera, by now, you probably met each other again; he never filled your eye, but he was a good husband."*

Her father had been the village blacksmith. He had never been impressed with the citified looks of his son in-law.

From what I was told, he must have been a kind and gentle man. Mother told me that I used to climb on his lap and ask him to play the bouzouki. I didn't remember any of it. I was about two-and-a-half years old when the Germans shot him, together with Kostas Liappis' grandfather and twelve other villagers, for not telling who amongst them was the Jew. For their silence, they got their names engraved on the marble obelisk. My grandfather's was right below the Jewish fellow's, whose son, years later, paid for the monument.

At the point where the road branched off toward the farmhouse, an arrow on a sign directed in English and German: To Paraskevi beach. I was wondering if the German soldier who took my mother's earrings and father's wedding ring ever came back for vacation.

A clay road now zigzagged its way down the mountain, passing behind our farm house on its way to the beach. We parked under a lemon tree.

The farm house stood in the middle of the olive grove, overlooking the sea. Nothing seemed to have changed all those years; the same cracks in the stucco, the same faded look on the green shutters, the same stoic look of endurance.

The tall mulberry tree by the chicken house and the table with the slate top from the

Propan quarry at the corner of the flagstone patio, were still there. And the quietness was still there. The constant murmur of the waves breaking on the shore and the occasional cry of a seagull only highlighted the silence. As a child I found that serenity suffocating; now it felt relaxing.

"It hasn't changed much," I told Dimos, but before he could answer, the ear-splitting noise of a small engine shattered the tranquillity. I looked toward the road and saw a guy riding a small motorcycle, with a mountainous bundle of freshly cut hay on the back of it, struggling to make it up the hill.

Dimos waited till he went by. "That was Spyros Kouvelos. His father had the gray mare that limped, remember?" he said when he could be heard.

We were soon assigned our chores. Mother had the work list already drawn up in her head. We started with the fireplace chimney. "It hasn't been done since it caught on fire years ago; need to do that first before we clean the rooms," she said.

Dimos volunteered to cut a supply of holly tree branches. We tied them in a bundle in the middle of a thin rope. Then, out of concern for my safety, he volunteered to climb on the roof and drop one end of the line down the chimney.

The bundle fit snugly inside the chimney and as I stood inside the fireplace pulling the line down, the stiff, curly, leaves of the branches scraped the walls clean, depositing decades of accumulated soot on my head. We pulled the rope up and down a few dozen times and I declared the chimney: "clean as a gun barrel." Katina had a good laugh when she saw me step out of the fireplace. She ran and got Mother, who managed to crack a smile. Just for that, it was worth it, and I gave up thinking how to get even with Dimos.

When we finished with the fireplace, the women started cleaning the room, running a damp cloth over everything, changing the curtains, taking the mattress and blankets outside and giving them a vigorous beating. I helped Dimos cut and stack firewood.

It was early in the afternoon when somebody suggested that we stop for lunch. We had been going strong since early in the morning. I went over to the lean-to on the north side of the house, where Mother was doing the washing, got a bucket of hot water from the caldron and tried to shower while standing behind the bed sheets hanging on the clothes line. For pouring water over my head, I used an enamel-coated cup that had been my own drinking cup when I was a kid; now chipped and leaking, it was demoted to laundry service. It took some vigorous scrubbing to rinse out the strange smelling lather from Mother's homemade soap. She didn't like the scented soaps Dimos and Katina brought for her. She kept them in Taxiarhes for the guests.

"It's a sin to waste what God gives you," she always said. And so, every year when Mr. Gourgiotis would press the olives that God gave us, she would take the oil that was not fit for cooking or the church lamps and make soap.

I cleaned up in time for the *trahana* to be served.

186

Trahana is the area's version of survival food. It has the consistency of runny oatmeal and tastes like cheesy grits. Mother had given me the recipe to pass it on to Margaret. Margaret never attempted to make any. The recipe is stored, together with lots of other recipes, on the inside cover of "The Art of Greek Cooking" cookbook, that somebody gave her as a wedding present. It goes something like this:

> *Put two kilos of boiled goat's milk in a clay pot (tsoukali), with a pinch of salt and let it sit four to five days, till it sets. Keep turning it with the spoon till curdled. Add semolina flour till it's thick and can be kneaded into patties (It takes about half a kilo of flour). Knead into patties about the size of your palm and about the thickness of your small finger. Spread it in a sunny spot, turning over so it dries evenly.*
>
> *Break into small pieces and pass through coarse sifter (koskino). Spread again in sunny spot till completely dry. Take care to keep bugs, birds, cats, ants and mischievous kids away from it. (Dimos and I used to make cat paw imprints on it with our thumb and two fingers, then watch Mother fuss, thinking the cat had walked across it).*
>
> *Store in cloth bag, in dry place. For better preservation and longer life, put in oven at high heat, for about fifteen minutes. To prepare, add one part of trahana to three parts of boiling water and cook for about ten minutes.*
>
> *It tastes even better when pieces of spicy home-made sausage are cooked with it.*

Every woman in the village has her own secret ingredient she puts in it; some add crumbled dry feta cheese, some yogurt, even ground pepper, but I am sure my mother's *trahana* would win ribbons at any county fair.

Katina made a salad with lots of onions, olives and tomatoes and Dimos brought out some of his wine. It was dark-red and had a smooth taste. He and Uncle Apostolis, my mother's brother, collaborate in making wine every year from our grapes, which they nurture with religious devotion.

"This is the last of this year's tomatoes," said Mother. She stood by the table, cutting the round loaf of home-made bread and passing it to us. "With your father sick most of the time, I didn't get to plant a big garden." She finished cutting the bread and sat down. "And if I did, who was going to eat it? All of you were too good to stay in the village."

When lunch was over, the women started washing the dishes before retiring for the afternoon nap. Dimos was already in bed upstairs. The sound of his rhythmic snoring, like small waves on a pebble beach, rolled down the steps.

Midday naps were something I never got used to. As a child, I would invent all sorts of excuses to get out of it.

187

I said I was going to walk around the farm.

"I hope you remember where the boundaries are," said Mother. "Your father's biggest fear was that none of you would care about the place and the neighbors would take it, little by little." She was standing in the middle of the room, drying her hands on her apron. Her brown eyes misted as she struggled not to cry.

"He was lying over there," she pointed to the bed by the fireplace. "I was sitting on that stool talking to him and rubbing his hand. He turned and looked at me, as if he was going to smile, then tried to squeeze my hand and whispered: *"Kane kalo koumando"* (steer a good course), then his hand went limp and he was gone." She was sobbing and wiping her eyes with her apron. I hugged her and sat on the freshly made bed with her.

"At least he is not suffering any more," I said.

The crying slowly eased, she laid her head on the pillow and soon she dozed off.

I went outside, lit a cigarette and walked towards the road. A rooster was fertilizing a hen's eggs in the chicken coop. When I was ten, I forgot to close the door of the roosting shed the evening before New Year's eve. The fox came during the night and took all fourteen of the chickens and a big rooster, the one mother was going to stuff for the New Year's meal. Instead, we nibbled on vegetable stew while everyone looked at me as an outcast and kept repeating that it was an omen of a bad year.

I walked toward *Lithos*, a small olive grove by the sea, about fifteen minutes walk from the house.

The narrow path leading to the grove was overgrown. Everybody lived in the city now and those who live in the farms drive noisy motorcycles.

The path went by *Kria Vrisi*, (cold spring) the big stone fountain, in the little ravine, at the bottom of a strawberry tree forest. At that time, it was the area's only water supply. Coming here to fill our clay jug for the house's drinking water, was a chore done at least once a day. Through the years, I remember at least four broken jugs and three whippings.

In those years the water gushed from the rock onto a cistern at the roots of a centuries-old plane tree. Now it was reduced to a small, smooth flow, like a kitchen faucet. I stooped down and drank out of the marble bowl. It was crisp and icy cold. Above the bowl was chiseled in a marble slab: Built by expenditure of Athanasios Gourgiotis, year 1935.

In the summers this was the coolest place around. People working in the fields would come here on their mid-day break to eat their lunch and doze off under the cool shade of the huge plane tree. The water was gathered in the bho (cistern), and the farmers would drain it three times a day to water their crops, in a sequence that had been established generations ago: One farmer would open the cistern in the morning and when emptied, the next one would close it and open it at noon. Then the next guy would do the same, and in the evening, the lucky farmer would close it and open it following morning. That was the most desirable turn, since it accumulated the most water.

In this dry, water-starved area where each drop of water was a precious commodity, opening the cistern too late or closing it too early was a cause for heated, drawn-out disputes. Always, someone from the farmer's family, would guard against the next guy opening the crude cistern plug too much, which would make the water jump out of the ditch, or closing it too early, trapping a few extra drops in the cistern. If the wives were lucky enough to be too far along in their pregnancy, they got to stand guard duty in the cool ravine under the thick shade of the plane tree, otherwise they, or the children did the irrigating and the farmer did the guarding.

Nobody was irrigating now. The cistern was open, the water running in the creek.

A few yards from there was Mr. Gourgiotis' olive pressing plant. During harvest time this used to be the busiest place around. Farmers brought their sacks of olives on their mules, then sat on the benches around the furnace watching the donkey turn the millstones and the men work the press that squeezed the olive pulp. The oil, golden-green, flowed from the press to the collecting vat and from there, under the vigilant eyes of the farmer, was poured into containers to be loaded for the trip home. While waiting, they swapped war stories and munched on bread toasted by the roaring cauldron fire and dipped it into fresh oil.

The breeze carried the aroma of the freshly pressed oil down the little valley and I remember my grandmother whenever she got a whiff of it, she would cross herself and whisper thanks to God.

The place had been sold to some crazy German who had turned it into a strange looking vacation house. The two mill-stones used to crush the olives were now laying flat, on either side of the door, like benches, their center holes serving as ashtrays. I felt my stomach tightening.

I kept on going through the winding footpath, when I realized I was almost running. I slowed down and smiled as I looked at the cause of my running: I was passing the Themelis house. There was no danger now, old Mr. Themelis and his wife were long dead. I never attempted again to imitate the sound of the *bourou*, (the shell that sailing ships use as a horn), that caused such a turmoil so many years ago.

I passed Agei Anargyri, the small white-washed chapel surrounded by large oak trees that the original owner of our land had built over a hundred years ago. A short distance from there was the olive grove which we called *Lithos* (boulder), on account of the huge boulder in the middle of it. It was my favorite place of solitude and contemplation.

Many years earlier, I had made a throne at the top of the boulder, from where I stared at the horizon. Someone had done the same thing long before I came along. He had carved: M.N.K. 1919, on a clear, smooth spot on the rock. I'd wondered who he might have been. Next to it, I had spent two days carving out in neat, large letters: Nikolaos K. Pilios, with the year under it. I framed the whole thing in what was supposed to be the outline of a sailing ship. Then I'd spent some time admiring it; from now on, whoever saw it would know that I had been here. Then the neighbors' shouting snapped me out of my daydreaming. The sheep had gotten into his garden and were destroying the bean rows.

That night I paid dearly for my attempt at immortality.

The fig tree that caused Father to break a mulberry switch on me when the goat ate the graft, was still there, at the top of the field. The graft had re-sprouted and grown into a twisted, knobby, tree that looked like something out of a Japanese painting. Father had made a bed of fern under it and used to sit with his back resting on the trunk. From there, he could see the entire field.

I poked around the bed with my foot to scare whatever might be sleeping under it and sat down. The fern was dry and crumbled. Father hadn't been here for quite a while. I leaned back and rested my back on the trunk.

The last time I saw Father happy was on this spot. It was on the second week of my first visit, after being away for twelve years. On the advice of Dimos, I had driven to Volos and bought Father's birthday present: a three horsepower McCulloch chain saw. He seemed very pleased with it.

"I was afraid you might get me some fancy-smelling soaps and fluffy towels," he joked, alluding to "sissyish grooming habits of city people."

Later that day, while Margaret and the girls were at the beach, father suggested we try out the chain saw. "The last storm uprooted a couple of apple trees over in *Lithos*; we could initiate your gift on those," he said.

Dimos and I cut up the two trees, and then, since the new toy was working so well, we cut some olive tree branches that had broken, and some wild chestnut trees to make grape arbor poles. We stacked the firewood to be loaded on the donkey, and we burned all the thin stuff.

Father had re-lined his bed under the fig tree with fresh fern, slowly eased down on it and watched his two sons work; sleeves rolled up, sweaty, with ashes and saw dust stuck all over us. He would recall some joke about city life or city men and then he would laugh heartily at it. I am sure at that moment, in my father's mind, life presented to him its ideal setting.

At mid-day, Mother brought lunch.

"I thought you would be too busy playing with your new toy, to come for lunch," she said. On a fresh bed of fern she laid a blue and white checkered table cloth and spread out the food.

"Something to hold you till supper," she said.

Father broke the tomatoes into quarters with his fingers which made the torn parts look like they were sugar coated. He said they taste better cut that way than when they're cut with a knife. Then he pounded a couple of onions with his fist to rid them of the burning juices and cut them in quarters. Mother had also brought olives, feta, a round loaf of bread, fresh out of the oven, and three smoked herrings that Dimos roasted lightly on the fire. She even brought a bottle of Dimos' wine and four glasses. Father crossed the back of the bread-loaf with the knife and cut big pieces for everyone.

Under the shade of the old fig tree, overlooking the olive grove and the blue Aegean beyond, that tranquil autumn afternoon, we munched on simple food, toasted to each other's health, to the joy of the reunion and the fulfillment of everyone's dreams. I offered Father and Dimos American cigarettes, we leaned back against the tree and smoked in silence.

It was a rare tranquil moment. Everything we could see and hear was soothing: A few white puffy clouds moving slowly with the soft breeze, a sheep bleating in the ravine, the murmur of the waves gently breaking on the shore. And further out, the white sails of a caique passing in front of the gray silhouette of the island of Skiathos.

"This is the life," declared Father.

For once, we had both agreed on something.

When I got back to the house the others were just waking up.

The next day, my brother and sister returned to their homes and their jobs.

Chapter | 19

*T*wo days after the funeral, when Mother went upstairs for her midday nap I went to the Bellmaker's house. I lingered in each room, looking at the cracked plaster, the faded flowery designs on the ceiling and the remnants of the carved molding. In my mind, I saw everything glow with fresh paint and shiny fixtures. Tenderly, as though caressing, I run my hand over the door frames and the stair rails. It felt like home, it felt like cuddling in mother's lap.

When I got out, the sun was about to set behind the village of Xourihti. In the yard, Kyra Amalia was concentrating in untangling a rope from a large blackberry bush in the middle of the patio. She turned towards the sound of my steps and let out a startled cry as she stood up.

"Oh Mr. Niko, I didn't hear you coming," she said then continued, gingerly, to unweave the loose end of the rope out of the thorny bush while mumbling curses at the sheep. "Don't know how the demonized animal gets itself so tangled up all the time."

The entangled black-faced sheep stared at her busy hands, showing neither remorse nor gratitude. Kyra Amalia gave the line a final tug then pulled the sheep behind her and tied it further down the field.

"Your father, God rest his soul, was a good man, I cried for hours when I heard he left us. God rest his soul" she said when she started back, then crossed herself.

"Thank you," I said. "I still can't believe he isn't here."

I lit a cigarette and gazed at what used to be the patio of the Bellmaker's house. It was covered with blackberry vines, nettle weeds and sheep droppings, but back, way back, in the glory-days of the house, this patio was where the great the feasts had taken place — where acetylene lanterns transformed the night into day, and important people visiting from far-away places danced to the tunes of the best musicians on the mountain. Why couldn't have Father have lived just for a little longer? Soon I'll be starting the renovation and I'll have it just like it was before; even better.

After a couple of puffs I started coughing and I ground the cigarette in the dirt.

Kyra Amalia sat on a tree-stump with a basket and a mound of apples in front of her. She cut the apples in quarters with a long knife and put them in the basket. "They like the apples, but I have to cut them because they'll choke." She nodded towards the goats. Then noticing that I was looking at the apple trees surrounding the house, she hasten to add: "They didn't have very good crop this year, and what little they had, it was all shriveled and wormy. I picked all these off the ground." She held one in my direction, as proof that it had worms. "The trees need to be plowed and manured and pruned."

A brown-and-white goat was standing on her hind legs nibbling at the lower branches of an apple tree. Kyra Amalia picked up a stone and hurled it in her direction. "Ah, you greedy demon, don't you like what's on the ground?" She chastised.

She resumed the apple cutting. "You should come more often, your father, God rest his soul, his biggest heartache was that you settled in foreign land."

"I'll be coming," I said.

"You should, your poor mother, she's going to be all alone. She's not so young anymore. Farms and houses, they need their masters to look after them; when they're left on their own they go to waste."

She stood up and scanned the area, making sure the sheep and the goats were all accounted for. She loosened up her black kerchief, pushed some of her gray hair back and re-tied it.

"Mr. Niko," she said when she started her apple cutting again, "I wanted to ask you, when are you planning to start fixing up the house?

"Soon," I said. "soon; probably the next time I come here."

"My sister's boy, Panos Stenos, remember him? You grew up together. He is a contractor, he'll do you a good job. Talk to him when you get ready."

I said I would, and went for a walk around the property.

When I got back from the Bellmaker's house Mother showed me the invitation. "You should go," she said, "somebody should represent our family, but don't stay when the music starts; it wouldn't be proper."

The invitation was handwritten, in calligraphy style, with lots of tails and curlicues: "Come, help us celebrate the opening of our new addition to the famous VILLA GIANNIS. Great food and dancing to the music by the Progidis band, after prayers by Father Pandelis."

"Katina Patekas' daughter, Niki, wrote them," said Mother noticing I was examining the hand-writing. "She's the oldest of the two. The other one is just as smart; they're both at the top of their class. They get all kinds of awards and honors." She sighed: "Some mothers, are so lucky. You wanted to be the smart-aleck, you used to call her Mount Katina and say she had 'a nose like cucumber and a mustache like a pirate,' remember?" (this last part in a squeaky imitation my teenage voice). "He's having his open house the day before I leave," I said, "I'll be packing, I won't have time to go."

"It won't kill you to stop for a few minutes to tell him 'congratulations' and wish him 'good business,' we're relatives, you know?"

I went to Giannako's place after Sunday's church service. I walked up the hill slowly and stopped often to look at the view. It was one of those balmy, fall days when the sun and the breeze and everything else seem soft and gentle and you wish it would last for ever. The leaves of the chestnut trees had just begun to turn reddish-brown. Higher up, the beech trees had covered the mountainside with a golden blanket that glittered in the breeze.

At Giannako's place it looked like everyone in the village had come for the open house, all dressed in their Sunday clothes, talking lively and joking and laughing loudly. Even the new mayor, who was elected a month earlier, was there, (the only one with a tie, the clip-on kind).

There were blue-and-white streamers stretched on the underside of the grape arbor and small Greek flags tied on the arbor posts. A big Greek flag, was fluttering from the second floor balcony.

At the edge of each step of all the stairs, and along the patio perimeter, flowers were in full bloom, planted in white-washed square feta cans - mostly gardenias. Spyros, the gardenia producer, closely scrutinized them to determine their origin.

On the far side of the patio, two lambs were slowly roasting on spits turned by the Giannakos sons. Patekas' oldest daughter, the calligraphy artist, was standing next to the oldest one, smiling and dreamy-eyed. Her mother, still firm and curvy and sensuous enough to tempt a saint, was examining the Giannakos establishment with the critical eye of a competitor. When she saw me, she came over and gave me a hug making contact with all the curvy parts, and kissed me on both cheeks. (No sign of "cucumber nose" or "pirate mustache." Was the prolonged hug a sympathy hug, or was she really glad to see me? Maybe she was just rubbing it in.

On a long table at the end of the patio, there were platters, loaded with mounds of olives, and cheeses and meat balls and spinach triangles and stuffed grapevine leaves and fancy pastries, enough to feed an army.

Tables covered in checkered blue-and-white plastic tablecloths were set up in rows, in the parking lot and around the patio, leaving an open space in the center, under the arbor, for the dancing.

Progidi, the best clarinet player in the area, and his three-man band were tuning their instruments at one corner of the patio.

People wandered in and out of the "new wing," looking awe-struck, as if they had toured the cathedral of Saint Sophia. I remembered when old Manetas used to keep the mule and the goats in that "new wing," till he gave the house to Giannis Giannakos as a dowry. All Giannis did was to white-wash the walls to kill the manure smell and divide it up into closet-size rooms. He hewed a few chestnut poles for rafters, because they didn't cost him anything, coming from his father-in-law's grove, and the newspaper guy and some of the schoolteachers were congratulating him for "preserving the architectural style of the area." Some people have all the luck.

Father Pandelis got there shortly after I did. Giannakos' wife, plump and radiant and constantly in motion, ushered him into a room where he changed into his priestly clothes and when he came out he stood by a small table covered with white tablecloth that Mrs. Giannakos had set up.

The new mayor whistled by putting two fingers in his mouth, then shouted: "Quiet everybody, the priest is going to read."

The priest read his prayers, sprinkled the building and everyone with the blessed water, wished *kaloriziko* (may it bring you good fortune), to the beaming Mr. and Mrs. Giannakos and stepped aside to make room for the mayor.

The mayor cleared his throat a couple of times, then loud enough to be heard on the next mountain, he thanked God on behalf of the village for sending us progressive, hard-working citizens like Mr. and Mrs. Giannakos, who contribute so much to the advancement of the community and spread the good name of Taxiarhes far and wide. He rambled on about how close friends he and Giannis were, how they both shared the same vision of turning our village into something that would make the people in Switzerland die of envy.

"Somebody should tell him that election time is over," whispered a guy next to me.

The Giannakos couple stood next to the mayor, both with smiles that exposed every gold and silver tooth.

He ended his speech just as one lamb came off the fire and was being cut up. There was a surge towards the food table and people started loading their flowery paper plates.

I didn't feel hungry. I sipped on a Coca Cola and listened to a guy talk about how many baskets of mushrooms had gathered the day before. Giannis, wearing a big red rosebud on the lapel of a dandelion-green jacket, came over and gave me a hug. "He was like a father to me," he said, "I still can't believe it."

I mumbled something that sounded like thanks and congratulations and then I said I have to go get ready for the trip.

On the way back, I stopped at Kostas Liappis' bakery. He was one of the few that were absent from Giannako's "bragfest." He had campaigned hard for mayor and was still grieving over the loss.

I didn't see anybody inside the bakery so I walked towards the back of the building calling Kostas' name. I found him hanging laundry on a line stretched between two linden trees.

"The wife is still in the hospital and the daughter has to study for the university entrance exams," he said while clipping pins on a shirt. He dried his hands and gave me a hug. "It's a good thing I was in the army, you learn to do these things."

I followed him into the bakery. He seemed to have aged more than the few years that it had been since I last saw him. His walk wasn't as springy as before, and there were quite a few gray hair above the ears.

"Sit down," he said pointing to the bench across from the counter. "I've been planning to do some renovating and get some more furniture in here, but always something gets in the way."

"I didn't know your wife was in the hospital," I said, "nothing serious, I hope."

"When God wants to test you, He puts you through trials like mine; but anyway, this too shall pass," he said with a sigh. "She slipped down the front door steps and ended up with a broken hip and three broken ribs. It happened the day after your father's funeral, God rest his soul. I still say thank God it wasn't worse." Then apologetically, "I didn't ask you, what can I offer you?"

I said I'd have a lemonade.

He took two bottles of EPSA lemonade out of the cooler and sat next to me. We clinked our bottles. He wished me welcome and condolences for my father: "He was a good man." He drank some of the lemonade and continued: "Now, the doctor says she needs to stay in the hospital one more week for observations, and I am driving back and forth to the city to be with her."

He took out a pack of cigarettes, offered me one and after we both lit, he went on. "It would have been nice to have a hospital in our village, our clean air can heal better than any city doctors. And it would create permanent jobs, and people wouldn't have to put up with the city noise and pollution and traffic to go to the hospital. It was going to be my top priority when I got elected, but that windbag promised to make everybody rich." With his head, he nodded towards Giannako's house from where the Progidi's clarinet was blaring down the mountainside.

"Eh, well, I'll do it next time; it won't take long to find out what a blabbermouth they voted for."

We talked about the village, and about mutual acquaintances who now lived in Germany or other parts of the world, and about our kids and about our own younger days. It was late afternoon when I got up to leave.

Mother was sitting by the kitchen window, knitting something with white yarn. I gave her a full report: Who was there, what they wore, what food they served.

"The church was almost empty, but for the free food and the drink, they show up. That's why God has turned his face from us," she said.

I told her that Giannakos and the new mayor plan to put the Swiss out of business.

"Ah, that clown, he fooled the village into voting for him; people can be so stupid sometimes." She put down her knitting and changed yarns. She carefully connected a golden yellow roll of yarn.

I asked her what she was knitting.

"It's going to be a blouse for your sister's oldest," she said, showing me the twelve inches of knitted material; fluffy white, with golden yellow stripes.

"It will be pretty," I said.

"Yours are too far away for their grandmother to do anything for them." She started moving the needles faster, looping the yarn with her fingers at a speed that would make a court stenographer envious.

She let out a sigh. "And if I did, they would be too embarrassed to wear something made by their strange grandmother." She let out another sigh. "Who would have guessed it that Giannis Giannakos would turn out to be so Big and Great. It was your father's heartbreak: other people's sons making great prokopi and his getting lost in foreign lands."

I couldn't think of anything that would be appropriate to say at the time. After a while, I said that I felt tired and I was going to bed and went upstairs.

The next day, with the expert help of Dimos, we grafted about two dozen trees around the Bellmaker's house. I wanted to have every fruit tree the climate would support. We grafted *firikia* apples, *riglotes* and *tzanera* plums, and apricots, and *kristalia* pears, the sweet, juicy kind whose juices run down your face when you bite into them.

I made copies of the property plot and spent quite a bit of time sketching the layout of the landscape: One acre for vegetable gardens on a well drained, sunny spot, a couple of acres for fruit trees, a wooded strip about fifteen meters wide around the property to give it depth and privacy, and a couple of acres around the house for flower gardens.

I looked again into another house Pavlos Stenos was building and again I was pleased with the kind of work he was doing; I made up my mind that's who I was going to use for the Bellmaker's house renovation.

TWA flight No. 564 took off from Athens at eleven in the morning. Estimated time of arrival at Kennedy airport: three in the afternoon. I took a long sip of the scotch and water and leaned back.

I reached into my shirt pocket for my cigarettes, then I remembered that I swore: starting today, I would quit smoking. (Dimos had told me that father died of throat cancer.)

I sucked on my pen, then scribbled on the napkin.

Next to me sat an elderly woman in a dark-blue, almost black, dress and matching kerchief that seemed not to know what to do with her hands. After a while she asked if the evenings in America were at the same time as in Greece. Her son had told her that the plane arrived in the evening. He was going to meet her and they would drive to *Kon-ne-kti-kat*. She was going to America for the baptism of her grandson, she said. Her son was a big boss in a big company. She showed me his business card: NEW ENGLAND RESTAURANT SUPPLY, INC., George Thompson, Sales Representative.

"His real name is Giorgos Tomarakis, but the Americans didn't know how to say it and he changed it," she said. "His company sends him all over the country, he does not have time to come visit any more."

"He must be an important man," I said and reached for my brief case.

"He is, he is. They couldn't keep the shop open without him. He paid for my ticket in America and they had it waiting for me at the airport in Athens." She paused, then went on: "His sister came out real smart too, she is teaching school in Mykonos. Both my kids have made good *prokopi*."

I didn't answer. I pretended to be absorbed reading my notes. I had called Margaret from the airport and she had brought me up-to-date on what was happening at home and in the shop: I need to have a talk with Maria, she's getting too independent; Nicole's team won the volley ball tournament, Katerina is going to need braces. Antonios called in sick two days last week and Floyd ran the shop, the guy from Gulf States Fasteners called and said the stainless steel bolts had to be special-ordered from Chicago and it would take a week to get them and Pete Carras brought a telex the other day from Hios Shipping. "It wasn't from Captain Emons this time, it was from a Laym-by-days," Margaret said.

"Lambidis," I corrected, "what did he want?"

"Says to contact him regarding the *Halcyon* account. He called again this morning and left a number for you in New Orleans."

As I read my notes again I felt the need for a cigarette. The mention of the tanker Halcyon always had that effect on me. That heap of rust which by some miracle it was still kept afloat, had given me one of the worst scares of my life.

Hios Shipping had talked a group of gullible investors into rescuing her from the scrap yard, then slapped some fresh paint on and appointed themselves her managers. Captain Emons had talked Captain Stewart of ESSO Petroleum into giving her a three year charter. We had done the cargo piping modification to bring the ship into compliance with the latest pollution control regulations; a hot, dirty job under the best of circumstances. It consisted of adding huge new sections of pipe, some three feet in diameter, while she sailed from Corpus Christi to Aruba, then back to Houston.

We worked at the bottom of the hold. Although the crew had washed the holds, there was still a film of oil coating everything, making every step feel like an attempt to climb an icy slope with rubber boots. Simple things, like turning a wrench to tighten the flange bolts, or walking a few steps, required major effort. Swinging a hammer or pulling on the chain hoist became a painful, tortuous operation. We were all covered in slimy, smelly, crude oil.

We would work for a couple of hours, then slither up the ladder a hundred and twenty feet straight up to the deck, collapse for about thirty minutes, cool off, and dive back down.

Victor Easterman was one of the new helpers who started when I got the *Halkyon* job. Victor, with glasses thicker than lighthouse lenses, was also a poet, a philosopher an intellectual and a few other noble, nonproductive things. He said he was working on a maritime novel and was gathering material. I told him not to talk to anyone about it and to watch his step on the ships. One time while climbing the ladder to the deck, he froze half way up. He wrapped his hands tight around the oily ladder and was not planning to move from there till they scraped the ship. Antonios, coming behind him tried to help: "Don't look down, just keep your eyes to the top, one more step, we are almost there," he urged pushing gently.

It took the ship's bosun a whole hour to hoist him out.

From then on, he stayed on deck, cleaning things and passing tools to those below.

We got a lot of compliments about the job from the ESSO representative who came to do the inspection before agreeing to charter the ship. I sent my regards to Captain Stewart and we got the hell off that ship as fast as we could.

We were supposed to get paid within thirty days, but two months later, we still hadn't seen a penny.

I got up from my seat and stretched for a while. It seemed that sitting slumped for a long time made my chest hurt and made it hard to breathe. Margaret had said I should see a doctor about it, but I figured it was nothing but a muscle cramp.

When I got back to my seat, the old lady was looking at a stack of photographs. As soon as I sat down she started showing them to me, with long explanations about every one of them.

I agreed, the baby had his father's eyes, and her son's house (with him standing in front) was a palace, and her daughter's daughter looked just like her grandmother, and her daughter's lawyer-husband looked very prosperous and she did deserve to be proud of the success of her children. I kept yawning and pretending to be falling asleep.

Margaret met me at the airport.

At the shop the next day, Antonios told me that he needed to take a couple of weeks off for "important family reasons." I told him he picked a hell of a time to get in a fight with his wife.

Chapter

20

Next day, I called the New Orleans number and asked for Mr. Stelios Lambidis as soon as I finished with my rounds in the shop. He was out, and I left my number to call me back.

"I have been authorized to settle your account," a wise-guy style voice said when he called back near the end of the day, "but first there are some adjustments that will have to be made."

I never liked it when port engineers make "adjustments" to my invoices; they are always downward.

"Where is Captain Emons?" I asked.

The quick, blunt answer startled me, then I felt sad. The heart attack was one deal Captain Emons couldn't negotiate his way out of.

"I am handling all of his projects now," the overconfident voice said, then started listing what would have to be deducted from my invoice because, as he put it, "they were owner's expenditures for my account." By the time he got to the penalties, I would have to pay back most of the advance I had managed to squeeze out of them.

I told him what I thought of his "adjustments," in plain waterfront vocabulary.

"It's all documented," Stelios Lambidis said, calm and sure. "The dates your men missed work, the cost of feeding your people, everything. I have the file with me."

"Damn it, it was your captain and that idiot you have as a chief engineer that made things difficult; and the only days we didn't work were when nobody could stand up."

"The captain's log says the sea was calm."

"Bullshit!"

"Listen," he said, "I will be in New Orleans till tomorrow night. If we have a meeting, we might work something out."

"It doesn't look like I got much choice," I said.

"You know where the hotel is. I'll be expecting you around ten o'clock tomorrow then. Ask for me at the desk."

The receptionist of the New Orleans Holiday Inn said Mr. Stelios Lambidis was expecting me and she pointed him out, sitting at a center table at the restaurant. I walked up to the table and stood across from him.

He was in his mid-forties, plump, with two shifty eyes that I swore could X-ray a wallet through a lead jacket.

The waitress had just unloaded a plate with three eggs, sunny side up, surrounded by home-fried potatoes, a steak the size of Texas and another plate with a stack of toast.

"Sit down," he said when I introduced myself, and with a loaded fork on his left hand he pointed to a chair. "You want something to eat?"

"Just coffee," I said.

"One American coffee for my friend and some tomato catsup for me," he told the waitress, standing by the table.

His English showed he had been educated in England. To me, Stelios spoke in Greek, with the accent of a Piraeus native.

"This is today's breakfast and yesterday's supper," he said catching my glance of the plate. He unloaded the fork, spread ketchup over his eggs and started sawing into the steak. "The ship did not leave until early this morning. Had a hell of a time with the cargo pumps," he added when he could speak.

"I didn't know the *Halkyon* was in port," I said.

"No, it was a ship we chartered. The *Halcyon* is in Europe, she is not coming to America anymore. Too many regulations."

"Let's talk about my invoice," I said.

He dipped a piece of meat into the egg yoke with a twisting motion, then brought it slowly to his mouth and chewed with relish while staring at the plate.

"You have to agree," he finally said, "the job took much longer than you had said in the beginning. And the workmanship was very poor."

That was a familiar line. The "discount by intimidation" approach. It must be in every port engineer's training manual. A pompous ass named William Petersen had introduced me to it when I first started in the business.

"The weather was shit! I don't care how much your captain is doctoring the log, and the help you promised never came. Anyway, it was a fixed-price job, so it's my ass. As for the workmanship, it was excellent; the charterer's inspector said so. And if you had seen the damned job, you would agree."

He concentrated on loading his fork.

"I could approve the invoice as is," he said finally, "but then... you know... business is business." He unloaded the fork.

"Yes..."

"You know... the port engineer's commission will have to be double the usual ten percent." He said that very casually, while using the napkin.

"Balls, Emons never asked for any percent," I yelled. "That's blackmail! You know damn well I lost money on that fuckin' job. You had promised you would give us all kinds of help, then we couldn't get anybody from your crew to do anything. Now you got me all the way over here for a shake-down. Bullshit!"

"Quit crying, you made a killing. What were you paying those bums? Minimum wage?"

"I am going to do something, I'll take some action against the fuckin' ship, or something," I leaned on the flimsy table to get up, making the cups rattle.

"I told you, the *Halcyon* is not coming back to the United States." He sounded unshakably confident.

"I'll think of something; I can't afford to kiss that much money good-bye." I threw a dollar on the table. "Don't want you adding the coffee to my bill," I said and stomped out.

During the long monotonous drive back to Bigport, I ran through my mind the whole *Halcyon* job. It was definitely the kind of job you wish had gone to the competition.

I passed an Esso tanker-truck and that reminded me that I hadn't spoken with Captain Stewart for quite some time. I could mention the good conversion job on the *Halcyon* and maybe he would throw some work my way.

I called him the next morning. After some small talk about the sex habits of southern belles and about the oil business, I told him that I had seen his assistant a couple of months back onboard the tanker *Halcyon*. "Did you guys end up chartering that ship?" I asked.

"Yeah," he said, "that was a big brain fart. The old man got talked into it. She is a dog, and the owners are a pain in the ass; I wish we could get the fuckin' charter canceled."

I told him about my problem.

"That's little league stuff," he said, "I thought you were smarter than that." He laughed as if the fix I was in was one of his corny jokes.

"That's a lot of money to me; I am not a big conglomerate like you guys. I can't afford to lose it and I can't afford the lawyers either."

Captain Stewart knew all that, but he liked hearing it.

"If I tell you what to do, you'll owe me. Next time I come down there, you'll have to fix me up with one of those young Southern Belles."

"I'll fix you up with Miss Magnolia Blossom," I said.

"You'd better. Listen, this is what you'll do."

I listened carefully, and I did exactly as he told me.

Two weeks later Pete Carras called to say there was a Telex for me. I went right over.

"It's on the machine," said Pete when I got there.

I glanced at it and then, without asking for permission, I grabbed his phone, dialed the bank number and asked for the person handling my account.

"What's the matter?" Pete looked at me concerned and perplexed.

Bravo, I shouted when I hung up, loud enough to make everybody jump. "You hear that? you little prick. Did they fire your shity little ass you fuckin pimp?" I was waiving the Telex paper in my hand and I was jumping up and down facing out the door towards New York, towards the Hios Shipping head office. "I accomplished what I wanted, and you little shit got nothing. I got paid every penny of it and then some. Fuck you, I never want to do another job for your shitty outfit again."

Pete, Stavros and Ramon were staring at me. With billy-goat agility I jumped on a rope spool and did a Zorba dance and when I got back down and caught my breath, I told everybody: "Let's go to lunch, I am buying."

"That must've been some news," said Pete.

I showed him the Telex. It was a short, curt message informing me that payment was made to my account by wire transfer. I was also informed that I would never do another job for the Hios Shipping Company.

"I want you to find me a hooker that looks and talks like Scarlet O'Hara," I told Stavros when we got to the "Wharf Restaurant."

"Your wife kicked you out?" he asked.

"I promised it to somebody and he earned it."

Captain Stewart had earned his southern belle. Hios Shipping had paid the invoice in full, the way the lawyer had revised it. Captain Stewart had suggested that I get a lawyer to write a letter to Hios Shipping, with a copy to him, informing them that if they did not pay the invoice as submitted we would proceed to arrest the vessel when she arrived at the next U.S. port.

Captain Stewart would then telex Hios Shipping that if the ship, which was calling regularly on US ports regardless of what that scum-ball Lambidis said, was delayed because of any legal dispute, it would constitute breach of contract per section blah, blah... paragraph blah... blah... and the charter agreement would be voided.

Bobby Carras had used the same lawyer six months earlier, to arrest the ship of another deadbeat.

"Smart boy, my Bobby," Pete had said, while looking up the phone number for the law firm of Edmont, Hairston and O'Brian. "He no take running around from nobody. Next year, he run the shop and I go to Andros for vacation."

The lawyer wasn't bashful about piling on the charges. He included interest from the day the job was completed, telephone and telex expenses, his fees, even one day's pay and expenses for my trip to New Orleans to meet with the Lambidis character.

We clinked the glasses and toasted to health and to business success.

Chapter

21

*M*oe walked into the office during the lunch break one day, a week after I got back from Greece: "Boss, need to talk to you about something," he said.

I knew it was important; he was still on his own time.

"I think your home-boy is fucking with you."

"What are you talking about, Moe?"

"Jack Foshier, the dude you fired, about a month ago."

"Yeah, what about him?"

"I saw him last night. Says Antonios hired him to run his shop. They'll be building the same kind machines we are, for the same Chicago outfit."

"That's bullshit, Antonios wanted his vacation because he's having problems with his wife. They went to some kind of family counseling. He'll be back in a week."

"Like I said, I think he's fucking with you."

"You guys like to stir things up, that's all," I said.

Later, when the mail came, there was a registered letter from Antonios. It was one line long: "Effective immediately I announce my resignation for personal reasons."

When I finally calmed down, I called Chicago Modern Machinery. The project manager, a smart-ass, greedy bastard, said that the conveyor job for Virginia Pulp and Paper went to a new company called Bigport Metal Works.

"Their bid came in a bit lower than yours," he said.

"Who the hell are they?"

"Don't know, might be that Greek foreman of yours; I am not sure."

Moe was right: The sonovabitch was fucking with me. I could feel the anger rising to my head and I poured out the curses. The sonovabitch, after all I had done for him, all the "emergency" loans, all the times I let him stay home with pay to look after his sick wife, all the times I had both of them over to my house. All the crying on my shoulder and pouring out of his heart about his wife and about his family, was nothing but a smoke screen. The sonovabitch! I treated him like a brother, gullible idiot that I was. I felt my chest tightening. I wanted to cry, I wanted to yell, I wanted to hit somebody, I wanted to kick something. I got in the truck and went for a long drive. I drove till dark.

The next day, I stayed home and made life miserable for Jim Farmanis, the Greek community's handy man, who was laying brick in the patio of the new house we had just moved into.

Philip Chalmers, a real estate salesman from Margaret's church, concocted a deal where he sold our old house to somebody who got a fat insurance settlement, then turned around and used that money as partial payment on this house which Margaret had fallen in love with. It was a two-story colonial, that looked like something out of a plantation photograph, with red brick and green shutters. There were master bedrooms and guest bedrooms and bedrooms for each kid, and enough bathrooms for every one to get the runs at the same time.

It was in an uppity neighborhood, with stuck-up neighbors, tall oaks and manicured lawns, next to a golf course. This house was even bigger than Pete Carras'. The mortgage amount almost gave me a heart attack, but the silver-tongued Mr. Chalmers insisted we could afford it. He also made a big deal about how hob-nobbing with all those rich neighbors would be good for my business.

We had been in the house for two months. Now with Antonios stealing away the biggest part of my work, I was in for some tough times. After eight years of struggling and agonizing to build up the business, I was back to where I started. Only now, I had to make mortgage payments to Margaret's *Taj Mahal* in America and to my *White Elephant* in Greece. I could become the laughing stock of the Greeks on both continents.

I kept venting my frustration to Big Jim, who kept saying he was shocked too, he didn't think Antonios would do such a thing, but don't let it get to me, it happens all the time to all kinds of people. He kept looking at his watch.

About a week later, Pete Carras came by the office to pick me up to go to the AHEPA meeting. I told him that right then, I didn't feel like seeing or socializing with any Greeks.

"You are the treasurer, you've got to go. Besides, it's my turn to set up the food and I need your help."

While getting ready for the meeting I kept glancing at the door, expecting Antonios to show his face and announce to everybody that he was a big businessman now.

He never showed up.

After the meeting, while helping set up the table for the social hour, Pete Carras told me that he heard Antonios got a loan from Christos Pittas to get started in his business.

It dawned on me that that slimy, double-crossing, back stabbing sonovabitch had been planning this thing for a long time, and a bunch of these people who acted like my friends, knew about it. They had probably been talking about it and laughing behind my back, and played me for a sucker. I might end up losing everything I had worked for, but to them it is just a fresh piece of gossip.

I asked Pete for a cigarette.

"You said you cut smoking cigarettes; don't let it get to you, it happens all the time."

"Somebody else told me the same thing," I said, "it doesn't help."

"Here, have a beer instead."

John Alepakis walked up holding some papers. "Brother Nick, you think you can help us with the convention program again this year? Last year you bought a half-page for two hundred dollars. Think you can get a whole page ad this time?"

He handed me the order form.

I threw the paper back to his face. "Go ask Antonios for your fuckin' ad! And you can take your fuckin' membership and brotherhood crap and shove it where the sun doesn't shine. You are a bunch of hypocrites and liars and I don't want to have anything to do with any of you!"

I stormed out.

For a long time after that I wouldn't have anything to do with anyone who was doing business with, talking to, or even knew Antonios.

One day, I called a trucking company I had been doing business with, to make arrangements to take a load of hatch covers to New Orleans.

"Is this the Virginia load, Anthony?" the dispatcher asked.

"What the fuck are you talking about?" I barked.

"Oh, I am sorry Nick, I thought you were Tony; you two sound just alike."

I told him to go to hell and almost broke the phone slamming it down. I never gave them another load.

Soon, every one in the shop discovered a new way of entertaining themselves. They would casually work into he conversation that Antonios got another contract, or that he was hiring people, then watch me blow my top. Better than the movies.

Chapter
22

A week after she graduated from high school, Maria started working as a full-time drafting and engineering assistant in the company. She was planning to go on to college and major in Mechanical Engineering, but she said she wanted to use the summer to build up her work experience and spending-money reserves.

I admired her level-headedness.

The first think she did was to talk me into buying a bunch of new stuff. She got a shining, metallic-gray, Facsimile machine, which she put next to a telephone of matching color, with lots of speed dial buttons, bells and lights, that contrasted nicely with the bone-colored computer with its big screen and laser printer next to it. Everything sat snugly on an L-shaped, imitation cherry wood desk, the first thing you saw when you walked in the office — a sure sign of a young company on its way up.

There are lots of people who are impressed with new gadgetry. They go around carrying anything that bleeps, blinks and buzzes, and when everybody is looking, they'll use it, acting as if the world will come to an end if they didn't do it right away.

I had made a sales call to a company called Multiplex Industries about a month earlier, trying to get a conveyor order, and I noticed that the purchasing manager, a super-conservative religious fanatic, had every electronic gadget on the market piled on his desk. He would peck on one adjust the other and answer a third, while he was talking to me.

I guess I didn't impress him because the conveyor order ended up going to someone else and I almost forgot about it till about a month later, when clear out of the blue, I got a call from him saying he wanted to come by to see my facilities and discuss my old quote.

I did some snooping and found out that A&B Fabricators, who had gotten the order, was a little behind schedule. Multiplex was going to use that as an excuse to take the order away from them, because the manager found out that the two guys who owned the company were queers.

I made the appointment for four-thirty. "The production crew will be off and the shop will be quiet then," I explained. I asked Maria to put a multi-color graph on the computer screen and show me where the on-and-off button was.

I stood by the window and when the Multiplex man parked and was getting out of his car, I went and sat in front of the computer till I heard him breathing behind me. Acting startled, I turned and apologized for not noticing him earlier. "I was doing a workload projection for the next quarter," I said and quickly, before he asked to see anything on it, I turned the gismo off.

I served coffee and started singing to him about what a hard working, God-fearing, super-conservative outfit we were. He was soaking it up.

We had gotten to the part where we were talking about delivery dates and trucking arrangements (my price was within his budget, he had said) when, of all the people, Big Jim Farmanis, the mountain man, walks in.

"Halo my friend, how are you doing?" he said in macho Greek, coming up to me. "You look good, look real good, *ftou ftou ftou sou*." And before I could duck, he pinched me affectionately on both cheeks. The purchasing manager of the Multiplex Industries stared awe-struck. To the uninitiated, Big Jim's words might have sounded like silly lovers talk, and his spitting sounds could probably be taken as Greek air kisses.

The manager cleared his throat, said he was running late for an appointment, and dashed out the door. That was the last I saw of him and his conveyor order.

Maria declared my old, battered metal desk obsolete and replaced it with a new one, the size of a city block. It was cherry-colored wood with a leather top and came with a leather chair and a matching credenza, whose bottom drawer was just big enough to hold all the photographs, notes and drawings for the Bellmaker's house I had accumulated.

In some remote corners of the world, there were still companies communicating the old fashioned way and for those, from time to time I had to go to Pete Carras' place and send a Telex.

That was the reason I went over there at noon that Wednesday.

There was a deathly stillness in the warehouse. The only sound was the faint humming of the meat freezer. Stavros and Ramon were sitting across from each other on plastic olive barrels, their elbows resting on the rope spool that served as a table, smoking and staring into their coffee mugs in silence.

Through the glass I saw Pete Carras sitting at his desk staring at a calendar that showed a Greek island with white-washed houses and windmills. It was the calendar of Atlantic Cordage, whose owner was Petro Zervas, Pete's old friend. A cigarette was burning undisturbed between his fingers, the gray smoke spiraling toward the vent.

"Where is Bobby?" I asked Stavro.

"Don't know, he didn't come in today." He spoke as if we were in church.

"I needed to send a Telex to Karenis Shipping," I said.

"I'll do it," he whispered and reached for the paper.

"I'll go say Hi to Pete while you are doing it," I said.

"I wouldn't go in there, if I was you, Mr. Nick," said Ramon. "Mr. Pete is very angry."

"What happened?"

"Don't know. Every time I speak, he tell me to go to the devil. He tell Stavro to go to the devil too and throw the coffee cup to him this morning. The cup Bobby bring to him from London."

Pete kept staring at the calendar when I walked into his office and sat on the couch.

"Did Zerva's cancer get worst?" I finally asked.

He turned toward me. His face looked tired. "I speak to his boy this morning; he is manager of Atlantic Cordage now, you know? He say his father take *chemical therapy* and is O.K. now. He go back to work soon."

The cigarette burned his finger and he grounded it in the overflowing ashtray, then wiped the ashes from the desk with the edge of his palm. The phone rang but he didn't move for it.

"To the devil with the damn business! We go eat; I buy." He started walking towards the door.

"You are not sick, Pete, are you?" He ignored the sarcasm.

I got my copy of the Telex from Stavro and caught up with Pete.

"Are you all right Pete?" I asked when we got in the truck, this time seriously.

"Zerva's boy told me today," he started as if he hadn't heard me, "that they buy the Maryland Wire and Rope company. They have *distributions* all over the country. Big company. God damn it, why is it some men are lucky to have sons with good sense and some others to have sons that are ungrateful?"

He ran a stop sign and somebody blew his horn at us.

"Go fuck yourself," answered Pete, then he went on,

"Zervas invited me to the wedding of his boy. I got the invitation this morning. He's marrying Captain Gerassimos Valitsas' daughter next month. Valitsas has office in New York and London, owns two tankers and one freighter. I bet Zerva's son gets a ship for dowry. I'm sure he will, Captain Gerassimos doesn't have other children."

He made a sharp right in front of the driveway of the Wharf Restaurant, with two wheels going over the curb, and parked in the front of the building taking up two parking spaces.

"You didn't lock it," I said, as we were walking away.

"Shit on it vre," he answered.

The place was almost empty; too early for the lunch hour rush. We sat at a table in a corner.

"Two whiskeys," he startled the waitress.

George Skoufos was standing a couple of tables down, a white napkin over his left shoulder, bent slightly forward, explaining to four older women with bluish silver hair, about the "Snapper George."

Pete nodded in his direction. "His boy didn't want to stay in the restaurant, he go sell insurance; stupid kids."

"The Americans say: 'The apple falls under the tree,' but some times I think it rolls down the hill a little," I said.

"Fuck the Americans and their America." He grabbed a glass from the tray before the waitress got a chance to set it down.

"To your health," he said clinking it with the one that was supposed to be mine. He took a long sip.

"What's bugging you Pete?"

"He invite me and his mother to his house for dinner," he started, as if talking to someone I couldn't see. "He said he wanted to talk to me. I said if want to talk, talk here, in the office. He says better in his house, his wife will fix dinner. Then I know is serious, he knows I don't cuss in front of women. Back home they say if you want to screw somebody on a deal, you invite him to your house." He was gazing at the far wall, as if the other person was out there somewhere, far away. "It is my fault, I should have put my foot down and make him learn Greek when he was young. Their mother don't speak any."

The waitress stood ready to take the order.

"Two more whisky," said Pete.

"We got to go back to work, Pete — bring us two bowls of gumbo," I told the waitress.

Pete drained his glass. "Bring me another one," he called after the waitress, holding up his empty glass. He glanced around the dining room; it was beginning to fill up. "Look at it, this place is a gold mine and his son go sell insurance; stupid kids."

"That's not what's bothering you, Pete, is it?"

"If Bobby speak Greek maybe be different. Maybe he wouldn't marry a foreigner."

"Pete, she is a nice girl, from a good family, you should be proud of them."

The waitress brought two bowls of gumbo and Pete's whisky.

"You know she call me Mister Carras? No papa, no father, I'm Mister Carras to her. Bobby start to go to her church now. She is Baptist; they are different kind of Christians."

"Is that what's bothering you? That the priest lost a customer? Eat some gumbo, it's good."

He stirred the soup slowly with his spoon, while talking. "He wait until we finish eating. Good food; he knows I like pot roast, and that girl cooks good. He give me a big piece, with small onions and potatoes, and green asparagus and salad, and he had red wine on the table too. He said it was from California, but it was good. When we finish, he says Papa, we go in the living room to have our coffee, let the women talk about their stuff. All the time I try to guess what problem he has. Maybe he is going to tell me he is getting a divorce, then I say 'no, no look like'. Maybe he want me to sign a loan for bigger house. The family of the girl is rich and maybe he want to move in a rich neighborhood."

He crumbled a cracker in his soup. He lit another cigarette, took a long puff and started stirring the soup again with slow circular motions.

"When we were drinking the coffee," Pete started telling the invisible person who was now inside the bowl of gumbo, "he says: 'Father, I love you and I respect you, and I know you have worked hard to make the business what it is, and I know you want me to take over someday and make it even bigger. When I went to London and New York, all the shipping people speak very well about you and I would like very much to make you feel proud of me.'

"I don't understand what he means with all that mushy talk. I am afraid maybe he'll say he is queer; maybe that's why they have no children; we have a few of those in our community, you know? I hear one of Vervatos' sons is one of them. I know it is serious because he says father, all the other time he calls me dad."

"Pete, you don't make any sense."

"Anyways, he tells me: 'Father, I have been thinking a lot about it and I talked with my wife and I have decided that the ship supply business is not for me. I want to do something else.'

I spilled the coffee all over me. I said: 'Bullshit, ship chandlering not good enough for you? What are you going to do? Go to work for your father-in-law in his fancy car business?'

He says he is going to be manager of the Sage Real Estate company. They have business in six states. Big salary, big bonus, big company car, real big-shot he thinks.

I say to him: 'You are going to be *ipalilos*,' but he don't speak Greek. I try to explain: 'You are going to be working for others, *i-po-ali-lous* means 'under others,' now you are your own boss.'

He says real estate is what he likes to do. *Arhidia Calavrezica*; what kind bullshit is that?"

He took a spoonful of the soup, then pushed the bowl away and took a last puff on his cigarette. "I was sure Bobby was going to keep the business," he said, smashing his cigarette in the ashtray. "The other two don't even know where the shop is. The old one became fancy lawyer, now is a big-shot District Attorney. The girl, she married a foreigner, an American who knows nothing about real life. He works for the government. Bullshit."

He was staring in the middle of the table, as if there were a porthole there, and he could see far away.

"You... you... you freeze your ass waiting for the godamn ships to dock in the middle of the night, you fight every sonavabitch that's trying to cut your throat, you become a pimp and a clown, and you let every captain, steward, port captain, any whore's son, play billiards on your back, so you get the order, you spit blood till you get paid from the sonovabitch owners, you..."

The anger was choking him, the words were trying to jump out all at the same time, getting stuck at the opening, like sheep in the barn door. He lit another cigarette.

"You... sacrifice your health and your life to build the business and when you get it where it can run by itself, you give it to them on a silver platter, and they choose to go and take orders from strangers. What prokopi can he make like that? Who the hell is this *Mr. Sa-ge Re-al Est-ate*?" He intentionally slaughtered the pronunciation of the last three words.

"He's going to be *ipalilos*. Bullshit. I tell Bobby, 'I don't want to know you any more.' I got out and told his mother she can stay with him from now on. I walked one whole hour, all the way to my house."

He took a long puff, then ground the cigarette vindictively on the side of the bowl of gumbo.

"The other day," he went on, "the little shit, Stavros, told me he could get a mortgage on his house and buy me out if Bobby doesn't want to keep the business. He come to me barefooted and bare assed; I turned that low class scum into a human and now he has the nerve to think he can buy me out. Bullshit."

The waitress asked if there would be anything else.

"No, no more else, we go back to the goddamn job," said Pete. He glanced at the ticket, threw a twenty dollar bill on the table and with short, defeated steps, shoulders sagging, he shuffled out.

Chapter
23

*T*rade shows are where the big boys strut their stuff. They spread it in fancy booths, have seductive, curvy women in tight dresses snare those passing by, and they have smiling, fast-talking salesmen to hand out the tons of propaganda and write up the orders. It's where every ambitious, progressive, modern business person goes to check out the competition, to make business contacts and to stock up on key chains, yardsticks and breath mints.

In my line of work, the *Poseidonia* is the biggest of the big trade shows. In the shipping business, anybody who is anybody, or thinks he is, or wants to be, puts in an appearance every two years at that show in the port of Piraeus, in Greece.

Poseidon Marine Services, Inc. had grown. We had been in business for twelve years. We had all kinds of modern tools, labor-saving gadgets and colorful propaganda flyers, and like all modern outfits, we blamed every screw-up on the computer. It was about time I went and saw how other people were doing things. I could find someone to be my representative in that part of the world, and with the same tax deduction, visit the village. The loan with the Greek bank was almost paid off.

Having a representative in major maritime centers around the world is very important in my kind of business. Every self-respecting ship repair outfit has overseas representatives who beat the bushes and steer customers their way. The back page of Dixie's brochure is full of the names and addresses of their representatives; some of them in places even mapmakers haven't heard of.

I loaded Floyd with instructions on what to do in the shop and I got to Greece a week before the trade show opened.

Margaret had exhorted me as strongly as she could: "Don't get us in another mess like last time." She had never warmed up to the Bellmaker's house. Everything that was wrong in the world was because I had the cockamamie idea to buy that white elephant.

On one of our rare quiet evenings, while watching Gone with the Wind, I told Margaret I had come up with a name for the Bellmaker's house. "Phoenix," I said. "What do you think of that? After being almost a pile of rubble, it will rise to a bigger splendor than before."

"That's not the bird I had in mind," she said pulling away from our snuggle on the couch. "Albatross seems more fitting."

I spent most of my time in the village, at the Bellmaker's house. I used up two rolls of film taking pictures of the outside, the inside and the property around the house; in close-ups and far away views.

Kyra Amalia chastised me for taking so long to visit Mother. "None of us is getting any younger you know? I had to sell two of the goats; couldn't take care of them any more."

Then she pointed out that the field needed to be plowed and the trees pruned and fertilized. I told her I was planning to landscape the property when I finished the house. "I have it all planed, Kyra Amalia," I said.

She reminded me again about her sister's son who was a contractor and built palaces for rich people from Athens and Germany, and from all over the world. He was building one now in the next village, I should go and see it. It was almost finished.

I went to see it and she was right; it was for a rich customer. She was also right that he did good work; his craftsmen worked with zeal and Panos Stenos was paying attention, even to the smallest detail. I told him that I would like him to renovate the Bellmaker's house when I got ready. He said he'll make me a good price.

I tried to talk Mother into coming with me to Bigport but she wouldn't hear of it. "Eighty-year-old people should sit on their eggs and not go gallivanting all over the world," she said. She rode with me as far as my sister's house, an hour away from Taxiarhes.

I got to the Poseidonia trade show the second day it opened. I was awe-struck. It seemed that anybody who had anything to do with anything that floated in the sea, from every corner of the world, was there: Ship suppliers, ship builders, ship repairers, ship agents, ship engine manufacturers, tug boat operators even seamen services outfits. They were all in shiny booths in brightly lit halls, showing films, photographs, mock-ups or their actual products — the best their company had to offer. People dressed in suits, jeans, robes and sarongs were walking up and down the carpeted aisles chatting with the salesmen, flirting with the "booth assistants," sampling the snacks and stuffing the plastic bags they carried with freebies and product literature.

I signed a representation agreement for Greece with a company that went by the acronym AMEN. It stood for Advanced Marine Enterprises Network. I thought it might be prophetic.

The next day I signed a reciprocal agreement with a repair outfit out of Rotterdam, who shared a display booth at the show with a hatch cover manufacturer. After the paper signing, we stopped at a quaint little ouzeri, in the old section of Pireus, to toast the deal and show Helmudth Sholtz, the head of the Dutch company, the Greek version of "schnapps."

The bar was not any bigger than an American house-closet, but in front of it, in a small square, were a dozen round, blue metal tables, with blue plastic chairs, arranged neatly in rows under a blue and white striped canvas canopy. Next to it was another ouzeri, almost identical, in a dark green color scheme.

The waiter brought our ouzo and a plate of bite-sized pickled octopus as appetizers.

I put a few drops of water in my ouzo, turning it milky white, and drank it in small sips. Helm drank his in one swallow and chased it with a glass of water.

We ordered the second round. The waiter called in the order in a singing tone that would rival any opera tenor. This time the appetizers were stuffed grapevine leaves. The Dutchman liked the pickled octopus; he asked why they changed it.

"It's the custom," I explained, "they serve different meze with every new order. That's why when we ordered, the waiter called in 'One second,' so the guy preparing the order would know to put in a different appetizer. It's going to be different on the third, the fourth and so on."

"Let's see how many kinds they have," said Helm, emptying his glass and quickly reaching for the water.

"That might take awhile. It's bragging rights for these bars to have the customer pass out before tasting the same meze twice."

At the next table, two men in their fifties, each twirling a thick beaded comboloi, were sipping ouzo and discussing the American involvement in the Cypriot crisis. A couple of sparrows were searching for crumbs under the tables. Further down, the hustle of the port: freighters and passenger ships coming and going, horns and whistles blowing. I felt relaxed, confident, optimistic.

The appetizer for fourth ouzo order, was tsitsirava (the pickled buds of a wild tree, the ultimate in meze cousine.) After that we took a cab to our hotels.

It hadn't taken much driving around the streets of Piraeus for me to see the benefit of using taxis. I had gotten used to driving in Dixie, so the kamikaze spirit and hunting instinct for pedestrians, both necessary qualifications for successful driving in Greece, had died in me from malnutrition.

I turned the rented car in at the end of the first day I got back from the village and rode taxis from then on.

Years earlier, riding a taxi was a sign of affluence; rich people rode taxis and commoners rode the buss. Some philosophizing thinker had said once that his dream was to become so wealthy as to be able to afford to hire two taxis, one ahead of him and one following him while he walked in the middle as a show of disregard for personal comforts.

On one of the cab rides between Athens and Piraeus, I felt I knew the driver from somewhere before. He had a trimmed, lightly grayed beard and under the Greek fisherman's hat protruded a flock of brownish-gray curls. There was something familiar in his manners and in his Bohemian philosophy. The relaxed way he was navigating the cab through the pandemonium of the *Leoforos Kifisias*, the soft music he was listening to, his smooth unhurried tone of talking, brought back a faint memory of something pleasant, something that was lost and missed; only I couldn't remember what.

Then as we were driving along, I saw at an intersection a tall man with a wild beard, holding a bottle, and with drunken gestures, pretending to direct traffic, and I remembered: My driver was Elias Matheos, or Barba Lias as we called him, the ordinary seaman on the old freighter *Maritihi*. I asked him a few questions to confirm it and then I let him talk, and as he talked, my mind was reliving that crazy, first year at sea. He was the modern Greek version of Diogenes. Clever and philosophical, he liked to read a lot and didn't like taking orders. He was the best tipper in all the bars and whore-houses of every port we visited.

"It's only money," he used to say.

What got him a prominent spot in my small, crowded memory box was that October night in Surabaya.

The ship had gotten into port the night before, after thirty days at sea and everybody was spending their overtime. While rushing to get on board on time for my midnight-to-four shift, I saw Elias in the middle of a small parade, moving toward the dock.

There was one rickshaw in front of him and one behind, paddling slowly, to keep up with his funny kind of walk. On the first rickshaw sat a bleached blonde in a bright yellow dress holding a radio that blared out a jazz tune. A red-head in tight white shorts was on the rickshaw behind him. Both were blowing kisses and calling out: *"Elias se agapo."* He waved me over and I sat next to the blonde. A few yards further down we saw one of the firemen returning to the ship, and Elias got him to sit next to the red-head. He kept on walking his funny walk between the two rickshaws, to the rhythm of the jazz music, till we got alongside the ship.

The whole crew lined up at the bulwarks to take a look at the spectacle.

"You don't mind if we pick up a passenger, do you?" Elias interrupted my reminiscing, and before I answered, he stopped next to an old woman with a cane, bent and bundled in black, shuffling along a dusty stretch of road. He walked around and opened the front door for her.

"Were you going to walk all the way over there in this heat?" Elias asked her when she told him where she was going.

"They took my daughter to the hospital and her little one is going to be by herself when she gets back from school. I go with the bus, but the pension check is late again this month."

He zigzagged between noisy busses and trucks that must have been coal-fired, ignoring the pesky motorcycles, while humming along with the classical music on the tape, moving his fingers as if conducting the orchestra.

When he let the old woman out, she searched in her bag. "I don't even have any change to give you," she said apologetically.

"Don't worry grandma, it's only money," he said.

When I got off I left him a big tip, but never told him who I was. Maybe I was afraid I wouldn't measure up to his standards, or maybe it was envy; I don't know.

Pete Carras, kept saying half-jokingly, half-serious, how he envied a rich man like me going to Greece for vacation. When I asked him to come with me, he brought up a mountain of excuses to keep from telling me he was afraid of flying.

"Bobby is a smart boy but needs more experience. In this business, even your ass must have eyes. Maybe he come with you this time. He can go see some customers I have problem collecting."

That was before Bobby dropped the change-of-jobs bomb. Since then I hadn't seen Pete. Stavros said he went to visit some relative in California.

He showed up at the shop, one day before I left for Greece, with half a dozen letters.

"These are some of the people I have trouble with the money," he said. "If you go speak to them, maybe you collect something."

I promised him I'd try and when I finished with the *Poseidonia*, I started on the collection route.

The first company I visited, Prosperity Shipping Corporation, was nothing like its name. There was only one person in the office, a bald, skinny guy around fifty, reading a newspaper.

"The company is broke," he said. "We expect a court settlement on a large claim and when that comes, we will take care of all our bills."

"He'll take a partial payment," I said. "He has some taxes that are due and needs the money."

"I understand. I haven't received anything from the company for my own expenses either."

"He is not Bethlehem Steel," I said. "He needs the money."

"You are welcome to take whatever you want," he said gesturing toward the few rickety furniture pieces scattered in the small office.

At the next office, a middle-aged, prune-faced receptionist asked what it was about, and when I told her, she tried to fake disappointment. "It's a pity Captain Mareas is in Germany, I am sure he would like to meet you," she said in a loud voice as if I was hard of hearing. She was trying to make eye contact with the people at the surrounding desks. "Give our best to Mr. Carras, Captain Mareas speaks very highly of him," she added, handing me back the envelope I'd given her.

"Could I come back another day? I am going to be here four more days," I said, immediately realizing it was a dumb thing to say.

"He will not be back for two weeks," she trumpeted. "The job will take that long, maybe even longer."

"Could someone else in accounting take care of this?" I shouted, thinking she might be hard of hearing.

"The only one from accounting who is in now is Mr. Pashalis, the gentleman in the corner," she said, in the same town-crier's voice.

The office consisted of one room, its desks arranged in rows, all facing the receptionist. A pencil rolling off her desk would be heard at end of the room, clear as a bell.

I approached the gentleman in the corner before the secretary could make eye contact, gave him the envelope, and repeated my earlier monologue.

He smiled, glanced at the envelope, and with the confidence of someone who knows exactly what to do handed it back to me.

"This is addressed to Captain Mareas personally," he said. "I can't do anything with it. He is visiting a ship that's unloading in port right now, but if you want to come back later, he will be here."

Either the guy had not been paying attention earlier, or his hearing was bad. I would bet my life that one of those guys looking at me over their glasses was Captain Mareas.

I didn't do any better on the other three stops.

The last company was one that I had also done some work for, but my bill was paid by the insurance. I told the receptionist that I was in town for the *Poseidonia* and stopped by to thank Mr. Karenis for his business.

She ushered me into a large office with Oriental carpet and dark paneled walls on which hung a couple of oil paintings of sailing ships, an icon of Saint Nickolas and two large portraits of old people who looked like Lefterios Karenis. Three models of freighters in glass cases were in the center of the room. Lefterios Karenis came out from behind a large carved desk by a window overlooking the port of Piraeus and greeted me with a smile and a handshake as if we were old friends.

When the conversation came around to the location and size of my shop, I mentioned that it was located about a block away from Pete Carras' place.

"Great guy, Pete. How is he doing?" he asked with professionally artificial interest. I repeated the hardship monologue and handed him the envelope.

"You mean he hasn't been paid off?" he exclaimed. His surprise and anger could be mistaken for genuine. He took the invoices out of the envelope, glanced at them and then turning his head toward the door, he called out in a loud voice:

"*Vre Pandeli*!" he waited a few seconds and repeated: "*Vre Pandeli*! he is the chief accountant, has been with me for ages," he explained. "I am going to get him in here and get this thing taken care right now. This is inexcusable especially when Pete has been so helpful. "Vre Pandeli," this time a loud shout and receiving no answer, he walked out of the office with the invoices.

"At last I am going to get something," I thought.

He returned a couple of minutes later.

"Pandelis has gone to run an errand. He will be back in about an hour; just missed him." He sounded sincerely disappointed. "Could you come back later and pick up the check?"

"I have another appointment for today," I said with some regret, "but I could stop by tomorrow."

"That will be fine, whenever you get here, just come right in." He put his hand around my shoulder and we walked to the reception area like two old school buddies.

"Despina," he instructed the receptionist, "when Mr. Pilios returns tomorrow, send him right in. I'll be expecting him."

He pressed the call button and while waiting for the elevator, asked where I was staying.

I told him.

"Neptune is one of the best seafood restaurants and it's only a block away from your hotel. Try the charcoal-grilled snapper, it's excellent."

I thanked him for the tip.

The next morning the receptionist ushered me to Mr. Karenis office.

"How was your evening?" he inquired with interest. "Did you go to the Neptune Tavern?"

I told him I did, and that I enjoyed it, and I thanked him for suggesting it, and then I reminded him about the check.

"Ah... the check, Pandelis already mailed it. I jumped on him as soon as he got back yesterday and he told me, he paid up all the US Gulf accounts last week. I should have looked into it myself, especially Pete's account, but I have been very busy lately."

We both proclaimed that we enjoyed meeting each other, he assured me that next time one of his ships needed any repairs I would be the first he would call, and then the elevator door opened.

"Give my best to Pete and my apologies for the mix-up," he said as we parted.

Over some home made ouzo and *mezedes* I had brought back from the village, I reported to Pete Carras about my bill collecting attempts. He grinned when I told him about my visit to Karenis' office.

"The goddamn *apateonas*, last month, when Stavros went to see him, the chief accountant's name was Leonidas. I bet he does the same trick to everybody asking for money. Apateones (crooks), all of them," he said in disgust. Then almost in a whisper: "Bobby could have collected from these *apateones*."

I told him about Prosperity Shipping and the expected settlement that was going to pay off all their bills, his first.

"Oh, yeah, sure. *Arhidia Kalavrezika* he'll pay. Let me tell you a story my mother used to tell me when I was a kid: A bill collector knocks on a guy's door and the wife answers. He asks to see her husband and she tells him he has gone to the fields to sow thorn bushes. 'Why would he want to do that?' he asks. 'Well,' the wife answers, 'the bushes will sprout and grow, and when the sheep run through them, their wool will get caught on the thorns. My husband will collect it, take it to the market and get the money to pay your loan off.'

The bill collector laughed. 'Aha, now that you've secured your money your heart has lightened up,' said the wife.

I think that guy has a better chance of getting his money from the farmer than I got from Prosperity Shipping," said Pete, chewing on a sun-dried octopus tentacle.

Chapter
24

"God must have told her to do it, I am sure of it, why else?" my sister's excited voice jolted me from a peaceful sleep at two o'clock on Saturday morning. (She always forgets about the time difference.)

"Of all the times I asked her to come and she wouldn't. You should see the house, half of it is demolished. She could have been crushed to death. She just took it upon herself to come and stay for a few days to help me with the twins. It was God's will, I am sure of it. I knew the *karydia* was going to come down some day."

"What are you talking about?"

"Of course, now she will have to stay here; she likes it in the back room with the twins."

It took me a while to figure out what my sister was talking about.

During a storm the previous day, the aged, arthritic roots of the huge walnut tree on the neighbor's sloping plot above our house, relaxed their grip and the Goliath of trees came crushing down. A branch of it had done some damage to Mother's house.

"Now is a good time to bring Mother over for a visit," I told Margaret later, while discussing my sister's call.

"Are you going to stay home to do the translating? You never found the time to teach any of us to speak Greek."

That too, was my fault. Anything in my family that wasn't to everybody's liking was my fault. Margaret and the girls blamed me for being a bad teacher; my relatives for marrying a foreigner and then not being man enough to make her learn my language and join my church; my father for giving up after three girls instead of keeping on till I got a son; my mother-in-law for taking her daughter to a far-away, strange state; my kids for inheriting my imperfect genes.

I had tried to talk my father into coming to the States for a visit, but he wouldn't budge from the farmhouse. He thought Paraskevi was the center of the universe; travels to other places were a waste of time.

Mother crossed the county line only once, in the thirties, when she visited her brother in Larisa, a city about seventy miles from the village. She would date everything in her life from that event, the way other women tracked time by their pregnancies and child births.

A couple of years back, when I was in Greece for the *Poseidonia*, I had tried to talk her into coming with me but I think she was afraid of making such a long trip.

This time I had a negotiating edge.

"It's an omen," I told her. "God wants you to come over here."

In the end, she agreed. She would stay with us while the house was being repaired. I could pick her up in early March on the way back from a business trip to Suez.

In its death, the old walnut tree had done me one last favor. When we were kids, it used to be our favorite play area. In the summer, we played under its thick shade and later, when the leaves were gone, we would compete for the highest look-out posts. I called mine "The Crow's Nest," from a pirate novel I had read. Pavlos Stenos called his "The Eagle's Nest," just because the eagle was a bigger bird, not that his was any higher. He hoisted some boards up there and built a floor and a seat. Dimo's look-out was lower, among the thicker branches. He called his "Filakio" (guard post), after the few concrete machine-gun shelters still found in some overlooks, remnants from the civil war days. From there, armed with a chestnut tree stick, he would gun down any bandits approaching within a hundred meters.

We used to carve our initials in its bark and the tree would slowly erase them and we would carve them again.

Sometimes a wind storm would break a branch and send it gliding to the houses below.

"I wish the American would cut that tree down," Mother would say then. "Some day it's going to crush right on top of us."

"That tree has roots going deep down, all the way to China, it's gonna outlive us, all," Mr. Vargaritis would answer when someone suggested cutting it down. "My grandfather planted it when he got back from America."

His grandfather had spent a few years in the States, long enough to saddle his heirs with the nick-name "the American" and to pick up some strange gardening ways. They said he had turned over the soil in his whole garden using a spade instead of the *dicheli*, the fifteen pound, two pronged, back wrenching mattock that everybody else used. He planted the walnut tree and a bunch of other trees, so that his grandchildren would remember him.

It was on this walnut tree that one fine autumn, I shot with my sling my first bird, a black-cap titmouse. (A fact, I made certain everyone in the village, including George the Mute, heard of in detail, the same evening.)

I will always be grateful to the old *karydia*.

THEODORE PITSIOS

Next Monday morning I found in the post office box a small yellow piece of paper that said there was a registered letter for me. A chill went down my spine. Usually registered letters were from lawyers or the IRS. I went inside to pick it up and stood in a line that moved slower than stagnant water.

I glanced at the letter as soon as the guy finally handed it to me. It was from the U.S. Navy. A month earlier, I had submitted a bid on a big navy contract for the fabrication of some special components. I signed the receipt, stepped aside and tore it open. In formal government-ese, I was being notified that Poseidon Marine Services had been declared the low bidder on solicitation Number so and so. "A team of representatives will be visiting the facility on… date for a pre-award survey and conference," it concluded.

I let out a shout that startled everyone shuffling in line.

At the time we were building a couple of chain conveyors for Howard Demming's company. After visiting and pleading with the big wheels of Chicago Modern Machinery, I had managed to take away some of the work they were sending to Antonios' outfit. Just enough to keep four guys from standing still. The navy contract would get things going big time.

A week later, four men and a woman in starched blue and white uniforms with lots of gold ribbons and bars, arrived to do what they called "the pre-award survey." They spent the whole day going over the books, writing the names and addresses of the bank and a bunch of suppliers and looking at every corner of the shop.

"Want me to stop the guys making a racket while the wheels are in the shop?" Floyd had asked.

"Hell, no." I said, "Keep them grinding and banging."

"How come all this poking around?"

"They want to make sure we know what we are doing and that we didn't bite off more than we can chew."

"Hell, there ain't nothing to it, we can whip them babies out without even breakin a sweat. Don't see why you had to go hire four more guys. What you want me to do with them? They'll be done soon."

"Lay them off as soon as the navy brass leaves."

"Don't see why you brought them in just for a day, we could've finished them conveyors in a couple of days without any help."

"I have my reasons," I said.

I needed that contract. I had waited too long for my *prokopi*. The contract was about making some strange contraptions that looked like giant mushrooms, which the navy was going to use to transport some kind of hush-hush stuff. They never told me what it was, but I had to sign a stack of papers that I wouldn't tell anybody about it.

It would be easy work, with a decent profit margin, for many years; just what I needed to start the renovation on the house in Taxiarhes.

Two weeks after the navy visit, in a letter that had me leafing through the English-Greek dictionary for an hour, I was told that as a result of the satisfactory "pre-award inspection," I was awarded contract number such and such. I was to sign and return the original and three copies. There was also a purchase order for a number of units that made me swallow a couple of times, to be delivered subject to the terms and conditions of section C, paragraphs one, two and three.

Section C, with its paragraphs and their tons of references, was something that worried me a lot. It was the section covering what the navy called "First Article testing." The specifications for the test, containing many long, fancy words, were an inch thick, the gist of which was that after we built the first mushroom, we had to put it through all kinds of torture to make sure it didn't fall apart. I had never done anything like that before and it seemed I was staking a lot on Moe's welding.

When I got to Taxiarhes to pick up Mother, spring was just arriving. After the long winter hibernation, all vegetation was coming to life. The earth was covered with a blanket of soft, virgin-green, grass and wild flowers were blooming among the rocks. I spent quite some time visiting with Kostas Liappis. We reminisced, bragged about our kids and promised each other when we retired we would take two long trips together. I would be his guide in America and he'd show me what I've missed in Greece.

To Giannis Giannakos I expressed, as believably as possible, my regrets for having to miss his son's wedding. His oldest son was marrying Niki Pateka, one of Stefanis Patekas' daughters. It was promising to be a big event and I was glad to miss it.

I coughed and my chest ached most of the time I was in the village. Mother said it was because I had gotten used to the soft climate of America. She had overcome her earlier fears about flying and was informing those who came to visit: "We are going to fly from *Athina* to *Frankfurti*, the city where Marika's son is living, and from there to *Nea Iorki*, where they have the big sky-scrapers, and from there to *Atalanta* and then we will go to Nikos' town. He lives in the south part of America, where it doesn't get cold in the winter."

Fortified by lots of advice from everyone in the village whose travel experience extended beyond the mountain ridge and by lots of wishes for *kalo taxidi* and safe return, we drove away — handkerchiefs waving, eyes misting.

On the drive to Athens Mother asked if we would go by the place they stopped for lunch on the trip to Larisa.

"Mother, that was back in 1939, you still remember it?"

"It was a big restaurant. It had fans on the ceiling that were turning and kept the place cool even though it was the middle of the summer."

"You just wait, when we get home, I'll show you things you will be talking about for years."

"Home is Taxiarhes, where we are going is *xenihtia*," (foreign land), she replied.

Every time we passed a church mother crossed herself and murmured a short prayer. She would do the same when we passed one of the votive stations along the road-side that mark the spot where someone's spirit left the earth after a car wreck and lately, seem to be getting denser than the trees.

Quite a few times she would recognize the name of a town: "So this is Almyros; my it's a big town. Siomos' youngest daughter married a boy from here and she was telling her mother she didn't like it one bit. She said the place was too flat." Farther down, somebody's son had married a girl from that village and gotten an olive grove and a guest house as a dowry. Now he lived there and his mother was heartbroken, and so on.

"Some go to Volos, some to Germany, some to America; poor Taxiarhes isn't good enough for them anymore," she would murmur. She scrutinized the gardens and the orchards we passed, with the critical eye of a colleague. "It looks like they are irrigating their olive trees down here; I bet they make olives as big as plums."

It was dark when we got to Athens. We got a hotel room and after a simple dinner, she was ready for bed. The city traffic awoke her at about three in the morning and, thinking we had overslept, she shook me awake.

"Must be time to get up, people are going to work," she said. I told her that there was always traffic in the city and talked her into going back to sleep.

When I woke up at dawn, she was already dressed, had her bed neatly made up and was sitting by the window, reading her Bible.

We took a taxi to the airport and an hour and a half later we were sitting in the plane, Mother scrutinizing everything she could see out of her window. On take-off, she whispered a little prayer and crossed herself. Soon, the rhythmic humming of the engines lulled her to sleep. She woke up when the plane started descending near Frankfurt and looked out of her window at the checkered farmland below. "It looks like a regular place," I heard her whisper to herself as I leaned over to fasten her seat belt. There was a trace of bewilderment in her voice; I guess she had been wondering what kind of land was it, that produced the cold, heartless, killing machines of the past.

While waiting for the connecting flight, we had lunch at one of the airport restaurants. Mother got an order of French fries and a tomato salad. She stared at my mouth when I was ordering, probably wondering how these strange sounds could mean normal things.

At the waiting lounge, an old black man sat next to Mother. She examined him from top to bottom and I could tell she was fighting back the urge to touch his skin.

"I've never seen one this close," she whispered. "When I was little, somebody from the Ahilopoulos family lived in Egypt. They visited the village one summer with their two black servants, a man and a woman. We used to peek through the fence to see what they looked like."

I told her she didn't have to whisper, that black man probably didn't understand Greek.

On the flight to New York, we sat next to a family from India. The husband and his wife were dressed in their traditional costumes: turbans, saris, the works. They said they were from Calcutta on their way to visit relatives in Washington. Their kids, a boy and a girl about eight or nine years old, played with an electronic game the whole time they were awake. They smiled at Mother and she smiled back.

"I used to see pictures of them in the newspaper, now I am sitting next to them," she whispered to me.

I would have loved to be able to read her thoughts at that moment.

At the John F. Kennedy airport she proudly handed her passport to the immigration officer. He glanced at the picture, looked at her, and with a broad smile told her "Welcome" and waived us on.

"Nice boy," she said, as we walked away.

Our connecting flight was on the next concourse. To get there faster I put Mother in a wheel chair and pushed her along. As I helped out of the chair in front of the escalator, she balked. "Are we going down there?"

"Just hold my hand and we will step on it together," I said.

She handed me her purse, looked at what the other people were doing, touched the moving rail gingerly as if it would shock her, and then held on to it. I could feel her palm perspiring.

At the bottom, she took a few steps then turned her head back to take another look at the monster we had just dismounted. *"Doxassi Kyrie"* (Glory to You Lord) she murmured and crossed herself.

She dozed off on the flight from New York to Atlanta and again on the short hop of the last leg. It was almost midnight when we got to Bigport. Margaret and the girls were waiting at the gate with a large bouquet of flowers and a sign: "Welcome Grandma" in Greek. It brought tears to her eyes.

At home, we called Greece and Mother talked to my sister "from the other side of the world."

When she woke up the next day, I gave her the tour of the house.

In Taxiarhes, even after the village was "discovered" and there were more *tavernas* than stables, Mother almost never ate out. The few times I suggested it, to save her the trouble of cooking, her answer was: "What will the people say? That I don't know how to cook?"

In Bigport, I wanted to show her all the variety that was available. We tried everything: Chinese, Italian, Greek, American/Greek and American/American. Always her portion was too big and mine too small. One night at a neighborhood restaurant, the owner came over and talked with us for a few minutes.

"He doesn't speak like the other Americans," said Mother when he left.

"He is from Turkey;" I said. "He came here about fifteen years ago. His daughter goes to school with our Katerina. She's the little girl who slept over the other night."

Mother didn't say anything. On the way out she confided: "The Turk is not a bad cook."

"His wife does the cooking," I said. "She is Italian."

She fell silent again.

Mother made friends with the ladies from the Greek church in Bigport, who would pick her up and take her to all the church functions, the Philoptohos meetings and the cooking preparations for the Greek Fest. When I could, I would drive her around and show her the sights of the town.

Sometimes we had friends over to our house for dinner or went to theirs and on most of those occasions I would ask Mother to come along to see how Americans lived. One day we visited Joe's house and that visit seemed to confuse Mother a lot. Joe Simmons is a contractor who has done well in the construction business and likes to show it. He goes to Margaret's church and I met him at one of the fellowship dinners Margaret dragged me to. He insisted on having Mother over for dinner. I tried to talk him out of it but in the end I said, "What the heck? It will be a chance for Mother to see me keeping company with rich people." So we set a date for a Sunday, after church.

It was a nice sunny afternoon and after dinner Joe gave us a tour of the place. His castle was in the middle of five acres on the outskirts of Bigport. Roaming in that acreage were two ponies, two goats, two peacocks and a flock of chickens. About a dozen colorful ducks were gliding on the small lake at the edge of the property.

Mother said the goats looked like the ones she had in Paraskevi a few years back. She called them, holding out a small, leafy twig and the goats came up and nibbled on it.

"They speak Greek," said Joe, laughing.

She asked if they make cheese with the milk and I tried to explain that they keep them as pets. I don't think I did a good job of it.

The chickens were roaming around, and at night, Joe said, they roosted on the trees.

"I guess they don't have foxes in America," said Mother.

"What did she say?" asked Joe who was standing next to her.

I translated.

"Funny she should say that," he said chuckling. "Just yesterday evening, a fox came out from those woods over there and grabbed a big rooster. He was so big, she had to drag him, and the rooster was clacking and flapping and there were feathers flying all over. It was something to see. I ran in the house to get my video, but by the time I got back they were gone. Yah, we got foxes, tell her."

I translated for Mother. She gave me a blank stare and didn't say anything. Then later, walking toward the house, she asked me in a low voice: "A while ago you meant to say he ran in the house to get his gun, didn't you?"

"No Mother, his movie camera."

"Oh, his movie camera," she echoed, sounding as if her voice was coming from far away, then she remained silent.

After the coffee, Joe's wife took Mother to show her the house. She did a thorough job of it; and the more awestruck Mother looked, the more bedrooms and bathrooms Mrs. Simmons would open up. She even included her walk-in closet with the tour.

"My, it's as big as a store," Mother exclaimed; which seemed to please Mrs. Edwina Simmons very much.

On a long weekend, we decided to take trip to North Carolina to visit Margaret's brother.

"One more place for my soul to travel through when I die," Mother mused.

On the way, she was fascinated by the wide open, uninhabited spaces, the abundance of water in the rivers and the lakes, and by the sheer size of the country. After we drove for about ten hours, she asked: "Are we still in America?"

We made a rest stop in Cherokee, North Carolina. At the entrance of the town, just past the souvenir shops selling authentic Indian tomahawks and headdresses made in Taiwan, we came to an authentic Indian teepee, next to a picturesque creek under a large hickory tree. In front of it sat an authentic Indian, in full ceremonial uniform; feathers and all. A sign stuck in a Coca Cola bottle, just out of camera range, informed us that for one dollar, you could have your picture taken with the Chief; or for five dollars you could get a Polaroid photograph, taken by the chief's grand-daughter. A young woman, also in native costume, was sitting on a bench under the tree, with a camera by her side, reading a fashion magazine.

I told Mother that these were Indians.

"They don't look like the Indians on the airplane," she said.

"These are American Indians," I said and recited the explanation of how Columbus thought he had arrived on the West side of India when he first came here and by the time they found out different the name had stuck.

"Ehm, if the cursed man didn't know where he was going why didn't he stay put? Would have saved lots of mothers the grief," she said.

It took some coaxing, but I got her to stand next to the chief for two dollars worth of pictures.

Later back home, the grandsons would show off the photographs at school and boast that their grandmother was close friends with Geronimo.

Chapter

25

*U*ntil the year of Mother's visit, I had managed to dodge all attempts to chair the Greek Festival, the annual fund-raising affair put on by the Greek church in Bigport. When someone nominated me to chair the affair, I would quickly stand up, thank them and say I regretfully had to decline because my workload, my other duties in the parish council and my frequent travels, would not permit me to do a good job, but I would be glad to help the person who was chosen in any way I could. Just like most of the others were saying.

This year, for reasons I couldn't explain to myself in the endless agonizing hours that were to follow, I didn't decline. When Manolis Vervatos stood up and said: "I nominate Nickola Pilio for chair for Festival," and Mrs. Irene Pappas (the Omaha Pappas), in her fine plantation-matron accent added: "I do second it, I most certainly do," I grinned and said: "I'll give it a try."

It was late March, two weeks after I came back from Greece. Mother didn't know what the festival was, but she said it sounded important and that "People must think a lot of you to put you in charge. Pray to God you live up to it."

The first Festival meeting, with last year's department heads, was a pandemonium; everyone wanted to either change jobs or change their help. After a lot of debating, pleading and old-fashioned arguing, we ended up with an updated organizational chart that would be the envy of the United Nations. There were committees and sub-committees, with their chiefs and sub-chiefs, and everyone had someone else to blame when things were not getting done.

Sofia Marks was always in charge of publicity. She wrote some kind of cooking column in the local paper and knew how to talk to the newspaper and television people. As soon as the sacrificial lamb had been selected, she would put the chairperson's photograph in the paper with a little write-up about the event.

My picture was in the paper two weeks after the general assembly meeting. Mother cut it out and sent it to my sister.

I asked Polyxeni Mavros to be the volunteer coordinator. She had one of the most valuable ingredients for the success of the affair: she knew who was not getting along with whom and who was not speaking to whom.

The second festival meeting was on a Monday night. The Saints were playing Atlanta and only half of the people showed up.

Irene Pappas, of the Omaha Papases, had asked to make a presentation. She did not chair anything, (she probably thought there wasn't enough prestige in it), but had called and asked if she could come to the meeting because she had a great thing for the gift shop and she wanted to show it to us before we made other plans. She sat at the end of the table holding on her lap a box with a blue bow on top and kept tapping her fingers on it, waiting to talk.

"I just returned from Corpus Christi," she started, "and while I was there they happened to have their Festival. My sister who runs the gift shop, gave me this to bring back. She says they sell lots and lots of them every year." She had the kind of southern belle-ish voice that northern comedians love to imitate.

She finished untying the bow and held up with two fingers of each hand, a light blue, short-sleeved T-shirt. "Isn't this something?" she beamed.

Everyone looked at the shirt, then at each other but nobody spoke. In the front of the shirt was the figure of a Greek Goddess, clad as befits a bosomy Goddess, in a thin, flowing, semi-transparent robe. She posed as though throwing a javelin, but instead of the javelin she was holding a long shiskebab. The cubes of meat and the chunks of onion and green pepper were in bright, vivid colors. The caption under it read: "The Greeks are throwing a party."

"Isn't this something? They sell lots and lots of them every year. I wanted to show it to you, so you can put your order in early." She passed it to her right, scrutinizing each person who examined the shirt. "They pay four dollars apiece and they sell them for ten, all sizes."

The shirt was being passed down the table, everybody holding it up, looking at the front, then the back, but no one said anything.

"In the back, they put the year of the Festival and they become collector's items," said Irene. Nobody spoke.

"Is it cotton?" our gift shop person finally asked.

"I think so, I am sure we can sell lots and lots of these."

Silence again. I could almost hear everyone's brain running on overdrive, trying to think of something to say.

231

"Thank you for bringing it to our attention," I finally said. "We will definitely discuss it and let you know."

She said she regretted she had to leave early but she was needed at a gala somewhere, and I escorted her to her car.

When I got back, John Alepakis, the history teacher, choir singer and Calamari booth chairman, asked to have the floor.

"The tentacles of the squid are scaring the Americans. We could have made double last year, had it not been for that. This year we leave them off and we charge fifty cents more."

"I no think the *Mericani* gonna pay four dollars for calamari. Besides, that's the best part of the *meze*," protested Big Jim Farmanis.

The person in charge of making the *dolmades* said she is going to need more help this year. "Like I told you before, it's getting harder and harder to find people to work."

"We could get some of the food already cooked," somebody suggested.

That got a lot of people stirred up. There were cries of: "You know nothing about food," and "Where are you when we need the help?" and "If that's the way you want to do it, you do it yourself."

The young professor of economics who had recently changed his name to Leonard Chartouche, because Lambros Kapsokalyvas didn't sound professor-ish enough, interrupted his scribbling. "If we opted to procure some of the items ready to serve and we held the Festival for three days, I am certain we could double the profit," he said.

"If I am you father, I ask for my money back from that fancy school he send you," answered Big Jim Farmanis. "You learn a bunch of fancy words but nothing about life. The *Mericani* no come here to eat store food, they can go buy it in Food World. That's my '*pinion*."

Jimmy Loukas, the chairman of the *souvlaki* booth, cooked and passed around samples of chicken souvlaki for everyone to taste. "We can make twenty-five percent more profit if we sell this instead of pork," he said.

Big Jim Farmanis almost swallowed his cigar. "There is no respect for nothing no more, we sell our ... our *paradosi*, our history, for a few pennies profit. We make us like the *Mericani*, everything for the dollar. You make me sick, I no want to do nothing with you no more."

He threw the chicken *souvlaki* in the trash can, grimacing as if he just discovered it carried the plague, and stomped out.

"He's got a hundred bucks riding on the Saints," said somebody.

Jenny Xanthis was responsible for the cultural activities.

She waited till Jim was out of the parking lot, then she said that we need to get someone else to do the church tours. "Last year we got a lot of complaints from people not understanding Mr. Farmanis' accent."

"It's a Greek church tour, with a real Greek, what do you want? Somebody that talks like James Bond?" someone asked.

"You think you could give Big Jim some coaching?" I asked Jenny when the laughing stopped. She looked at me as if I had asked her to walk on water.

"Are you kidding?" she said. "He is Greek. The only constructive criticism a Greek will accept is praise."

After a while people started saying they have to be somewhere, or the baby-sitter will be leaving. I suggested we study the church tours and the chicken souvlaki problems further at in the next meeting.

"It's a miracle the thing comes off," said Jenny as we were walking in the parking lot. "Everybody seems to disagree with everybody else."

Jenny Xanthis, tall, blonde and good looking, was a converted Greek. She had moved to Bigport a few years earlier from South Africa, when the Greek she was married to was hired as the head doctor at a local hospital. She had a delightful accent and a cheerful personality, but hadn't fully fathomed the Greek way of debating and deciding things. The genes for orderliness and discipline had been planted in her brain by her Dutch ancestors, deep enough to have survived ten years of marriage.

The next festival meeting had to be rescheduled because Margaret and I had to go to Pompano Beach for Joe Carroll's funeral. During the long drive, we kept repeating to each other as if it was the first time we said it, how unbelievable it was. He seemed in perfect health a couple of months earlier at the family reunion, when he was telling everybody about an old houseboat he was going to buy to go island hopping when he retired in a couple of years. Then all of a sudden, he had a massive heart attack and died.

"That goes to show you," we kept saying, as if it were a brand new statement. "You never know when your time will come."

We managed to settle the festival layout in two meetings.

A week before the festival, the preparations got into high gear. Monday evening was *souvlaki* preparation time. We prepared eighteen hundred servings (a big jump from last year).

Dr. Xanthis, with some of his surgeon friends, were the cutting group. Carefully and methodically, concentrating on finger preservation, they cut six hundred pounds of pork loins into cubes. Leo Marks, working as a courier, transported the cut meat to the next table, where another group did the skewering. Then Big Jim Farmanis would immerse the souvlaki in his special marinade, while praising my good sense not to go for the chicken suggestion.

The star of the evening was Leo's visiting brother, Stavros Marks, a reporter for a Miami newspaper. He was in his late fifties, tall, slender, with a "high gloss" shaved head and the manners of a British aristocrat. He spoke like Cary Grant and had the women hanging on his every word.

When somebody reminisced about their parents, it prompted Stavro to tell how his parents had met and married.

"My mother told me the story a couple of times but I liked the way Father would tell it; Mother put a romantic spin to it.

Anyway, here is the consolidated version of it: Mother was born in Mani, the rockiest, most God-forsaken place in all of Greece.

When she was eleven years old, my grandparents sent her to live with her aunt in Alexandria. In those days, lots of people migrated to Egypt. Her aunt wasn't rich but she was well educated and made sure Mother got a good education also. When the aunt died five years later Mother returned to the village, broke and over-educated. She could speak English and French, play the piano, recite poetry and do a lot of other useless stuff. My grandparents argued and blamed each other for sending her away and getting her ruined.

My father saw her planting flowers in front of the house, six months after she came back from Egypt. He was twenty years old then. 'That's a good spot for cabbages and peppers,' he said.

'Flowers are pretty,' she told him. Father thought that was a stupid answer. He asked for a drink of water and Mother washed her hands and went into the house. He was wondering, he told me later, how come she didn't have enough sense to keep a tin cup by the well so a person could scoop water out of the bucket to drink.

She came back bringing water in a glass, on a tray no less.

He went back for water many more times that summer and in early fall send word to Grandfather that he wanted to marry her.

Grand father thought it was a miracle.

A couple of months later they came to America. They arrived in Boston in the middle of the winter. My father washed dishes for some Greek and Mother got a job at a bank. Later, her boss helped her find my father a job at a textile mill where he earned more without having to talk much. He never learned how to speak English — always planned to take his money and retire to the village. He sent the money to build a big fountain in the village square. It's still there, I saw it. The *Makromeritis Vrisi* they call it. They have his name on a marble plaque. That's my old man's mark on the village.

Stavros took a sip of his root beer and continued: "When he retired, my old man went to the village planning to stay there for good, but after three months he packed up and he was back in Boston. 'They don't know how to live their lives over there,' he said."

At the same time we were preparing for the Festival at the church, I was making preparations for the navy inspector's visit at the shop. The navy brass was supposed to come on Friday of the Festival to witness the "First Article test" of the navy gismo. Before I went to the church-hall on Wednesday morning, I stopped by the shop to check on the preparations. We had been working on that thing for months and now it was almost ready. It stood in the middle of the shop, nine feet tall and twelve feet round at the top, looking like a super-mushroom, puzzling everybody that came by.

After a walk around the shop, I told Floyd to call me at the church if he needed me.

At the church grounds, the guy from the tent-rental outfit kept asking me if I was sure I wanted the tents set up. There was a hurricane in the Caribbean that could be heading this way, he said.

There was a refrigerated truck parked at the side of the church hall packed with gyro, souvlaki and marinated chicken. The refrigerators, freezers and walk-in coolers, were full of the things the women of the community had been cooking for months. I didn't want to think of what we would do if the hurricane decided to come this way.

Mike Athan, working since dawn, had all the booths set up. The little blue and white flags had been strung and were now fluttering in the light breeze.

When I got home, late that evening, I tuned into the weather channel. The hurricane had wreaked havoc in the Caribbean, had run the whole length of Cuba and was getting close to the Florida Keys.

"As of five o'clock this evening, the center of the hurricane was ..." a weather girl with a short skirt was pointing to a little, two-bladed propeller on the screen. Then pointing to a line of dots behind it: "If it continues on the same path, it is projected to make landfall Friday evening, here, in the city of..." And as she tapped the city with her stick, it felt as if someone was hitting my head. "In Key West," she continued...

I switched to a local channel. Here, the weatherman, a portly fellow with gray, thinning hair, was showing on a more detailed map of the area the possible path of the hurricane. "If it maintains the present course, the center will pass right about here." He pointed to a spot which in my mind was right over the big tent. They were advising people how to get ready for the hurricane: Secure all patio furniture, have a full tank of gas, have a flashlight and a radio with good batteries and stock up on canned food. Nothing about stocking up on souvlaki and pastitsio, so this year's chairman, who was trying to show off to his mother, wouldn't get crucified at the general assembly meeting.

"There is some possibility of relief though," he continued, "this cold front" (pointing to a wavy green line on the screen) "is moving south behind this low pressure area, which if it gets here soon, could force the hurricane to change course.

I made a silent prayer for a cold front.

Thursday: day one of the Festival.

I got to the community center as soon as it was light. This morning, the television people were coming to broadcast the weather report from the kitchen of the community hall; it was another one of Sofia Marks' publicity gimmicks. I had changed shirts three times, until I found one that met Margaret's approval. In my head I rehearsed many times my moment in front of the camera. I was going to look relaxed, preoccupied with my work and act as if the television crew had just happened to come by, instead of being scheduled three months in advance.

I told Margaret to make sure that Mother was watching.

The television crew arrived thirty minutes after I got there. The portly weatherman was relaxed and casual, and tried to make everyone around feel the same. Then when he put the microphone in front of me, my thinking stopped. When I spoke, the words echoed inside my head as if someone else was in there, doing the talking. Like a trapped bird, I kept glancing back and forth to the camera lens and to the microphone and to the fellow behind it. I was supposed to point to my left, to the serving counter with the white table cloth, where the pans of pastitsio, dolmades and all the other delicacies had been placed by Marie, tilted at just the right angle toward the camera, with miniature Greek flags behind them. Instead, I moved the right hand and pointed to the sinks, where a mountain of dirty pots, pans, ladles and spatulas was waiting to be washed. Then I was supposed to hold up a plate of pastries and explain what they were, but I forgot to do it. Instead I held the plate with my left palm in a tight grip as if someone was trying to yank it away from me.

The experienced weatherman made the disaster seem scripted. He picked up a cookie from the plate, held it up, nodded towards the sink and said: "As you can see, it takes a lot of work to make these delights." Then took a bite, and looking into the camera, he declared: "Yum, yum, good stuff, hurry up, come and taste some of these before the hurricane forces them to close up."

The interview lasted only a couple of minutes, but by the time it was over I was sweaty and exhausted.

Margaret said I looked tense and I forgot to say what hours we were open and what we were offering.

"I think you got people confused," she said.

Mother thought I looked peakish. So much for stardom.

Kyra Katina offered me a glass of water and a cookie.

"We might end up eating most of these if the hurricane keeps coming this way," I said, holding the kourabie.

"It will go away, I am sure. Last night I dreamed I was talking to Father Thomas. Every time I have worry, I see him in my sleep and everything he tells me, always comes true. He told me that the big storm will go away."

"From your mouth to God's ear, Kyra Katina."

I drove to the shop, had a quick look at how they were doing with the navy mushroom and went back to the church.

By eleven-thirty the line to the hall entrance was stretching to the end of the block.

Everybody was in high gear and high spirits, smiling, making silly jokes, feeling brotherly to everyone.

I was going from station to station, making sure everybody had supplies, helping where shorthanded, resolving disputes and calming down tempers.

The *bakalico* was doing a thriving business. People were buying everything on the tables. Nick Podakakis, a retired cook, fit the part of a village grocer as if he were cast by Hollywood: a white apron snug over his round belly, his thick, long mustache moving in tune with the chewing strokes of his plump cheeks - always sampling the samples.

I got a message that Marika Simons was looking for me. I found her in the kitchen, tossing salad in a huge metal bowl; with pieces of lettuce stuck all over her, she looked like a camouflaged marine.

"We are running out of tomatoes, Costas was supposed to bring them this morning and he hasn't shown up yet. There is no telling when this guy gonna show up. I am already on the last box, we have nothing after that." She was talking panicky fast, as if the calamity was about to crush her.

"We just started, Marika, how come we are out already?"

"Don't yell at me, I didn't want this job to begin with." She looked as if she could burst out crying at any moment.

"Even if we get them now, we've got to clean them and cut them up; we don't have the time, did you see the line? This is it, next year I'm coming in as a visitor, that's it, for sure."

"And I'll join the Hare Krishnas, they only make you sell flowers at the corner," I joked.

Leo Marks offered to go get a box of cherry tomatoes and that pacified Marika.

Voula, the young divorcee, had problems with the machine making the *loucoumades* (those delicious, round honey puffs with an eighty percent profit margin). She tried to adjust it and ended up covered with flour and dough from the top of her blonde curls to her red, high-heeled shoes. She looked like a little girl trying to make cookies. She finally unplugged it and started making them the old-fashioned way: squeezing the dough in her left fist, scooping with a spoon what comes out between the thumb and the pointer and dropping it in the hot oil.

It works fine this way except it doesn't look very appetizing and the things come out in strange shapes.

I told her to be careful not to splatter too much oil and she got mad, threw her frilly, pink apron across the booth and said she would go and work somewhere else. I got Mike Athan to fix the machine and I went looking for someone to run it.

I asked Manolis Vervatos if he knew of anyone that could run the *loukoumades* machine.

Vre si, you mean *that's* shut down? People are buying that stuff like crazy, got to keep it going." He walked with me to the booth. "Look at this," he said, pointing to the people standing in line waiting for *loukoumades*. "Give me an apron."

"Don't have one, we've run out," I said.

"Never mind, I'll use this one." He put on Voula's pink apron with the white frilly edges and started loading the machine. Soon he had more dough on his mustache than in the hopper, but he was popping out the loucoumades faster than a machine gun.

Big Jim, working the wine booth, called me over to tell me that he liked this job better than the hopeless task of explaining the church to the *Mericani*. "You know, I bet you ten to one, the hurricane is going to go to Texas," he announced with a grin as he poured me a glass from the source of his optimism. Big Jim is like the Oracle of Delphi when he gets a couple of glasses of wine in him.

Friday, day two.

I turned on the television as soon as I opened my eyes. The hurricane was still churning out there. The trail of little dots was showing that all it did in the last twelve hours was make a loop.

I drove to the shop. The guys trickled in as the starting time approached. The ones coming in early would walk by me, say "Good morning," ask how the festival was going and what I thought about the hurricane. After the whistle blew, I greeted those who tried to sneak by and listened to their excuses. I walked around the shop, to make sure everything was ready for the test. The Washington wheels were coming this morning. We had been preparing for this "First Article Test" for days. The huge, rust-colored, mushroom-like contraption, with a dozen yellow hydraulic jacks around it, resembled something out of a children's book. Floyd and Moe could be the dwarf cartoon characters playing hide and seek, as they were stepping in and out of it, securing the fifty ton jacks and the measuring instruments.

An engineer, with walls full of diplomas and membership plaques, had charged me a fortune to write the "First Article Test Procedures." It was a book an inch thick, full of drawings, graphs and calibration tables; bound together with a plastic binder, with my company's name and logo on the glossy blue cover. It looked big time.

We were supposed to push the top of the oversized mushroom with a force of two thousand pounds and then measure how much it bent out of shape and check if the weld cracked. It seemed I was putting a lot of trust in Moe's welding.

I kept running through my mind: Three mushrooms per month, at three thousand dollars profit per mushroom the first year, then so much more the next year and every year after that for five years. The house in Taxiarhes would be finished, just the way I want it.

There was a lot riding on the success of this test.

I walked around the mushroom for the zillionth time, checking the location of the jacks and every inch of the welding.

"It will be all right boss, you had the best welder on it," said Moe.

"We will know pretty soon, the inspectors will be showing up any minute now."

They didn't. Instead they called, saying their plane got delayed and they would be arriving around noon.

I told Floyd to have me paged at the church when they came.

I listened to the radio on the way to church. The hurricane still hadn't made up its mind where to go.

The lines started forming around ten o'clock.

This year, Mike Athan installed a paging system. Through it, Sofia Marks would announce the starting of the church tours and the cooking demonstrations or give a plug for some slow-moving item. Ourania Vervatos used it to page people, always giving a long-winded explanation: "Mike Athan, you are needed in the carry out booth, to hook up another warmer for the pastichio, because the other one is not working and the food doesn't stay warm and Mr. Lourakis says..." a full five-minute news bulletin.

I was getting a cup of coffee when I heard the loudspeakers scream my name. "Nikos Pilios, Vasilis Larkeas needs to talk to you at the calamari booth right away, about his relief not being here yet and about..."

I got there, started talking to Vasilis and she was still broadcasting.

"George was supposed to be here an hour ago and hasn't made it yet. I told him I got to pick up the kids from school. I need to leave right now." He handed me his apron and walked away. He turned around after a couple of yards and called back: "There is something wrong with the second burner, the oil won't get hot."

"I'll fix it," I growled. The damn guy, he had promised to stay the whole day. It was the only time he was asked to do anything for the church. The rest of the year, if he ever came to church, he would spend his time in the community hall, dishing out wisdom and drinking coffee.

I put a batch of calamari in the fryer and took a look at the ailing burner. The gas was not open all the way; the knob was sticking a bit. He hadn't even tried.

I told the guy in the gyro booth to keep an eye on it and went looking for the volunteer coordinator. I found her arguing on the phone.

"But Dimi, I have you down for the evening slot at the pastries. You promised... but couldn't you have made some arrangements beforehand?... I know, but Dimi this is the second day in the row you make me look bad. O.K. then O.K.!" and she slammed down the phone.

"I thought we were not going to have squid this year," she said. Nobody asked me for people for that booth. It's your job to make sure everybody knows what is going on." She wasn't much help.

"I'll run the damn booth myself," I said and stumped away, looking straight ahead without really seeing anybody, zigzagging through masses of slow-moving people and silently cursing those who blocked my path to stare at every piece of pastry and every stupid poster.

The music was blaring, the dancers were dancing, and people were clapping. I slapped the squid in the flour mix pan as if it was fighting back. "They are all an uncaring, ungrateful bunch of people," I kept muttering. "All they care about is themselves and nobody else. When this nightmare is over, I am not going to have anything to do with the Greeks, their festivals and their parish councils. They are all a bunch of selfish egoists who want somebody else to do their work and then criticize the hell out of him. Boby Carras had the right idea to join the Baptists. I should have learned my lesson when Antonios shafted me. Now he's in charge of the lamb spit, acting pious and running for Christian-of-the-Year. If the hurricane blew this joint off the map, it will serve them right."

A fellow from Margaret's church with a plate full of pastries walked by.

"Great festival," he said, "so big, yet so well-organized."

I just grinned.

In the afternoon, Margaret came in for her shift at the gift shop and brought Mother and the girls. Margaret was active in her church, but she would come with me on major holidays and sometimes lend a hand with the activities. Later she would call in the IOUs.

I gave Mother a tour of the festival ground. I showed her the different booths, the grocery store, the gift shop, the children's playground, the big tent and the behind-the-scenes operation of the kitchen. "It's bigger than the county fair back home," she said in awe. Then she scolded me for standing in the draft when I was all sweaty; I would never get rid of that infernal cough that way.

For the rest of the afternoon, Mother sat in the pastry booth helping with the packaging and chatted with Kyra Dora, fresh from Athens visiting her son. Her son had come here as a student and ended up marrying a woman almost the same age as Kyra Dora to keep from getting deported when somebody squealed on him about having a full-time job. Mother and Kyra Dora spent most of their time lobbing curses at Columbus.

Maria and Nicole came over to the calamari booth. They thought what I was doing was "cool." I showed them what to do and left before they changed their minds.

Everybody kept asking for the latest news on the hurricane. Saturday was expected to be our biggest day. If the hurricane came this way, we would be stuck with the mountains of food and pastries.

Some years earlier, a hurricane had turned out to be a savior. It saved Poseidon Marine Services from bankruptcy, its foolhardy owner from getting humiliated in two continents and his parents from the heartbreak of realizing they had raised an idiot.

Maybe this was the payback.

I kept calling Floyd every thirty minutes, asking if he had heard from the navy people, but they never called.

It was after midnight when I got home. I was asleep before I even hit the bed.

I dreamed I was being chased by a huge angry mob, waving spatulas and eggbeaters and throwing shishkebab spears at me. I kept turning back to see if they were catching up, tripped and fell into a vat with loukoumades dough. I yelled for help and Margaret shook me awake.

Saturday, day three.

As soon as I got out of bed, I ran downstairs and turned the television on. I flipped through the channels, listened for a moment, then I let out a shout that knocked everybody out of bed.

"What happened?" called Margaret from the top of the stairs.

"The hurricane is heading west!"

"Praise the Lord," she said.

I drove to the community center with renewed optimism. The sky was clear, a gentle breeze was blowing and the hurricane watch was lifted. It was a perfect fall day. With a little luck we would have a good turnout at the festival. Maybe they wouldn't nail my ass at the general assembly. Maybe I wouldn't look so bad in front of Mother after all.

I was whistling a peppy Greek tune, pulling into the parking lot. The tune died as soon as I stopped the car. Ourania Vervatos was next to me before I opened the door.

"I reported it, I went across the street and reported it, but who knows when they are going to come; don't even know if they work on Saturdays; people were already calling for carry-outs when it got knocked out. Without the phone we are dead, we are dead, dead dead. Why that had to happen today, when..." She hadn't taken a breath yet.

"Calm down, Ourania, it will be all right, what happened?"

She took a deep breath.

"The garbage truck was picking up the dumpster. I told Mike when they brought them here the other day, I said: 'Mike, I don't think this is the right place for the dumpster, it don't look good.' I parked my car there, trying to hide it and now look at it, it's covered with..."

I walked toward the truck. The driver, still in his seat, was talking to someone on the radio.

"What happened?" I asked.

"The little car was in the way, tried to miss it and the box hit the pole."

The dumpster was hooked to the truck, half open, puking plastic plates, chicken bones and pastitsio over a cherry red Volkswagen.

The telephone pole lay broken in half, on top of the overflowing dumpster, half buried in "Sunshine" lettuce boxes and black garbage bags.

The telephone company guy who arrived a half-hour later was not very optimistic.

"It'll be Tuesday before we get a new pole up. We are short on equipment. Sent everything to Texas to help with the hurricane."

There were frantic phone calls to the telephone company and to the garbage company; to Nick Matrapas who never came to church but was a big businessman and knew a lot of politicians; and to Andrew Carras' son the local District Attorney who had nothing to do with the telephone company but was the biggest Greek wheel I knew in Bigport. In the end, the phone company put in a temporary line until the pole installing crew could get to it.

Margaret called the community hall around nine-thirty and got everybody looking for me. She said a navy guy called about the test. He left his name and phone number.

It was one of the Washington wheels. I called him from the pay phone in the community hall. He said their plane got diverted because of the hurricane and they were stranded in Pensacola. They could drive over and "get this test business over with" today, if I could do it; that way they could fly home this evening and salvage something of the weekend.

I told him I would have a crew in the shop by one o'clock. I called Floyd, Moe, Tuan and Leonidas and had them at the shop by twelve-thirty.

The Washington people drove up at two o'clock.

They said no to the coffee and pastries, got their drawings, measuring tapes and calipers out and started examining the mushroom. They measured every little piece of it, looked at their drawings, read through all the paper work and finally around four o'clock, they said we could start the test.

I had eight hydraulic jacks and four guys standing by them. Each jack had a large pressure gauge. On the glass of the gauge we had drawn a red line, marking the spot where the expensive engineer had calculated the pressure would equal the required force.

The goal was two thousand pounds of pressure.

We started pumping. Each guy, handling two jacks, would pump two hundred pounds, call it out and wait till all stations reached that point. Then they did the same thing all over again to the next line. The needle slowly moved from one line to the next, each line representing two hundred pounds.

Every four hundred pounds we stopped and one of the navy guys measured the deflection of the mushroom top. As the pressure increased the pumping got harder. After eight hundred pounds the metal started flexing and making groaning sounds, like a dragon resisting torture. Flakes of mill-scale began breaking off, fluttering down.

My handkerchief was soaked.

At fourteen hundred pounds, a bracket holding one of the jacks broke, making a loud, heart-stopping noise as the jack tumbled on the floor. In a flash, I saw in my mind the lopsided force ripping the welded seam and popping the mushroom top like a sardine can. I yelled at everyone to dump the pressure from the other seven jacks.

"Let's get a coffee break till we get the bracket re-welded," I said keeping my hands in my pockets and acting cool. My hands were shaking and felt sweaty.

I got everybody a cup of coffee and passed around a tray of *baklava and courabiedes*. I couldn't think of anything I could talk about with the Washington people so I went to keep an eye on Moe welding the bracket.

"Don't look at me, the Cuban dude welded that," said Moe.

"I'm sure he did Moe, put some more weld on the rest of the brackets while you are at it."

"Already done it, boss."

I went back in and told the navy wheels we were ready.

They finished munching on the cookies and told me they were delicious. I told them I baked them myself from an old family recipe, we had a courteous laugh and everybody went to where they stood before.

We started pumping again. Every stroke took an eternity to complete. We got to the fourteen hundred pounds and I held my breath. A couple of mill-scale flakes fluttered down.

"We are almost there, guys," I said, "let's go up two more."

We went up to sixteen, the metal grunting as we pumped. We stopped. Nothing happened. The navy guy took his measurements and called them out to another guy who was writing them down on a chart. When he finished, he stepped out of the way.

"Almost there," I said again. "Let's go up two more." We started pumping again. The jack felt tight. We had to put all our weight on the handle to make it go down. The hydraulic hoses rattled with every stroke. Everybody was drying the sweat off his forehead.

It was the last pumping.

"Two thousand pounds." Floyd's voice rang through the shop. "Two thousand," repeated Moe. "Same," said Tuan Nguyen, conscious of his accent. "*Dio Hiliades*, two thousand," an excited Leonidas echoed the magic number.

"We are there folks," the navy guy said. "Keep it there for fifteen minutes, we take another set of measurements and then you can take the load off."

Some headed for the Coke machine, others lit cigarettes and sat down.

"Don't start it again boss, it'll be all right," said Moe, when I reached for his cigarette pack.

The muscles in my chest were aching. I didn't realize that I had strained myself pushing on those jacks.

I remembered that the festival was going on and went in the office and called the church. The phone was busy. I figured I would wait a few minutes and try again. I sunk into my chair, with my elbows on my desk and my head in my hands. I needed this contract and by all methods of judging I deserved this contract. I made a pledge: If I ended up getting this contract, out of the first year's money, I would buy a big chandelier for the church in Bigport.

I got up and walked outside. "And I'll buy one for the church in Taxiarhes too, bigger than the one Kostas Liapis bought," I added.

In the shop, Floyd was talking with one of the navy guys about deer hunting. I looked at my watch and walked around the shop coughing and massaging some aching muscles around my chest. About time I started taking it easy, I thought, I am not getting any younger.

"Ready to take the load off," I heard the senior navy wheel saying. I rushed back to the mushroom.

"We go down the same way we did it coming up, guys — two hundred at a time," I instructed. We released the pressure slowly till it got down to zero. Then we took the jacks away.

The navy guy stepped in and started taking measurements again, calling them out to the fellow who wrote them down, then all of them went in the office and compared the measurements before and after pumping. I wished I hadn't given up smoking. Finally they broke their huddle:

"Looks good, no visual damage, no permanent deformation," the senior wheel said. "Now if we hurry, we might catch the last flight to Atlanta and maybe we'll make it home tonight. You will get the official report in a week. You did it. Congratulations."

I said "Thank you" and tried to act cool. I would yell later.

I told my guys I would buy them a beer if they came to the festival, and I went back to the church.

The crowds were coming in hordes, buying everything in sight. It felt wonderful seeing the mountains of baklava boxes and bags of coulourakia melting away.

Margaret came at about five-thirty to help with the evening crowd and brought Mother and Kyra Dora. They sat at a section reserved for senior citizens, and every time I walked by I could feel Mother's eyes following me. A couple of times our eyes met and she smiled. Her look was a mixture of longing and admiration; very much like her look the first time she saw my house and longingly whispered: "Ah, if only your poor father could see it."

I ran into George Papas on his way to the counting room.

"With this deposit," he said, raising his hand holding two money bags, "we are breaking all past records." I felt like kissing him.

One by one the stations were running out of things to sell. All the *bakalico* had left were a few bottles of olive oil and about a dozen packages of *manestra*. The gift shop was down to its last komboloi. Even without the T-shirts of "Shiskebab Athena," they took in more than any year before.

John Papas, the hospital accountant, stopped at the gift shop table and tried on the last "authentic" Greek fisherman's hat.

"Buy it," I said, "it looks good on you."

"Well, I might, since it is for the church." Then while writing the check, he said, "Next Saturday, I'm taking some colleagues from the hospital out on the boat for a few hours fishing. Care to join us?"

I said I had already made plans.

I hadn't really planned that far ahead, but somehow being accepted in his inner circle, didn't seem to give the satisfaction I thought it would.

At around nine o'clock, most of the booths had closed down.

Everyone was grinning and everyone was telling everyone else (hoping the words would bounce back): "You did a great job, Congratulations."

We gathered by the dance floor and I thanked everyone for their hard work and presented a bouquet of roses to Ourania Vervatou and a box of cigars to Christos Pittas he was responsible for running the kitchen. The Greek Fest was the only time he would stay away from the Andros restaurant for a whole week except when he was in Greece.

A feeling of wanting to hug everybody run through me.

The lamb on the electric spit was turning slowly under the watchful eye of Antonios Vrahis, who kept basting it with a long brush. The slime-ball does a good lamb on the spit, no argument about that. Actually, he is not too bad of a guy. With the exception of the lucky ones who inherited their business, most of us worked for somebody else in the beginning. He'd probably gotten some bad advice about how to start up on his own.

By the time I finished my talk, Antonios cut up the lamb, someone poured some wine to toast the occasion and everyone said: "*Kai tou hronou*" (may we do it next year).

The music started and people got up to dance.

Someone pulled me to the dance floor.

Chapter | 26

"Morning boss, heard you went to see a doctor last week, what's the verdict? You pregnant?" It was Friday morning, last week of September. Moe had already clocked in and was now sitting on his tool bucket by the shop door, smoking a Camel and waiting for the bell to ring. Then he would slowly stand up, stretch a couple of times, transport the bucket to his work station and turn around and head for the bathroom. Nikos was getting out of his truck. He knew there was sincere concern under the crude joke; they had been together for almost fifteen years.

"He said, two more payments on his Mercedes and I am going to be as good as new," he answered walking towards the office.

"That's good, so long ain't nothing wrong with your check-signing hand."

"Nothing wrong with that," answered Nikos over his shoulder. Then before he got into the office, he added, "Anyway, you aren't getting a paycheck this week Moe; the garnishments ate it all up."

He told the secretary to get his coffee, then he watched her putting the cup on edge of his desk. He wandered, not for the first time, if she fooled around. She was still young-looking, with a firm, curvy body; that goofy old husband of hers couldn't keep her satisfied. Nikos would bet on that.

He took a sip of the coffee, put his feet on the desk and watched his cigarette smoke rise towards the ceiling.

Margaret had been on his case to see a doctor about his cough and his muscle aches. By some careful planning, she arranged for him to meet Doctor Milhowser one evening when her church group met at their house. The doctor, after talking to Nikos for a few minutes, said he should go in for a blood test and a physical. Nikos let Floyd look after the shop and had taken almost half the day off last Tuesday for a visit to the doctor's. He knew the doctor was hustling business for himself but he had agreed, just to keep Margaret happy. He already knew what the cure for all his aches and pains was: a few weeks in Greece, eating food worth eating and taking it easy. He had been thinking and planning about that trip for a long time. His mother had returned to the village a few months back and was telling everybody how she got lost in his big house trying to find a closet, and what a wonderful, huge place, America is, and how it couldn't run without her son.

The navy "mushroom" contract was over a year old. The crew working on those super-secret navy gismos had almost run out of mistakes and was humming along, pumping them out like donuts. Every month, the navy made an electronic bank deposit to Poseidon Marine Services' account and Nikos discovered it had turned out to be even more profitable than he had originally estimated. It kept everybody busy and for quite some time now, he only took on additional work if he liked the price or the customer. He was relishing the fact that he didn't have to go hat in hand, to ass-kiss pompous purchasing agents who mispronounced his name or pretended they didn't understand his accent. Now they came to him.

The loan from the Greek bank had been paid off, and the way the navy money was coming in, Nikos figured he could renovate the whole house without borrowing a nickel. Margaret was only coming to the office two days a week now to check the books. The rest of the time she kept busy managing the apartment building that Philip Chalmers, the hot-shot, real estate wheeler-dealer she knew from her church, had talked them into buying. Nikos had to admit: it was a good investment; it was paying for itself and then some.

A couple more years like this, he thought, and he would give the finger to the world. It had taken fourteen years of fighting, scraping and struggling but damn it, he had made it. This time, when he got to the village, they would know he had arrived. Buying a round of *tsipouro* for the guys at the Festorias *cafenio* is little league; he's going to invite everybody from the village for a big picnic at the Bellmaker's property, with two, three, four, as many lambs as it will take, roasting on the spits and a band playing for everybody to dance.

First, he's going to get the priest to do the pre-construction *agiasmo* (blessing), of the Bellmaker's house. Then, he's sure, Kostas Liappis, who got re-elected village president a few months back, will make a short speech, without any prodding, and christen the house the "Nicolas Pilios Manor." Also, he'll probably say that the village is grateful to its native son who made such great *prokopi* abroad and came back to share it with the people of his birthplace. Then there will be eating and drinking and dancing, for as long as there are people standing. Nikos could almost see his old man nudging Saint Peter at the Paradise cafenio in heaven: "That's my boy, down there, I knew he would make it; never doubted it."

It's going to be great. He is going to arrange it so he can go there next month; October is the best time of the year to visit the village.

The renovation will start the day after the celebration. Pavlos Stenos is going to be the contractor, he does very good work. Nikos has spent a fortune on telephone calls to him.

Last month, he sent two boxes full of brochures, photographs and product literature to Greece with Stavro Rigotis of Carras Ship Supply. Nikos had been gathering it for years. It was all numbered and cataloged to match a master list he had made for every part of the house. He put the list on the top of one box and had also mailed an extra copy to Pavlos. Everything was spelled out, item by item:

Interior doors : per enclosure No. 3

Dining room chandelier : per enclosure No. 12

Stair rails : per enclosure No. 22

Patio flagstone : per enclosure No. 15

And so on, a full note pad; no guessing, no chance for mistakes.

Stavros was going to Greece for a month, and since he was traveling light Nikos got him to carry the boxes. "When I go anywhere with the wife, it looks like we are moving; the blessed woman packs everything in the house. They'll charge me a fortune in overweight for these two boxes," Nikos had explained.

"Women take a lot of clothes and beautification junk with them," Stavros, who had never been married, informed him.

When Nikos took the boxes to Carras he had left them open, so Stavros could see there was only paper in them and wouldn't worry about the custom inspectors. Since they were open, he showed Pete Carras some of the things he was putting in the house: the paneled study with the tall book shelves, the large carved desk that would be by the corner window overlooking the Aegean, the flagstone patio and most of the other things. Carras liked the large Jacuzzi that would be installed in the front room, by a large window.

"It might be too late to try for a son, but Margaret and I will be soaking our aching muscles while taking in the view," Nikos had said.

Within a week, every Greek in Bigport had heard about the "palace" Nikos was building in the village.

A few days later, Pavlos called to say he had picked up the boxes. Nikos told him to put them in the front room of the house; it was going to be the field office during the renovation. "And make sure they don't get wet, it took me a long time to gather all that stuff," he had instructed.

After a while he put out the cigarette and went to see who was goofing off in the shop. Around eleven o'clock, when he was at the far end of the shop, checking how the work on a chain conveyor was going, he heard the secretary page him: "Mr. Pilios, line three," her voice rang over the welding machine hum. Nikos picked up the shop phone.

"Mr. Pilios, this is Yolanda from the Diagnostic Center. Dr. Milhowser would like to know if you could come in for another blood test." Her voice was young, soft, friendly and Southern.

"What did you do with the gallon you sucked out of me last week?"

She chuckled. "Dr. Milhowser thinks the lab got it mixed up. He would like to get another sample. Also since you will be coming in, he would like you to have some X-rays taken. He will leave instructions at the desk."

"We must be hiring from the same place; my guys don't seem to get it right the first time either." She didn't laugh.

"Dr. Milhowser would like you to come in tomorrow morning at seven-thirty, could you do that?"

"I guess I could. It's a hell of a way to start the day; visiting the vampires. Is there anything else the good doctor would like me to do?"

"Remember, nothing to eat or drink for twelve hours before the test," she added.

Nikos hung up and mumbled something nasty about incompetent people and went to help Floyd and Tuan fit the plates on the chain conveyor.

"I am going to be a little late tomorrow morning," he told Floyd, "when Bigport Steel delivers the angle-iron make sure you count the pieces before you sign the ticket."

"Always do, chief," said Floyd, and with the sledge hammer hit the wedge to bring the two pieces of plate together. He hit it a couple of times, but nothing moved.

"Here, let me have a go at it," said Nikos. "You watch the line and tell me when it's in place." He got the sledgehammer and banged hard a couple of times on the top of the wedge.

"Two more hit and will OK," said Tuan, watching the chalk line.

Nikos raised the hammer over his head, ready to strike the wedge again, when suddenly he felt a sharp pain across his chest and his arms went numb. He lost his grip on the handle and the hammer went flying away, almost hitting Tuan on the head.

"Are you OK, chief?" Floyd asked.

"I'm all right," Nikos said, "it's that damn muscle I bruised last week, it's more stubborn than I am."

"We finish it now, anyway," said Tuan, then hit the wedge a couple of times and started welding the plates together.

Nikos went to his office and got two Tylenol tablets from a large bottle in the desk drawer. The damn muscles seemed to be getting sore more often now. "When a man gets over forty, it's all downhill," Nikos thought. He leaned back in the chair. The Tylenol was slow in taking effect. It seemed everything around his chest was hurting. He hoped it would have gone away in the next couple of weeks; he didn't want to go to Greece a cripple.

He stared across the wall at the painting of the Bellmaker's house he had had made in New Orleans, long time ago. He thought the apricot color of the stucco had faded some but he liked it better that way; it was more delicate. As soon as it was finished, he'd be dividing his time between the village and the shop. It's time to slow down a bit and enjoy life, he thought; do some of the things he always wanted to do. Joe Carroll: the closest he came to his dream was the flower arrangement in the shape of a house-boat his wife got him at his funeral. He didn't want Margaret getting him one in the shape of the Pilios Manor. Maria seemed to be learning the business pretty well; she could run the company while he was taking some time off. Who knows? Maybe he'll get lucky and she'll marry a boy that will run the shop; their children and Nicole's and Katerina's children will spend their summers at the Pilios Manor, in Greece - there will be plenty of room for all of them. They might be calling it "the ghost house" right now, but when it's renovated the way Nikos saw it in his head, they will love it, all of them, Nikos is sure of it.

Three days after the sledge hammer incident, Nikos left the shop an hour earlier feeling a cold coming on. When he got home, Margaret fussed at him for leaving his shoes in the middle of the floor. She said Dr. Milhowser would be coming by later in the evening. He happened to be in the neighborhood visiting a friend, he told her, and he wanted to stop by to talk to both of them about the tests.

He came around eight o'clock. All the kids were out of the house. Margaret had made a fresh pot of coffee, but Dr. Milhowser said he didn't want any. "Just a glass of water," he said and sat by the kitchen table. He took a sip of the water, cleared his throat a couple of times, and then asked if they could join hands for a prayer. People from Margaret's church were always doing that when they came to visit and it always bugged Nikos, but he went along to keep Margaret from griping.

They held hands across the table. Doctor Milhowser thanked the Lord for His blessings and for looking after this Christian family all these years and for blessing him with the privilege to be their friend. Dr. Milhowser's hand felt sweaty in Nikos'.

"We know Lord," the doctor went on, "that you have a reason for everything you do. We just pray that you give us the strength to pass the test. We know, Lord, that you suffered and died for us, and we ask that you give your servant Nick the strength to pass the test and glorify your name." "This guy is good," Nikos thought, "I wonder how much he's clipping my insurance for this sermon." He wished the doctor would hurry it up, there was a World Cup match on television.

Finally the doctor said: "In Thy name we pray, Amen," and Nikos did a couple of up-and-down strokes, crossing himself.

Doctor Milhowser took another sip of the water and cleared his throat a couple of times. "Now, we are not absolutely sure," he started, "we will have to have more tests made, and of course the medical science is constantly making progress in cancer research and we should never give up hope... and..." He kept on talking; Nikos could see his lips moving and Margaret's face wrinkle and get soaked with tears, but Nikos' head started buzzing and he couldn't hear anything.

He mumbled something, got up and slumped on the living room sofa. He leaned his head back and stared out of the window. A small, puffy cloud was sailing across the evening sky. The branch of a pine tree could be seen through the lower pane, moving gently. On it, an energetic sparrow was searching for something.

The world was silent.

Nikos didn't go to the shop the next two days. Margaret told everyone he had a cold. When he went, he felt like a spectator at a game where he knew neither of the teams. He walked around the shop looking at machinery, as if he was seeing it for the first time. How long had he had the iron worker? How much did he pay for that saw? How long did it take to pay off the shear? He sure had to kiss ass to get the loan for it.

Around ten, a blabber-mouthed machine salesman came to see him about an angle roller Nikos had been looking into buying. Between corny jokes and loud laughter, he was plugging his machine:

"The dies are guaranteed for five years. If any one of them chips or cracks, sixty months from now, you call the dealership and they'll get you new ones for nothing."

Nikos told him he would let him know.

When he left, Nikos went to the bathroom and threw up. A strange feeling that was a mixture of sadness, anger, betrayal and abandonment, was sitting heavily on his chest. He sat at his desk and stared at the Bellmaker's house for a while, then went to the bathroom and threw up again. His legs felt weak. He told Floyd he would be back tomorrow and went home.

Margaret packed for the trip to Greece in mournful silence. This time she didn't bother Nikos with questions if she should pack something formal, something casual, something for warm or something for cold. She even managed to fit all of her things in one suitcase.

The kids gave them a going away party and kept making jokes about the "second honeymoon."

They hadn't been told about the cancer.

Maria drove them to the airport and helped with the checking of the luggage. Nikos got a window seat and after a scotch and water he tried to sleep.

Margaret read her Bible.

They spent the night in Athens and the next morning, rented a car and drove to the village. Nikos' mother had a big spread waiting for them. She kept saying Nikos looked tired and he kept telling her it was the long trip.

On the afternoon of the second day, Nikos and Margaret went to the Bellmaker's house.

Margaret had made some sandwiches, Nikos got a bottle of Dimo's wine and they had a picnic on a clear spot of the patio. The trees Nikos and his brother had grafted a few years earlier had grown. Two apple trees of the firikia variety, near the patio, were loaded with the fruit. Nikos picked a few, the most ripened ones, reddish and yellowish and sweet smelling and peeled them. Margaret agreed they were the best apples she had tasted.

When they finished eating, they climbed slowly up to the top floor.

On the way up they passed by what was going to be the temporary construction office. Pavlos Stenos had built a large plywood desk in the middle of the room and on it were the two boxes with all the pictures, drawings and notes Nikos had collected over the years.

Margaret's eyes were examining everything and Nikos thought he heard her mumble to herself: "It will take lots of work to bring it into shape, lots of work and lots of money." After a while, Margaret said she thought she forgot to close the food basket and went back down. Nikos cleared the cobwebs from one of the corner windows of the study and sat on the wide sill looking out.

The sun was sinking behind the village of Xourihti; the last rays brightened the golden leaves of the chestnut tree-tops and brushed orange patches on the light blue sea. A sailboat was passing in the distance, cutting a path through an orange patch. A soft old song was coming from a distant radio. A group of children were playing war on top of the ruins of the Venetian castle. The bell of Agios Taxiarhis started to toll, announcing it was time for vespers; its heavy sound rolled down the mountainside and spread out to sea. Everything seemed so peaceful, so normal, as if nothing was about to change.

Somewhere Nikos had read that somebody had asked some Italian guy who went on to become a saint what he would do if he found out that he had only three days to live.

"I would continue to hoe my garden," the saint had answered.

Damn it, that's taking things lying down! Nikos couldn't go on "hoeing his garden." He wanted to yell, to fight, to punch somebody's lights out. It was not fair, it was not just, it was not right by any measure. He didn't care how the priests, the preachers and all those who earn their keep by peddling words, tried to explain it. He deserved what he got and he deserved to live and enjoy it. There are millions of people who hadn't busted their asses near as much as he had and they were living long, uneventful lives. A few more years: that's all he wanted.

Now that the shop was running smoothly (the water was in the ditch, as Nikos' mother would say), he could do some of the things he and Margaret had always talked about doing.

For all the suffering, the endless hours of working, the constant scrimping, the countless times Margaret and the girls wanted to do something together but he didn't want to pass up the overtime or miss out on the big job, for all that struggle and misery, is this the reward?

All of a sudden, without any warning, tears started running down his face. He let loose and cried, a heart-broken child's crying.

Oh, if he could do it all over again.

He thought of his whole life and what he would do differently if he had sixty years ahead of him instead of six months. The staying in America wouldn't change; that was something he never regretted. But he would go back to school and learn how to speak the language right. And he would learn how to run a business by administering and letting other people do most of the work, and he would spend more time with his family.

At the going-away party he had looked at the girls and realized how little he knew of their lives. He looked at their photographs in their ballet costumes, their little league uniforms, their cheer-leading outfits and prom dresses, as if he was seeing them for the first time.

His whole life, he thought had been a constant hassle of striving to pay something off, to meet a deadline, to survive the day-to-day living. But then again, how else could he do it? He lived the only way he knew how. Maybe more schooling would have taught him how.

He thought of all the people he knew who were now dead. The boasters and the shy ones, the scheming, the optimists, the hard working and the lazy ones; all of them in their day, thinking they would live forever.

In somebody's funeral he had heard the priest say in his eulogy: "We are like a falling star, one brief sparkle and then we are gone." What was his brief sparkle in this life? Was it when he outsmarted Bubba Smith and took the barge of Caribbean Shipping away from Dixie shipyard? Was it the tanker Halcyon? when he outmaneuvered the shake-down of the port engineer? Or was it his interview with the weatherman at the Greek Festival? Everything seemed so insignificant now.

A few months back, Stavros Rigotis told him that Bubba Smith dropped dead one day while walking in the shipyard. It took a while for Stavros to remember Bubba's name. He kept saying: "You know, the big man that talked real loud and used to chase you from the shipyard."

How long would it be before everyone forgets about him? It will be as if he never existed.

After a while he got up and slowly went down the rickety stairway. He found Margaret trying to carry on a conversation with Kyra Amalia, who had limped over to greet them. Her back was bent and she looked frail. She was pulling a gray goat on a long line; she said it was the only one she had kept.

"What's the use of having a lot? I am not going to take it with me," she said.

Nikos translated for Margaret.

"That's right," said Margaret, "the Bible says a man should also be content with little."

Nikos translated for Kyra Amalia.

"You have a sensible woman there," said Kyra Amalia, "a very sensible woman."

On the way back, they stopped at Kostas Liappis' bakery; Margaret said they needed a loaf of fresh bread. Kostas asked them to stay a while.

The bakery had doubled in size since Nikos was there the last time. It was made to look like an old fashioned village kitchen.

There was a coziness and warmth that made one feel at home. Nikos felt as if everything in there was inviting him to cuddle up and stay forever: the wide, weathered floor planks, hand-hewn chestnut tree rafters, the massive stone walls with their shelves and old-fashioned niches, the wooden racks loaded with loaves of bread and cookies, the aroma of freshly baked bread, the burning fireplace with the two deep chairs on either side of it, covered in home-woven cloth. It was homey.

Kostas told a helper to finish taking the bread out of the oven and joined them at an old table by the fireplace. "You two — both of you, look more pretty and more young every time I see you."

Margaret laughed and thanked him.

After a while Kostas walked over to a cupboard and brought a carafe of *tsipouro* and three glasses.

Next to the cupboard, mounted on the wall, was an old photograph. It showed Kostas' and Nikos' grandfathers, and a couple of other village men in their forties, back from a successful hunt. They were posing with big smiles, displaying their guns and their bandoleers; two wild boars lay at their feet. They looked jovial, strong, immortal.

"To your health," said Kostas and they clinked their glasses.

Margaret clinked but did not drink.

"And to yours, wishing is all we can do," said Nikos.

They started reminiscing about their youth, then later Nikos congratulated Kostas on his re-election as village president.

"I thought you gave up politics," he told him.

"I was sick for a long time and I couldn't do much; no use being in it if you can't make a difference. Thank God I am all cured now. I don't mind telling you: I was scared. I pledged a chandelier to Agia Marina and She made Her miracle." He crossed himself reverently.

Nikos kept staring at the old photograph of their grandfathers.

"I hear Pavlos Stenos is going to renovate the Bellmaker's house for you. When is he starting?"

"Soon," said Nikos.

"I am glad you bought it, instead of some foreigner." They clinked their glasses again, this time without Margaret. Nikos sipped slowly. The tsipouro spread a pleasant warmth across his chest. In the fireplace, the playful flames sent a bright glow through the room.

"Ah my friend, there is nothing like having your health. When I got sick last time, I got scared. It was quite a hardship for the family too, having to come all the way to the city to visit me. Remember what I told you about trying to get a hospital built here? I still think that's what the village needs. And it would give about sixty people work, year-round. This time, most of the council sees things my way; we can do some good things for the village."

"I am sure you can talk them into it, you are a persuasive man, Kosta. Remember when you were the captain of our football team? You always convinced the others you were right." Nikos sighed.

"Ah, those were the carefree years; we were young and healthy; there is nothing like good health," answered Kostas in a thinking tone, "that's why we need to have a hospital here. If we had the land, we could get the construction money from the government easy, but land prices have gone crazy around here. The foreigners are buying up everything, the Kambanaris land is now worth ten times what you paid for it." His voice, even in imperfect English, had the zest and conviction of someone who knows what he's talking about.

Nikos was still looking at the photograph of their grandfathers.

"You can have the Kambanaris property," he heard Margaret saying. He turned and saw her looking at him, looking at the picture.

Kostas' glass of *tsipouro* had stopped in mid-air. His eyes kept darting between Margaret and Nikos. "Serious?" He finally asked, almost in a whisper.

"We can go to a lawyer tomorrow and sign the papers," said Nikos. "Just keep it quiet for a while." He sounded relieved, like a man who has just unloaded a heavy sack off his shoulders.

Kostas jumped up rattling everything on the table, gave both of them a rib-cracking hug and kissed them on both cheeks. There were tears in his eyes.

After a couple more rounds of *tsipouro* they started home. A full moon was shining bright. They stopped at the straight, half-way part of the path and Nikos leaned against the old chestnut tree with the hollowed trunk, catching his breath before starting up the steep hill. The Villa Giannis could be seen at a distance. Without knowing why the meeting with Giannis Giannakos, the first time he returned to the village came into his mind. He grinned, almost smiled. "Yes, Gianni, to believe, is to see," he said out loud. Then startled, he mumbled an excuse to Margaret and said, "Let's go".

"I'm sure the kids will be proud of you when they grow up," she said and gave him a hug. They started up hill with lighter steps.

He nibbled on the supper his mother had waiting, then took the chamomile tea she had made for him, because she was sure something was wrong with his stomach, and went out on the balcony.

There was a light, cool breeze blowing, rattling the few leaves that clung to the apple trees. The moon hung over the island of Skiathos, shining a golden path on the calm sea, to the cove of Fakistra and up to Kambanaris house. Nikos leaned back on the chair, put his feet on the railing, and stared at it. Maybe in the years to come, people would look in that direction and think of Nikos Pilios.

The next day, Nikos heard his mother talking to Margaret when she thought he was taking his mid-day nap.

"Nikos not well, eh? You tell truth to me."

"*Nickolas lost big contracto, lost big job, apolia mega ergo, lost many money, many dollaria,*" Margaret was summoning all the Greek she knew to make a believable answer.

A few days later Nikos and Margaret started on a trip around Greece. They were going to all of the places Nikos had always wanted to see.

They returned to the village after two weeks. Nikos was ready to go home. He told his mother there was an emergency in the shop and they had to get back in a hurry. She could say the "good-byes" for them to people in the village. She said he looked tired, and seemed to doubt his emergency explanation.

"There is something you are not telling me isn't there?" she kept asking him and he kept telling her there wasn't. He gave her a big hug, pulling all of the courage he could muster to make it brief, and told her they would try to come for Easter. Then he got behind the wheel and drove off quickly.

A few minutes later, he parked by the Kambanaris house. They had started clearing the property. Kostas Liappis had called the previous day to say that the ribbon-cutting was set for eighteen months from now and that he should make sure to be here.

Nikos sat on a rock and watched as a noisy yellow grader leveled the cobblestone path and the flagstone patio to make a road for the trucks. After a while, it clanked its way to the end of the property and somebody yelled something, soon followed by the muffled sound of dynamite. In seconds, a large pile of rubble and a cloud of dust was all there was left of the Kambanaris house.

The mountain breeze picked up a mass of loose pieces of paper, twirled them up high and then sent them gliding down the mountainside toward the cove of Fakistra.

"There go your remodeling instructions," said Margaret. She hugged Nikos' shoulder.

"Let's go home," said Nikos.

He got on the passenger's side. "You drive, I feel tired."

He handed her the keys.

THE END